THREE LEGS OF THE CAULDRON

By
R. L. Cherry

With poetry by
Morgan Mullins

*To John & Vicki —
Enjoy this Celtic Journey!
Sláinte*

**The three highest causes of the true human are:
Truth, Honor, and Duty.**

Traditional Celtic Triad

ACKNOWLEDGEMENTS

No book is truly a solo work.   I had many sources that I consulted, so many that I hesitated to name them all.   Instead I have provided a suggested reading list that gives but a few of them.   Morgan Mullins provided all the poetry, not my strong point, and advice. Cindy Grubbs did a fine editing go-through.   My wife, Kelly, did so many editings, as well as enduring my obsession with this book. She is my Aislinn, my beloved Irish warrior woman.

INTRODUCTION

Sometime in the late 4th century or early 5th century, according to lore, Gaels from Ireland sailed across the Irish Sea to what is now western Scotland.   They came from a kingdom in what is now the Antrim region of northeastern Ireland that was then called Dál Riata, and so their lands in western Scotland had the same name.

It was a rugged land they came to, rocky islands and coastline.   Why they did so is a matter of speculation.   It may have been to expand their lands, establish trade routes, or just a sense of restless adventure.   Since there is no written record, we cannot know for sure.

Whatever the reason, these Irish settlers, known as Scotti by the ancient Romans, eventually gave their name to Scotland.   Their Gaelic language became the tongue of the Scottish Highlanders, those kilted warriors that inspired awe and story in later centuries. The Dál Riatans are the ancestors of the Scotland of legend and romance.

With them, these travelers brought their myths and legends. The filidh, those who memorized all the classic tales of their ancestors and created poems about the deeds of their heroes, were honored and respected.   It was because of them and their abilities that we have today the great stories of the Irish.   These oft tragic tales spoke of heroic and noble deeds.

And what of this tale that follows here?   It is the tale of a father, Fergus, an aging warrior who was a taoiseach, the chief of his small clann.   It is the tale of Ciarán, his eldest son who lusted for power.   It is the tale of Cathal, the warrior second son, and Aislinn, his only love.   It is the tale of Connaire, the impetuous youngest brother, who learned the pain of a hero's life in finding the woman to be at his side.   It is the tale of a journey across land and sea, as well as through this life.   It is a tale of the three legs of the cauldron of society: Truth, Honor and Duty.

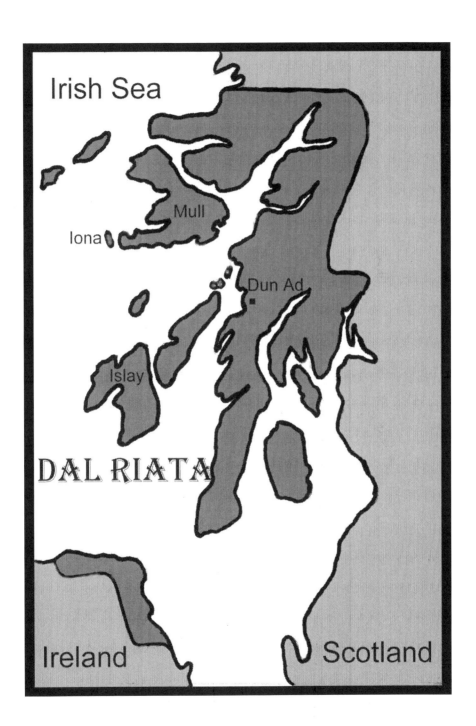

I. FROM EIREANN TO ALBA

Chapter 1

With no moon penetrating the storm clouds, Ronan steered the currach across the sea by instinct alone, heading to where he felt the sun would rise. The rowers determinedly plied their oars to keep the craft steadily moving toward their goal, the land of Alba. Cathal, the man they had all followed on this journey across the sea, came to him, doubt in his voice.

"With no stars, how do you know we are on the right course?"

"I just know," Ronan said with more confidence than he felt. "But I think the storm is lifting on the horizon and the moon will give us some light to see our guides to the isle on the way to my mother's people."

"The rocks of Lugh and the Three Fairies? I do not understand how rocks could look like anything but rocks."

"Your problem is that you only know the poetry of words.

"No, I know the poetry of battle."

"If that is poetry." Ronan snorted in derision. "The sea is a poem from the lips of the god, Manannán mac Lir. The sea is my favorite of the Three Realms." Ronan looked out over the dark, pitching waves. "The sea, too, is a battle, a battle against the power of the gods, not mere men."

Cathal grunted. "I'd rather fight a handcount of trained warriors any day, but on dry land."

Ronan knew that Cathal had no love for the sea. If anything, it was one of his few fears. Yet, he encouraged the others, showing a belief that they would succeed, even if he had serious doubts. That was a man worthy of being taoiseach, the chief of their small clann.

The sail on the single mast of the currach was furled to keep it from being shredded in the violent winds. Six children had surrounded it, huddled together on the narrow plank deck that ran along the ribs of its hull. Woolen blankets were wrapped around them to keep them warm.

The oldest was a girl who had seen but seven Samhains, the Celtic new year festivals. The youngest was a boy who had not yet seen two. Using the bundled goods around them as a protective fence, they futilely tried to escape the storm's fury. Not one, however, cried from the terror they all must have felt. The oldest clasped the youngest to her drenched chest, her down-turned mouth quivering. Cathal knew that it was not merely from the cold that she shook. He knelt beside her and brushed her wet hair from her face.

"You are a courageous lass, Eavan," he said, shouting to be heard above the howling wind. "Your strength comforts the others. You have the makings of a warrior. When we settle in the new land, would you like me to start training you?"

The young girl only nodded, but her eyes lost some of their fear and a slight smile touched her lips. The quivering lessened. Cathal smiled back and rested his battle-calloused hand on the top of her head.

As the clouds lifted, the full moon shone on four rocks, Lugh and the Three Fairies. Pulling hard on the steering oar, Ronan maneuvered safely past them to the shore. When the boat's greased-hide hull hit the beach, Ronan pulled back on his oar, digging it into the sand. He wiped the salt water from his face and his trim, black beard with the back of his hand. Two rowers from the front of the boat leapt into the chilling sea and waded to shore, pulling the vessel forward onto the beach before the angry waves could suck it back into the sea. He sighed in relief. They had survived. While some may have thought they would not, they had made it to a safe shore. Maeve, a dark haired woman with flashing green eyes who was sitting on a rowing bench close to him, managed to give him a smile through the heavy rain and he smiled back.

Manannán's Curse had stricken about half of the two handcounts of rowers, including some of the strongest, sending them to the sides of the boat as they emptied their stomachs during the voyage and they were still not recovered. Ronan chuckled. Perhaps that was Manannán's way of forcing an offering from the proud.

Cathal helped the auburn-haired Aislinn towards the front of the boat, calling to one of the men ashore to help her. Shrugging off Cathal's hand, she dropped over the side of the craft, landing in a sprawl. Quickly she rolled onto her hands and knees and rose shakily to her feet. With as much of an air of dignity as her weakened state would allow, Aislinn plodded up the beach and rested a moment on one of the bundles lying there. Cathal knelt beside her.

Aislinn angrily shook her head. "I should be working, not sitting here like a helpless babe."

"Rest, Aislinn. This sickness that you suffer will soon pass. It does not shame you."

"The other women are not sitting here with me." She swept her hand around to indicate eight women, one of whom was beginning to show the signs of pregnancy, who were helping to unload the boat. "I alone of the women do nothing while others work.   It is not the way of our people.   Besides, I'm a warrior and stronger then they."

"And is it our way for the strongest men to lie in weakness while the women work?" Cathal asked, grinning as he pointed at a groaning, black-bearded giant and a brown-haired, trim-bearded man, not much smaller, who had stumbled ashore and were sitting on the sand.   "Gruagach and Cairbre have always thought themselves far stronger than any woman.   This sickness of the sea has laid them low as well.   Perhaps that's the way of the sea: only those proud of their might are stricken."

"That is . . . ."   She grabbed his arm.   "Oh, Cathal, help me to the sea.   I don't think I can make it."

Cathal helped her stagger to the water and she retchingly tried to empty an already empty stomach into the sea.   Coughing and gagging, Aislinn finally spat out a few drops of bile. Exhausted, she dropped to her knees on the damp sand.   After a few moments, she shook Cathal away and crept to the pile of bundles.

Ronan stayed on the boat, tossing the remaining cargo to those on the shore.   Maeve worked alongside of him, laughing when they bumped each other while they worked.

Suddenly a gust of wind hit the lightened craft, turning it and breaking it loose from its tenuous landing.   It happened so quickly, so unexpectedly, that almost no one reacted.   No one except Cathal.

Lunging, he grabbed the side of the currach as it slipped back into the sea.   Unstoppable by even one as powerful as he, the boat dragged him with it as it headed toward the waiting rocks less than a hundred feet from the shore.   Those on the beach stood in stunned horror.   Ronan and Maeve watched helplessly as their small craft was impaled by a protruding rock, holing its side.

The impact sent Maeve stumbling across the deck and over the side.   Ronan leapt after her, grabbing her cloak as she fell into the water.   The force of her weight and the tipping of the boat threw him into the sea with her, but he was able to grab the gunnel as he fell.   The boat skewed around, almost pinning Ronan against the rock.   His arm was numb from the wrenching it had suffered when he grabbed the gunnel.

The waves crashed over him and tried to pull either the boat from one hand's grip or Maeve from the other hand, but he clung to the wood frame and to the young woman tenaciously.   With great effort he was able to pull her to him and, when a lull between waves allowed, slipped his arm around her waist to hold her more securely. At that moment, he saw Cathal working his way towards him, holding onto the side of the currach.   When the warrior got close enough, Ronan called to him.

"Take her, Cathal!   Try to swim to shore with her!"

When Cathal got next to Ronan, he looked at Maeve. "Let her go, Ronan.   I will try to get you ashore."

"What?"   Ronan's eyes blazed   "Save Maeve!"

"It is too late, Ronan.   Let her go and I will try to get us to shore."

Ronan had been concentrating on keeping Maeve's head above water.   He looked at her and saw her green eyes staring sightlessly ahead.   Her black hair floated around her face, half covering a bloody red gash.   In the battering sea, her head had struck the rock.

Cathal put his hand on the young man's shoulder.   His heart was heavy, but he knew they were now in danger of dying there, too. "You cannot do anything for her.   Let her go to the ancestors now. We've got to try for the beach.   I will help you."

Like many sailors, Ronan couldn't swim.   He had told Cathal that it would only prolong the inevitable if his craft went down.   Cathal, however, was an able swimmer.

"No!" It was both a denial and a refusal by the young man. Releasing his grip from the boat, he dropped into the sea.

Cathal grabbed him as he dropped and pulled him to the surface, but had great difficulty holding him up. Ronan still held Maeve and thrashed to free himself from Cathal's grip. Letting go of the boat, Cathal swung his fist at Ronan's jaw. The crashing blow stunned him and he let go of the lifeless Maeve.

Cathal, holding onto Ronan's tunic at the back of the neck, struggled with his free arm and his legs to make the shore. Already tired from the day's rowing, an overwhelming fatigue sapped his strength and made each stroke a supreme effort. His wet tunic and woolen trews were weights that tried to pull him under. Never had he known such weariness. He wondered if it would take long to die by drowning. He had heard that it was almost like falling asleep. Perhaps it would not be so bad to just stop, to let the water take him to the ancestors, to rest.

Then he saw her. As he looked toward the shore, Aislinn was wading out, fighting the waves to reach him. Her long, auburn hair streamed behind her and her wet tunic and overskirt were plastered to her body as she struggled against the sea.

Redoubling his efforts, Cathal fought his way toward her. His sodden cloak choked him, pulling him under the cold, salty sea. With his free arm, Cathal wrenched it from around his neck, tearing it from its securing brooch. Without it, the winter nights would be frigid and deadly, but with it he could not save Ronan.

Aislinn called to him, encouraging him to keep swimming, and he did. As he reached her, she and others who had waded out grabbed him and Ronan, pulling them to the beach. As he lay panting in the sand, Aislinn clasped him to her, giving him her warmth, and wrapped her cloak around them.

"You've lost your bratt," she softly said, referring to the warm, woolen cloak. "I'll have to weave a new one for you. Tonight, you will share mine."

When he had recovered enough that he might be able to speak, she asked, "What happened to Maeve?"

"Dead." He gasped the sad tale between ragged breaths. "Her head hit the rock . . . . Ronan almost killed us both. Would not let go of her body."

"You would have been the same."

Cathal drew back, still panting from his struggle. "What do you mean? . . . I saw that she was dead . . . . I'd have let her go, if Ronan were trying to save me."

She brushed his cheek with her hand. "But what if it had not been Maeve? Would you have been sensible enough to let me go?"

Looking up at her in surprise, Cathal started. "You mean . . . ."

"You have not noticed how they looked at each other? How his hand often brushed across her? How they seemed to laugh at whatever one said to the other? Why do you think Maeve was the one who stayed on the boat to help Ronan?"

"No . . . no, I guess I missed that. With all the . . ." Cathal stammered.

Aislinn kissed his cheek. "You were so worried about all of us that you never saw any of us."

Cathal silently chastised himself for his lack of perception. Pulling himself to his hands and knees, he crawled away from Aislinn to check on Ronan. He was lying face down in the sand, sobbing. The others, seeing that he was still alive and safe, found tasks to keep themselves busy.

Cathal rested his hand on the young man's shoulder. He

could think of nothing to say, but knew Ronan needed some comfort.   Aislinn came up to them and sat down, slipping Ronan's head into her lap as she stroked his hair.

"It's my fault," Ronan said in a choked voice.   "I should have grabbed her before we hit the rock.   I should have made sure the currach was higher up the beach.   I should have had someone else help me unload."

"You are not at fault.   It was the end of her turn of the wheel.   There was nothing you could do."   Cathal knew it would not be of much comfort as he said it.

Ronan rose on one elbow, screaming.   "It is my fault!   I killed her!"

Motioning for Cathal to leave, Aislinn stroked Ronan's head as she gently pressed his head back onto her lap and cooed comforting words to him.   Cathal paused, then shook his head at his own shortsightedness.   Maeve's death was a tragedy, a tragedy for which he felt a personal responsibility.   She had trusted him with her life in this journey and he had failed.   But before he could mourn her, he had to see to the living.   With heaviness in his heart, he set about his role as leader, checking on what was lost or damaged.

Chapter 2

Almost none of the cargo had remained on board the craft when it had slipped off the beach, so Maeve and the currach itself were the only real losses. And Cathal's cloak. Although it did not compare to the loss of the young woman's life, Cathal knew he would sorely miss his bratt.

As he stood, surveying the survivors and their goods, another boat beached itself nearby. Cathal sent a messenger to warn them that they must pull the boat completely ashore as quickly as possible. He did not want a repeat of their tragedy. It was Maille and her crew.

As the new arrivals began to unload their craft, the winds diminished. Rain began to fall. Not a mere sprinkling, but heavy drops that thudded heavily on the voyagers' heads. Even though they pulled their woolen cloaks over themselves, soon these were sodden and not much help. Although they had been splashed by the sea for the entire trip, this cold drenching multiplied their misery.

Cathal squinted as he glared into the cloudy night. Did the sea-god Manannán have some special enmity for his small band? First the rough crossing, then the loss of his boat and Maeve, and now this. The sea was descending from the sky. And the last boat, his young brother Connaire's, had not yet arrived. Knowing that he had to get his people out of the storm, he sent several search parties to find shelter.

A short time later, Gruagach, Cairbre, Tian and Maille approached Cathal as he stood anxiously watching for the missing third boat. Maille had been on the second boat at her insistence, in command even though her sword arm was useless, but she seemed none the worse for the trip. Gruagach and Cairbre had recovered somewhat from their sickness, but still looked unsteady on their feet.

"Cathal, leader of the bravest men and most desirable women in all Alba and beyond, we have found shelter for our dauntless party," Tian said with flourish of his hand. "There is a cave nearby, not like an inviting warm hearth nor the commodious Hostel of Da Derga, but large enough to house us for the night, protected from these cruel elements. Might I suggest that we move our goods to this rude shelter with all speed?"

Cathal rolled his eyes and smiled at Maille, Gruagach and Cairbre. They grinned back at him. Such verbiage was expected of Tian. In truth, he was as eloquent as any of the filidh Cathal had ever heard. If he were not such a fearsome warrior, he might have been one, a poet who lived by his craft.

Tian was not nearly as large as his two male companions, with brown hair and a drooping mustache, but was sinewy and agile. His swordplay was as well-respected as Gruagach's axe and Cairbre's spear. The three together were a formidable combination.

"The leader of our people in Alba am I?" Cathal shook his head sadly. Leadership had become less of an honor and more of an onerous duty. "As your leader, I command that you get everyone into the cave. But we will need a fire to signal our last boat."

"Ah, then you will tell me how to make one in this foul night, with no warm, dry hearth?"

"We will make it there, under that overhang." Cathal indicated an outcropping of rock, making a roof about ten feet above the ground that gave enough shelter from the rain to start a fire. "The rain is just starting, so the fallen timber will be dry inside the bark. If you dig under the top layer of leaves, there should be usable kindling. Hurry, though, if this rain continues as it is, we will have little time to act."

Everyone set about the necessary tasks, some taking goods to the cave and others gathering fuel. Even those who had had the sickness of the sea found the strength to contribute. To survive would take much work and there would be no place for any who would not.

Although, due to the youthfulness of the voyagers, there were not many children who usually gathered kindling, everyone not hauling goods to the cave brought what dry leaves and twigs they could find. Eavan staggered with an armload of branches. She had several other children in tow, all with more than their share of kindling, and called encouragement to them as they struggled along the sandy beach. She would be a great warrior and he swore to himself that he would make sure that she was properly trained.

The other boat now safely beached and secure, more hands fell to the chores. Soon their goods were safely stored in the cave, a fire was started and enough timber to last the night was piled in a reasonably dry area under the outcropping. Mercifully, the rain subsided to a steady drizzle.

As he paced the beach, still looking for the missing boat, Cathal could not help worrying about Connaire, his younger brother. Connaire was the dreamer of the family. It had been his idea to leave, to find a new place for those of the clann who would not have Ciarán for their chief, ruling through his demented father. Barely more than a boy in Cathal's eyes, Connaire was not yet a skilled warrior.

Youthful and brown-haired, he did not even have a proper beard. It was thin and faint, common for a lad his age. Yet it did not bother Connaire, who seemed to feel himself a fully a man. He was always laughing, teasing and flirting, and women loved him. Cathal had thought they wanted to mother him but the look in their eyes often betrayed other than maternal desires. He seemed to have tapped the powers of the Otherworld of which he often spoke, dazzling the women with his charm and wit. But, Cathal felt, Connaire could not protect himself. Not yet. The tongue was no match for the sword and swords ruled.

Now Connaire was lost. Cathal had broken the small band into groups of three handcounts of adults to man the three boats, with a leader for each boat. Connaire, as Cathal's brother, was the leader of his boat. Now he was lost, perhaps still battered on the sea, perhaps crushed against the rocky coast. Whether he had perished, been injured or was still alive and unharmed, Cathal did not know. While night reigned and the storm raged, he could do nothing but hope for Connaire's safety. Too young and inexperienced, Cathal thought.

The bone-chilling night sent a shiver down his back and he walked to the crackling watch-fire where some of the others were seated, having a meager supper. His tunic was soaked and the cold had penetrated him to the marrow, but he had not realized it until he came to the warmth of the fire. Aislinn met him as he approached and tried to put her bratt around him.

"No." Cathal shook his head. "My loss will not be yours."

"But we share."

"I must bear this alone. They followed me. Now one is dead and more are missing." However he did allow, even welcome, her warm presence next to him as they dropped onto a log next to the fire.

"This is a clann. We are kin. You are never alone."

Cathal shook his head, but said nothing. It was true.

Aislinn reached into a basket sitting near them and took out some oat cakes, cheese and dried herring. "Here. You must eat. You must be strong to help your people."

By habit rather than with appetite, Cathal dully ate.   Tian's tenor voice floated from the darkness beyond the light of the fire, singing the beginning of a tale.   The story of their journey, of Maeve's sad death.

Cathal of the mighty arm leads his people now to flee
To the lands that he will rule, out beyond the Eireannach Sea.
Ronan sails the currach that sets Cathal's people free.

The sailor's skills are rewarded, the lookout gives a screech.
Alba's craggy shore appears, waves crash upon the beach.
Life and land on Alba's shore, far from Ciarán's evil reach.

Through the water's pitch and toss, landing in the gloaming,
Over the side of the currach, Cathal's people swarming.
From the sea Cathal pulls kin; from rough and windy foaming.

Bright Maeve does strong Ronan watch, she stays, helps and hovers.
A sea-born romance has now blossomed and created fresh new lovers.
But yours will be a different fate, declares Danu the Mother.

Maeve mounts up against the side, she throws a parcel on the heap.
A wave catches the currach square; she falls down to forever sleep.
Down to the western sea, to Donn's house, beneath the deep.

Ronan the brave and swimless will save his love from the wave.
He jumps in, Cathal reaches again and Ronan's life does save.
He grabs Ronan's bratt; Cathal tugs and Ronan parts from Maeve.

As the last notes faded, a hush descended.   Only the sounds of the crashing waves and crackling fire continued. A few of the party were already in the cave, exhausted from their trip and wrapped together for warmth as they slumbered. The rest soon joined them, escaping the pall of Maeve's death and the dread of the missing boat by drifting into a tired sleep.

Aislinn stood and tugged at Cathal's arm, saying, "Come. You're tired and cold. We'll wrap with others tonight and share warmth."

Shaking his head, Cathal said, "No, the fire must be tended. I'll do that and keep warm by it as well. My léine and trews are already dry." As he pressed his hand against his knee-length linen tunic and woolen trousers to demonstrate, water dripped from them. "Almost. I will stay here until they are dry."

"Then I'll stay too," she said with resolve in her voice. "My place is at your side."

"No. Go with the others and sleep. This is my vigil. Only mine."

"We both are responsible for this journey of our clann." Aislinn's voice bristled. "You cannot bear this alone."

"Please." He paused, not trusting his voice. "Go to bed. I will be there as soon as the others arrive."

"Cathal . . . . The others . . . . They may never arrive." She said it softly.

For several minutes Cathal stared into the fire, watching pictures of what might be Connaire's fate in the dancing flames. Aislinn waited silently. When he finally spoke, it was with a quiet resignation.

"I know. I know."

She sat with him for a while, but he neither looked at her nor said anything more. At one point, he reached behind where he was sitting, grabbed a heavy branch and laid it on the fire. It was as if

14

she were no longer there.   Or he was not.

Silently she rose and turned to go.   Then, almost as an afterthought, she gently rested her hand on his shoulder, where his muscles were knotted and tight.   "I love you," she whispered, and touched his cheek before slipping away.

Cathal did not stir.   In his mind, he had returned to Eireann, to the time before they had left.   Once again he was at his father's hearth.

II. EIREANN

Chapter 3

Fergus had been a mighty warrior and a father to admire, even fear. He had fathered three sons, one from his first wife and two from his second, and had outlived both wives. In Celtic tradition, the second wife had accepted and treated the one from the first wife as her own until her death. All had been equal to her.

Ciarán, the eldest and having seen five handcounts of Samhains, was of medium stature with dark hair and eyes that gave a brooding and closed look to his face. His every move, every word, seemed to claim some imagined status merely by being the eldest son of the chief of the clann. Although no position or title was given him by his birth, he did display a leadership of sorts, but one of arrogance that drew mainly the weaker-willed youths of the clann to him. An expert at manipulation, he could artfully play one person against another, while always managing to appear blameless. By creating constant dissent, he neutralized any opposition. It was likely this skill would have made him the main leader of the young men and women if he had not had charismatic brothers. And they had been the cause of great displeasure for him.

Cathal was the day to Ciarán's night. Having had a different mother, he had fairer hair, wider shoulders, more impressive height and had seen three fewer Samhains than Ciarán, but those were not the main differences. It was how he extended a welcome to all, whether it might gain him something or not. Hunting, drinking and laughing were his favorite pastimes. Whether it be pursuit of the wild boar or the laughter of a light-hearted companion, the pleasure of the experience was to be enjoyed, to be relished and remembered. Cathal was the warrior

16

who loved life as much as he loved flirting with death, for who could know the depths of the pleasures of life as well as one who was unafraid to lose them?

The youngest, Connaire, had the coloring and disposition of Cathal, but a quicker wit and sharper tongue. He was tall, but his youthfully wiry frame was that of a lad who had seen but three handcounts and two Samhains. He understood the minds of his siblings and preferred to be with his open-handed and open-hearted brother, gravitating toward Cathal early in his life. This only increased Ciarán's dislike of his younger brother, but would have had little to do with clann chieftainship if not for a hunting accident.

Fifteen years younger than Fergus, Faolan was his half brother and the uncle of Cathal and Connaire. A vigorous warrior and hunter, he was a man who worthily and effortlessly commanded the respect of the whole clann. His herd of cattle was not quite the size of his half brother's, but its quality was better. When Fergus died, his herd would be divided among his sons. Although each son would have a sizeable herd of cattle, none would rival that of Faolan. These factors, when combined by the great love Fergus had for Faolan and that he was the only surviving male of their generation, made his future as the next chief very likely under Brehon Law. Since he was only a few years older than Ciarán, he might well hold that honor for many years. Might have, but for the unfortunate accident.

Boar-hunting was a favorite sport of both Fergus and Faolan. In keeping with their warrior spirit, the thrill of pursuing the dangerous beast through the forests and underbrush gave them the heady experience of a life-and-death struggle in times of peace. The large, wild pigs had been known to knock men from their horses, shatter spears men thrust at them and gore the unsteady hunter with their powerful tusks. It was mid-spring, just after the Beltane festival in early May, and Cathal was with Fergus and his herdsman, taking their herds to a new pasture when Ciarán came with word of a huge boar in the woods just to the north of them. Sending Ciarán to take word of this and where to meet to his half-brother, Fergus finished his tasks with the herdsmen before he took several of his household with him and rode to the rendezvous point, near where the boar had been seen.

Ciarán found Faolan with his herds, not far from where the boar had been sighted. "Uncle," he yelled from his horse as he approached, "a boar worthy of a hero is here, such as has not been seen in our forest for many years. It is near Cormac's ravine. Father said to fetch you."

Before Ciarán had a chance to dismount, Faolan had grabbed his spear and had leapt onto his horse. "What are you waiting for, boy?" he demanded. "If we are not quick, others will make the kill without us. Ride!"

With that, he rode off. Ciarán hesitated, but then followed.

Soon Ciarán and Faolan saw the boar: a massive creature with bulging shoulders, a shaggy hide and a bristling mane. He was rooting for food in the undergrowth at the base of a rocky cliff when the men saw him and he swung his heavy head to confront them with beady, black eyes and dirt-smeared tusks curving on each side of his thick skull. With a rashness that should have passed with his youth, Faolan ignored Ciarán's well-known ineptitude as a hunter and attacked.

As Faolan gripped the sides of his powerful, roan stallion with his knees and was preparing to charge, he heard wild snorting from Ciarán's horse. Suddenly a blow from behind struck him on the back of the head, knocking him to the ground. Dazed and dizzy, he was vaguely aware of hearing the sound of two horses galloping away from him. As he looked up from where he lay on the rocky, forest floor, he saw the boar rushing towards him, intent on ending this threat to his territory.

With no time to draw his sword, the warrior saw that his spear had landed near his hand. Without time or the steadiness to rise to meet the challenge, he grabbed the spear and jammed the butt of it between two heavy rocks, aiming the point just below the head of the charging beast. The skull would be too bony and sloped to penetrate, and he did not trust his groggy state to try any more difficult target.

When the boar struck the spear, his sheer weight and momentum carried it forward even as the weapon pierced his heart. The shaft of the spear splintered and the half of the shaft, embedded in the wild pig's chest, raked Faolan's face as the impetus of the dying animal's charge carried it over the prostrate warrior. The heavy animal landed on Faolan's chest, pinning him to the ground. Hot blood from the boar's wound pulsed out as he squealed his death song. Miraculously, Faolan escaped further injury from the thrashing hooves or the crushing weight of the dying pig. For a moment, hunter and prey lay still on the blood-soaked ground in a grim tableau of sport.

As Faolan struggled to extricate himself from under the foul-smelling carcass, the blood from his lacerated face mingling with that of his dead prey, he heard horses approaching. Cathal, Fergus and their retinue arrived just as Faolan crawled free. Ciarán rode up to him from the opposite direction.

"My uncle," Ciarán cried as he flung himself from his horse and knelt next to Faolan, "are you hurt?"

Faolan was still on his hands and knees, his face to the ground. With all the blood from the boar, it was hard for anyone else to know how much, if any, was from his wounds.

"Where were you?" he demanded. Dazed though he still was, Faolan remembered the blow and that Ciarán had not been there when the boar charged.

"My horse had never been on the hunt. When he saw the boar, he bolted. My spear struck you accidently as my horse turned and ran. I could do nothing to stop him until I was some distance from you. As soon as I had him under control again, I hurried back to you." While Ciarán had been speaking, Faolan raised his head. Ciarán gasped. "Your eye! Uncle, your eye!"

"It is gone," Faolan said, simply and stoically.

By this time Fergus and the others had dismounted and surrounded Faolan. Fergus mutely took his dagger and cut a large strip from his own léine. With it he bound his brother's wound. When he had finished, he softly said, "We will get you to a healer. This wound must be treated as soon as possible."

"It is my fault," Ciarán wailed. "Name your honor price, Uncle. I will pay whatever you ask."

"It is not for me to ask. Even if it were, I want nothing from you, nor will take anything. You are my brother's son and will pay me no honor price."

"I insist. I must pay something."

"He has spoken," Fergus told his son. "He will take nothing. Let it be. It is more important that we get him to the healer."

With an anguished yell, Ciarán unsheathed his sword and swung it with all his strength. Its sharpened edge cleaved deep into the neck of his horse, severing the jugular and sending blood spurting to add to the carnage on the leafy ground. With a look of startled incomprehension, the beautiful black stallion sank to its knees. As its life quickly ebbed, the steed attempted to shake its head, as if to deny the charges and the injustice of its death.

"If you will not accept an honor price, then I will pay one to the gods," Ciarán said.

Faolan gave him an accusatorial glare with his good eye as Fergus helped him back on his own horse. The now-dead stallion had been from the line of Faolan's own mount: a spirited line, not given to bolting at danger. Unlike Ciarán. To accuse his nephew, however, would mean a challenge to combat. He knew the younger man was no match for him, missing the sight in one eye or not. But to kill him would sever his relationship with his brother, and Fergus meant more to him than avenging the wrong. Whether the blow to the head had been accidental or a willful act, he was not absolutely sure. His suspicions were, however, quite strong. He, like all of those present, knew what this wound would cost him.

All those in Eireann were familiar with the tale of Nuada, the king of the Tuatha dé Danann or People of Danu. He led the invasion of the island by the descendants of the goddess Danu in the time before the Gaels.

With his fellow gods and goddesses, Nuada fought a tremendous battle against the Filborg, who had previously settled the land, and in that battle he lost an arm. Although the physician god Dian Cécht fashioned a silver arm and hand that functioned as well as a real one, Nuada could not serve as king because he was not then without blemish. The Tuatha dé Danann were oppressed by a king of alien lineage, but nothing could be done until Miach, the son of Dian Cécht the physician, was able to restore Nuada's original arm, regenerating the decayed flesh. Then Nuada was able to resume his rightful position.

What was true for the gods was true for the Gaels. Unfortunately, no human healer had the powers of the legendary Miach. Because Faolan was maimed, he could never be chieftain if

Fergus died or was incapacitated.

Although most blamed Ciarán for Faolan's injury, many were impressed at his act of atonement. Considering the value of such an animal, the sacrifice of his horse was considered more than just compensation. And Ciarán had every appearance of sorrowful regret at the banquet that night.

He stood, banging the table with his fist to get the attention of the boisterous crowd that had gathered. "My uncle shall have his rightful hero's share, the haunch of this monster." With a sweep of his hand, he indicated the boar that was roasting over hot coals. "And I challenge any and all who might dispute this to trial by combat."

Then he bowed his head. "If I had only been able to control that skittish beast of mine, he might not have paid so high a cost for our feast. I take responsibility for this . . . this great tragedy." Then he dropped to his bench, evidently overcome by emotion.

"You could almost believe Ciarán found it unfortunate rather than opportune that your uncle lost his eye," Tian whispered to Cathal.

Faolan sat in stony silence through the evening, eating little and drinking much.

Not long after the accident, Faolan slipped away at night, taking little but his horse and his weapons. There were those who thought he went to join some band of noble and independent warriors, like the legendary Fianna of Fionn mac Cumhail and those who thought he sailed across the sea to Alba to fight for the Ri of Dál Riata across the sea and there were those who said he drowned on the way, but no one really knew.

Chapter 4

Cian, the father of Aislinn, had been a trusted friend of Fergus for many years. Although only a few years older than the chief, his body had borne the ravages of time less kindly than his friend. His hands had become twisted, gnarled and painful with an evil that the healer found impossible to halt. While his mind was still functioning well, his body was not. With no sons and only one daughter, he looked for a son to come by marriage who would help tend the herds.

Although a beauty, Aislinn had a tinge of red to her brown mane that told of the fire in her soul. She was a wild horse, spirited and untamed. When her duties at home permitted, she would roam the fields and forests, often bringing home game to supplement the table. Riding on her dappled mare, with her thick hair streaming behind her and her léine bunched at her thighs, exposing shapely and muscular legs, she was the image of Scáthach, the legendary woman warrior who trained Cú Chulainn, the most famous and powerful of all the heroes. Although permitted by law, only a limited number of women displayed the necessary instincts and talents, practiced enough or were strong enough to achieve the status of warrior.

Like Muirne, her mother, who had started her training, Aislinn was better with weapons than many of the male warriors, equal to most and surpassed by few. It was not by strength that her abilities were known, but by skill. With her light-weight javelin, she could hit the stump of a tree at fifty paces, three out of four throws. Most men could hurl their weapons farther than she, but not as accurately. In swordplay, she used quickness and strategy to overcome those far stronger than she. Many a man had found his blade cleaving empty air as she side-stepped and swatted him on the buttocks with the flat of her sword.   With a bow, she was unrivaled.

She intimidated would-be suitors who feared such a woman and embarrassed suitors who failed her challenges.   She would set the test and any contender who failed would owe her a price, although normally she made it merely some trinket or a verbal admission that she was the better warrior.   All who tried had failed. Ciarán was one, missing a stump with all three of his attempts with a javelin while Aislinn scored three hits.   From him, she had demanded a fine steer.

Behind her back, Ciarán and his friends called her Medb, after the legendary banrion of Connacht whose pride had led her to a disastrous war against Ulaidh.   Although Aislinn had not spread her thighs to gain her will like Medb had, there were those who thought her as arrogant.   They urged Cathal to compete with her. They hoped that, like Cú Chulainn in the *Táin bó Cuailnge*, Cathal would be this Medb's undoing.   But he had his reasons for not doing so.

Aislinn had seen but eight fire festivals of Samhain when Cathal had come to live with her family.   Her mother was having severe problems during her pregnancy and had been forced to her bed.   It was an ill-fated pregnancy, one that resulted in a stillborn son and a mother who never fully recovered.

Aislinn's father, dividing his time between caring for her, her mother, managing the household and overseeing his herd, found it difficult to manage.   Aislinn tried to help where she could, but was still a child.   Often more of the meals were burned to the sides of the cooking kettle than eaten when Aislinn was in charge of minding the fire.

Cian and Fergus had long been close friends, sharing their bratts on cold nights when on campaign. Seeing his friend's plight and not wishing to dishonor him, he had asked Cian to foster Cathal for a time, to raise him as his own son, as was the way of their people. Ciarán had recently returned from a fosterage with another family in the clann, a family that came to dislike him greatly. Stating that three sons were impossible to properly train, Fergus asked if his friend would assist him with his second son. Cian had agreed, since it had been worded in such a manner that he would be helping Fergus rather than taking aid.

Cian wanted do all that he could to instruct the youth who was but four Samhains older than his daughter, but he was hard put to find time to do so. But then, Cathal was one who would see a problem and act to solve it. If the roof began to leak, Cathal immediately organized the re-thatching. If the herders were shirking their duties, Cathal saw it and admonished. It did no harm when he reached puberty, gaining a physique and deep voice that was worthy of any man. Cian found the strong youth a very useful addition to the hearth and welcomed him as a son.

If Cian acted as Cathal's father, then Aislinn acted as his little sister: pesky and combative. While he tried to attend to his duties with the seriousness of youthful authority, she would harass him with the joy of youthful abandon. When he was helping with the herd, she pelted him with stones from the branches of a nearby tree. When he was training in the use of the sword or spear with Cian, she would yell taunts and gibes from the sidelines. When he struggled to bridle an unruly mount, she would roll on the grass in laughter. Yes, she was the little sister he never had: a spoiled brat.

Even so, there was an admiration behind her actions and he did feel a brotherly affection for her. In time, she might have found less antagonistic ways of showing it, if they had not had the incident at the river.

It happened some three festival cycles after Cathal had come to Cian's house, when Muirne was again experiencing a difficult pregnancy. That warm summer day, Aislinn had been sent to fetch Cathal for the evening meal. Aislinn came upon him at the river where it was wide and slow, floating on his back in languorous ease in a deep pool that was sheltered from the currents by a hollow near the bank. He had stripped and jumped into the near-by, cooling river to cleanse himself of the filth of the day after a difficult tending of the herd in the far field. A large and ancient oak, overhanging the river, provided both a place to tie his horse and a cooling filter of the warm August sun. As he drifted, the water must have muffled his hearing, because he seemed unaware of her approach.

Aislinn tied her horse next to Cathal's and shed her léine. Stealthily, she climbed the oak tree and crawled out on a limb above him. Her slim, willowy figure was yet that of a girl, without the thatch of hair and swelling hips and breasts. When she was over the relaxed young man, she jumped. Aiming for a spot right next to him, she curled herself into a human ball. When she landed, the waves she created swamped Cathal, filling his nose and mouth. Aislinn surfaced, shaking back her long hair with a quick flick of her head and breaking into wild laughter when she saw what had happened. He was sputtering and choking as he treaded water, looking for the cause of the sudden turmoil in the pool.

Cathal's temper flared as he remembered all the taunts and torments of days past. Before the girl regained control of herself, Cathal was upon her, forcing her head under water. It would have been normal horseplay, but she had not taken a breath before being submerged.

In panic, she fought to regain the surface, but he would not let her up yet. Obviously, he wanted a little retribution and his superior strength dominated. Her right hand happened to find his groin and she grabbed his wrinkled sack. Knowing that males were vulnerable there, but not the full extent, she squeezed to get Cathal to release her. In her near-hysterical fear, she squeezed hard. Very hard. Cathal released her.

As she regained the surface, gasping for air, Cathal fought to keep from choking. Slowly, painfully, he swam to shore. She easily reached it first and slipped on her discarded léine. As Cathal got to the side of the pool, he crawled out of the water and collapsed, groaning and curled on his side. Seeing him that way and worried that she had injured him far more than she had intended, Aislinn cautiously approached him.

"Can I help you?" she asked in a quavering voice.

"Get . . . away," he managed to grunt.

"Do you want me to get your léine for you?"

With great effort he managed to haltingly vent some of his feelings. "Get away . . . or . . . I . . . swear . . . I'll . . . drown you."

With that, he struggled slowly to his hands and knees. Hearing this, and the tone of his strained voice, the young girl ran to her horse and rode away as quickly as possible, glancing over her shoulder many times on the way back to her home. Cathal was a much better rider and his horse much faster. She was sure he would catch her before she reached safety and wreak vengeance on her. It did not happen. When she returned, her father asked of Cathal. She told Cian that the young man should be arriving soon. Very soon.

She was wrong. After a half hour had passed without Cathal appearing, Cian sent her to find him. When she found him, he was walking, leading his horse. Even walking, he should have covered the distance to the house in that time, but he was walking slowly, with an ungainly gait.

"Father sent me to see how much longer you will be," she said, warily keeping her distance in case he put on a burst of speed to catch her.

"As long as it takes." His voice was strained, unnatural.

"Why aren't you riding your horse?"

"Because I can't."

"Why not?"

"Haven't you done enough to me for one day?" he asked with barely-restrained rage. "Are you going to torment me all the way back as well? Can't you leave me alone?"

Without a word, she turned and went back to the house. Confused, she knew that she had hurt him more than she had first thought. She wanted to ask someone about what she had done, but did not know whom to ask. Her mother would have been the person. But the healer had given her a potion that helped her sleep. She might have asked her father, but felt a man might not understand her confusion. She feared that what she had done was something that would anger a man. So she decided to ask Bevin, their servant.

Bevin had been with them as long as Aislinn could remember. She had seen about ten more Samhains than Aislinn. She was small and slender, with dark hair and dark eyes that seemed to harbor an ever-present fear. Around Cian, Bevin hardly spoke and always in a soft, hesitant voice when she did. Although she was a slave, the family treated her kindly, especially Aislinn's mother to whom Bevin was devoted. Ever since her mother's illness, Aislinn had noticed that the servant had seemed distraught, paying little attention to the girl.

Aislinn went to Beven, who was cooking a stew in a cauldron over the hearth fire.

"Bevin, I need to ask you a question."

"What?" Bevin seemed to have been unaware that Aislinn was around. "A question? About what?"

"About what is between a man's legs."

"Do not even speak of such things," Bevin said. She sounded upset. She fingered a pair of crossed sticks that hung on a leather strap around her neck. "There is only cruelty and pain there."

"I just wondered--"

"Hush child." Bevin's voice was stern, almost angry. "Do not speak of such . . . such vileness again."

Then she patted Aislinn on the top of her head, a gesture that Aislinn felt was childish and demeaning. "Now go and play while I cook the meal."

With a sigh, Aislinn wandered out of the house. She would wait until her mother was well and ask her.

When Cathal finally returned, hobbling through the door, Cian asked what was wrong. He told a lie about climbing a tree and slipping, straddling the branch, protecting her from her father's anger. This and her father's solicitous concern for Cathal's injury confirmed Aislinn's opinion of how a man would view her action. She wanted to thank Cathal for the false story, but the glaring look he gave her convinced her that it would not be a good time. She would wait, talk to her mother, then make things right with Cathal. That night her mother went into labor.

The baby's birth cost Muirne her life. Cian never stopped mourning the loss and dismissed friends' suggestions that he follow the custom of taking another mate, instead devoting himself to work. With a wet nurse to tend to the baby and to the domestic chores, quarters seemed cramped and uncomfortable to Cathal. Since Cian would no longer be tending his sick wife, he did not greatly need Cathal anymore, so the young man returned home.

Cathal and Aislinn didn't say a word to each other when he left. Fate had left him bound by his self-righteous indignation while she was bound by uncomprehending guilt.   The baby, sickly from the difficult birth, died not long after, but Cathal never returned to live at the hearth of Cian.

Years passed without any peace overtures from either Cathal or Aislinn.   They settled into a pattern of cold politeness.   They would speak to each other, at least as much as was necessary to conduct whatever business they might have, but nothing more. Inside, she ached to explain she had not known what she had done and he longed to tell her that a childhood prank was of no lasting consequence, but the wall of pride is a tall one indeed.   If not for the cattle raid by Eoghan's clannsmen, that might have never fallen.

Chapter 5

Cathal was with his father when the herdsman reached Fergus's hearth with news of a cattle raid against the clann. More a boy than a man, the youth had collapsed with exhaustion from his run back to the settlement.

"Speak, boy," Fergus said.

"Raiders . . . cattle raiders." The herdsman raggedly gasped as he tried to speak. Breathing heavily from his long run, his eyes bulged with the effort of trying to deliver his message.

"Take a moment, lad," Cathal said. "Get your breath. We will wait."

"No!" The youth's eyes were wide, wild with panic. Gulping air, he continued. "They're killing . . . everyone. We . . . have no weapons. Those who cannot . . . run fast enough are . . . already dead."

Fergus jumped to his feet, roaring. "Who would kill defenseless children? What beast would do this?"

"A . . . a boar," the young herdsman managed to say.

"A boar?" Fergus said.

"A boar. A man like a boar . . . big, with black, bristling hair. Even his bratt is black."

"Bran," Cathal said, through clenched teeth. Bran was the nephew of Eoghan, the chief of a rival clann. They had met before and Cathal knew him to be cruel and arrogant. In games, he was known to gouge and bite while wrestling. Cathal had experienced it. "This time he has gone too far."

Cathal summoned his brothers and their council of battle was quick, since hesitation would mean the loss of more life and much of the clann's wealth. Cathal paced the floor of the roundhouse, hands folded across his chest, anxious to be in battle with such a dishonorable foe.

Fergus had wanted Connaire, as the youngest, to summon the other men of the clann to the defense of their cattle. Since they were all grazed on land common to all in the clann, everyone stood to lose if the raiders were not stopped.

"Let Ciarán take the word to the clann," Connaire said to his father. "Cathal needs me at the reins of his chariot."

Cathal's charioteer had suffered a broken arm a few weeks before and could not handle the fiery team that drew the chariot. His lightweight war chariot, a wicker-fronted platform with a single axle of wood-spoked wheels, was drawn by two ebony-black stallions that all knew could not be controlled by a weak hand.

Connaire pleaded with his father. "Cathal is known to all as a fearless warrior, worth three men. Seeing him ride into battle on his war chariot will inspire the clann and put dread into the hearts of these base raiders. No one else can handle the chariot as well as I. I have practiced with him many times."

For a change, Ciarán agreed with Connaire's plan. "This is wise, Father. I can summon the clann."

"No, no." Fergus shook his head. "You are the oldest. You should be at your brother's side."

"Because I am the oldest, the others will respond to me," Ciarán persisted. "I can get them there more quickly. Let me go to the clannsmen. And with raiders in our lands, there might be great danger in this task that I am more able to handle than a youth."

Fergus seemed uncertain, confused even, and he looked to Cathal. "This is unclear to me. Cathal, you decide."

Cathal had seen this happen more and more in the last few months. He was not sure why, but of late his father had become less of the commanding chief and more of a weak-willed, old man.

He stopped his pacing and turned to his brothers. Even though Connaire stood as tall as Cathal, his youthful frame was wiry rather than muscular like his older brother. Even his brown beard had not grown to the bushy fullness of an adult. Yet Connaire displayed a natural ability that boded well for his future standing. Ciarán, fighting a tendency for pudginess, was shorter than the other two and not even close to the warriors they were. Nor did he inspire awe. In council, however, he could be a formidable opponent. His mouth was to be feared more than his arm.

Cathal smiled. "Let Ciarán use the weapon with which he is most able. Connaire will drive my chariot."

Ciarán glared at Cathal, but said nothing. Fergus nodded his assent.

So Ciarán rode to rouse the men of the clann to defend their cattle and Fergus led those who had been at his hearth to delay the raiders until help arrived. In the fore was Cathal's chariot, with Connaire at the reins and Cathal holding several spears as he rode beside him.

The grim-faced contingent headed west, towards distant, steeply rising hills, from which a broad stream flowed. Between the forked branches of that stream lay the spring grazing land for the clann's cattle. Although not very wide, the steep-banked sides of the flowing waters kept the cattle from wandering across. Between the branches was a tract of gently rolling, green hills with few trees by the high banks of the north fork, where the waters kept the cattle in check on two sides while the field provided ample feed. Across the open end of the "V" formed by the dividing river, a high, rocky ridge formed the last natural barrier of a triangular, several-hundred acre field. There were three sandy fords and these were what the herdsman watched to keep any of the cattle from wandering. This made the herdsmen's task containing the herd easy and just a few youths were needed to do so.

As they approached the grazing land, Cathal signaled the warriors to halt.   From his chariot, he shouted to them

"The bare fields bordering the grazing land will be against us.   With no forest to shelter us, our enemies will see us and how few we are.   They will be able to overwhelm us with their greater numbers.   But if we stay on the far side of the low hills, we can use the ridge to prevent them from seeing our approach.   Then we can surprise them and use their confusion to our advantage.   We will drive them from our land and take revenge for the murder of our helpless lads."

With a roar, the gathered warriors gave their approval and followed Cathal as Connaire spurred the team forward.

Dark clouds covered the sky, giving an ominous foreboding to the day.   Lightning struck across the distant skies and the rumble of thunder gave warning of what was to come.   As Fergus and his men neared the ridge, rain began to fall, lightly at first but rapidly becoming a downpour.   It was a warm, spring storm with much force, but little wind.   As the water cascaded from the heavens, it was blinding and deafening.   Footing, he knew, would be difficult for both the attacker and the defender.

Only seven in number, Cathal knew surprise was their only hope.   They must surprise and hold their foes until reinforcements arrived.   If help arrived quickly enough, the herds could be saved. The passage of time was their ally and their opponents' foe.

As they crested the ridge and came into view of the raiders, Cathal and his men gave a yell and fell to the attack.   With the rolling thunder and the deluge, Bran's men had evidently not heard the sound of the galloping horses and were unaware of Cathal's small force approaching. The raiders on the far side of the field did not respond at first as the clannsmen crossed the rise, more concerned with trying to control the uneasy cattle and getting them moving as quickly as possible.

To Cathal, his enemies were mere shadowy forms, obscured by the curtain of rain, but there appeared to be about four times their own number scattered around the herds. Fergus went to the right, taking four of the others with him. Cathal and Connaire went to the left, the light, two-wheeled chariot becoming airborne as it cleared the rise. As it landed, it skidded on the soaked grass, sluing sideways as Connaire fought the reins for control. Although trained in the handling of a chariot, the youngest brother was not as adept as Cathal's own charioteer and not used to handling the powerful team in such adverse weather.

As Connaire struggled, the chariot came to the first enemy horseman who had just begun to draw his sword. Cathal hurled his first spear, piercing the chest of the man. In their careening ride, Cathal and Connaire were upon the next two raiders in but a moment. One, his spear raised, was ready for a fight but fell to Cathal's second spear before he could throw. The other horseman fled, closely followed by the chariot under Connaire's headlong and barely-controlled pursuit.

Urging the horses on, the youngest brother doggedly chased the fleeing raider. Cathal started working his way down the center pole of the chariot between the horses, intending to leap from it to the horse of the raider. He drew his sword and used his other hand to steady himself as the chariot jolted along the gentle slope.

Nearly blinded by the heavy rain, Connaire saw the raider veer sharply to the right and tried to follow. As the team turned, the chariot swung wide in the rain-slicked grass and the left wheel hit a large rock, half sunken into the ground. The wheel was not made to take such a side impact and the spokes snapped. The wheel disintegrated, burying the end of the axle in the sodden soil and bringing the left side of the chariot to an abrupt halt. With the hard-pulling team in full gallop when this happened, the chariot pivoted as the left side of the axle dug deeply and held firm, pitching the chariot into the air.

The chariot careened wildly to the left as the platform broke from the yoke and the team. Cathal, on the pole when this happened, was tossed violently forward as the horses were abruptly slowed by the drag of the damaged chariot. Although he tried to grab the reins while still clutching his drawn sword, his forward momentum pitched him off the chariot pole.

Cathal tried to control his roll as he hit the ground, but was bruised and stunned as he tumbled to a stop. Getting to his hands and knees, he tried to clear his head. Nothing seemed to be broken, but everything ached from the battering he had taken. His sword lay several feet away, but at least it was unbroken. He knew he must get to it as quickly as he could.

As he struggled to rise, Cathal saw that the horseman that he had been pursuing had seen what had happened and had stopped fleeing. With spear brandished high, he was galloping to attack the staggering warrior and closing fast.

Cathal had no time to reach his sword, with his only hope being to dive away from the spear at the moment it was hurled at him. Cathal was strong and agile, but in his dazed state and on wet grass, he had little hope of escape. As the gap between them closed, he could see the horseman's expression of glee, having trapped a stunned and weaponless opponent.

Just as Cathal started to leap aside, he saw a spear sail through the air and sink deeply into   is attacker's side, under his upraised spear arm. The doomed man's expression change to one of painful surprise as he fell heavily from his charging horse. Cathal regained his feet and he looked to see who had saved him.

There, like the legendary Fionn mac Cumhaill's warrior foster mother, was Aislinn. Astride her horse, with the rain plastering her long, thick hair to her head and her léine to her body, her muscular, female form was clearly outlined. As if seeing her for the first time, he realized the allure of her swelling hips and jutting breasts. With difficulty, Cathal forced his mind to focus on the battle at hand.

As he grabbed his sword from where it had fallen, Aislinn recovered the riderless horse of the dead raider. Bringing it to him, she offered Cathal the reins.

"You'd better check on Connaire. If he is safe, we could use your help near the far river," she said.

She sounded disappointingly brusque and cold to him, without even inquiring of his condition. He was standing, sword in hand, so that was enough. Instead of offering concern, she wheeled her mount and rode to rejoin the fight.

By then, enough of the clann had arrived to make the odds more in their favor, but Cathal could see through the mists that they were still outnumbered and he was needed. Leading his newly-acquired mount, he jogged unsteadily to his fallen brother. Kneeling beside him, Cathal found Connaire bruised, bloody and in pain.

"I'm sorry," the younger brother apologized. "I've destroyed your chariot and now I cannot even rise to help in the battle. I think my leg is broken."

Quickly checking his brother's leg, it lay at an odd angle and Connaire winced when he gently probed. Looking around, Cathal found a spoke from a shattered wheel of his chariot. Since it was fairly straight, he used it as a splint for Connaire's leg, binding it with strips torn from the young man's léine.   Making sure his brother was as comfortable as possible, Cathal leapt to the back of his mount and galloped to help his clann.

By the time he reached them, fighting was mostly finished. More warriors had arrived, coming singly and in groups as the summons had reached them.   As they had appeared, the raiders had broken from battle and fled across the river.   Cathal was sure that he saw Bran's stocky dark form among the fleeing raiders.   They had come for cattle, not for battle.

The warriors had wanted to pursue, but Fergus knew that the protection of the herds, the wealth of the clann, took priority.   If they were lost, it would be the ruination of all.   Eoghan had far more warriors than the few raiders they had just dispersed and the aging warrior-king knew that this could easily be a trap: sending a small party of raiders to draw the main body of warriors away. They would be ambushed by the main force of Eoghan's warriors, waiting for a rash pursuit.   Then the herds would be totally unprotected and at the mercy of Eoghan.   Instead Fergus had them calm the restless cattle, who had been disturbed by the clamorous weather and the clash of battle, as well as search for the herders. Only one had reached his house to give the alarm, so many were missing.   As was Ciarán.

He had never arrived at the scene of battle.

Chapter 6

With the fighting over, Cathal summoned the healer to see to those in need. The battle, such as it was, had been brief, but not bloodless. Six of the raiders had fallen, while Fergus's clann had lost two dead and two to serious wounds, not counting Connaire's leg. With the aid of the healer, Cathal organized his brother's return home. He was relieved that his brother had lived. He realized that he was even more relieved that Aislinn had lived. A cart had been brought for those needing it and Connaire, in spite of his protesting that he could ride a horse, was loaded with the dead and wounded. Cathal's team had been recovered and he traded the now-dead raider's mount for his favorite stallion from his team.

After seeing his brother safely away, Cathal felt the effects of his tumble. His shoulder was sore from his hard landing and his head ached. Grass, mud and even cow dung covered him, both body and clothes. With the river close at hand, he decided that at least he might remove the filth from himself. Riding upstream from the others, he tied his horse to a tree, hung his sword from a branch and plunged into the cool water without taking off his léine. Its cleansing effect reached his mind as well as his body, helping to clear the remnants of grogginess from his brain. After a few moments in the slow-moving water, he swam into a still pool to relax and recover. As he did, he heard a horse approaching.

Cathal was sure all the remaining raiders had fled, but he realized that his sword was too far from him. With powerful strokes, he swam for the shore. As he reached the land and rushed to his sword, the rider appeared. It was Aislinn. Seeing Cathal's hand reaching for his sword, she smiled.

"You need not worry. I'm here for the same reason as you: to wash off the battle." Blood was on the front of her léine, not her own.   Dismounting, she tied her horse and waded into the water. Looking over at Cathal, standing as if frozen with his hand grasping the hilt of his sword, she cocked her head and said with a slightly-mocking tone, "You really won't need the sword.   I am unarmed now, you know.   Unless I frighten you that much."

Cathal released his grip on the haft of his weapon and quickly waded back into the water.   It had not been fear that had stopped him where he stood.   It had been shock.   Shock and admiration.   Until this day, in spite of all physical evidence to the contrary, he had continued to think of Aislinn as a mischievous, pre-pubescent adolescent, the naked child who had humiliated his youthful manhood.   During the battle, when he had seen her on her horse when she had saved his life, a small voice in his mind had told him differently.

Now, as she waded into the water with her wet léine clinging to her body and revealing every curve of her form, he was forced to see her as a woman.   A very beautiful woman.   It both startled him and made him uneasy.   No longer could he dismiss her from his mind as a child.   He had to consider her as desirable.   The most desirable woman he had ever seen.   It was unexpected, and he hurried deeper into the river before she could see the evidence of his newly-acquired appreciation through his own wet léine.   He wanted to speak, to thank her for coming to his aid, but did not trust his voice.

Swimming over to him, Aislinn reached up to his forehead, softly asking, "Are you all right?   That was quite a tumble you took.   You have a terrible bruise."

He reached up to stop her hand, not trusting himself under her gentle touch.   As his hand grasped hers, their eyes locked.   For a moment, they stared intensely at each other and said nothing. Then he drew her to him.

Their bodies touched, separated by their clothing yet electrically aware of each other. Their lips met with open mouths, frantically probing, teasing and meshing. Her arms went around his neck, clinging to him, engulfing him. They both realized that the distance they had placed between each other had been artificial, a mechanism to protect themselves from admitting the passion they both had felt. Desire had been sublimated, transferred to icy aloofness. Each had been afraid to admit to him or herself the craving inside. Now, with the adrenaline of battle still coursing through their veins, these walls were gone.

One of his hands went to her breast, gripping and kneading as her nipple pushed back with a life of its own. His other hand went down. Her léine had floated up in the currents and he grasped her bare buttocks. As he pulled her tightly to him, his hand slipped into the cleft between her legs and she softly moaned. Slipping one hand between their bodies, she reached under his léine. Her fingers slipped down his hardness and grazed the sack at his crotch. Surprised at the suddenness of her touch, he flinched slightly. Pulling her lips from his, she gave a soft laugh.

"Don't worry," she reassured him. "I won't squeeze this time."

With only a muted grunt, he covered her mouth again with his own. His fingers probed and pressed. In response, her body pushed more intensely against him. One leg wrapped around his as she rocked and ground herself against his fingers. His other hand teased her hard nipple and rolled it between thumb and forefinger. Throwing back her head and fiercely panting, her face flushed red as waves of passion overwhelmed her. Cathal licked and gently nibbled her throat as she did. Uttering a satisfied groan, she leaned her head on his shoulder.

While Cathal had been at work on her, Aislinn had kept a

41

firm grip on his hard shaft. As she had squirmed in delight, her hand had pulled and tugged, bringing him to the edge of the great pleasure. Pulling her up high against his body, he was ready to slip inside her when she suddenly pushed away from him.

In frustration, he started to pull her back, but heard voices calling his name. As horses and riders appeared at the river's edge thirty or more paces downstream, Aislinn moved farther away from him. The riders were his friends, Tian, Gruagach and Cairbre.

"We wondered if you had been lost," Tian said with a wry smile. "But I can see you have been found. Maybe a little too found."

"I don't know what you're talking about," Aislinn said abruptly. "We both needed to wash the grime of battle from ourselves and happened to meet. Nothing more."

With that, she turned and waded to the shore. Cathal watched her, stunned.

"You are needed at the Dal of the aire," Tian said, referring to an assembly of the nobles of the clann. As he glanced from Cathal's startled face to Aislinn's closed visage, Tian's voice lost its usual flippancy. "We are to decide upon what action we should take. This was worse than we thought. They killed the herders. Most of them were mere boys, unarmed. This was not the way of warriors. We cannot let it pass."

"We will be there," Cathal said, indicating Aislinn and himself. If she would be a warrior, let her speak as one. She had shown the ability and valor in the field already. "Ride on. We will join you shortly."

Without another word, the three turned and left, obviously glad to be away from a situation that appeared to be problematic.

As soon as they had gone, Cathal waded out of the river, grabbed Aislinn by the arm and held her firmly in his grip. His tone of voice expressed his hurt and rage.

"What is this?   Am I nothing but a toy?   First you act as though you care for me, then you deny me to my friends."

"You, a toy?   I'm the one you wish to make a toy, to brag to your friends that you have been between the willing thighs of Aislinn, that she is like Maille, whose thighs have sheltered any who seek haven.   I will not have it.   Many have sought to delve into me, but I have denied them.   I will not be made a servant to any man."

"Nor would I want it."   He reached out with his other hand and gently brushed her forehead.   "I want a warrior who is my equal in all things.   That is you.   I want you."

"What do you mean by that?"   The quiver in her voice showed that she knew.

"I would oath to you.   Will you oath to me?"   His eyes were steadily holding hers in their gaze.

"Yes.   Yes, I will."   Her voice was almost inaudible, quivering just above a whisper.   "I give you my oath."

"And I give you my oath of love and fidelity."   His voice was as soft as hers, but firm and sure.

As they stood by the river, staring at each other and saying nothing more, the bond was made.   She reached up and, wrapping her arm around his neck, pulled his lips to hers.   Their kiss was long and deep.   Tongues intertwined as his arms pulled her close.   She could sense, feel, that he wanted to go further.   She did as well, but knew they would have to wait.   Unwillingly, she halted his advances.   Pulling back, she looked deep into his eyes.

"We are each other's now.   You have a council to attend, so this will have to wait."

"You only say that because you have been satisfied," he said with a slight smirk.   "You are right, however.   But you forget that you are to be at council as well."

43

"You go. I will follow shortly." As he equivocated, she added, "I need a moment. Please."

After a moment's hesitation, he left.

As she watched him ride away, Aislinn remembered when she had seen Cathal pitched from his chariot in the battle. How her heart had risen in her throat. How she had ignored the battle, all that was around her, and had ridden to him. How she had hidden her inner relief that he had not been badly injured or killed. Her harsh exterior had been her way of keeping herself from running to him, from embracing him and telling him of how much he meant to her.

Was her relief at his survival why she had decided to oath with him? Was it nothing more than an emotional over-reaction? She had always been independent, the equal of any man. True, Cathal had not asked subservience, but to join with a man was to risk it. But then, risk was what she wanted of life. With Cathal she felt that the risk to her individuality was minimal, even if other risks were high. The other risks she could stand. No, she would relish. It was a good choice. They would face all, good and bad, together. As for now, he would need her support in council.

Wading out of the river and taking her sword, she mounted her horse. Suddenly she felt the hair on the back of her neck rise in alarm, like the hackles of a threatened wolf. She was being watched. The rain had stopped some time before and the warm air caused a ground fog to rise, partially obscuring the far bank. A horseman across the river turned and galloped away. She thought it looked like Ciarán. A shiver ran down her spine. With a feeling of foreboding, she galloped home to prepare for the council.

Chapter 7

The Dal was held in the large hall of the briugu, a wealthy man who was entrusted with the clann's hospitality and hosting its meetings. When he arrived at the rectangular hall, Cathal pushed past those standing by a bonfire lit in preparation for the coming darkness and entered the hall. The heads of each hearth were closest to the center to act as spokesmen. His father was in the center of the gathering, sitting on a chair with his druid and brehon close at hand. A large fire burned brightly next to them, with the smoke filtering through the thatched roof. A number of torches flickered around the room, giving an eerie, hazy light.

Ciarán rushed in and sat next to Fergus. Of late, Cathal had seen that Ciarán had Fergus's ear more than his traditional advisors, his brehon and his druid. It was said that currying favor with Ciarán was one's key to having a dispute decided in one's favor, that Fergus had grown too dependent, and that it might be time for Fergus to step down from his chieftainship. It was not good for the clann for his father to continue in his condition. While that was true, Cathal hesitated to speak against his own father.

As the last of the clann crowded into the room, the murmur of voices grew to a loud drone. Cathal knew that this was a crucial moment for them. Eoghan and his clann had been at odds with Fergus's clann for many years. Normally, there had been posturing by warriors when they met, occasional fights and a few head of cattle stolen from time to time. These were not the acts of war.

Now all had changed. This last raid had been an attempt to steal most of the herds of the clann, to leave them impoverished and starving in the coming winter. That alone would have been just cause for war, but the killing of the unarmed herders, youths from the households, was even worse. It was a challenge, an insult, to them and could not be left unanswered, no matter what the cost. Yet, as valiant as the warriors of his clann were, Cathal knew they were outnumbered by clann Eoghan and would have to be very fortunate to triumph in an out-and-out war.

Fergus stood in the smoky light and glared. Silence fell. He spoke.

"Everyone knows what happened today. If not for the valor of Ciarán in rallying the warriors all would have been lost." A murmur of disagreement arose, but Fergus's stern gaze brought back silence. Although many had begun to wonder if his mind, like a rusty sword, had lost the keenness of its edge, his presence still commanded respect. His powerful chest and thickly-muscled arms were still formidable. "I have asked Seanan, the keeper of our laws, to tell us if we have cause to take this battle to the very hearths of Eoghan."

Seanan, the brehon, stood. A friend of Fergus since both men had been boys, he lived with the clann when not judging some dispute in other clanns. As a most learned anruth, his wisdom and knowledge were widely respected. Age, however, had taken its toll on his body, while not his mind. Although still tall and erect, his height the equal of Cathal, his spare frame had become gaunt and his cheeks hollow. He walked hesitantly, using a staff to steady himself. A fine fringe of gray hair circled a shiny pate. Only his beard was still full and hearty, though now gray as well.

Any impression of weakness, however, was dispelled by his flashing almost-black eyes under thick, shaggy brows. Before speaking, he scanned those gathered, holding their eyes to his in a hypnotic stare. For a moment, he said nothing as he studied them. Then, with a sigh, he finally spoke.

"It is true that you have cause to take this battle to the very

hearths of Eoghan.   Killing the young boys has violated honor, one
of the three legs of the cauldron of society."   A roar swelled from
the assembly, a roar of hurt and anger.

Seanan merely raised his hand and within seconds silence
was restored.   "You have just cause, but you should consider.   If
you do so, many will die.   Clann Eoghan is strong.   You may lose
all of our bravest warriors and then your clann would be
defenseless.   Would you be violating the third leg of the cauldron,
duty, duty to preserve your clann?   Your duty is to keep those
within the clann safe.   You can go to the ri.   We can tell him what
has happened and exact an honor price, a heavy one that will
compensate us for the loss of our cattle and for our young men.   By
doing that, we would keep all three of the legs of the cauldron: truth,
honor and duty."

"No!"   It was Fiach, one of Ciarán's companions, a gaunt
warrior with little skills other than a loud voice.   "We should ride
now, burn every house and steal all the cattle of Clann Eoghan."

"Brave words from a man whose sword only gathers rust,"
Tian muttered.

Fiach turned to him.   "Are you calling me a coward?   You
are fortunate that weapons are forbidden in the Dal."

Tian stepped close to him, his stare icy.   "No, you are lucky.
But this meeting will end and we can meet any time you wish to
settle this."

Fiach dropped his eyes.   "I meant no offense.   I only want
revenge on the killers, as any warrior must.   I am a warrior, as you
are."

Tian spat on the ground.   "When you disrespect Seanan,
you act as a coward. Act like a warrior and I will give you the
respect of one."

The voices of those assembled rose, with some loudly

supporting Seanan's suggestion and others yelling for immediate action. Hotheads wanted to attack at that moment while the calmer ones urged seeking the intercession of the ri before any rash action. The council might go either way.

Cathal stood and raised his hands. Those that respected him and followed his lead soon silenced the crowd.

"Clannsmen," he said, turning to face all in turn. "I feel the same rage that all of you do. We cannot let this slaughter go unpunished. My heart says that we should ride after those foul murderers and woe be to any who come in our way." A roar of approval filled the night air. Again, he held up his hands for quiet. "But we live by laws, laws handed down to us by our ancestors. Laws that Seanan spent many years to learn and to give to us advice in times like this. Seanan says we should first appeal to the ri to hold Clann Eoghan to our laws." A few muttered in disagreement, but Cathal pressed on. "But if the ri does nothing, I will lead the fight into the very hearth of Eoghan himself. My sword will know no mercy."

First a few, then almost all there began to cheer. Cathal's words had swayed even the hotheads to follow the wise words of Seanan.

Then Ciarán stepped forward. Clasping his hands behind his back and looking up at the smoky roof, he calmly waited until the crowd had quieted enough to hear him.

"Clannsmen. My cautious brother bids us do nothing until the ri deigns to hear our plea. We mourn, with no revenge, for our slain boys." An angry murmur started among the hotheads, then spread. Ciarán was feeding the fire of their anger. He raised a clenched fist and shook it as though he were brandishing a sword. "We act now! I am not afraid to ride at your head against the clann of Eoghan!"

"Like you were when we fought them earlier, hiding in the back until the killing was done?"

The question came from the back of the crowd and brought silence. This was an assault on Ciarán's courage, a challenge. Darkness had fallen and the speaker was hidden by it. Those in front of the speaker parted, giving him a path to the center where Ciarán stood. Connaire, using a forked stick as a crutch, hobbled forward to confront Ciarán.

"That is a challenge to combat, Brother," Ciarán said. His eyes darted along the faces illuminated by the torches. "I cannot take advantage of your injury, though, so you can insult me with no consequence. It is not honorable. As you know, I was summoning the warriors. I arrived, but only after you had been injured in the battle. You did not see me because I was at the far end of the field."

"I did not see you either. How many did you slay?" This time it was Aislinn who spoke. She stood, wrapped in her father's bratt, and legs wide spread, as if ready for an attack. Others were beginning to murmur, asking each other where he had been during the fight.

Ciarán took the offensive. "I said that I was there. If you dispute my word, again I can do nothing. I will not kill a woman. You should not even be speaking in the Dal. This council hears only the heads of the hearths. Your father is the one to speak for your hearth. You are nothing but a woman."

Some of the voices rose in agreement, but others were just as vocal in dissent. Aislinn's eyes flashed with anger and her fists clenched at her sides. It was fortunate for Ciarán that weapons were forbidden in the assembly, but her eyes sent spears at his heart when she replied.

"As you know, my father is ill and will die at any time. By

our custom, another free person may then speak for the hearth. As I am the only other warrior in my hearth, it is I. You have allowed many warriors who are not the head of their Fine to speak, so I also have the right to speak as a warrior. And, as a warrior, I am able to challenge the words of any other speaker here. That is also the way of our people. As a warrior, I can also fight to defend my honor. This 'woman' will meet you at any time on the field of combat."

Ciarán was momentarily without words. Ciarán's speech had silenced Cathal by making any further protestation seem an admission of cowardice. His wording had been enough of an insult to quiet any wise words, while not enough to warrant a challenge. It had worked, until Connaire and Aislinn spoke so effectively. Aislinn had spoken the truth, as had Connaire. Ciarán was saved, however, as Fergus stood, pounding the arm of his chair.

The aging chief's powerful frame was unwithered by the years, though his beard and long hair were now gray. His green plaid bratt flowed off of his broad shoulders like a field of grass flowed down a mountainside. Steel gray eyes flashed angrily as he spoke.

"I'll not have these attacks on my son! Ciarán had the reins of my chariot in this battle. He shielded me from the spear of Cormac. If any challenge him, let them first challenge me! If any dispute my word, let him challenge me! Even if it is a woman, let her challenge me!"

Silence fell on the assembly. Cormac, a brother of Eoghan, had been dead for ten years, dead from the sword of Cathal as he had guided the chariot of Fergus. It was that very chariot that now lay damaged in the field of the day's battle.

"Father," Ciarán said, as he moved closer to Fergus, "should we not ride against Clann Eoghan? Should we wait for the ri who might do nothing? Are we cowards who wait for others to fight our battles?"

"No!" Fergus roared, his word echoed by the hotheads. "We ride at first light tomorrow. This clann is proud and strong. No one can slaughter our youth without knowing our swords and spears. It is a clann of heroes, not cowards. Are there any of you afraid to fight?"

A resounding "No" echoed in the night. All there were swayed by the resurgence of Fergus's charisma. No one dared to speak against him, not even Seanan the brehon or Miach the druid. The crowd's wish had swung to war and war it would be. Ciarán smiled.

"Look to your hearths now," Fergus said, "and sharpen your weapons. We ride tomorrow."

With a cheer, the crowd dispersed. Men and women moved away in small groups, excitedly talking of coming battle glories. Soon only Fergus, Ciarán, Cathal, Connaire, Seanan, Miach and Aislinn remained.

Fergus looked around, confused. "Where is Betha?"

"She is dead, Father," Connaire said. "Mother has been dead for many years."

All the power seemed to leave Fergus. His shoulders hunched as he turned from face to face, bewildered.

"She isn't dead. I slept with her last night. I remember the stew she made for dinner before we rested. She is somewhere. She might be lost. Ciarán, will you help me find her?" he said, turning to his eldest son.

"Of course, Father. I am always here to help you." Ciarán wrapped his arm around his father's shoulders. Taking one of the torches, he led his father away. The others stood in silence as Ciarán guided Fergus through the darkness to his house.

Chapter 8

As Cathal watched Ciarán take his confused father away, his heart ached. As much as he loved his father, he wished that he had died in the battle. Then the old warrior's dignity would have stood intact, enshrined by an honorable death. Soon, Cathal feared, he would be forced to stand in the Dal and state that his father was no longer fit to be chief. And that would kill the old man. Cathal's love of his father kept him from acting in the best interest of the clann. But how much longer could he hesitate?

"I should have protested," Connaire finally said. "Father is not well. To attack Clann Eoghan in the morning, after they have prepared, will mean the death of many and no victory. We are brave and skilled warriors, but so are they. I fear the result."

"No, it is I who should have spoken," Cathal said as he shook his lowered head. "I held back because Ciarán manipulated me and I did not want to show the clann how Father is slipping. I take the blame."

"If you are both finished with the self-flagellation," Seanan said, eyes probing each brother in turn, "we should consider what must be done to prevent the clann's ruin. The truth is that nothing either of you could have said would have made any difference. The Fergus we knew is gone. He is becoming Ciarán's hound, obeying his master's will without thought, and something will have to be done soon. For now, we must find a way to save this clann from a bloody defeat."

"I know what must be done." It was Miach. His druidic tonsure of shaving the front of his head from ear to ear and leaving it long in the back made his round, ruddy, clean-shaven face look even rounder. Because of his short stature and battle against portliness, someone who did not know him might easily underestimate his wisdom and strength of will. A mouth that was often turned up in a grin hid the iron that was in his green eyes. While his years were shown by gray hair and lines on the face, his mind was as alert and able as ever. And when he knew what he must do, he was not to be thwarted. "I will go to clann Eoghan and call them to account for what they have done."

Aislinn shook her head. "You cannot be so rash. They might kill you."

"I appreciate your concern, but it is unwarranted," Miach said, as he rested a hand on her shoulder. "Even if Eoghan were as evil as some here think he is, he would never harm a druid. And I know Ailin, his druid. I will speak to Ailin."

"But we ride against clann Eoghan at dawn. What can you do before then?" Connaire asked.

"Much, I hope. All of you try to delay the attack. I'm leaving now. I will return as soon as possible. With luck, I will have good news. If I fail, may Morrigan give you success in battle." With that said, Miach took a torch and strode toward the horses. Cathal thought he looked taller, that the druid had grown in physical stature by his determination.

After a moment, Cathal shook his head and said, "We cannot rely upon such a wild hope to save the clann. In the morning I will confront Fergus and get him to change his mind."

"That hope is wilder than your stallions," Seanan said. "This is not the Fergus we have known. This Fergus is ruled by Ciarán's manipulations. If you try to stop him, you will lose. He has roused the bloodlust of the clann and once aroused, like Cú Chulainn in a frenzy, they will not be calmed.

"When we have resolved this war, you must confront Fergus. Miach and I will support you. He cannot continue as taoiseach. We should have done this before. We did not. Until

Fergus is replaced, we must tread cautiously. He is still much loved. For now we will rely upon Miach's great skills."

Cathal started to protest, but stopped. He would act only after the problem with Eoghan's clann was resolved, when the very life of the clann was no longer in jeopardy. "It is late. Whatever happens, tomorrow will be a difficult day. Let us get some rest."

As they scattered to their homes, Aislinn walked with Cathal. They walked close to each other, but not touching. She wondered if the magic of their river encounter would be lost. Finally Cathal put his arm across her shoulders and pulled her to him.

"As soon as we have finished with the business of tomorrow, we will publicly oath," he said, before giving her a kiss on the forehead.

"I will go with you now," she said. "I will be with you tonight."

"What of your father? Will he not worry?"

"The healer has given him a potion to ease his pain and he is always asleep or groggy," she said sadly. "He never even knows I am around anymore. I fear this disease will soon take him to our ancestors, the next turn of the wheel."

"I fear that I will be poor company tonight. Too many specters to haunt my dreams. Perhaps we should wait until this is over."

Aislinn stopped and pulled away from him. Clouds covered the stars, enveloping their world in a cloak of darkness. Without having to see his face, though, she knew what he was thinking.

"You fear you might die tomorrow. You are trying to protect me from mourning you."

He said nothing.

She grabbed his arm, clenching his bicep. Her voice was taut. "If this is all we have, then that is as it shall be. Do not deny me this time together. Do not deny yourself. We should be with each other for as many days as we have life."

Silently, they walked with arms encircling each other's waists to the house where Cathal lived with his brothers and Fergus.

The roundhouse had a short, windowless stone wall with a log-beamed, pitched roof on top of it. The floor was excavated a few feet to give more headroom inside. A central communal area of about twenty feet had sleeping stalls on the sides shielded from view by hides. A fire in the central hearth, vented only by the porosity of the thatched roof, gave a smoky light and warmth to the house.

As they entered, Connaire caught Cathal's eye and smiled. Fergus was not to be seen, but snoring came from his sleeping area. Ciarán, though, was banking the fire in the hearth as they entered and glared before turning back to his task.

Cathal and Aislinn pulled back the hide divider as they entered his sleeping area. They slipped off their léines and crawled under the fleeces of his bed. Cuddling against Cathal's powerful body, Aislinn reached down to find that Cathal was not aroused.

"What's wrong?" she asked. "Do you no longer find me desirable?"

"I . . . I'm sorry. It's not you. The worries of tomorrow press hard on me. After tomorrow, I'm sure I'll be . . . normal again." His concern over what he saw as a weakness was evident in his voice.

"Do not worry. You are tired. Rest."

She cradled him in her arms, holding him close to her breast.

"I can try to-" he started to say.

"Hush." Slightly rocking, she gently cooed a soft song her

mother had taught her before she died. A song from when she was a young child. She heard him start to breathe the deep, regular breaths of sleep. She stayed that way, holding his head to her breast, for hours. A dread, a foreboding of the next day, filled her heart. When she finally drifted to sleep, it was fitful and restless.

Chapter 9

Dawn broke cold, cloudy and windy. Although it was not raining, the chill, damp air promised that it soon would and Ciarán pulled his bratt tightly about his body. As he walked through those gathered by the house of Fergus, he saw warriors sharpening their swords and spears while others in the settlement prepared a coarse, flat bread and cheese for the journey to Eoghan's land. While the best warriors had horses, this effort was to drain the settlement of all who could fight and the majority of them would be on foot. With those on foot holding back those on horseback, it would take six hours to reach their destination, assuming that they were not met by the enemy in route. After the raid, Clann Eoghan would surely expect a reprisal and might try to strike first. Ciarán knew he must control the battle. Everything depended upon it.

As he entered the informal council of war being held in the home of Fergus, Ciarán saw that Fergus, Cathal and Seanan were already there. Evidently Connaire was seeing to helping the warriors prepare for battle, knowing that he would be sitting at the settlement while the fight raged. No one mentioned Miach's absence. Fergus didn't seem to notice and Ciarán was glad not to have his voice to speak against his plan.

Ciarán wanted to move a solid force, placing all their hope on finding the enemy either still at their own settlement or on the same route Fergus's warriors were taking. Cathal argued for using a screen of outriders surrounding those on foot. The horsemen could quickly come to the aid of the main body, he said. Without the screen, the enemy might slip past and raid the clann's defenseless lands, or possibly circle around Fergus and catch his forces by surprise. Fergus, as the chief, would lead the warriors and decide the battle tactics.

As Ciarán and Cathal angrily argued the best course of action, Fergus looked from one to the other with bewildered incomprehension. Ciarán saw this and knew what to do.

"Father," he said, "you must decide. Will you not allow my greater age to give the wisdom in this?"

"Age has nothing to do with it," Cathal said. His face was flushed as he spat the words. "Your plan is insane."

"Ah, Father, now Cathal says the aged are insane." His dark eyes glinted at this verbal coup. It was the type of comment that would evoke an angry response from Fergus. It might have worked, if not for Seanan.

As brehon, he knew he was to avoid taking sides in intra-clann arguments that had nothing to do with points of law or tradition. Perhaps it was the obvious attempt by Ciarán to use flawed logic that goaded the aging legalist to intercede.

"I too find your plan flawed, Ciarán. Would you claim the wisdom of age over me?" While Ciarán glared, Seanan reached out and placed a comforting hand on the shoulder of the confused chief. "Fergus, my friend of many years, each of your sons is different. Each has special abilities. Cathal is our best young warrior. Trust Cathal on this. If not, trust me."

"Yes," Fergus said with a sudden sureness. "Yes, we will do as Cathal suggests. Cathal can command the outriders and Ciarán and I will ride at the head of the main column."

"I can see the wisdom of our brehon's words," Ciarán said with unexpected graciousness. Cathal's and Seanan's faces betrayed their shock as he continued. "Since this is Cathal's plan, he should ride with you at the head of our main force. I will command the outriders. I know the very men for such work. The rest of the mounted warriors should be with you."

"Very good, Ciarán," Fergus said. "You show great honor

by bestowing this position on your brother. Let it be so."

"Father," said Cathal, alarmed at having only Ciarán and his picked men as outriders. "Let Ciarán ride by your side. I desire no honors. I will command the outriders."

"Do you countermand me?" Fergus's voice rose, but a tremor gave it a quavering nature rather than one of strength. "I have said that you ride by my side and Ciarán shall command the outriders. That is how it shall be."

"But, Father . . . ." Cathal began, but stopped. He could see the irritation in his father's eyes and the gloating in Ciarán's. Switching tactics, he said, "As you wish, Father. But let the outriders be the women warriors. They are smaller and less easily seen. They are also quick on their horses. Then we will have the strongest warriors in the main force." He had said this knowing of his father's prejudice: women warriors were not the equal of the men and should be used as auxiliaries.

"Father, no," Ciarán said with alarm. "I must choose my own men."

"This is wise," Seanan said with a hard glance at Ciarán. "You know women are best used to ride around the battle rather than fight."

Cathal knew that Seanan had not spoken his true feelings. Although women were a small minority of the warriors, they were neither less valiant nor less bold in battle than a man. But the waning of Fergus's mental powers required treating him more like a child, playing to his fears and prejudices, than talking to him like the chief he was.

"Yes," Fergus said, nodding in agreement. "That is true. That is how it shall be."

"But Father--" Ciarán began, visibly upset.

"So it shall be," Fergus interrupted, with a raised hand to

prevent further argument. Enough of a spark of the old Fergus was there that Ciarán said nothing, but glared at Cathal and Seanan before he stalked out.

Fergus sat a moment, staring after him. Then he suddenly said, "I must see to my warriors," and left the house.

Cathal was about to follow when Seanan grabbed his arm. He still had a grip of iron hidden in his thin frame.

"We have delayed too long," he said. Although his voice was firm, his eyes were sad, almost tearing. Something Cathal had never seen in the brehon. "For the sake of the clann, we must select a new taoiseach. As you must know, it will most likely be you."

"No," Cathal said, violently shaking his head. "I do not want to be the one to challenge my father."

"Miach and I will support you. We have been his friend for longer than you have lived, but we also know that the clann must have a taoiseach who is strong in mind as well as body. With our voice added to yours, we can force the Dal to face reality."

Cathal stood in silence a moment, head bowed, before he said, "For now we have a more immediate problem. When it is over, I will talk with you and Miach about my father. Not until then."

Without another word, Cathal walked out of the house. Seanan stood a moment, staring after Cathal. His eyes were sorrowful. Slowly he shook his head, and then followed Cathal.

Chapter 10

There was an infectious excitement in the settlement. It was almost as though the people were preparing for a festival rather than a battle. Still, there was an edge of worry and concern. As mates were embraced and children were kissed, those leaving and those remaining knew they might not meet again. Cathal found Aislinn checking the bridle of her horse.

"I need you to watch Ciarán," he said to her.

"I love you too. Is that all you have to say to me?"

"I am sorry. I have just met with Father and Ciarán. For some reason Ciarán has had Father make him the leader of the outriders as we move out. Only with the help of Seanan did I persuade Father to have the women warriors, rather than Ciarán's cronies, be the outriders."

Pulling his mouth to hers, Aislinn deeply kissed Cathal. Looking into his eyes she said, "I understand your worries. I will watch Ciarán, and I will have some of my friends help. Trust me. And love me."

"I do love you," he said, kissing her. "There is something happening here that I do not understand and worries me. But we will win, both in this battle and the one with Ciarán. Then tonight we can be together."

"Until tonight." She said as she reached out and gently stroked his cheek. "But now I must join the other outriders. Take care. Our time together has just begun."

With that, she leapt onto her horse and, clasping his sides with her knees, rode away without looking back.

Fergus and a number of mounted warriors were to be in the vanguard of the main body, followed by those on foot. Connaire was with those gathering to ride against Eoghan, painfully astride his horse. Just before they left, Fergus handed Cathal a bow and quiver of arrows.

"What is this for?" Cathal asked. "I have my sword and spear. I have no use for a bow. It is not honorable to kill another warrior from afar."

"Just carry it," his father said. "Your brother says that we will quickly win this battle and he intends to hunt boar on our return for a victory feast."

Cathal looked questioningly at Connaire. He gave a half smile, raised his eyebrows and shrugged.

"It was not I," he said to Cathal. "With my leg in this condition, I cannot ride any distance, much less hunt. I will be remaining here at the settlement. Ciarán came by with the bow, claiming that he did not want to carry the extra weight of the bow while an outrider. It is not very heavy. I told father that there was no reason Ciarán could not carry his own bow, but neither of them cared for my opinion."

Fergus's face turned red with anger.

"Is this so much to ask," he said, his voice quivering in rage. "Your brother is in the most danger and asks for this small favor. You would eat of the boar he would kill, yet you begrudge him this. Will you defy me as well as insult your brother?"

With great difficulty, Cathal restrained himself from telling his father that he was being duped. He remembered how his father had favored him for so long: two warriors from the same mold. Since his father's memory and reason had started to fail, Cathal had seen Ciarán worm his way into his father's graces and turn him against him. Cathal considered speaking honestly to his father about his concern that Ciarán had some ulterior motive to having him carry the bow. Of late, any disagreement merely sent his father into a rage. Instead, he angrily slung the bow and quiver on his back and rode silently off, his father following.

The advance toward lands of Eoghan's clann was unhampered. As they passed the field of the previous day's battle, where armed men and women now watched with wary eyes for raiders, Cathal sadly studied his chariot. The severity of the damage to it looked even worse than before. One wheel was shattered, the tongue broken away and the basket crushed.

He wondered if he would ever again feel the thrill of riding behind the snorting stallions that pulled it, know the excitement of walking the center pole to attack an enemy or feel the joy of heady speed as he rode it across a meadow.

Although he hoped that he would, he doubted it. Fewer and fewer warriors used chariots. The horse was now favored. The wheel had turned. Would the time of the mighty war chariot ever return? How much of what he held dear would pass with time?

With a shake of his head, Cathal decided it was best not to know.

After almost three hours, several outriders galloped to the main body. Maille, a powerfully built woman warrior of Aislinn's contingent, rode up to Fergus.

"Eoghan and his warriors are just over the next rise. They form a line and just wait. What I cannot understand is that they do not seem to be ready for a fight. No spears, no swords. They just wait, like calves to the slaughter."

Fergus turned to Cathal, puzzled.

"Is it a trap?" he asked. "Do you think they want us to attack? What is Eoghan's plan?"

"I have no idea. It makes no sense." Cathal slowly shook his head as he studied the ground. "Have the outriders form one body and stay in the trees to our left. Then, if Eoghan attacks, they can hit his right flank by surprise."

"Yes," Fergus said, turning back to Maille. "Have the outriders ready on our left."

Without another word, Maille turned and rode away. After passing the word to the other warriors to be on the alert, Cathal joined Fergus as they rode over the grassy rise. What they saw on the other side was Maille had described.

Eoghan sat astride his horse at the front of his warriors, unarmed and flanked by Miach and another druid. His face was grim and resigned. None of his warriors appeared to be armed. As Fergus and his riders crested the rise, Eoghan and Miach rode toward them. Eoghan reined his horse to a halt in front of Fergus.

"We owe you honor price," he said, bowing his head. "We have a debt for our offenses."

Fergus seemed confused, unsure of what to say or do. Cathal rode forward and spoke. "There are those in our clann who feel that an honor price is not enough, that those who would slay unarmed boys should not escape so lightly."

"They are right," Eoghan said, bowing his head. "What was done was without honor. I had no knowledge of what happened until Miach came to me. Still, I am taoiseach and will pay what price you demand."

"Why?" Fergus asked. "Why did this happen?"

"My nephew, Bran, led the raid," Eoghan said. "He never told me of it. Most of us knew nothing of it and regret the deaths of your boys. The Dal has told Bran that he is no longer of this clann. He and his followers have been made outlaws. None of them are under the clann's protection any longer. But that is of no matter here. What would you have of us?"

With his enemy prostrate before him, warriors unarmed,

Fergus sat erect on his horse and took control.

"Your brehon will meet with my brehon. They will decide the honor price. It will be done with truth and honor."

"So be it," Eoghan said, raising his eyes to meet Fergus'. "We have often fought, but always with honor. You have shown great kindness. I hope that we might never fight again. Let our clanns be allies from this day on."

Before Fergus could reply, Ciarán rode up to them, accompanied by Aislinn, Maille and several women warriors. His eyes were hooded, dark and angry. There was a bow slung across his back.

"Why do you hesitate, Father?" he demanded. "The man responsible for the slaughter of our boys is right before you. Kill him."

"No." Fergus spoke strongly, with the firmness and purpose for which he had been known in days past. "Honor price will be paid and the matter will be ended. He is not the one responsible. It is Bran who bears the burden of responsibility."

"Speaking of Bran," Aislinn said, looking toward horsemen visible on the ridge behind Eoghan and his warriors. "He is there."

Unslinging his bow, Ciarán, notched an arrow and drew bead on a figure on the ridge.

"No!" Fergus roared. "You will not dishonor us by killing him in this way. If you do, I will kill you myself. Go and meet him in single combat."

Ciarán lowered his bow, but made no move toward the ridge. His eyes darted from Fergus to Eoghan.

"If Eoghan is to pay honor price, then I should do nothing," he said. "Bran is of Eoghan's clann and will be covered by that price."

"Bran is no longer of this clann," Eoghan said. "What he

has done has removed him from us. You may kill him at will without worry from any here."

Ciarán said nothing. Cathal stifled a smile. Bran the Boar, would have destroyed Ciarán with one blow and Cathal knew Ciarán was not one to act in such a heroically fatal way.

Aislinn pushed forward and, blandishing her spear, shouted, "I will fight him and his warriors. Will any join me?"

With a roar, Fergus's warriors showed their support. Cathal gave her a sardonic grin. He should have been the one to issue the call, but had hesitated. Although he agreed with the desire for revenge, he feared that their mounted warriors would be too few against the numbers he saw on the ridge. Nonetheless, he would ride in the fore of the attack. Better to die the hero than live the coward.

"I will not need this for the battle," Cathal said as he flung the bow Ciarán had given him to the ground at the foot of Ciarán's horse. Ciarán said nothing, but glared at Cathal as he dismounted to retrieve the bow.

Then the most unexpected happened. Nuallán, the most noted of Eoghan's warriors rode up to them and said to his chief, "Eoghan, many of Fergus's warriors are on foot. They will be of no use in catching Bran. Our warriors have brought no weapons, but, if those on foot will loan us theirs, we will ride against Bran. His actions have brought dishonor upon all of our clann."

Eoghan turned to Fergus. "What he says is true. If your warriors on foot will do as he asks, our warriors will ride with yours. Will you allow this?"

"Yes," said Fergus. "We will fight Bran together. Or least our young warriors will." He smiled grimly at Eoghan. "I fear we old warriors cannot keep the pace of the young ones and Bran will escape us."

Eoghan nodded his agreement. Quickly, his warriors gathered arms from those of Fergus's clann on foot. As one body, the warriors of both clanns rode toward the crest where Bran and his warriors were watching them. Seeing this united force, Bran and his contingent turned and fled. Aislinn, Cathal and the others pursued, soon out of the sight of Fergus and Eoghan. Cathal glanced back, seeing that Ciarán stayed at Fergus's side, two bows now slung across his back.

It was two days before Cathal and his warriors returned to the clann, tired and frustrated. After a full day of riding, they had tracked Bran to the lands of the Uí Néills. Just as they had closed upon Bran and his men, a large body of Uí Néill warriors had appeared from behind a grassy knoll and interposed themselves between the pursuers and the pursued. They outnumbered the warriors from the clanns of Fergus and Eoghan by at least two handcounts of their number. It was a powerful contingent from a powerful Cenél forming a line at a rise between Bran's riders and those of Cathal. They made a wall of horses, men and flashing swords. The young warrior at their head had as commanding a stature as Cathal, sitting tall and proud on a prancing horse as he waited their next move.

Halting their own warriors, Cathal rode alone to meet the leader of the Uí Néills.

"You are on Uí Néill lands," the warrior said. "You have no claim here."

"Our quarrel is not with you," Cathal replied, "but with one of our own. He is from the kingdom of Dál Riata and has acted without honor."

The warrior frowned, as if uneasy with his role. "If you have a complaint, you must take it up with Uí Néill. Only he, our taoiseach and king, can allow you to continue your pursuit. And he has told us that you must not enter our lands."

Bran, secure behind the fence of Uí Néill swords, had ridden to where Cathal and the Uí Néill warrior were speaking. His smirk showed that he knew he felt no fear of his former clannsmen.

"Oh, mighty and proud Cathal," Bran said with a sneer. "What will you do now that the Uí Néills block your way? Will you turn like the cur that you are and flee back to Fergus and Eoghan?"

"I will take you, coward," Cathal said, reaching for his sword. "The Uí Néills will not protect you when they learn of your treachery."

Aislinn reached out to restrain Cathal, but the Uí Néill warrior had already drawn his sword, followed by the rest of his warriors. Cathal's and all those with him responded in kind. Tension sparked the air like a summer thunderstorm. At any moment, the lightning of pride might ignite a battle.

"Hold," Nuallán firmly told Cathal. "We have ridden with you to help avenge the wrong of Bran, but our fight is not with the Uí Néills. We will accomplish nothing but create mourners by fighting them, and it will bring no honor to us. We will die and Bran will still go free."

"Listen to him," the Uí Néill said to Cathal. "I have no desire to fight you, but I will if you force me. I wish that matters were different, but they are not. Let it be. You cannot win this battle and you will only cause sorrow for both of our Cenéls."

"What battle has Uí Néill lost that you would protect one such as this?" Cathal asked the warrior, gesturing at Bran.

"It is not in the battling, but the bedding," Bran said with a laugh as he turned and rode back to his followers.

"My ri has promised safe passage for these ... refugees while they are in our lands. I must protect them if you attack," said the Uí Néill, shifting uneasily on his horse. His eyes were downcast, not meeting Cathal's. "If we are to fight, let it be another time and for another cause. I ask you, as one warrior to another, let this not be our time to battle."

Cathal hesitated. It was not from fear. If he died, this turn of the wheel would pass. Cathal saw something in the Uí Néill warrior's eyes that gave him pause: shame. Not personal shame, but for another's pledge that he was bound to uphold.

Cathal had little doubt that, if he attacked, few of his warriors would survive. The best in both clanns would perish. They would be so weakened that it would be easy prey to any renegades such as Bran that might be looking for herds to raid. How would the death of the clann serve truth, honor and duty?

Still, to let Bran escape without even trying to stop him . . . . If only the Uí Néills had attacked them instead of blocking their path the way would have been clear.

"Cathal," Nuallán said softly. "We have come with you to fight Bran. I will fight with you here, against the Uí Néills, if you choose. But I must warn you that all my warriors may not. They might see this as your clann's battle, not theirs."

Then Tian joined them, sword in hand. He smiled at Uí Néill, but there was no mirth in it. "So, slave of Bran, are you ready to die for your master, the killer of boys? Is it your duty to defend dung?"

Anger flashed in the warrior's eyes. He had sheathed his sword and he reached for it, but stopped. Then he dropped his hand. "You taunt me, but I will not be the one to start this slaughter. If it comes, I shall fight until I die. And I hope I shall die if it comes to that. Even if your ri makes an unworthy choice, he is your ri. You must follow his will or kill him."

This loyalty struck deep into the heart of Cathal. Was he as loyal to his chief, to his own father?

Tian rode close to the warrior, so close that their horses almost touched. He spat on the ground. "Then let the slaughter begin. I will be glad to make you the first to fall."

"Hold!" Cathal's voice rang with authority. "You will do nothing until I say." He rode to Tian and gently placed his hand upon the other's sword arm. "It is not to be. Not this day. There will be another time. I know there will."

Tian slowly sheathed his sword. Fighting tears of frustration, he shook his head in bewilderment. Then he spoke softly to his friend.

"You are no dishonorable coward. You must see a reason to hold back that I do not. I will trust you with what is greater to me than my life: my honor."

Tian turned his horse and rode back to the rest of the clann's warriors.

Turning to the warrior, Cathal said, "We do not fear you, but I do respect that you would not fight this fight. I do not understand why you and the mighty Uí Néills would protect one such as Bran. As a man of honor, you will have to find a way to live with that."

Having said this, Cathal turned his horse to return to his warriors and Aislinn followed. Before they had gone but a few paces, the Uí Néill warrior called to them.

"Wait," he said. "My name is Breandan. I am the son of the Ri of Cúige Uladh. I would like to know your name."

"I am Cathal. Fergus is my taoiseach."

Breandan guided his horse to them.

"I thank you for not making me shed blood dishonorably. My father is an honorable man, but he is old now. When a . . . desirable young woman played to his vanity, he was led as easily as a child into making foolish promises," he said, turning as he spoke to look with disgust at Bran in the distance. "I must protect them, but not their plans. As I understand matters, we are a temporary refuge to be used only if some plan went awry, as it evidently has. Currachs will take them somewhere across the sea."

Aislinn turned to Cathal with a knowing look. They both knew to whom Bran was going for refuge. Although a small kingdom in Eireann, Dál Riata spanned the sea. Cenéls in Dál Riata had clann ties on both shores. Both Eoghan's and Fergus's clann had blood ties with Cenél nGabrain in Alba. Bran was going there.

Their ride back from the lands of the Uí Néills was one of disappointed silence. To have attacked a force that, counting Bran's men, outnumbered them by thrice their number would have been foolish and there was no dishonor in their restraint. Yet, the warriors felt a sense of frustration, of failure.

Aislinn had stayed with the other women warriors during the most of trip back, as though riding with Cathal might usurp his position of leadership, but her real reason was not wanting others to know that she and Cathal were pledged to each other. After so many years of proud independence, she feared the gossip once it became known that the mighty Aislinn had fallen. But she could sense Cathal's despair of failure and finally rode up to him, pacing her horse to his. Reaching over, she rested her hand on his arm.

"There is still a chance. We can secure boats and pursue them across the sea."

She said it with more hope than she felt. In her heart she knew that this would not happen. Even if the two clans decided to mount such a seaborne effort, they were warriors, not sailors. If they took the time to recruit sailors and outfit boats, Bran and his followers would easily reach Alba before an avenging fleet could even have sailed from Eireann.

Cathal turned to her and smiled sadly. "We both know that it will not happen. It is over."

Aislinn started to object, but stopped. Cathal was too intelligent for her to continue to pretend. She knew that they both were aware that Bran had escaped justice. She stayed at Cathal's side for the rest of the ride back to the clann.

Chapter 11

When Cathal and Aislinn reached their settlement, they found Bevin speaking with Labhras, the healer, outside of Cian's house.

"What are you doing here?" Aislinn asked the healer.

"It is your father," Bevin told her, resting her hand on the younger woman's shoulder. "He has come to help him."

"Are his hands worse? Is he aching more?" Pausing, Aislinn suddenly knew it was far more dire. "What is wrong?"

Bevin tried to pull her close to herself, as she had done when Aislinn was a child with a bruised knee or some other minor injury. Aislinn impatiently pushed her away.

"What has happened to my father. Tell me."

"He is dying," the healer stated. He said it simply, as Aislinn wanted.

"Can you help him?"

The herbalist sadly shook his head. "I can only relieve his pain. This turn of the wheel is almost over for him. Say good-bye to him, then leave. He fears that his body will disgrace him and would not want you to see that. He wants his dignity."

"Why are you not at his side?" Aislinn demanded of Bevin. "Why are you not there with a cup of cool water?"

"Fergus and Ciarán are with him. Ciarán ordered me to leave. He said no woman should see Cian in such a condition and that he would see to his needs. All I can do is pray to God ease his suffering." She stopped for a moment, choking back the tears. "I have been praying for him. He was the only man who has been good to me."

"This is one woman Ciarán had better not order away," Aislinn said with a snarl.

Aislinn rushed inside, Cathal following close behind. They found Cian lying in his bed, covered with sheepskins. Although it was not cold, he was shivering and sweat beaded on his brow. Aislinn felt a knot in her chest, knowing that her father must be near the end of his journey. The powerful man who had been her father had been reduced to a shivering husk. She knew that soon even that remnant of her father would be gone.

Fergus was bent over his friend, softly talking. Ciarán was next to his father, also hovering over Cian. Ciarán looked up at her and gave her a cold, reptilian smile and she felt a shiver of dread run down her spine.

"Father," she said as she knelt by his bed, "what has happened?"

"Nothing, child," he said as he patted her head with a trembling hand. It was a gesture he had not done since she had been very young. His voice was weak and there was a rattling deep inside him as he spoke. "It is almost my time. But you need not worry. I have had good advice for your care."

"My care? What care?" Aislinn involuntarily recoiled from her father's hand. She was a warrior, not a child. She looked back to Cathal as she spoke. "Father, I am of the age for a mate, not a guardian."

"Hush, child, you are not to worry." Her father's thready voice was almost inaudible. His breathing came with great effort, in long, weak gasps. He tried to say more, but only was able to make small, gurgling noises. Aislinn leaned over, getting closer so that she might hear him better. His hand weakly touched her hair, then dropped to his bed. He was gone.

For a few moments, Aislinn did not move. She had loved her father as greatly as he had loved her. With an angry shake of her head, she fought back the tears that welled at the corners of her

74

eyes.   Let other women wail and keen for their fathers; she was a warrior.   She would mourn him as one warrior mourns another, by asking the filidh to regale the warriors with the tales of Cian's cattle raids and battles for years to come.   And by celebrating his life with feasting and games.

Chapter 12

Cian's funeral games were to be truly of legendary stature. So was their cost. Word of what Aislinn was spending on them quickly spread through the clann. One afternoon, Ciarán stopped her as she was leaving her house.

"You cannot trade away Cian's cattle like you have been doing without Fergus's approval," he told her as he blocked her way.

"Cian is dead. They are my cattle now. I trade them to get what I need for the games to honor Cian." She spat the words, barely restraining herself from shoving Ciarán into the ditch next to the path.

He gave Aislinn a smug smile. "Cian appointed Fergus as your guardian before he died. You must have your guardian's approval before you do anything with your herds."

With a shiver, she remembered her father's dying words. Now she understood what had happened. Then her anger flared. "I do not know how you got my father to agree to such an abomination, but hear me well, little man. I will do as I wish with my herds and I will honor my father's memory. If Fergus objects, let him come to me himself." Then she grabbed the front of his léine with one hand, almost raising his feet from the ground. "And if you try to stop me, I will pin you to the nearest tree with my spear like the insect you are."

Then she shoved him into the ditch and strode away without looking back.

Fergus never came to her. And Ciarán never spoke to her again on the subject, giving her wide berth when their paths crossed.

The games were held. There were competitions in running,

horse racing, spear hurling for distance and accuracy, stone putting, archery and wrestling. Most competed, many for multiple events. Connaire, still on a crutch, watched unhappily as Tian won the gold arm band for the foot race. Connaire knew that he was normally the fleetest afoot.

Cathal won the horse racing and spear competitions. Gruagach's stone put outdistanced his nearest competitor, Cairbre, by the length of three spears and surpassed any puts within the memory of even the oldest of the clann. Aislinn presented the arm bands to the winners with a pleased smile.

When Ciarán won the archery competition, Aislinn took up her bow and shot an arrow that bettered Ciarán's best, then tossed the gold arm band on the ground in front of him as though it were a worthless trinket. Ciarán glowered at her as he stooped to pick it up.

The wrestling was the most hotly contended of the games. By luck of the draw, Cathal was in the first round, easily defeating Ronan. From then on, he had to take on each challenger selected by the draw. He had little competition and was not even winded until he wrestled Cairbre. Even then, Cathal was obviously the better of the two, but they wrestled long and hard until Cathal finally pinned his friend.

The final challenger drawn was Gruagach, known as the Bear. Gruagach walked to the straw-covered clearing in the center of the field that served as an arena. The crowd surrounded them hushed, knowing that the match would be short and one-sided as the Bear studied the tired and battered Cathal. He was panting as he bent over with his hands resting on his knees, exhausted from his last match. Then Gruagach turned to address the crowd.

"I concede this match. Cathal is the winner," he bellowed.

Although most cheered his nobility, some shouted in protest.

77

The loudest protest was from Cathal, given between gasps for air.

"No! . . . You will not give me that . . . which I did not earn . . . . Do not dishonor me this way!"

The huge man walked over and laid his enormous paw on Cathal's heaving back. "It would dishonor me to wrestle you now. I would gladly beat you if I were your first opponent, but not as your last."

"Then I concede to you as well." Cathal was still breathing hard, but slightly recovered. "The whole match is forfeit."

Aislinn stepped between them. "Wait. I have a solution. We will delay the match for a time until Cathal has rested. Will you both agree to that?"

Gruagach grinned at Cathal and nodded.

Cathal, still wheezing, grinned back. "We agree."

Cathal walked wearily to a nearby oak tree and dropped to the cool grass. His breathing had returned to normal, but not his strength. Aislinn brought ale to him and massaged his aching neck and shoulders as he drank deeply. She kissed the back of his neck and whispered in his ear. "He is physically stronger than you, but you are quicker. He is slower of body and mind. Use it against him."

"I know that," he said a little too quickly. Then, after pausing a moment, he added, "But I do appreciate that you have brought it to the fore of my thoughts."

She slapped him softly on the side of his head and whispered in his ear, "See that is stays there."

After a little while, Tian brought his harp to the place Cathal and Aislinn sat.

"I will sing the tale of Cian, the right arm of Fergus. It is the tale of a great warrior. 'Mighty Cian.'"

Tian's tenor voice carried through the air.

In Tir na Og a warrior sleeps
Tired by his journey through watery deeps
From Donn's house, under western sea,
Brought by Manannán to bright company
Of warriors, maidens, and immortal gods
Cian wakes to life in Tir na Og.

Cian wakes, brave Ailin's son,
To bard's sweet lay of battles won.
Feast and rest, you've earned respite
From the tests and trials of warrior life.
From the wheel you've earned a rest;
Farewell brave Cian, Ailin's best.

Feast and rest until life reborn
By Danu's call and the Dagda's horn
Then drinking deep from Seagais well
Clearing your mind of tales to tell.
But Danu's wheel has yet to turn;
Enjoy the rest that you have earned.

Mighty Danu has yet to assign
The wheel's turn that's Cian's time.
Feast and dance, make love and drink;
Into carefree sleep you'll nightly sink.
For mortal life you will not yearn
Until Danu's wheel begins to turn

Into mortal life then will Danu send
Mighty Cian back to the world of men.

As the last notes died in the afternoon, all were quiet; held rapt by the story. A tear slipped down Aislinn's cheek. Angrily she shook it away. Cathal turned back to her and took her hand.

"I am ready. Let the match continue."

Aislinn looked at him with concern. "It is too soon. You must rest longer."

"I am ready." Cathal stood. He smiled down at Aislinn. "If we delay any longer, Gruagach might fall asleep."

Gruagach was sitting not far from them. The mountainous man heard his name and yelled over to Cathal. "So, you are talking about me. I hope you are trembling at my name."

Cathal walked over to him and placed a hand on his massive shoulder. "Not exactly. I was commenting that a mighty tree can be felled with a small axe, if properly handled."

Gruagach roared with laughter. "Then let us see if you are an axe or an ox, tamed and yoked by this tree."

The two friends walked to the straw-covered wrestling field. Warily, they watched each other and looked for an opportunity for a hold. Cathal slowly circled his powerful foe, who kept turning to keep Cathal always in front of him. Several times Gruagach attempted to grab Cathal, but the quicker man sidestepped the attack.

Tiring of the game, Gruagach ran, arms stretched wide, full-tilt at Cathal. Just as one of the Bear's massive hands closed on Cathal's léine, the smaller man grabbed the thick wrists and fell backward, stuffing his foot into the big man's stomach to propel him over the top of him. Turning in flight, Gruagach landed with a thud on his back, momentarily stunned.

Quick as a fox, Cathal leapt to his feet and pounced on his opponent, landing hard on Gruagach's stomach. The Bear grunted, but swung a mighty fist that caught Cathal on the side of his head.

Knowing that he had lost the advantage, Cathal struggled to his feet and staggered back, trying to recover.

With surprising quickness for one so large, Gruarach was on his feet and rushed Cathal. Wrapping his arms around his opponent's waist, the big man locked his hands around Cathal's waist and squeezed with all his strength.

Unable to breathe, Cathal knew that he would soon lose consciousness. With all his might, he swung both fists toward each other, catching the sides of Gruagach's neck just below the jaw between them. The bear-hug weakened, allowing Cathal to push back with one hand to get enough room to drive the heel of the other hand hard up under the Gruagach's chin.

As the Bear staggered, Cathal slipped from his grip and backed away. Both were panting hard, cautiously watching each other as they tried to recover.

With a roar, Gruagach charged Cathal in more of a stagger than a run. Cathal returned the roar and rushed at Gruagach. At the last moment, Cathal threw himself at the Bear, diving low and tackling him below his knees. The big man went down like felled tree.

Just after Gruagach hit face first on the straw, Cathal lunged on his back, wrapping his right arm around the other's thick neck. Grabbing his right wrist with his left hand, he pulled hard, cutting off Gruagach's air. The big man rose to his knees, ineffectively clawing at Cathal's arm, trying to break the neck lock. In desperation, the Bear flung himself on his back in an attempt to stun Cathal, but could not break the hold. As he felt himself starting to black out, Gruagach signaled with his hand that he conceded defeat. The match was over.

Both men sat on the ground with their heads hanging, exhausted. Aislinn rushed to Cathal, kneeling to embrace him.

"I feared that you had no chance." She gently caressed his brow. "You surprised me."

"Surprised you?" he gasped. "I merely followed your advice: use his strength against him. Of course, I may have a broken rib or two."

Aislinn laughed. "I said it, but I did not expect it to work." She helped him to his feet. "I will bind your ribs."

Ciarán pushed his way through the crowd and stood before them. "I challenge the victor."

Aislinn rose and confronted him. "You did not put your name on the list. The match is over."

"I told you I wanted to be on the list," he said petulantly. "If you do not remember, that is not my fault. Is Cathal afraid of me?"

Cathal looked up, glaring angrily at his brother. "I have no fear of you. Let us wrestle, list or no list."

Aislinn shook her head in disgust. "He is injured. I will bind his rib and he will rest first."

"No!" Ciarán's voice was insistent. "Let it begin immediately. It is my right to demand it. I do not want to wait."

"That would not be fair!" Aislinn faced Ciarán with clenched fists. "We will wait."

"He must face me now or forfeit." Ciarán gave her a smug smile. "I do not agree to a delay."

Cathal looked up at his brother. It was a look of disdain. "I accept. So you want the bout to start at this moment?"

"Yes. No delay. It starts right now or you forfeit."

Cathal immediately lunged at Ciarán, hitting him solidly in the stomach with his shoulder. Stunned and gasping for air, Ciarán fell back onto the straw. Cathal threw himself on top of him knocking the breath out of him. With his right hand, Cathal shoved

Ciarán's chin back against the ground and pressed his left forearm against his brother's windpipe. Ciarán grunted and waived his arms in concession. The match was over.

Hurrying to Cathal, Aislinn helped him to his feet again. "The coward. He knew he had no chance against you unless you were exhausted."

Cathal smiled through bruised lips. "And he lost anyway."

Aislinn helped Cathal stagger away, leaving Ciarán moaning on the ground. Gruagach, leaning on Cairbre, limped over and looked down at Ciarán. He spat, hitting Ciarán on his left cheek.

"I should squash you like a bug, you coward." the Bear snarled. "It would be a favor to the clann."

Cairbre came to the big man's side and stared at Ciarán with undisguised disgust, then turned to Gruagach. "If you squash him, he will make an awful mess on the bottom of your foot. And some poor person would have to bury the wretch. Let us go and drink ale with the fine women I see over yonder instead."

With a last angry glance at the prone Ciarán, Gruagach allowed himself to be led away.

After the two warriors left, Ciarán slowly rolled to his stomach and pushed himself up to his hands and knees. He stared after them, his face contorted in rage as well as pain.

"You win today, but my day will be here soon," he muttered as he wiped his cheek. "I will be taoiseach. Then see who spits at me."

Slowly he rose, brushed the dirt from his léine, and stumbled off.

Chapter 13

The feast to honor Cian was as extravagant as the games. Aislinn had slaughtered two of her finest cattle and they were roasted to perfection.   With the help of her warrior women, Aislinn had tracked down a massive boar.   But the kill had been hers alone. It hung on a spit, its juices dripping to sizzle on the hot embers below.   The aroma of the cooking meat permeated the whole yard in front of Fergus's house, where tables and benches had been arranged.   Rather than ale, she was serving stronger and more costly mead.

As Samhain, the beginning of a new year, approached, the days had grown shorter and the nights cooler.   Rains often came, so there was a risk in feasting out of doors.   With the entire clann, both free and servant, being fed, even the briugu's house would have been overcrowded,so Aislinn was willing to take the risk.   But the weather had stayed dry and everyone braved the cold to honor Cian and enjoy the wake.

Bonfires roared all around the yard.   The low stone wall that surrounded it gave no protection from the chill night breeze, but with everyone pressed close together in their woolen bratts, warm camaraderie and free-flowing mead, no one minded.

Aislinn went from table to table, making sure that the trenchers were piled with meat and the pitchers of mead were filled. She laughed and joked with the boisterous diners, adroitly warding off any of the men who tried to get too friendly.   She neither ate nor drank herself, devoting herself to her guests and watching for the one person she most wanted to see.

When Cathal arrived, bathed and wearing a clean léine, she moved casually, but determinedly, though the crowd to his side. She noticed that his wounds and bruises had been salved with herbs and oil and felt a pang of jealousy. No doubt Maille, since she acted as healer for minor injuries at times, had applied them. No doubt Maille had enjoyed rubbing her hands on Cathal's powerful muscles. No doubt that any further application of salves would be done by different hands, her own.

Cathal wrapped his arm around her waist when she reached him. He smiled and bent to kiss her, but she slipped away. Cathal looked puzzled.

"What is wrong? Have I offended you?"

Aislinn touched the three gold arm bands he was wearing, the ones he had won that day. Then she stroked his cheek and smiled.

"You have not offended me in any way. But I must keep my wits this evening. Come. Let me get you the hero's portion of the boar. You have more than won it."

As she started toward the roasting boar, Cathal grabbed her arm and pulled her back. He held her tight against his chest, her hardened nipples pressing against his flesh through both of their léines. His breathing was as ragged as hers. She wanted nothing more than to forget everyone else and take him to her bed. With great effort, she pushed away.

"Sit at the table and I will get your reward for winning."

"I would prefer a different reward," he said with a grin.

"Later you will get another hero's portion," she whispered in his ear. Then, looking at the swaying Tian, she added, "If you do not drink too much mead."

Cathal plopped unhappily onto a nearby bench, next to Tian who obviously had been greatly enjoying the abundant mead.

When she turned to go for Cathal's haunch of boar, Aislinn saw Ciarán standing in the shadows by one of the fires. His bratt was wrapped tightly around him against the cold air, but his right arm was exposed to display his gold arm band.   In the flickering firelight, she could barely see his face, but he was looking directly at her and Cathal.   And he was smiling.   An evil smile. Just like he had been smiling after her father died.   She started to say something to Cathal, but shook her head and walked away.   What threat could that worm be to either of them?

As the evening wore on and all had sated themselves on the feast, three men entered the yard from different directions, walking at a slow, stately pace.   Each carried a fiery brand, held at arm's length.   They had their bratts pulled over their heads so that their faces could not be seen in the shadowy light.   They met at the center of the yard where there was a large pile of wood.   At the same moment, each thrust his brand into the pile and the dry wood burst into flames.   Then they flung off their bratts and turned to the watching crowd.

One of them had black hair, a blackened face and wore a black léine and trews.   His eyes shone white as two stars as he solemnly surveyed the crowd.   Then he broke into a load roar of laughter that stopped as suddenly as it had begun.   Without another sound, he crossed his legs and sat upon the ground, facing the fire.

The next man had long, stringy hair as white as snow and wore a white léine.   He had a bag slung over his back, which he dropped to the ground and began to rummage through.   A number of short daggers were thrust in a belt around his waist.   While he was doing that, the last of the troop stepped forward.

He was taller than Cathal, with a frame that was both slim and powerful.   He wore only trews of a pale yellow color, with no léine to shield him from the cold.   The man had no hair on his head or body and had dyed himself yellow.   His muscles tensed as he raised his arms and began to speak in a stentorian voice.

"Warriors! Craftsmen and craftswomen! Herdsmen and herdswomen! Even kings and taoiseachs, if any dare haunt this ill-begotten group! Servants! Idiots and dolts! Druids and brehons! Oh, I repeat myself! Randy men and loose women! Especially loose women! Enjoy us! We are the Sun, the Moon and the Night, here to amuse you!"

They were Crossans, who traveled from place to place and were paid handsomely to provide entertainment. A load roar of approval rang through the yard.

The tall one, the Sun, leaned over backwards until his hands touched the ground. Then, with a kick, he stood upon on his hands and started to walk on them. He went to the table where Cathal sat next to Tian. Tian's head lay across his crossed arms, which were resting on the table.

The Sun turned, displaying two black dots and a black arc that had been stitched in the seat of his trews to make a grinning face when he stood on his hands.

"Valiant Cathal," the Sun said. "You have three trophies on your arm from this day. Sun has shone on you with favor, have I not?"

Cathal laughed. "It is true. You have shone upon me most kindly."

"Then would you be willing to give me one of those trophies that I have helped you to win?"

Cathal shifted uneasily on his bench. The Crossans were to be honored, feted and never harmed. Yet this request was unreasonable and Cathal felt his anger rise. Silence fell on those close.

The Sun laughed. "I jest. You have rightly earned your rewards. I would, however, appreciate an ample reward of mead for my part."

Cathal sighed. "Done. You shall have all the mead you desire." All around applauded.

"But first I must talk to your inebriated comrade," the Sun said, walking on his hands to confront Tian with his stitched smile. "Poet! Awake! The Sun is shining upon you and you must bask in my presence."

Tian raised his head slowly. He seemed to have trouble focusing. He blinked several times, as if trying to discern what was the apparition before him. "By the gonads of Lugh, what is this?"

"I am the Sun. The light that gives you inspiration. The light that gives you hope. The light you will curse when you wake in the morning with an aching head."

There was laughter from all who heard.

Tian rose unsteadily to his feet. His hands rested on the table to steady himself. But his speech was clear and sober. "You are no sun. You are nothing but a man who thinks he can speak through his ass."

"Have you not led the way? I hear that your breaking wind has often bored this clann. Do you not call it poetry?"

There was laughter, but it was subdued and nervous. Tian was known for his poetry, his swordplay and his temper. No weapons were allowed in this feast, but Tian's house was not that far away.

Before Tian could speak, Cathal laid his hand upon the bard's arm. "He is Crossans. To do him harm would bring disgrace upon both you and the clann. Use your wit, not your sword."

For a moment, Tian glared at the Sun with obvious hostility. But then a smile crept upon his face, and finally he began to laugh. Then he sat back down on the bench and leaned back against the table.

"Sun, you have presented me with your best: your best wit, your best end and your best odor. I even know from that odor what is your best meal. At least your most recent. Cabbage, was it not?"

The Sun laughed. "True enough. There was no meat to be found on our way here. But is your breath any better?"

"I have had no complaints from any women. And is that not the most important? I daresay I have had more kisses upon this face than you have had upon the one you present to me. Perhaps it is because my nose is on the front of my face?"

With a laugh, the Sun flipped back onto his feet. "Well said. Perhaps now the women will kiss my face." He turned to the crowd and clapped his hands twice. "Let the Moon shine upon you."

Solemnly, the Moon paced in front of the blazing bonfire. His léine was loose and baggy, billowing a little in the breeze. In his hands he held three silvery balls. He started to juggle them, slowly at first, but soon at whirlwind speed. His hands were a blur in the firelight. The Moon's expression never changed and his eyes stared straight ahead. It seemed to Cathal that the balls were changing color, that they began to have a gold cast to them.

The Sun again clapped his hands twice. He shouted to be heard above the noise of boisterous talk and laughter of those who were enjoying the show. "To the victors of this day, a reward."

Suddenly four balls flew from the hands of the Moon, out to the crowd, two to Cathal, one to Gruagach, and one to Tian. They barely had time to react, but each caught his ball in midair. They were of gold, but Cathal could tell by their light weight that they were hollow. On his ball, he could see there was what looked to be engraving. Leaning toward the firelight, he could see that one of them had a man on horseback and the other two men engaged in wrestling. Tian and Gruagach were holding theirs in the light to see them better and laughing. No doubt Tian had a runner and Gruagach a stone putter.

Ciarán pushed his way to the firelight by the Sun. He folded his arms across his chest so that his gold armband glinted in the firelight and glared up at the yellow man. "And where is my reward? I won for archery."

The Sun's smile had an impishness about it. "Let us see what we can find hidden in the Night." With that, he stepped back and clapped three times loudly.

The Night roared out a loud peal of laughter and slowly rose. He walked slowly towards Ciarán and the Sun. He paused at the first table and gently stroked the hair of the most beautiful woman there. Before she could react, a silver broach suddenly appeared in his hand and he pinned it on her bratt. She gasped in happy surprise at its intricate beauty. With a short laugh, he moved on.

The Night repeated this act with another woman at the next table. This time it was Maille and she grabbed the Night around his neck, pulled him to her, and gave him a long, deep kiss. When she finished, the Night stepped back, his eyes wider and whiter than ever, and gave a long, loud laugh before moving on. The crowd applauded.

Cairbre was at the next table. He tugged on the Night's léine.

"Does the Night only favor lovely women? What of lusty men like me?"

The Night passed his open hand over the top of Cairbre's head. As he did, a small fieldmouse appeared, perched on top of the warrior's hair. For a moment, it remained still, then scurried down the side of Cairbre's head, jumped from his shoulder to the table and from there to the ground, escaping into the darkness. As the mouse made his run down his head, Cairbre had realized something was on him and had leaped to his feet, almost knocking the table over onto those across from him. Those at the table there grabbed their cups of mead to prevent them from spilling. As he saw the mouse scurry away, Cairbre turned angrily towards the Night. But the Night silently wagged his finger, then broke into his quick, loud laugh. Cairbre shook his head and joined the laughter. He gave the Night a good-natured slap on the back that sent the dark man staggering forward.

The Night finally reached Ciarán, who was scowling and drumming his fingers on his crossed arms. Solemnly staring into Ciarán's eyes, the blackened man first turned his hands palm up to show he held nothing. Then he turned them palm down and slowly pulled Ciarán's hands out in front of him. The Night gave his laugh and turned away from Ciarán.

Looking down at his hands, Ciarán said, "What are these?"

Connaire limped up on his crutch and looked at what was in Ciarán's hands. Then he took something and held it high for all to see. Speaking through his barely-suppressed laughter, Connaire shouted to the crowd, "They are the bollocks of a bull. A bit shriveled now, but they are better than what you have. Or should I say do not have?"

Hoots and yells filled the night. Gruagach laid his head on one arm and pounded the table with the other as the tears of humor streamed down his cheeks. Tian pummeled Cathal on the back as he doubled over in laughter. Almost everyone was convulsed in their guffaws. Almost.

Ciarán started toward the back of the Night, but the Sun slipped between them, towering over the angry man. Ciarán glared at him, then at all those who were enjoying the joke. His mouth twitched. He turned as if to leave, but stopped. Instead he grabbed a piece of firewood, stepped onto a nearby bench and began banging on the table. Slowly, the laughter died and everyone looked to him. He smiled. But his eyes did not.

"My clann, I am glad you found humor from my . . . discomfort. It is good to laugh. But now is the time to be serious. My father, your taoiseach, has an announcement."

Ciarán looked down the table, to where his father was sitting. Fergus looked around in obvious confusion.

"Father, remember what you told me? About the honor you are going to bestow upon your ward, Aislinn?"

"Aislinn?" Fergus rubbed his forehead. "There was something. Yes, there was. Aislinn." He turned to Ciarán. "Who is Aislinn?"

"Cian made you Aislinn's guardian. And you decided a wonderful way to protect her. In the family."

"Yes . . . yes. I remember." Fergus slowly smiled. "My wife, Aislinn."

Ciarán looked directly at Aislinn. His smile grew bigger. "Yes, Father, she will be your wife."

Aislinn stood, stunned. What was he talking about?

"What rubbish is this?" Tian asked Cathal. "Everyone knows she loves you and you her. What is Ciarán's think he is doing?" Others at the table began to voice their thoughts, rising in cacophony of confusion.

Cathal rose and pushed his way towards Ciarán. "This is nonsense! Aislinn needs no guardian. She will choose the man she wishes."

"It is the law. She will have to follow the ruling of the brehon. He is the keeper of our laws and she cannot dispute his decision."

"Seanan will spit in your face, worm," Cathal said through gritted teeth. "I would never have thought you such a fool." He turned and looked around. "Where is Seanan?"

No one seemed to know. No one claimed to have seen him since early that morning. In the crowd, he had not been missed.

"No one will be spitting in my face, Brother," Ciarán said. "I summon the Dal to meet in the morning. Then this matter will be settled by law."

Aislinn forced her way to confront Ciarán. With great vehemence, she spat on his cheek. His smile faded as he wiped it away with the back of his hand.

"This is only one more insult for which you will pay." He turned to Fergus. "Father, what shall be the honor price for this dishonor from your future wife?"

"Dishonor? Wife?" Fergus seemed in a daze. "Is Betha here?"

"No, Father. Just me. Ciarán." He wrapped his arm over Fergus's shoulders. "I will take you home to rest."

Cathal stepped in front of them. "You are not leaving, Ciarán, until this matter is resolved. Aislinn will not be your weapon to attack me. Leave her be."

"Stand aside, Brother. Unless you want me to resolve this now." Ciarán looked to his side. About twenty men gathered beside him, weapons in hand. "My friends will do what is necessary if you force the issue."

Cathal stared at his brother with stunned dismay. "You have broken hospitality. You have brought arms to a funeral feast. I cannot believe even you would be so vile."

"Believe. And stand aside or die." Ciarán's smile returned. "I would gladly kill you now, but it would mean war within the clann. Is that what you want?"

Cathal hesitated, but stepped aside. Ciarán led Fergus away, flanked by his armed escort. Gruagach, Cairbre, Tian and a number of Cathal's friends had noticed that all was not well, that armed men were in their midst, but Cathal signaled to them to stay back. He wanted no deaths here, no civil war in the clann.

With some unhappy muttering, the crowd dispersed. The festivities had been ruined. Some blamed Ciarán, some blamed Cathal, some blamed Aislinn and some even blamed the performers. But all left except Cathal and Aislinn's close friends.

The Sun, the Moon and the Night stood by awkwardly. It was not their clann, so this was not their fight. The Sun came up to Cathal and Aislinn. "My apologies. We seem to have precipitated difficulties for you and ruined your feast."

Aislinn shook her head. "No, I imagine he had planned this for a while. Fergus had been coached. You just lit the kindling." Then she gave him a rueful smile. "At least your barb stuck him before he had his say."

He bowed. "Nonetheless, we will refund your payment with apologies."

"No. You did your part well. Ciarán is to blame." She clenched her fists as she spoke. "And he will pay for it."

The three men all bowed and silently slipped away.

"I am sorry that Ciarán ruined your father's funeral feast," Cathal told Aislinn.

She shook her head. "Cian is dead. This turn of the wheel for him is over. It is us that I worry about. What will we do?"

"Seanan and Miach would stop this nonsense, but Miach has not returned from Eoghan's clann and Seanan was not here tonight. I will send a rider for Miach, but there is not time for him to return. We must find Seanan."

"And if we do not?"

Cathal shook his head. "We must. With him on our side, very few will follow Ciarán."

Gruagach wrapped one arm over Aislinns's shoulders and one over Cathal's. "Then let us not just stand here, tossing words about. Let us go find Seanan."

Tian nodded. "For one who barely can put two words together, you said all that needs to be said. Let us go."

After getting their hounds to track Seanan's scent, they set out to find the brehon that could stop Ciarán's plan.

Chapter 14

Dawn brought little light. The sky was overcast and a misty rain had begun to fall. Cathal, exhausted from the night's hunt for the missing brehon, stirred the ashes in front of the briugu's house, in an effort the restart a fire from last evening's bonfire, but had no luck. The fire was almost as dead as his hopes of finding Seanan alive. He did not want to seek the warmth of his father's house, knowing that Ciarán would likely be waiting to relish in his failure.

He should go into the house, drag Ciarán out and demand that he tell him of what happened to Seanan. If his brother refused or told some obvious lie, he should hand the coward a sword and tell him to defend himself. Then he should kill him. But he knew he would not. If it had been in him to do so, he would have done it a few hours ago when he had returned there with Aislinn.

The others who had gone to search for Seanan had returned to their homes, going to their beds to get a few hours of sleep before the Dal would meet. Aislinn and he had been among the last to give in to the inevitable conclusion: Seanan would not be found alive. They had returned a couple hours before dawn. Connaire had been unable to help in the search, but had waited by the fire. By the time Cathal and Aislinn had returned, it had little life.

"What happened to the fire?" Cathal asked his younger brother. "Why did you not tend it?"

Connaire looked around, as if unaware of his neglect. "Fire? Oh . . . sorry. I was not thinking of it. But what of Seanan?"

Aislinn dropped to a bench left from the night before. "Dead, from the hand of Ciarán in all probability."

Cathal shook his head. "We do not know that he is dead. And even if he is, was not Ciarán with us?"

"Why do you defend him?" Her eyes flashed angrily. "You know what I say is true. Even if his hand did not hold the dagger, he is responsible. If the archer releases the arrow, it is not the arrow that murders. It is the archer."

Cathal turned mutely to the dying fire. He knew she was right. Seanan was dead and Ciarán was the murderer. Yet he had trouble accepting it. And even if he did, what should he do about it?

Aislinn wearily stood. "We should get some rest. The Dal will meet later today and we should all be on guard. It is obvious that Ciarán is on the attack with his favorite weapon, his tongue." She started to walk away and paused. "Cathal? Would you like to sleep at my house?"

Turning to face her, he slowly shook his head. "I . . . I will stay here. Until this is resolved, I should not sleep with you."

She gave him a wry grin. "You would be safe. I would not attack you. I am far too tired. But have it as you will." She turned to Connaire. "And you? Do I frighten you as well?"

"I do not frighten easily," Connaire said. He looked at his brother. "Neither does Cathal. But he so concerned with the clann that he lets Ciarán use his honor against him."

Aislinn took Connaire's arm to help him hobble away. Cathal watched silently as they walked off, agonizing over the truth of what they had said. Truth. Truth, honor and duty. The three legs of the cauldron that was their society. But was that society worth the sacrifice of one so pure of heart as Aislinn? Could he sacrifice the one he loved, truly loved, for that society, his clann? But was it the clann who demanded the sacrifice, or just his scheming brother? Then where was his real duty? He watched the fire until its last life was taken by a slow drizzle. The rain dripped from his hair and ran down his cheeks like tears, but he could not cry.

With the dawn, the clann began to rise. Although many who had helped with the futile search rose late, Tian and Gruagach were up early. When they joined him Cathal looked up for a moment, but returned to his silent study of the drenched ashes at his feet. They all stood without speaking, bonded by their friendship and their sadness. Before long, Aislinn and Connaire came quietly up to them.

Aislinn slipped her arm through Cathal's. "I am sorry for what I said. I did not mean that you are a coward."

Cathal shook his head. "Perhaps I am. I do not fear death, but I do fear acting wrongly. I fear what might happen if I do. I fear for my father. I fear for us. I fear for the clann. I do fear."

She gently stroked his cheek. "It is the fear of a brave man, not a coward. A coward cares not for anyone but himself. That is not you."

Cathal realized that one of his trio of friends was missing. "Where is Cairbre?" he asked Tian and Gruagach.

"He was gone when I awoke," Tian said as he stifled a yawn. "So was his favorite hound. I assume they are together, since I have heard of no women or bitches unaccounted for."

"No matter. I doubt that he could do anything here," Cathal sighed. "Let us prepare ourselves for the Dal. I fear it will not go well."

When Aislinn and the group of warriors arrived at the hall, it was already crowded. Representatives of all the hearths were present. There were a few benches scattered around for the eldest, but most were milling around in small groups. The din of their voices hovered as heavy in the air as the smoke from the fire that provided the only dim light for the gathering place. Aislinn noticed that their voices dropped when they saw her. She knew that she and her fate were the prime topic for their conversations.

Aislinn was relieved to see Connaire wave to them from across the room and moved toward him.

Connaire greeted them with a wan smile. "No word of Seanan?"

Cathal slowly shook his head.

"Then I may have found another way to stop Ciarán." Connaire leaned on his crutch and rested his hand on the shoulder of a young man next to him. "Do you remember Fergal?

Aislinn recognized him as from the clann, but knew little of him. Obviously not a warrior, the man was nothing impressive to see. Although he looked about the same age as Connaire, he was shorter and pudgier, with the look of someone that would talk rather than act. She saw nothing about the youth that impressed her.

"And how can he be of any help?" she asked. Noticing Connaire's embarrassed expression, she added, "Not that I do not appreciate the offer. Many warriors would willingly fight for us if we wished. But that would bring ruin to this clann and we do not want that."

Connaire gave a short laugh. "Fergal is no warrior. He would be of little help with a sword. But you can tell that. He has other value to us." He turned to Fergal and gave him a smile. "Fergal has been studying under Seanan to be a brehon. As a glasaigne who has done his first course of study of our laws, he can speak the words Seanan would use if he were here."

Cathal shook his head. "I remember Fergal. I know that he has been under Seanan's instruction. But he has not completed his study yet, has he?"

"The answer to that is not simple," Fergal said solemnly. "It is not determined purely by time, but I have studied the Senchus

Mór and the Book of Acaill and I have demonstrated to Seanan my knowledge of the laws and traditions of our clann. He had planned to present me to the next Oenach. He would have then formally conferred my standing as a dalaigh. I may not be an anruth like Seanan, but I am qualified to be a brehon"

Aislinn sighed. "But Seanan is not here to verify this. Without him, Ciarán will dispute your claim."

"And who would he say has more experience?" Connaire asked with a laugh. "Himself?"

Aislinn chuckled at the thought of Ciarán claiming knowledge of the law. The only law he knew was the law of subterfuge. "Perhaps it might work. We will surprise him with Fergal. He will not be expecting him."

At that moment, the voices around them became hushed, more subdued. Fergus had entered the hall, walking slowly with a long staff in his right hand. He was accompanied by Ciarán on one side and a stranger on the other. The man was tall, as tall as Cathal, but thin to the point of emaciation. He had long grey-black hair that was pulled tightly back to frame his gaunt, craggy face. A drooping mustache matched his down-turned mouth. Shaggy eyebrows cast dark shadows on his sunken eyes. He glowered at the crowd as they parted to let the trio through. Aislinn turned to her friends and raised her hands slightly in a silent question about the identity of this ominous visitor. They looked as perplexed as she was as to who this intruder of their council was.

Upon reaching his chair, Fergus turned and sat. He seemed confused, unsure of what to do. Ciarán leaned down and whispered in his ear. Fergus looked up questioningly at his eldest son. Ciarán again whispered in his ear. Then Fergus pounded his staff heavily on the ground three times.

"The Dal is assembled," he stated in a loud voice, "to decide if a father can appoint a guardian." Then he looked up again at Ciarán. Ciarán smiled at him and nodded.

Aislinn turned to Cathal. He smiled wanly. It was a smile of hopelessness. While it was not obvious what Ciarán's plan was, it did not bode well for them.

Chapter 15

The hall was almost silent. Ciarán stepped in front of Fergus and looked around.

"Is Seanan here?" he asked.

"You know he is not," Connaire yelled. "But his apprentice is. Fergal was to be named as a brehon at the next Oenach. He is here."

Ciarán turned to him with a disdainful glare. He clasped his hands behind his back and leaned slightly forward. "A boy speaks of a boy. I am addressing the men of the clann."

"And what of the women?" Aislinn called to him. "Do you discount the youth of our clann and the women as well? And why do you speak instead of Fergus?"

Ciarán's smile was most condescending. "My father is not well and has asked me to conduct this Dal. And of course the women who have a right to be in the Dal are welcome to speak. But girls and boys should not even be present, much less speak."

"You call me a boy," Connaire said, "but I have drawn blood in battle while you cowered behind Father. Young girls have more a right to speak here than a coward like you."

Ciarán's eyes narrowed and his face turned red. Voices rose, some agreeing with and others contesting Connaire's claim. Suddenly Fergus's voice rang out.

"Enough of this bickering! Ciarán speaks for me. Let this council begin."

The hall fell silent. Ciarán smiled coldly as he looked at Aislinn.

But Fergus had not finished.

"Let all have their say. Connaire is my son too and Aislinn is like a daughter. I want all my children to get along."

Aislinn expected Ciarán to protest, but instead he stepped back to his father's side, gently patted his shoulder and spoke softly to him. "Of course, Father. Everyone should be heard."

Ciarán paused, giving more emphasis to his next words. "But the voice of age and experience should always be heeded most. While Fergal should be allowed to speak, would not Seanan be given more credence if he were here?"

"But he is not, is he?" Connaire called to him. "We wonder why."

Ciarán ignored him, continuing to speak to his father. "Do you not agree that a brehon of age has more wisdom than a youth who has not been publicly acknowledged by his teacher as a brehon?"

Fergus nodded his head emphatically. "Of course. Wisdom only comes with age. Seanan is old and wise. But is Seanan here?"

"No, Father, he is not. But someone else can help." Ciarán nodded to the gaunt stranger, who moved quietly to his side. "We have an old and wise brehon, who was traveling through our lands. Father, I present Tairdelbach, a brehon of some note."

Near-pandemonium erupted. Most everyone there began to talk to his or her neighbor about this latest surprising development. How did this stranger happen to be in their lands? Was he truly a brehon? Would he solve this matter in a way that would mend the differences that had arisen?

Aislinn turned to Fergal and found his face as contorted as if he had just eaten a bad piece of beef.

"What is it Fergal? Is this man a fraud, not a brehon at all?"

"Worse, I fear." The young man sadly shook his head. "He is a brehon, but one without honor. Have you heard of Ruardi of the O'Conners?"

Aislinn and the others with her indicated that they had not.

"Ruardi was a fearsome man, strong, able and of vile temperament. There was a boar hunt and his brother, Adamnan's son, scored the kill. In honor of this, he was to receive the hero's portion, the largest haunch, at the feast. During the feast, Ruardi grew wild with drink. He accused Adamnan's son of stealing the kill from him. When the lad protested his innocence, Ruardi stabbed him with the carving dagger. The lad was of but twelve Samhains when he died.

"Adamnan was a weak man, but he did demand honor price for his son. With the boy's standing in their clann, it would have been high. Their Dal was summoned and Tairdelbach was the brehon who advised them. He said that the boy had dishonored himself by stealing the kill and Adamnan must pay Ruardi for this dishonor rather than Ruardi pay for the murder. No doubt Ruardi was willing to pay much for such a decision."

The friends gasped at this affront to honor price and the law. Fergal continued the tale.

"The Dal almost agreed to this. But even Adamnan could not take such a travesty of law. He challenged Ruardi to combat. Ruardi was a far better swordsman and accepted. He did not plan on Adamnan's righteous rage. The bereaved father flung himself in such fury at his brother that skill was defeated by heart. Ruardi died and Tairdelbach wisely fled. Since then he has gone to a number of Dals where a brehon has been absent, always seeming to render an opinion that favors a losing side. One that can pay, of course."

Connaire stamped his crutch on the ground and thrust his chin towards Fergal. "Then expose him for the base, mercenary fraud that he is. Then you can decide this matter for Aislinn."

"That is exactly what I cannot do," Fergal said with a sad

shake of his head. "I am not a recognized brehon, but Tairdelbach is. I have no standing or proof of what I know. It is from the mouth of Seanan, who I cannot summon to support me. I would be accused of a number of wrong motives, my friendship with Connaire being among them. No, Ciarán has planned this well."

The crowd was beginning to quiet. Ciarán was pounding Fergus's staff to regain order.

"Then I will speak," Connaire told his friends. "I will tell everyone how Ciarán is manipulating this Dal."

Cathal placed his hand heavily on Connaire's shoulder, almost knocking his brother to his knees.

"You will not. If you do that, it will be a challenge, a challenge that will lead this clann to fight amongst itself. We have been outmaneuvered by Ciarán, but we will not destroy this clann."

Aislinn pulled Cathal's hand from Connaire's shoulder. Anger and frustration rose in her throat like bile. "And what does that mean for us? For me? Am I to be left to the whims of your hideous brother? Am I to be the wife of your demented father? Was it all a lie? Do I mean nothing to you?"

Cathal put his free hand up and bowed his head, as if to ward off her attack. "Aislinn, nothing has changed. We just need to act with caution. Much is at stake."

"You tell me that much is at stake? Our very future is at stake, and yet you do nothing. Your brother is a far braver man than you are."

Ciarán's attempts to regain order had attained some success by this time and Aislinn's last sentence, almost screamed, was heard by many. Including Ciarán. He smiled, but said nothing. Instead he turned to Tairdelbach and said, "We are obviously in need of wise counsel. Tairdelbach, would you help us in this difficult matter?"

The gaunt man smiled, or grimaced rather, at those assembled. Then he turned to Fergus.

"Fergus, as taoiseach, you should decide if I am worthy to help you. I ask nothing but your hospitality. We aged ones need not much more than that."

Fergus looked up at Tairdelbach with a confused expression, then he looked to Ciarán. Ciarán smiled and nodded to his father. Fergus seemed to take heart.

"We are glad to take your counsel, brehon," he said slowly. There was an uncertainty to his voice, something once unknown. "Do you know the matter at hand?"

"I do," he assured Fergus. "It is a matter of guardianship. Ciarán has told me of it."

"Guardianship?" Fergus looked from Tairdelbach to Ciarán, who nodded to him. "Yes, yes. I remember. Do you have an opinion?"

The brehon's face became somber, judicial. "Yes, I do. The importance of guardianship should never be diminished. For in it is found truth, honor and duty, the three legs of the cauldron of our people."

Aislinn slowly shook her head, fighting back tears. "I am doomed," she softly muttered, "and there is no one who will save me."

Chapter 16

As Tairdelbach began to speak, Cathal found it difficult to concentrate on his words. He kept glancing over at Aislinn, torn by the hurt and abandonment he saw in her eyes. In spite of what he had said to Connaire, he was tempted to rally his friends and settle this matter with arms. He knew it would be bloody. Ciarán had friends, friends who would find courage only in a pack. And many still would find it difficult to go against Fergus, even though they knew he was being manipulated by Ciarán. The old chief's prestige was dying with his mind, a slow death. How sad that he seemed fated not to die honorably in battle.

"Tian," he whispered to his friend, "what chances do you think we would have if we decided to settle this with the sword?"

Tian turned to him and studied him in solemn silence a moment before answering. Cathal trusted his friend, but Tian would know the disaster to the clann such an action would mean.

"It would be close," Tian said. Then a slight smile cracked his lips. "But if Gruagach, Cairbre and I were at the fore, our chances would improve greatly."

Cathal turned back to the brehon, trying to listen. He knew what Tairdelbach would say, but until he did, Cathal would not be forced to decide between his clann and the woman he loved. Which would it be the greater dishonor to betray?

"I have not taken this matter lightly," he heard the brehon say. "I have considered whether the individual is more important than the laws and traditions. Yes, the young woman may be past the normal age of guardianship. Yes, she is a warrior who has fought as bravely as any other warrior. Yes, she is of age to be a wife. But there are larger issues here."

Tairdelbach paused dramatically, scowling at those

assembled. His bushy eyebrows lowered and his lips tightly pressed together, as if daring anyone to take issue with this observation. His head was tilted slightly forward and, with his beaked nose and deep-set eyes, he reminded Cathal of a buzzard eyeing its prey. Then his visage softened and he continued his speech.

"There is the matter of the tradition of guardianship itself. You send your children to each other's hearths, to be raised and nurtured by kith and kin. It allows us to understand each other with greater depth than otherwise possible. What would happen if a child could simply say 'No' when told to go to another family's hearth? What would happen to guardianship? What would happen to the authority of parents? What would happen--"

"Aislinn is no child, old man," Connaire loudly interrupted. "Are you blind as well as corrupt?"

A swell of voices rose in the room, some agreeing and some dissenting. Tempers rose and blows were sure to follow. But the roar of Fergus's voice quickly quieted the situation.

"What is this?" he bellowed. "Do you insult my guest? Are you challenging me, boy? Apologize to this brehon now or feel my wrath."

But Tairdelbach waved his hand with a smile. A vulpine smile. "It is not necessary. This youth has merely demonstrated my point: physical size does not prove maturity."

The tall, gaunt man crossed his hands behind his back and began to pace back and forth in front of Fergus. His head seemed to bob up and down as he walked. Cathal knew he was about to pronounce his opinion and wondered if he should act before the dooming words were spoken. But he waited as Tairdelbach stopped and turned to the crowd. Cathal could see Ciarán standing next to his father. A confident grin was on his brother's face.

Aislinn's fate was about to be sealed, but Cathal still found himself too torn to act.

Ciarán stifled a laugh. It was all too perfect. The faces before him had the appearance of anxious anticipation. Yes, they must know what was to be said, but there was an electricity in the air, like a thunderstorm, until the words were actually spoken. And Tairdelbach was giving them quite a show. He should be, Ciarán reflected, for the wages he was receiving.

"The guardianship of Aislinn," the brehon finally said, "is no easy matter. But she was in her father's hearth at the time of his death and under his rule. His final words were to convey guardianship to his friend, Fergus. Yes, she is of age to be a wife, but not one yet and Fergus has already taken the matter in hand. Therefore. . . ."

Voices in the back, near the door, began to rise. Their volume was steadily growing as more people were joining in. Tairdelbach had stopped speaking, solemnly waiting for attention to his wise words. Ciarán craned his neck, trying to see what was happening to cause the uproar. Fergus was sitting with confusion on his face. When Ciarán saw what was causing the disturbance, his blood ran cold. It was Cairbre, carrying the battered, lifeless body of Seanan in his arms, cradled like a helpless child. The old brehon's arms and legs were draped awkwardly over the warrior's arms, his head lolled from side to side with each step and his sightless eyes stared upward with a look of uncomprehending surprise.

When he saw his old friend in his Cairbre's arms, Fergus slowly rose. His jaw jerked up and down, but no words came. Tears streamed down his cheeks and then he let out a howl like a wounded wolf. Shoving his way through the crowd to Cairbre, he grabbed Seanan's body and hugged it to his chest. Slowly, he walked back to his chair and sank into it, staring at Seanan's face and softly moaning.

Ciarán saw that the moment of decision was slipping from his grasp. He leaned over and softly spoke into his father's ear.

"We are all shocked and saddened by this tragic accident, but we must continue. A decision must be made on Aislinn's guardianship. It is for the good of the clann."

His father looked up at him, but his eyes were empty. Ciarán wondered if he had heard and pressed on.

"Seanan would have wanted it," he said.

Fergus's stare turned focused and hard. Suddenly he backhanded Ciarán across his mouth so powerfully that Ciarán was knocked to the floor. On his hands and knees, Ciarán shook his head trying to clear it. His ears were ringing and dizziness threatened to overwhelm him. He tasted warm blood and his jaw ached. Something hard was in his mouth, like a rock. He spit out a tooth. Before he had recovered enough to rise, he heard his father's voice.

"This Dal is over," Fergus said. His voice was sure and strong. "There will be no further Dal until I bury my friend."

Ciarán watched his father carry Seanan's body out of the room. The crowd began to slowly follow, speaking softly and many glancing back at him as they left. Ciarán sat on the floor. Gingerly he tested for damage to his face. His lip was split, his face was swelling and his top front teeth were loose. Very loose. Looking over at Aislinn and Cathal, he saw them glaring back at him. Then they turned and left with Connaire and their friends.

Tairdelbach cleared his throat. "We will talk some other time. At this moment, I need some mead." Without offering a word of comfort or a hand of assistance, he left.

As the room was emptied, no one came to Ciarán as he sat on the floor. It was all he could manage to fight back tears of pain and of frustration. So close. "It is not over," he muttered.

Chapter 17

Ciarán wrapped his bratt tightly around him to ward off the night chill as he left the abandoned meeting house. He headed toward the house of the healer to get some herbs for his bruised lip and aching jaw. He hoped that he would not lose any more teeth loosened by his father's attack. Gingerly, he explored them with his tongue. They hurt.

"You cursed, old fool," he muttered, angrily shaking his head. "You cursed, sentimental, old fool."

Feeling a presence close behind him, Ciarán reached for a small dagger that he kept secretly at his side and spun around. He saw the vague outline of a large figure approaching.

"Ciarán," a voice softly called. "I need to speak to you."

Ciarán relaxed. "Brandugh. What do you want?"

"I have done as you wished. I have killed Seanan. Now I would like my reward."

Ciarán peered through the dark, but the stars only gave the dim outline of the man in front of him. But he could smell him. "What are you saying? I never asked you to kill Seanan, Brandugh."

"Do not try to play such games with me," the man said in a throaty growl. "You said that it would be worth much if Seanan were missing. Now I want my reward."

"I meant for someone to delay him, not to kill him, you fool." Ciarán spoke in an angry whisper, afraid of being overheard. "I should seize you for murder, not reward you. You killed him because of the judgment against you for assaulting Aed, son of Aed."

Seanan had awarded Aed Brandugh's horse as honor price for the attack. Since Brandugh was a metalsmith, not a warrior,

Seanan decided Brandugh must forfeit his horse as his only real wealth not needed for his trade.

"If you charge me with murder, I will tell everyone you paid me to do it. Everyone knows you wanted to use this Dal to ruin Cathal."

"That is false, cur of curs. You are a murderer and will pay," Ciarán said in a growl, as he silently pulled his dagger.

"Murderer I may be, but I do not have others do it for me and then deny it."

Ciarán saw a glint in the starlight and then felt the tip of a sword blade at his throat.

"Since I have murdered once," Brandugh continued, "a second time will mean nothing."

Ciarán sheathed his dagger. This called for a different approach. "You are right. I will give you two head of cattle to compensate you for your . . . efforts. But I ask one more thing."

"And that is?"

"Kill Cathal."

Ciarán heard a derisive laugh. He knew his ploy had failed.

"I am not suicidal," Brandugh said. "I will take three cattle to forget this whole matter."

"I will give you two now. I will give a third for keeping watch on Cathal and his friends. I feel that they are planning something. Keep watch and report to me. If you discover their plan and I am able to use it to my advantage, it is worth another two head."

Ciarán heard the sound of Brandugh spitting and then a moist palm was pressed into his.

"Done and done," Brandugh said. "Our bargain is made."

Without another word, the big man left.

Ciarán stood, staring into the darkness. He had made a deal

that could come back to ruin him, but it had saved his life. He had no doubt the Brandugh would have killed him as easily as he had Seanan. This bargain gave Brandugh reason not to harm him. And time for him to figure a way to kill Brandugh without being blamed. He had purchased time. And he also might get information that would be of use against Cathal. Yes, he thought smugly, he had turned a certain disaster into a possible victory. With that pleasant thought, he continued his path to the healer.

Ciarán pounded his fist on the healer's door. After a few minutes, she answered, her bratt clutched tightly around her thin frame, gray hair cascading down her shoulders.

"What do you want?" she asked in a sleep-clogged voice.

"I need healing for my mouth and jaw," Ciarán said.

"Come back in the morning. You will not die," she said as she started to close the door.

Ciarán held it open. "I am in pain tonight. I need healing."

With a sigh, she opened the door for him to enter. The dim glow of the hearth fire gave enough light to see the room. Ciarán heard the snoring of her mate as he entered. The healer rummaged through some pots and found what she sought.

"Open your mouth," she said.

Ciarán opened his mouth.

The old hag scratched her chin. "Hmmm, you seem to have lost a tooth. Another looks loose."

Suddenly Ciarán felt a searing pain in his mouth. He swung wildly, striking the aged healer and knocking her to the ground.

"What did you do to me, you old hag," he screamed.

"I gave you healing herbs and for that you struck me. Get out of my house." She was sitting on the ground, holding her head.

"Not until you get rid of this pain. Give me something for the pain," he demanded.

The healer crawled to her pots. She found what she wanted and poured some liquid into a vial. Without standing, she handed it to Ciarán.

"Now get out before I kill you, you ungrateful whelp," she said with an angry snarl.

Ciarán staggered out, drinking the liquid as he went. He headed toward his father's house, but had gone no more than fifty paces when his head began to spin. He grabbed a tree for support, but sank to his knees. Then he fell on his back and looked up at the starry sky, which seemed to slowly swirl above him. The last thing he remembered was closing his eyes in an effort to ward off the dizziness. The rest was dreamless sleep.

Chapter 18

As they left the meeting of the Dal, Aislinn and Cathal walked in silence. Aislinn was consumed with dread, knowing that the decision of her fate was merely delayed, that her doom was already determined. She knew what she must do. As they came to a bench by the remains of the now-dead fire of the evening before, Cathal slumped onto it and buried his head in his hands. Connaire, carrying a torch and accompanied by Gruagach and Tian, soon joined them.

"Cairbre is taking Seanan's body to be prepared for burial," Connaire said. "After that, the funeral games will be held. We have but four or five days before the Dal will be summoned again."

He grabbed his brother's shoulder, bringing Cathal's head up so their eyes met. "Now is the time to act. We can rally our friends and make a stand. Ciarán will crumple like a thin reed in the wind if he is met by force. Just say the word."

"No." Aislinn spoke with a firm, steady voice. She knew what she had to do, the only course open to her. "It would destroy this clann, all of you and many honorable people. There is but one answer: I will leave this clann. I will pack what belongings I can take without raising alarm and be gone."

Connaire shook his head emphatically. "We cannot let you do that. We will not let Ciarán drive you from us, to wander without a clann. You are a part of us. He is not."

Cathal suddenly stood, aroused from his stupor.

"She is right," he said. "She must leave." He raised his hand to stifle the protest that arose. "But she will not be alone. I will be with her."

"No," Aislinn said. "This clann is your very life's blood. You will be the next taoiseach. The clann needs you and you need

116

it. Without it, you will wither and die."

"In that, you are wrong." He smiled at her and gently brushed back her hair. "It is without you that I will wither and die. You are my clann. Without you, I have none. I will go with you, whether you want me or not."

"You know I want you," she said with a catch in her throat. She desperately wanted him to go with her, but feared he would grow to hate her for forcing him to leave his clann. "But you would be giving up what has been your life. Your friends, your family--"

"Not all of his family," Connaire interrupted. "You two are not going to leave me with Ciarán."

"Not me, either," Gruagach said. He shoved Cathal with a meaty fist. "If you try, I will teach what it is like to wrestle me when I am angry."

Cathal shook his head. "No, no, it would not work. A couple might find a clann that would accept them and they might hide from Fergus's wrath. But a whole group? And this clann needs all of you."

Tian stepped close to Cathal. He grabbed Cathal's chin and held it firmly, glaring into Cathal's eyes. When he spoke, his voice was low and determined. "You are my clann. Without you, I have none. I will go with you, whether you want me or not."

A smile tugged at a corner of Cathal's mouth. Then a grin. And finally Cathal broke into a laugh. The others joined him, the levity providing a needed relief.

As the laughter subsided, Cathal sighed and shook his head. "This decision should not be taken lightly. Whatever course we take, it is too late to decide tonight. We must meet again to talk of this matter when we are rested and more alert. Tomorrow, when the sun is halfway from its rising to its zenith, let us meet in the gorge past the sacred oak grove. For now, we need rest."

The others murmured their agreement as they headed to their houses.

Connaire walked with Cathal and Aislinn in the cool night. Although they carried no torches, the stars were so bright that they had no trouble finding their way. As they approached the house of Cian, now the house of Aislinn, they stopped. Cathal turned to Aislinn.

"Keep well," Cathal said softly, as he cupped the back of her head. Gently, he kissed her, a kiss that was long and slow.

Connaire poked his brother's shin with his crutch. "What are you doing?" he asked.

Cathal turned to him. "Kissing the woman I love. Are you blind or just simple?"

"I can see that. Why do you do it here? Or are you planning to drop to the ground and couple in the dirt?"

"If you were not my brother, and a cripple for now, I would swat you like a fly for that comment." Cathal felt his anger rise within him, giving a flush to his face that was hidden in the night.

"For what? I wondered why you stand here in the dark instead of taking the one you love to a more comfortable place. Like her house."

Cathal slowly shook his head. "You know I cannot do that. Not now, with all the problems."

"What do these 'problems' matter? We have set our course. What do you fear?"

"I fear nothing." Cathal's voice rose. He realized it and, lest others hear, quickly stifled his anger. "I am only doing what is best for the clann. Now that Father has claimed Aislinn as his wife, to go against him and . . . well, to act on my desire would be unwise."

"What of you?" Connaire asked Aislinn. "Would you take this man into your bed and enjoy the pleasures of his love?"

"I will beg no man to come to my bed," she said in a cool, steady voice.

"Surely you understand," Cathal pleaded, taking her hands in his. They were limp, not fighting but not confirming either. "It is not lack of desire, but a sense of duty. Duty to the clann. Duty to my Father."

"I understand that you do what you feel is right. I am not to be consulted." She pulled away from him and started toward her house.

Connaire grabbed his brother's shoulder and squeezed it tightly. "I have admired you from the moment I drew breath. To me, you have always been the bravest and most honorable. You still are. But too often you deny your passion, as you are doing now. Be a little more 'Connaire' tonight. Let your emotions rule your mind. Think less and feel more."

Cathal shook his head. So much was at stake. "If Ciarán realizes this and tells Father--"

Connaire punched Cathal in the shoulder. "Forget Ciarán. This clann will divide soon and many of us will follow you wherever you lead. But for now, let your heart lead you."

Cathal looked at the retreating figure of Aislinn, almost lost in the night. There was duty. And then there was love. But love had its own duty. "Wait, Aislinn. I want to be with you. It is now your house. Will you let me?"

He saw her stop. She did not turn to him. Had he waited too long? Then he heard her say, "I will wait a moment. But do not expect more."

Cathal grabbed Connaire by both forearms. "You are right, my brother. I am not used to being advised by you, but you are right. From this time on, never hold from telling me when I am unwise." With a smile he added, "Or falsely wise."

Cathal trotted to catch Aislinn. He heard Connaire call to him, "Do not worry. If I think Ciarán suspects anything, I will slit his throat." Cathal started to protest, but then chuckled. Connaire was merely jesting. And if he were not, then so be it.

Aislinn's house was almost ten paces across. Its conical, thatched ceiling rose the height of almost three times of a man and rested on a stone wall three hands less than one. Stall-like dividers created private spaces radiating from the central hearth area. The fire in the hearth had burned down to embers, but the smoke still hung heavy in the air as it slowly filtered through the porous thatch. It had once housed three handcounts of relatives, the extended family of Cian. A strange sickness had taken many and age took the others. Now Aislinn lived there with only Bevin, her servant, as a companion.

Raiders had captured Bevin, then named Mairwen, many Samhains before, when they had plundered a settlement on the British coast. She had been a young girl then and sold to Cian's father. Then he died and it had become Cian's hearth. When Aislinn's mother Muirne came to the house, she found a special kinship with her. Although Muirne was a warrior and Mairwen knew nothing of fighting, they became very close. There was kindness in Muirne's strength. It was Muirne who had given Mairwen the name of Bevin, melodious woman, because of the songs she sang. Bevin loved the family dearly. But not as much as God. The rough wooden cross she wore around her neck attested to her faith, a faith in one God rather than many. She touched it gently as Aislinn and Cathal entered the house.

"Bevin," Aislinn called to her. "Do we have any of the

120

wine that Father bought a few years ago? If not, we can have ale, but I want you to celebrate with us. Cathal and I are oathed and tonight we will be together for the first time."

"No wine, I am afraid. Only Gaulish traders have that and none have been here for many years. I gave the last to your father when he was near death. But I will get the ale."

As Bevin busied herself in the task, she listened to what was said by the two lovers.

"Do you think it is wise to be so forthcoming with Bevin?" Cathal asked Aislinn.

"Of course it is. Bevin has been my mother since my own died. I trust her more than anyone but you."

Bevin again touched her cross. It was true that she had raised Aislinn after Muirne's death. But she was still a slave. She was not free. She could never worship with other Christians. She had not been given the Sacraments since she had been captured. She was alone among pagans. And Ciarán had promised her freedom and passage back to her own people if she gave him any important information. What was the right thing to do? She pondered this as she went about her duties.

As Bevin set the cups of ale on the table, Aislinn suddenly grabbed her wrist.

"Bevin, I must tell you. Cathal and I will not be here for much longer. We are going to leave the clann so that we can be together."

"Oh, child," Bevin gasped. "Why would you do that?"

"Because I love him."

"But is he worth it?" Before Aislinn could answer, Bevin laid her fingers against Aislinn's lips. "Do not answer me. I know what you will say. But think. Then think again."

Cathal scowled. Bevin had not liked him since he had

shunned Aislinn those years ago.   Why should she trust him now?
He was like all men.   Like the raiders who had spread her thighs
when she had been but a lass and hurt her.   Now Cathal would hurt
Aislinn.   Perhaps it would be best to tell Ciarán and save Aislinn.
Except she knew in her heart that it would not save Aislinn.

    "It is late, child," Bevin said.   "Do you mind if I go to my
bed?"

    "No, no."   Aislinn patted her hand.   "Rest well."

    Bevin went to her section of the house.   She heard Aislinn
and Cathal as they coupled.   Aislinn's screams almost caused her to
leap to the child's defense until she realized they were cries of
passion instead of screams of torment.   For Bevin, those many
years ago, they had been only of torment.   Now her child had been
violated.   And she had done nothing.   Aislinn would have been
angry if she had done so.   Perhaps it was time to escape.   And
Ciarán was her only chance.   But to do so, she would betray the
child of her friend, her child.

    Quiet descended upon the house.   The fire in the hearth was
banked, so there was little light.   Tears crept from her eyes as she
fingered her wooden cross.

    "God help me," she muttered.   "God help me."

Chapter 19

Aislinn woke late. Dawn had already come. She stretched languidly, recalling the night before. Where was Cathal? With a rueful shake of her head, she figured that he had left early so as not to be seen coming from her house. Would he ever put the two of them before the clann? Likely not. It was part of him that she admired and hated. But she knew it was something she would have to accept. At least until they and their companions finally left.

She realized she had felt none of the pain most of the women spoke of after their first time. Looking down, she saw no blood. Some of the women warriors, the ones who spent many hours on their horses and serious training, had told her they had no first-night blood either. Being a warrior had some extra advantages, she decided. She felt no soreness, only a desire for Cathal. But he had left already. With a sigh, she rose and donned her léine.

Brushing her hair back with her fingers, she walked to the fire burning low on the hearth stones. A stew slowly bubbled in a pot set close to it and she dished some of it into a bowl. Looking around, she did not see Bevin. Where was she? She normally greeted her each morning. With a shrug, Aislinn grabbed a drying cloth and walked out the door. As much as she had enjoyed the night with Cathal, it had left her with feeling a strong need for a bath.

Ciarán sat on a bench outside his father's house, rubbing his temples. He had awakened lying on the ground with a hound licking his face. He was still groggy, but his jaw did not ache as it had the night before. He still resented the healer's attitude, but she had done her job. When he became chief, she would have to treat him with more respect, though.

Suddenly a pebble hit him on his temple. He spun around to see who had thrown it. Behind a tree, hiding from any passers-by, a woman motioned to him. It was Aislinn's servant. He just wanted to be alone and almost waved her away. Still, it might be worth hearing what she wanted. Anything she heard Aislinn say might be of value. Slowly, keeping a wary eye for any who might see him meet with the woman, he rose and walked to her. When he reached the tree she hid behind, he casually leaned against it, still watching for anyone who might wander by.

"So, Aislinn's slave, do you have something you wish to tell me?" There was a sneer in his voice. She was a tool, not worth anything except the use he could make of her.

The woman made no reply. He could hear her labored breathing, as if she were carrying a heavy burden.

"Come, woman, speak if you wish. I have other matters to attend, matters more important than you."

"I only speak to you that I may return to my home, that I may worship my God with fellow followers of the Christus, my family." Her voice was choked, as if she were fighting not to weep.

"Yes, yes. You are an honorable woman and taking the path of greater duty." Ciarán could hardly keep the disgust from his voice. He hated having to coddle fools such as this. "I promise that you will be returned to your people." He paused. "If the information is worth the price."

"What I have learned is worth far more than that. How do I know you will keep your promise?"

Ciarán reached down and shook a pouch that was tied to a belt that cinched his léine around his waist. A metallic jingle could be heard. "I have accumulated silver coins, coins with the image of a man. Coins that came from your land across the sea. They will pay your way home with traders. Now what did you come here to tell me?"

"They plan to flee."

"Who? Aislinn and Cathal plan to leave the clann?" Ciarán's mind spun with the possibilities. Should he let them escape and then use their flight to discredit them with the clann? Or should he just wait until they were gone, then alert his father and track them down like frightened prey? Or should he foil their escape before it happened? Whatever he did, he must make sure his information was complete and accurate. "When? And where are they going?"

The woman shook her head. "I do know yet." She stopped speaking for a moment. "The money you have, the coins you will pay me?"

"Yes?"

"How many coins?"

Ciarán considered his answer. If he said too few, she might refuse to help him. If he said to many, she would not believe that he actually would give her that amount. Of course he had no intention of paying her for the information. She was mere chattel. But she must believe that he would pay her for the information.

"Six," he finally said.

"Six?"

Too low. She was going to renege on their bargain. He had to up the prize. And do so without seeming to do so.

"Yes," he said. "Six hand counts of coins."

She gasped. Ciarán feared that he had offered too much.

"I know that it is more than you expected, woman, but I am feeling generous."

"Mairwen." She said it softly, just above a whisper.

"What?" What did that strange word mean?

"Mairwen. My name is Mairwen. It means Blessed Mary

in the language of my people.   Mary, like the mother of the
Christus, the son of God."

What was this nonsense?

"Mairwen.   Well, Mairwen, when you give me the full tale
of their flight, you shall have all of these coins."

Without another word, she turned and walked away.   He
thought he heard a short sob.   Tears of joy, no doubt.   He had
offered her both her freedom and a fine reward for the information.
Ciarán smiled to himself as he walked toward his father's house.   It
had been a rewarding meeting.

When Ciarán had stated the number of coins he was
offering, Bevin had almost cried out in horror.   Six hand counts.
Thirty.   Thirty pieces of silver.   The Judas price for her betrayal!
Betrayal of Aislinn.   Her betrayal of Aislinn's mother.   Her
betrayal of the only ones who had shown her kindness since that
horrible day she had been seized by those men, the men who had
taken her so cruelly.

Bevin did not know what to do.   If she told Ciarán that she
had changed her mind, he would surely learn the details of Aislinn's
plan.   He would still be able to stop her and Bevin would still be a
slave, away from her people and other Christians.   And if Ciarán
told Aislinn of her betrayal, that it was she who told of the plan, then
she might be sold or given to someone of great cruelty.   A man who
would use her for his pleasure.   She shuddered at the thought.
What should she do?

When she had been a child, safe at home, she would have
talked to a priest, a man of God.   He would have known what to do.
But there were no men of God here.   The pagan druid was nice
enough to her, but he would not know God's will.   No, she would
have to pray and fast.   Pray that God would reveal His will.   Pray

that God would not condemn her to hell for her sinful betrayal. She, named after the mother of the Christus, was now no better than he who sent Him to His death for thirty pieces of silver. Tears streamed from her eyes as she stumbled back to Aislinn's house.

Chapter 20

Cathal paced the small clearing in the center like a restless wolf. By midmorning, Cathal, Aislinn and their companions had gathered in the ravine as planned the night before. They had drifted in by ones and twos so as to not raise suspicion, knowing that Ciarán or his friends would likely be watching them. The ravine was sheltered by large oaks growing on the banks above it, hiding them from view of any possible passer-by. Finding a rough circle of large rocks, Connaire, Gruagach, Cairbre and Tian sat, while Aislinn and Cathal remained on their feet. He still paced, head down. Aislinn watched him, waiting for him to speak. Finally, impatient with Cathal's hesitation, she spoke to the group.

"If we are all to go, we must make a plan. Alone, I would take my weapons, my horse and some items for barter. That will not work if we all go. We will need a place to go and supplies to get us there. We will need to plan how to survive when we arrive."

Cathal stopped his pacing.

"You sound like a taoiseach," he said, giving her a bemused grin. Then he turned to the others. "But she is right. We must first decide where to go, where we will find welcome. But we must be careful that we do not ally ourselves with any clann that might war with our own. That would go against both our duty and our honor."

"We could ride south, far from the lands of our clann," Tian volunteered. "Perhaps find a clann far distant that would like strong warriors to aid it."

Cairbre shook his head. "Though we are strong, we are few. Riding armed and unbidden through the lands of so many other clanns might well lead them to believe us outlaws and rogues, to be dealt with by sword rather than words."

"And we will be outlaws," Gruagach added. "We will have left our clann without the permission of the taoiseach, with the woman he wishes to oath."

"We are oathed," Cathal stated belligerently. "We will stay oathed and go alone if necessary."

"Calm yourself, my love," Aislinn said, laying her hand on Cathal's shoulder. She feared he might say something that would offend the others to the point of ruining their plans. "They all support us, so that is not the issue. Gruagach is stating how we will be perceived. Nothing more."

"I know," he said, shaking his head. "But it seems we have no hope of finding safety."

"I have a suggestion," Connaire said, slowly stroking his chin. "My friend Ronan may be of help to us. His mother's clann lives by the sea. He has often gone there to visit relatives and enjoys fishing with them. They are of Cenél Loairn, across the sea in Alba. We could go there, find a clann that would welcome us or even start our own clann."

"We are not sailors," Cathal said, with a dismissive wave of his hand. "How would we get there? How would we take cattle and horses? We would be far from what we know, among people we do not know."

Aislinn saw that Connaire's suggestion might be their best course, their only course. She touched Cathal's arm. "We cannot take our herds from the clann without a battle. Even if we were able to, as Cairbre said, other clanns might consider us enemies and do battle to steal our herds. We are few in number. Our only hope is to go far away, to a place where we are not known, but not by passing through the lands of many other clanns."

Cathal stood a moment in silence, looking at the ground. Then he turned to Aislinn, resting his hand behind her neck and smiling.

"You do have the wisdom of a taoiseach, a wise taoiseach. Breandan might well let us pass. He seemed to feel a debt of honor at our last meeting."

He turned to the others and continued. "Connaire, if you can trust Ronan, send him to see if any boats might be purchased. We can sell our herd for tradable goods we can carry. Weapons, jewelry and such. It will have to be done in total secrecy. Do not talk to anyone you cannot trust entirely, anyone who cannot keep quiet. We must be ready to leave before the funeral games for Seanan are over. From now on, we meet away from the clann, where friends of Ciarán will not see us and tell tales. Surprise is our main weapon."

"What of others?" Tian asked. "There will be others who will not do well under Ciarán."

"Fergus is still taoiseach," Cathal growled.

Tian gave a soft, mirthless laugh. "Ciarán almost rules unhindered now. In time, he will control Fergus totally. Our escape will only speed the process. Do not abandon our friends to this fate."

"He is right," Connaire said, striking the ground with his crutch. "They need you."

Cathal stood, silently studying the ground for a few moments.

Aislinn feared his loyalty to the clann he was leaving would override his loyalty to his friends. If it did, she would have to speak against him, something she did not want to do. He would need all the authority he could muster, if they were to succeed in their escape. Finally he spoke.

"You are right. My duty to them, our new clann, must come first. Enlist those that you feel would come with us." Then

130

he raised a warning hand. "But be cautious in who you tell and where you do so. If Ciarán hears of this, he will do everything he can to ruin us. And likely would be able to do so. Let us hope we can leave without a fight. But if we cannot, then we will fight."

"You are the leader again, the warrior who knows the battle and is ready for it. And I will be at your side," Aislinn said to Cathal, then grabbed his head with both of her hands and gave him a deep, powerful kiss.

The others smiled as they rose from their rocky seats.

"It looks as though we will be assured of a next generation for our new clann," Tian said, nudging Gruagach.

But Gruagach looked suddenly grim.

"I have never been on the sea," he said. "Is it as fearsome as I have heard?"

Tian looped his arm through his friend's and led him away toward their houses. "Worse. There are sea monsters that the god Manannán sends to devour any who are not sailors that invade his realm. But do not worry, my fearful friend," he said with a laugh. "You are much too distasteful a morsel for them."

Gruagach shoved Tian so hard he almost fell. "You laugh now," he told Tian. "But when the winds howl and the waters toss us as leaves in the storm, you will look to me for help."

"Perhaps, my mountainous friend," Tian replied with a wry smile. "Perhaps. I fear no man, but the realm of Manannán is unknown. And it is the unknown that is to be feared most."

Soon only Connaire, Cathal and Aislinn remained in the ravine.

Connaire leaned on his crutch, speaking excitedly. "Of course not all of our friends will want to go with us. Some are too old for such a journey and some will not want to brave the sea.

Still, they are our friends and can help us."

He gestured wildly with his free hand as he spoke, looking to Aislinn as if he were swatting flies. She smiled at his enthusiasm: an enthusiasm of youth that does not bear the responsibility of such a decision.

"We can trade our cattle and horses to our friends who stay here for goods that we can carry with us," he continued. "Things like gold and silver jewelry. Torques, armbands, and the like. And weapons. Plenty of them. We can trade them for cattle and horses after we cross the sea. We can . . . ."

Aislinn leaned on Cathal's chest. His arms encircled her, holding her tightly. She could feel his heart beat. Connaire had stopped talking, seeming to have finally noticed them. His face flushed red.

"I, ah . . . I need to get back to Father before he notices anything is amiss," he stammered. "Do you mind if I leave?"

Aislinn stifled a laugh as Cathal said, "Very wise, my brother. We will be there soon." Then a pause. "Well, fairly soon."

"Yes, ah, . . . yes." Connaire started up the ravine, carefully picking his way with his crutch. Pausing at the top, he said with a laugh, "Do not hurry on my account." Then he disappeared from sight.

Cathal pulled Aislinn even closer and kissed her deeply. It was a heady moment for Aislinn. No longer did she feel that she had to push Cathal, no longer did she wonder if he would forsake the clann and his father for her. She knew that he was now as much hers as she was his. And she felt the fire of her passion burst into a roaring flame.

Pulling his mouth from hers, Cathal softly asked, "Do you want to find a grassy meadow? It would be more comfortable."

"No," she gasped, "now."

Without another word, she locked her lips onto his as they stood on the rocky soil. Then she felt him lift her léine above her waist. She felt his hands grip her waist and lift her from the ground. Instinctively, she wrapped her legs around him and, as he lowered her slightly, she felt him enter her. Her tongue intertwined with his as she rocked up and down, first slowly and then rapidly. Her fingernails dug into his back and she leaned her head into the hollow of his neck, eyes closed. Soon, all too soon, it was over.

For a moment, they stayed together, her legs wrapped around him. Then she slipped to the ground, but still held him tightly.

"I suppose we should get back," she finally said.

"Yes."

They stayed in their embrace.

"Really," she said.

"Yes."

Slowly, reluctantly they parted. Aislinn turned and climbed the rocky incline out of the gorge. With a satisfied sigh, Cathal followed.

Chapter 21

From his vantage point in an oak tree near the gorge, Brandugh watched Cathal and Aislinn untie the reins of their horses and ride away. Connaire had never noticed Brandugh as he followed him that morning, leading him to the gorge. He had not dared to get close enough to hear what was said for fear of being seen, but had been close enough to observe the entire meeting and its erotic aftermath. Now he would need to find a companion to relieve the tension of arousal that still churned in his loins. He would have gladly taken a go at Aislinn when Cathal had finished. Not that that haughty bitch would have had him. Still, he thought with a smile, there might come a time when she would spread her legs to keep him quiet. For now, he thought as he slipped down from the tree and wiped the sweat from his brow with a grimy hand, he would see what reward Ciarán would pay to know what he had seen.

When he reached the settlement, Brandugh saw Gruagach talking to Tian. It was a perfect opportunity. He sauntered over to the pair. They stopped talking when they saw him.

"Ah, my friends," Brandugh said, flashing a wide smile, "is it not a fine day?"

"I suppose it is," Tian replied, looking up at the sky. "But why ask us? Do you not know it is one or not yourself?"

Brandugh laughed. He would rather have struck Tian in his arrogant mouth, but he needed to get on his good side. "You have such a way with words, Tian. I am almost afraid to speak in your presence."

"Almost? Then I have not been successful."

Brandugh decided this was not going very well. Time to change his approach. He turned to the bigger man. "Gruagach, can you believe how that little worm Ciarán behaved in the Dal? Is there some bad blood between him and his brothers?"

Gruagach shrugged his shoulders. "Brothers often fight. And Ciarán likes to start things."

"To me, it seems that he does not have the manhood to do anything physical like you or I would, so he uses his mouth." Brandugh gave Gruagach a quick grin. "Or overuses it."

Gruagach gave a short grunt of agreement.

"I know you both are friends of Cathal and I like him," Brandugh continued. "He is a man of strength. I want you to know that if comes to a fight, you can count on me."

Tian's eyes narrowed. "A fight? What makes you think there will be a fight?"

Brandugh shrugged. "It seems like that is what Ciarán wants. Well, I must be off."

As Brandugh walked away, Tian thoughtfully stroked his mustache. "Why would he come to us now and say these things?" he muttered.

"Because he wants us to know that he will stand with us," Gruagach said. He slapped Tian on the back. "And we can use men like him."

Tian snorted. "A metalsmith? And a poor one at that. He is so poor at his craft that his drinking cups are used only as a last resort. And then as latrines."

Gruagach laughed. "Well, I am sure we will need those too. But he is strong and able. I have seen him use a sword almost as well as a warrior. And he could do very well with an oar. I wonder how well he does on the sea?"

Tian shook his head. "I do not trust him. Say nothing to him of our plans."

"You worry too much."

Tian wrinkled his nose. "And he stinks."

"Then I will dunk him in the sea for you if he comes with us," Gruagach said with a loud laugh. "Will that make you happy?"

Tian gave his friend a half smile. "Maybe if you keep his head under for a while. A long while."

When he found Ciarán, Brandugh indicated with a jerk of his head that Ciarán should follow him. The big man strolled toward the river, acting as nonchalant as he could. No one seemed to be following him, so he waited after he crested a low rise that hid him from view of the settlement until Ciarán arrived.

"I have news for you," he told Ciarán smugly. "I expect a good reward for it. Cathal and Aislinn are planning something."

"They are planning on fleeing," Ciarán said with a bored wave of his hand. "You will get nothing for such worthless information."

Momentarily taken aback, Brandugh said nothing. Then he forged on. "Did you know that Connaire, Tian, Cairbre and Gruagach are going with them?" He did not know that for sure, but it was a fair guess.

"Interesting," Ciarán said. "But not worth any reward."

"How about that Cathal is poking Aislinn? I saw them do it."

Ciarán laughed. "That is no surprise."

Brandugh nervously ran his fingers through his matted, black hair. "What of my reward?"

"For what? Consider your view of the lovely Aislinn rutting to be your reward for this meager information." Ciarán smiled. It reminded Brandugh of a lizard. "But if you can find when and where they are going, I will reward you well."

With that, Ciarán turned and left. As he did, Brandugh stared daggers at his back. If not for the expected reward, he would have broken Ciarán's neck as he had Seanan's. Then he spat on the ground. Better start to figure a way to become a part of Cathal and Aislinn's group, find the information that Ciarán wanted. And perhaps find a way to play both sides against each other. That was it. Use them both. What did it matter who won as long as he came out ahead?

As he walked away, Ciarán softly laughed. This was interesting news indeed. Now he could be rid not only of his arrogant brother and his she-wolf lover, but that whelp Connaire and their whole circle of friends. If he could sway his father to see them as traitors, out to destroy the clann, many would follow his father's lead to attack them. Many might die. Even if his brothers survived, they would be outlaws, pariahs shunned by the clann. So killing them would have no honor price. And then he could quietly offer a reward for their deaths. Or even do it himself. A swift arrow kills at a safe distance.

Chapter 22

The next meeting of Cathal, Aislinn and their friends took place that night, after many of the clann had gone to their beds. They gathered in the same ravine as before. No fire was lit for fear of its light being seen by someone who would betray them, but the full moon in the cloudless sky gave ample light. It was bright, almost like day. Connaire had brought his friend Ronan and several other of his close friends. The others had done the same. Their number had grown to over twenty. As Cathal surveyed them, he hoped that they could be trusted to keep quiet about their escape plans. Trusted to be loyal. Trusted.

Connaire brought Ronan to Cathal. "Brother, you remember Ronan?" he said, his arm wrapped across the other man's shoulder. "I have spoken with him about our need. He is sure that he can help."

Cathal studied Ronan silently for a moment. He was shorter than Cathal by half a head, with dark hair and dark eyes. Although slight of build, his arms showed wiry muscles. Even though he did not know this man, a man who looked more like a lad than a warrior, he sensed that Ronan would be agile and strong. He grunted his approval.

Ronan looked from Cathal to Connaire, as if seeking guidance, then took a deep breath and spoke rapidly. "My mother's kin in Alba are fond of me. I am very close to many in her clann and I am sure they will accept us, but we must reach them. I have rowed and sailed across the sea to them several times. I know the sea well. Not as well as the old men who are on it every day, but better than any in this clann. Not that I mean to dishonor this clann but--"

Cathal held up his hand to stop the flood of words. He gave

the young man a quick smile. "Two questions. Can we get the boats to carry us across the sea and can we learn enough about boats to sail across?"

Ronan took a deep breath. "Yes. I believe we can do it." Then more forcefully. "Yes, by Manannán, we can do it."

Cathal slapped him on the shoulder. "Then we will."

Ronan hesitated. "But I failed to get the currachs for us. Since I did not want to tell of our plans, I could not find enough of them without raising suspicion."

Cathal stroked his chin. "Perhaps I know of a way. Brandon of the Uí Néills might be willing to aid us."

Cathal, with Aislinn at his side, walked to the center of a clearing and he banged his sword against a tree to assemble the people. When he had gathered everyone around him and they had quieted enough for him to be heard, he told them of the proposed voyage across the sea. When he had finished, at first there was silence. Cathal sensed that they were surprised, maybe even shocked at the thought of leaving all, their cattle, their horses and most of their goods as well as their clann. This might be too much to sacrifice, too far to go. He hesitated to speak, to try to persuade them to follow him. Was it not too much to ask?

Suddenly Connaire hobbled over to him and turned to face the crowd. He scanned the faces, then spoke loudly.

"I know what you feel. We are not a sea-people. I have been on the sea but twice myself, with my good friend Ronan." He gestured toward Ronan, waving him to stand by him. "But what is the alternative? Ciarán has taken control of my father." Connaire shook his head. "I do not know what has happened to Fergus, but his mind is in the palm of Ciarán's hand. And we are in his hand as well, as long as we remain here."

A voice from the back called out, "Then let Cathal take this clann in his hand.   Let him have Fergus stand down and Cathal be taoiseach."

Those gathered roared their approval.   Connaire waited until the noise lessened, then raised his hand.

"That is not possible.   My brother, Cathal, follows the three legs of the cauldron of our people: truth, honor and duty.   If one is lost, then the cauldron falls.   He feels that to go against our father would attack the very legs of the cauldron."

A murmur of disagreement began to rumble, but again Connaire raised his hand and continued.

"You follow Cathal because of the man he is.   So do not criticize him now for being what he is.   My friend, Ronan, will speak to you of crossing the sea.   If you do not wish to do so, there will be no dishonor in that.   Just speak of these matters to no one."

While Connaire had been addressing the group, Ronan had come to his side.   He glanced at Connaire before speaking to the assembled crowd.   His previous hesitancy was gone.

"My brave friends, no one would dare to call you cowards. If he did, he would die in the fight afterwards.   And I do not to want be that man.   But now you are acting like cowards."

Angry muttering rippled through the people there.

"Acting like, but not cowards at heart," Ronan continued. "You know warriors who attack you as merely other men and women: defeatable.   It is because you do not know the sea that you fear it.   But I will show you how to defeat the sea.   I have done it and so can you.   Or do you think me better than you?"

A shout of "No!" roared through the ravine.

Connaire struck a tree with his crutch until the clamor subsided.   "Cathal is going.   Aislinn is going.   I am going. Ronan is going.   Who will go with us?"

Everyone there yelled their approval. Cathal smiled and shook his head. The matter was decided. And it was by the leadership of Connaire and Ronan. Taking his sword, he banged a tree until the noise abated and he could be heard.

"If anyone wishes to remain, it will be no dishonor. I will fight anyone who says it is." He paused to let the import of what he said be felt. "But all are welcome to go. It will mean ridding yourself of all that cannot be easily carried on horseback. We will leave tomorrow at this time. If you will go, be ready."

Tian pushed through to Cathal and turned to the crowd.

"I have arranged with friends in the clann who will not be going to give fair value for what you cannot take. Some are too old, some have obligations here, but all are friends and will trade with you honestly. But I caution all of you to speak of this to no one else. The more who know, the greater the chance of Ciarán learning of our plans."

Cathal nodded in agreement.

"Tomorrow, Tian will help you prepare to leave. Tomorrow night, when the moon reaches its highest point in the sky, we will leave from this place. Now go to your houses," he said. "Get some rest. But as you leave, go one at a time or in pairs. We must keep Ciarán from learning of this."

As the crowd dispersed, Aislinn leaned her head against Cathal's chest. He wrapped his arms around her.

"It went well," she said.

"Yes." He shook his head. "I hope that I am not leading them to destruction."

"You are leading them. After what has happened with Fergus, they need that."

Cathal sighed and held her more tightly.

When Brandugh reached the ravine, he saw people leaving. He waited behind a tree until most had left. He had been watching Aislinn's house, hoping to gather more information on what she and Cathal were planning. When she did not return to her house, he realized that she must be with the others at the ravine and hurried to find her. Seeing a number of people leaving the ravine, heading in different directions, he figured that the meeting was over. Unsure of what to do next, he waited by the tree.

Finally, deciding that he would gain nothing by doing nothing, he slipped into the ravine. There he saw Aislinn, Cathal, Connaire, Tian, Gruagach and Cairbre standing together. As he got closer, he heard Cathal say, "I will leave now so that I can make our arrangements and be back before midday tomorrow."

Then Aislinn saw him.

"What are you doing?" she demanded. "Spying on us?"

He saw the hands of the warriors, Aislinn's included, go to their swords at their sides. He held up both hands, showing he was unarmed and gave his most disarming smile.

"I wanted to join with you. I know you are leaving and I do not want to stay with Ciarán. I have nothing here, no wealth, no family." He saw distrust in their eyes and hurriedly continued. "Remember, Gruagach and Tian, I spoke with you about that."

The tension eased, but they still eyed him warily.

"Yes, we remember," Gruagach finally said. "What do you think, Cathal? Shall we tell him?"

"Of course, we should tell him," Tian said with sudden warmth. He walked over and put his arm across Brandugh's shoulders. "We do have a plan, but you must not speak of it to anyone."

Aislinn seemed upset and started to speak, but before she said a word, Tian continued. "You see, my friend, we have made arrangements to go to Mumhan, where we will be welcomed as warriors. They want us as much as we need them."

Gruagach looked uneasy. The others looked surprised. Brandugh suppressed a laugh. The fools did not realize that the glib-tongued idiot was sealing their fate.

"But when will you go?" he asked. "It will take time to get everything ready."

Tian sighed. "That is the problem. We are not sure. As you heard, Cathal is going to ride now to finalize everything. The rest of us are preparing. Are you with us?"

"Definitely." He smiled at Tian, then at the others. "I am with you."

"Good, good," Tian said. "Gruagach, Cairbre and I will meet you here at midday tomorrow. We will know the details then."

Brandugh spit in his hand and offered it to Tian, who seemed to take it with reluctance. Then Brandugh turned and hurried away. He needed to find Ciarán.

Chapter 23

Ciarán had retired for the night, huddled under his bratt in his bed in his father's house. He could hear the steady drone of his father's snoring as he tried to go to sleep, but his mind was too occupied. Neither Cathal or Connaire had yet arrived and he was sure that they were planning their escape. He hoped his spies would learn enough of their plans for him to thwart their efforts. A smile crept across his face as he imagined Cathal's dismay at being confronted by Fergus and his loyal warriors.

Then Ciarán heard a rustling near him. Before he could react, a hand clamped across his mouth. In the dark, he had no idea who it was. He started to struggle, but an arm slammed across his chest and held him down.

"Shh," his attacker whispered in his ear. "We need to talk."

Ciarán realized it was Brandugh by his voice and his stench. He stopped his efforts to free himself and the hand on his mouth withdrew.

"Let us go outside," he said to Brandugh in a low voice. "I do not want to wake Father."

When they reached open air, Ciarán followed the hulking man by the light of the moon to a tree a short distance from the house. When they reached it, Ciarán asked impatiently, "What reason do you have for dragging me from my bed at this hour?"

"I have won the confidence of your brother and his friends. I know where they are going."

"Well?" Ciarán almost grabbed the large man's léine in his impatience. "Where are they going?"

"Not until I get some guarantee. I want your promise of twenty cows and a bull."

Ciarán considered this request. It was far too high. He had

no intention of giving this fool anything, but if he agreed to such a demand, Brandugh would surely be suspicious.

"I will give you ten cows only, providing the information is true."

"Fifteen cows and a bull."

Ciarán knew that he had him.   Brandugh was going to talk. It was just a matter of negotiation.

"Twelve cows."

"Ten cows and a bull."

Bandaugh must desperately want the bull.   Time to seal the deal.

"Eight cows and a bull."

"Done."

Ciarán could hear Brandugh hawk and spit.   He knew the hand with its spittle would be outstretched and reached for it.   They shook hands.   The deal was done.   Ciarán could hardly wait until he could wash his hand, but first he needed the information.

"Now prove that the information is worth the price."

"They are going to Mumhan."

Ciarán considered this revelation.   Why would they choose Mumhan?   Then again, why not?   But to believe this, he must have some reason to do so besides the word of a self-serving traitor.

"And how do you know this?"

"I was with Cathal, Aislinn, and all their friends when they made their plans.   I heard it from them."

"And they trusted you?"

"Why not?   Look, here comes Connaire now.   The meeting has ended."

Connaire hobbled through the moon-lit night and entered the house.   Could this be?   Had Brandugh gained their confidence? Had he now the power to destroy them?   He must be ready when they fled.

"When are they to depart?"

"They do know yet, but Cathal has left to make arrangements. If you do not believe me, see if Cathal is not missing for much of the morrow. I will know when he returns." There was a pause. "Before I give you that information, I want payment for what I have given you. Have the cows and bull brought to my house tomorrow morning."

Ciarán silently cursed the big oaf before him. He was smarter than expected. He would have to comply. Still, he could gain from seizing his brothers' and all their companions' herds when they were caught fleeing. Even if they were not caught.

"It will be done. But I want to know as soon as you find out when they are planning to flee."

"Done."

He heard the hawk and spit, but turned and left before having to take the grimy hand.

Once inside the house, Ciarán made a point of yawning and scratching himself, as though he had been out in the night to relieve himself. Connaire made no sound, evidently trying to act as though he had been there for some time. Ciarán plopped into bed. Tomorrow he would speak to the slave woman and see what she might know. With a contented sigh, he rolled over and fell asleep.

By the time Aislinn reached her house, she expected Bevin to be asleep. She found her sitting in front of the hearth fire, a fire that was only embers, staring at the red coals. The woman looked up at the young warrior a moment before resuming her contemplation. Aislinn thought that she saw tears. She approached and laid her hand on her servant's shoulder.

"You should not have stayed up for me. It is late and you

are tired."

Bevin made no reply, only slowly shaking her head as she stared down. Aislinn knelt beside her and wrapped her arm across the woman's shoulders.

"You are worried about what will happen to you when I leave. You will be free to go or to stay. If you stay, I will find someone who will treat you kindly. You need not worry."

Aislinn felt Bevin's shoulders shake. She was crying. Aislinn held her for a while longer, unsure what to say. Fighting a battle was so much easier. So simple. After giving Bevin's shoulders a squeeze, she went to bed. She knew that Cathal was riding north and hoped that he would be safe. If the Uí Néills were not receptive, if they considered Cathal a threat, all would be lost. Cathal might even be killed. She knew sleep would not come easily that night.

Unable to bear being in the house with the woman she was betraying, Bevin fled into the night. Tears flooded her eyes and she could not see where she was going. Stumbling on a fallen branch, she fell to the ground and lay there in the oak leaves as if in a stupor. She did not know how long she lay there before she realized someone was kneeling over her. It was Miach. That pagan priest. Where had he come from? He was saying something.

"Are you hurt? What has happened?"

She shook her head, trying to clear her thoughts. He kept talking to her, asking her questions.

"Is Aislinn alright? Speak. Tell me."

She knew she must say something.

"Forgive me, Father, for I have sinned."

Miach hid a bemused grin. "I may not be a father, child, but tell me about this sin."

Chapter 24

Just before midday, Brandugh approached the ravine for his meeting with Tian, Cairbre, and Gruagach. The morning had gone well. The cows and bull from Ciarán had arrived at his house. He was now a man of property. And before this affair ended, he would have more property, and influence with Ciarán. He had little doubt that after the younger brothers were disgraced, or worse, Ciarán would be the next chief. He tonelessly hummed a tune, a lay of heroic warriors, as he walked.

The other three had already arrived before him and he saw Tian give a friendly wave as he arrived. Brandugh smiled and waved back. The other two looked uncomfortable. Odd that Tian would be the nice one to him. Brandugh shrugged and walked up to Tian.

"So, has Cathal returned? Do we know when we are to leave?"

Tian laughed and slapped him on the shoulder. It stung.

"I like that. Right to the point. Yes, he has just returned. We will be leaving during the funeral games for Seanan. We will enter a couple of events, and then slip away. Are you ready?"

"More than ever." Brandugh had trouble suppressing a chortle. The fool was such a talker.

Tian leaned close and dropped his voice conspiratorially. "You need to be packed and ready tonight so you can leave at a moment's notice. Pack lightly. We will need to cover much ground."

Brandugh nodded. "I will go now to prepare."

As he turned to leave, he caught Gruagach's eye. The big man solemnly nodded, but said nothing. Brandugh gave a quick nod and hurried up the ravine. He needed to find Ciarán as quickly as possible.

Gruagach snorted and spat. He glared at Tian. "This is not right. You have deceived him."

Tian raised an eyebrow and shrugged. "No harm done. We will wake him tonight and he can come with us. If you are right, it will be a pleasant surprise." He slowly stroked his mustache and his eyes narrowed. "And if I am right, it will be an unpleasant one."

As soon as he had returned to the clann, Cathal had sought Aislinn. He found her in her house, talking to Miach while she knelt by a cooking pot suspended over a smoky fire. She rushed to him when he entered, embracing him tightly and giving him a long, deep kiss.

"It is set," he told her, as soon as he could gracefully pull his lips from hers. "I have spoken to Breandan and we will have safe passage through the lands of the Uí Néills. It seems that Bran and his followers left a bad impression and the Uí Néill regrets not letting us take them at our last meeting." He gave a short laugh. "Bran's sister even stole a jeweled dagger of great worth from the ri himself when they left."

"I have told Miach all that has happened," she said. "Of how Seanan was likely murdered, of how Ciarán has manipulated your father into planning to make me his mate, of our plans to flee."

Cathal released Aislinn and looked to Miach. He trusted Miach, but feared the druid's loyalty would be with his father and the clann. "And what do you think of all these . . . these problems."

The old man shook his head slowly. "I see no way to save this clann. If you stay, matters will only worsen. Ciarán has made that inevitable. Your father has lost his senses and Ciarán uses him to speak his own will. Nothing I can say will change this." He

149

paused, leaning on his staff and staring at the floor. "No, you have taken the best path. And I will help where I can. How are matters with bartering your herds for goods?"

Aislinn sighed. "We have fared reasonably well. We have to be cautious. We may lose some cattle that we must abandon when we go." She knelt by the hearth and stirred a watery stew bubbling in the cauldron over the fire. "I fear that our meal will be less than appetizing. Bevin has disappeared and I am no cook."

"She is at my house," Miach stated.

Cathal looked at Miach with wonder. Since the death of his mate some years ago, the druid had not shown any desire to take another woman to his side. Had the fire been rekindled? But Miach continued as if unaware of the curiosity he had engendered.

"I may be of some assistance in this bartering. Let me know who has need of my help."

Cathal had no doubt that Aislinn was wondering about Miach and Bevin as much as he was, but she acted as if nothing were amiss, continuing a conversation that must have been in progress before he had entered.

"Tell me more about what happened with Eoghan's druid, Miach."

Miach went to a chair and slowly settled into it. He placed his staff between his legs and leaned forward with it as a support. His tone was one of instruction.

"I spent much time talking with Ailin. He acts as a druid, but in the new religion, the path of the Christus. It is the path that Padraig brought here long ago."

Cathal shook his head. "Is our clann the only one that still follows the way of our ancestors? What of our gods? What of Ogma, Dagda, Lugh, Manannán mac Lir and the Morrigan?"

"Ailin follows only one god, but one that is three at the same time." He waved his hand dismissively. "I know you will say this is nonsense, but is not the Morrigan three while being one? Did she not appear to Cú Chulainn in many guises? Why cannot there be a god that is a father, his own son and a ghost?"

Stunned, Cathal shook his head. "So you have decided to go the path of this new god?"

Miach chuckled softly. "No. Though we may be the last clann to follow the way of our ancestors, I am too old to even consider abandoning the gods of our ancestors and Fergus, his father and his father's father all have stood firmly for our religion. I only say that I can accept Ailin's path. Eoghan and all of his people have been ceremonially washed to follow it. At least, they claim to follow it. There will always be those who do what is in fashion, belief or no."

"What will this mean to Eireann when the way of our ancestors is lost?" Aislinn asked. "What of Danu? What of the Tuatha dé Danann, the clann of our gods that guides our people? If we no longer accept our beginnings from the gods of this land, what will it mean for the three legs of the cauldron: truth, honor and duty?"

Miach shrugged. "Those who follow the new path seem to value those precepts as much as we do. Their god makes laws that they must follow, laws like the ones the brehons learn to guide our people, and to violate one is to commit what they call a 'sin.' When Bran killed as he did, he committed a 'sin' and to have defended him would have defended his 'sin.' Ailin spoke hours on all this when I was with him. That is why I stayed so long. I see no danger for our people in this path, but it is not mine." He smiled at them both. "It is Bevin's, though. She came to me and I will take her to Eoghan's clann tonight when you leave."

"Ah, then you have not taken Bevin into your house for a

mate after all," Aislinn said, with a nod of her head. "So you would take my slave from me with no payment?"

Miach gently laid a hand on her shoulder. "I will pay what you feel is fair. She belongs with those who follow the same god as she does."

Aislinn waved her hand in dismissal. "Take her. I have grown weary of her morose look."

Gods and such matters were not of great interest to Cathal. But his stomach was. "Let us not talk of gods for now, new or old. Aislinn, is the meal ready? I have ridden long and eaten little."

She gave him a wry smile. "It is ready, such as it is."

When Aislinn had served him, Cathal sipped some of the broth from his bowl. He had never considered cooking to be an art, like fashioning jewelry or forging swords. Until now. He was afraid to say anything that might offend Aislinn. When he glanced at Aislinn and Miach, he saw that they had also tasted their food and were staring at their bowls.

Aislinn sighed and set her bowl on the ground. "I already miss Bevin."

Chapter 25

Brandugh woke with a start from his dream of forcing apart Aislinn's thighs. Someone was shaking his shoulder and it was not Aislinn. Light temporarily blinded him, adding to his disorientation. He struggled to rise, but felt a heavy hand keep him flat on his bed of a pile of sheepskins.

He heard a voice say, "When we leave, we should burn this place to get rid of the stench."

As his eyes adjusted to the light, he saw that it was a torch, held by Cairbre. Gruagach was holding him down. The voice had been Tian's.

Brandugh started to reach for his dagger that he kept by his bed, but decided the odds were against him. In the flickering light he could see all three had swords and daggers in their belts. It would be wiser to play for time until he knew why they were in his house.

"What are you doing?" His voice sounded choked with fear in his own ears. Hopefully, they would think it was from sleep. "Is something wrong? I did not expect to see you until the games, when we were to leave."

Tian smiled at him, but Brandugh saw no warmth in it. Then he spoke softly, calmly, as if nothing were amiss. "A change of plans. We ride now. Are you ready?"

Now? He had told Ciarán it would be during the games. What could he do? He must figure a way to remain, to warn Ciarán.

"I am not ready. You go and I will catch up with you later."

He saw Tian's hand move toward the dagger in his belt. When he looked to Gruagach for support, Brandugh saw suspicion in his eyes. The massive hand held him down with greater firmness. He must rethink this.

"And you said 'ride.' As you know, I no longer have a horse. If I did, I would go now, ready or no."

"Not a problem," Tian said coldly. "We have extras. So, are you ready to leave?"

Brandugh quickly assessed the situation. If he said no, he knew he would die. They were already suspicious and that would prove their fears. If he went, he might easily find a way to slip off in the night. If he got away, they would never follow him back to the settlement for fear of having the rest of the clann aroused. Best cooperate, at least for the moment. Besides, he would get a horse to keep after he escaped.

"If you will provide a horse, of course, I am ready. Why do we wait?" He said it with far more enthusiasm than he felt. He would have to watch carefully for his opportunity and he wanted the others to have their guard down.

Gruagach released him and he rose, took his bratt from the bed and clasped it on with a crude bronze broach. He belted on his dagger and sword. They were rusty, but serviceable. He had found the sword on the body of a warrior from another clann years ago, after he had helped foil a cattle raid, and Fergus had allowed him to keep it even though he was not a warrior. Much practice and his strength had made him formidable with the weapon. He hoped he would not have to test his ability with any of the three with him.

The warriors still watched him, but the tension in the room had eased. By no longer hesitating, he knew that he had cooled their suspicions. He clapped Tian on the shoulder, hard enough to almost knock him over, and smiled.

"If you have supplies packed enough for me, I am ready."

Tian rubbed his shoulder. "You seem to have changed your

mind rather quickly."

"That is how I am. It might take me a little time to make up my mind, but when I do I am ready to act." He looked at each of the others. "Well? Are we going to talk all night or ride?"

Brandugh saw Gruagach nod at Tian and Tian shrug in reply. Hiding a smile of satisfaction, he headed for the door and the others followed.

As Maille waited outside of Brandugh's door, she could see the flickering movement of the torch and hear the murmur of voices. She began to wonder if they would ever come out, but finally she saw Brandugh emerge, followed by Tian, Gruagach and Cairbre. As they did, she drew her sword from its scabbard. She assumed the ready position, blade pointing upward and tilted slightly forward, and the stance of one foot forward. The blade glinted in the moonlight and she knew they saw it when they halted just outside the door.

"You are fools," she called to them.

She saw them draw their swords.

Tian stepped to the fore. "You are the fool if you think you can stop us. There are four of us and I know three of us are a match for you in single combat."

Maille stood firm. "I have no quarrel with you, Tian. But you are fools to trust the other one, the metalsmith. He is a traitor. He is the one I drew on."

Instantly the three friends backed away from Brandugh. Their swords were now ready for attack from either him or Maille. Brandugh looked nervously at her and then his companions.

"She lies. I am no traitor."

"I lie?" She gave a short laugh. "This afternoon he came to me, wanting to share my bed. He told me that he had come into

wealth and that it was only the beginning.   Soon he would have
power and more wealth.   That he had information that would make
it possible."   Maille snorted her derision.   "He thought my body
could be bought.   He believed too many of the stories men tell
around the fire."

The swords now swung to face only Brandugh.   His eyes
darted like a cornered badger, from face to face.   Panic was in his
voice.

"She lies, I tell you.   She offered herself to me and I spurned
her.   She said she knew of your plans and would give me anything
if I told her.   Why would I go with you if this were not true?"

"Then explain to these three fools why you suddenly have
cattle with the mark of Ciarán still on them."

Brandugh said nothing.   His eyes widened with fear.

Maille pressed her attack.   "While you three were listening
to his lies, I checked behind his house.   The cattle are there.   He
has sold you to Ciarán for eight cows and a bull."

"She must have put them there to make me seem guilty."
His protest sounded weak, half-hearted.   He knew he was caught.
He looked to the men.   "Will you kill me on the word of a woman
who opens her legs for any man?"

"She has never opened her legs for me, much as I would
have enjoyed the experience," Tian said.   "For you, Cairbre?
Gruagach?"

Cairbre laughed.   "Only when I dream of her at night."

Gruagach shook his head, staring at Brandugh.   When he
spoke, anger rippled through his words like a flooded river.

"I trusted you.   You betrayed us.   Now I will kill you."

As he stepped toward Brandugh, Maille moved swiftly to
block him.

"He is mine.   I claim this as my honor price.   I will fight him in single combat."

"He is a powerful man and a fair swordsman," Tian told her. "But even if he wins, we will have to kill him to prevent him going to Ciarán. Why take the chance?"

"He will not win. But if he does, bind him securely and hide him. Then you will be far away when he is found."

Tian stroked his mustache. "It is more than he deserves, but I suppose that would be honorable. So be it. But why do you wish to risk your life?"

"Because I have another request when I win. I want to go with you."

Tian hesitated. "I will have to check with the others."

"Tian, you know I am a good warrior, that I am an honorable person. I have known something was happening by the bits of conversation I heard from those preparing to leave. I do not know where you are going, but I cannot stay with Ciarán running the clann." She saw indecision in Tian's eyes. "I also know that Aislinn is against me going. I am sure that she has spoken of it. She believes the stories as much as you did. But what does it matter with whom I have my pleasure or how many men it has been with? Am I still not a warrior of honor?"

Tian nodded. "That is true. But I will need to convince the others."

"You mean Aislinn." She cocked her head. "Maybe this will help. I can also be the healer. My mother was a healer and taught me that art. Unless you have another healer going with you . . .."

"We have no other healer." Tian stepped close to her, resting his hand on her shoulder. "You are welcome to come with us. You will be a great help and we will be glad to have you."

"And if Aislinn objects?"

"You will be with me." He grinned. "And perhaps you might like being with me."

Maille laughed. "Perhaps I shall. But then again, perhaps I shall not. We shall see." Then she became serious. "But first to the matter at hand."

"This is not necessary." He glanced over at the nervous Brandugh. "Let Gruagach handle him."

She shook her head. "But it is necessary. My honor is as important to me as yours is to you. I am a warrior."

Tian sighed. "Remember that he is strong. And he is no stranger to the sword, rusty though his may be."

She lifted an eyebrow. "I am no novice myself."

She turned toward Brandugh. He would know that his life would be spared, so he would be desperate. So much the better. Desperation can cause mistakes. The others moved away to form a triangle with the combatants in the center.

Suddenly, Brandugh sprang forward before she had assumed the ready position, swinging his sword down with both hands. Not expecting such quickness from the big man, Maille was taken off guard and parried awkwardly. She deflected the blade to her right, but was staggered by the force of the blow. Her left hand stung from the impact and had difficulty gripping. Before she had recovered, Brandugh swung again, a horizontal blow aimed at her right side. Maille swung her sword sideways forcefully to block, holding it only in her right hand. She stopped the blade with a loud ringing of iron as the swords met, but felt a pain shoot up her arm like fire. Fortunately, she had struck Brandugh's sword with so much power that it had knocked him off balance and he stumbled to the side. She had only time to switch the sword to her left hand before he recovered and faced her again.

Maille's right arm was useless. Her left hand still had

trouble gripping. One more attack like the first two and she knew she would be dead. She had not heeded Tian's warning. She had been overconfident, relying on her skill, and had underestimated her opponent. It was a flaw that often cost a warrior his or her life. And it looked like it would happen here.

Then she saw Brandugh's eyes. He knew her right arm was useless. He assumed that, like most people, her right arm was her favored one. He did not know that she could use either with equal skill. It was time to use her intelligence as well as her skill. Although her left hand still tingled, her grip was returning. Like a quail that feigns an injury to fool a predator, Maille pretended to be awkward with the sword in her left hand. She moved quickly, mainly staying out of sword's reach and weakly parrying when necessary. Pretending to be near collapse. Waiting, waiting for the moment.

Swinging a sword is hard work and, although Brandugh was strong, he did not have endurance. He was tiring. She could see it in the way his blows were less frequent and had less power. She felt his desperation. Trying to close in on the elusive Maille, he finally barreled headlong at her, sword extended. Maille danced to the side and swung her sword with all her might at Brandugh's neck. It hit bone with a jarring shudder, then went through. Blood spurted, a flood at her feet.

With his momentum and the force of her blow, Brandugh was decapitated. His headless body had pitched forward at her feet and his head rolled to the side. His unseeing eyes stared at Maille. She rolled the head over with her foot. Then she sank to her knees as pain shot through her right arm.

Tian rushed to her and lifted her up. She yelped, clutching her right arm with her left. Tian looked at her with concern.

"I thought your injured arm was a fake to draw Brandugh

out."

"Only in part." Her voice was taut, strained. "My right arm hurts like a speared boar and I can barely lift it. I feared that he would use that, so I had to lure him to close to me."

Tian rolled Brandugh's head with the tip of his toe. "Well, Brandugh does seem to have lost his head over you. Maille, you are as brilliant and brave as you are beautiful. If anyone ever speaks ill of you in my presence, he will answer to my sword. Or she, for that matter."

"And my sword," added Cairbre, smiling at her.

"And mine," Gruagach gruffly said.

Maille lifted her head and kissed Tian on the lips. He embraced her as she did, pulling her to him. Pain shot up her arm with a vengeance and she screamed.

Chapter 26

Sitting under a tree by the house, Ciarán used the polished brass disc that his stepmother had owned to study his image. He wished that his mustache were thicker. Although it was long, curving around his mouth and past his jaw, it was scraggly. All in all, though, Ciarán was pleased with his appearance. He had bathed that morning and had put on all his armbands and torques. For a moment, he wondered if he had gone too far, but decided the occasion warranted extravagance. This would be the end of Cathal as a threat to his position in the clann. Satisfied, he rose and dropped the disc into his pouch tied to his belt. He was ready for the culmination of his planning.

When he arrived at the field where the games were to be held, things did not look right. Although the straw had been laid out the day before for the wrestling, the course delineated for the races and the targets for spear toss and archery, no one was organizing the events. People were wandering about, a few were practicing. But no one was running anything. As he looked around, many of the athletes were absent, most conspicuously Cathal, Aislinn and all their friends. As was Brandugh. It was all wrong.

Ciarán grabbed the arm of a man walking by and asked, "Have you seen Cathal? Connaire? Aislinn?"

The man merely shook his head at each name.

"Have you seen Brandugh, then?"

Again, a shake of the head.

Something was terribly amiss. He hurried to his father's house, grabbed his horse and galloped to Brandugh's hut. As he dismounted, he saw a large stain in the dirt in front of the door. It looked like blood. Inside he found Brandugh.

His body lay to one side of the door, his head to the other. With a curse, he kicked the head. Howling in pain, he clutched his foot. He had not expected the big oaf's head to be so hard. He hobbled to his horse and rode back to find his father.

Fergus was staggering aimlessly about the games field. His clothes were disheveled and he was carrying a cup that kept spilling. Ciarán knew he was drunk. He dismounted and walked as quickly as his sore toe would allow to confront his father.

"Father, Cathal has fled."

"Fled? From . . . from whom?" Fergus shook his head wildly. "No. No. Cathal never flees." He squinted at Ciarán, his eyes seeming to be having trouble focusing.

Ciarán needed to jolt him, to make him angry at Cathal. "Cathal has taken your promised mate. He is going to . . . going to ravish her."

"Cathal is going to ravish Betha?" Fergus shook his head confusedly.

"No, you old fool," Ciarán yelled with an angry wave of his hand. "Cathal is going to ravish Aislinn unless you send every warrior to hunt him down."

Anger flared in Fergus's eyes. "You call me an old fool when you claim Cathal is going to ravish his own mother? He would never do anything like that to Betha. Why would you say that?"

"Not Betha. Aislinn." Ciarán almost stomped his foot in frustration. "Can you not understand that, you old fool?"

"I understand that you think me a fool. Do you also think me weak? Do you think you could best me in combat, too?" Fergus advanced on Ciarán. Ciarán stumbled back, falling to the ground. He had already lost one tooth to his father's anger and did not wish to lose more. He noticed his father's cup was tilted, empty.

"Father, you have no ale. Would you like me to fetch some for you?"

Fergus looked down at his cup. Then he looked at Ciarán, questioningly. A smile crept across his lips.

"Why, yes, I would."

He reached down and pulled Ciarán to his feet, handing him the empty cup. He wrapped his arm across Ciarán's shoulder and spoke warmly.

"Get me some ale. And when you see Betha, send her to me."

Ciarán eyed him warily. "Of course, Father. I will be back soon."

Fergus smiled and nodded.

Ciarán limped away, looking for his friends. He soon found one, only a rude herdsman, but better than nothing. He called to him.

"Iuchar, have you seen Bevin?"

"Who?"

"Bevin. The slave of Aislinn."

"Ah." The little, dark man smoothed his thinning hair. "She has nicely rounded hips, does she not? Is that why you seek her?"

"No, no." Ciarán waved off the very idea impatiently. "I just need to speak with her."

"Well, the last I heard, she was staying with Miach." He smirked. "I guess that the old twig still has some sap yet."

"With Miach? Has he returned?"

"Are you deaf? That is what I said."

This did not bode well. Miach was no friend.

"Find all those who are my friends and gather them by

yonder tree." Ciarán pointed to an oak not far away.

"Friends?" The herdsman gave a gap-toothed grin.

Ciarán wanted to throttle the man. "Just summon everyone who would be with me."

"And it will be worth doing?"

Ciarán inwardly cursed the rabble he needed. "Yes, yes. You will be rewarded. Now go."

As the man hurried away, Ciarán considered his plan. Cathal and his companions had left earlier than Brandugh had said. Was it because they had discovered Brandugh's duplicity or had that been the original plan? Brandugh had said they were heading to Mumhan. Bevin had confirmed this when he had last spoken to her. But was she already with Miach then? The only sure thing was that they had not gone north. After their last encounter with the Uí Néills, Cathal and the others would not even try to go through those lands. But where had they gone? Perhaps he could persuade Bevin to be more forthcoming. He saw Iucharba, Iuchar's twin brother, wandering close by and called to him.

"Iucharba, could I speak to you?"

The man smiled, stroked his long, thinning hair and went to Ciarán. "How can I be of service?"

"Go to Miach's house and ask Bevin, Aislinn's slave woman, to come to me."

"I cannot."

"Why not?" Would no one help him with payment? "I will make it worth your time."

Iucharba shrugged and concentrated on digging something from between his remaining teeth with a fingernail. "Because she is not there."

"What?" Dread crept up Ciarán's spine. Something was amiss.

"My sister went by this morning to see if Miach wished any help in the household and no one was there. They must have left in the night."

Ciarán stamped his foot in anger. His sore foot. Clutching it in pain, he fell on his side, moaning. Iucharba laughed. Ciarán glared at him. He would pay. But Ciarán knew he could never catch Cathal and Aislinn. He did not know where they had gone. Even if he did, without Fergus he could not gather enough warriors to defeat them.

"It is not finished, Brother," he muttered. "I will win in the end."

Cathal watched as the boats were loaded. Passage through the lands of the Uí Néills to the sea and the acquiring the currachs' had gone without a problem, thanks to Brandon. Perhaps the Uí Néills were trying to atone for protecting Bran. Ronan had handled the bartering of horses for boats and goods. It was not something Cathal knew how to do, nor wished to, and he was glad the young man had handled it.

"We may not have made the best trades ever made," Ronan had told him with a smile. "But neither have we made the worst. We will have enough to establish ourselves across the sea."

Then Cathal divided the people into crews for the three currachs that would carry them. In all, there were nine hand counts of adults and six of children and babes. Cathal assigned Ronan and two others who had some knowledge of the sea to master each boat. Connaire would command one and Cathal another. But Cathal needed one more person to be in charge of the last one.

He wrapped his arm across Tian's shoulder and smiled at him. "You can charm even the gods. Will you not charm your own crew for our journey?"

"I will be under your command." Tian gave him a wry smile. "We have followed you thus far, so if we are to die on the sea, you will lead us there too. But I know nothing of the sea and am loath to command. I am afraid that I speak for Cairbre and Gruagach as well as myself."

"I will command the last boat."

They all turned to see who had spoken. Maille stood in the water by the currach, one arm bound with cloth strips to a splint and the other grasping the side of the boat. "I said that I will command."

Tian walked to her and rested his hand on her hip. "I thought you would be with me on the voyage."

"With my arm as it is, I cannot row. But my other arm will suffice to command." She looked first at her uninjured arm and then at Tian's hand. "Or to handle any who might think me easy prey."

Tian quickly removed his hand. "I meant no offense. I only wanted you to know I wished you to be with me."

Maille reached over and touched his hand. "I took no offense, but it is good to know that you meant none. However, it is enough that I come when Aislinn would have me stay. Let us not rub salt in the wound by having me on the same boat with her. I can prove my worth by this."

Tian shrugged his shoulders and smiled. "You have already proved your worth. Then would you allow me to serve under your command?"

Maille returned his smile. "Not this time. We both need to have no distractions from our tasks." Then she turned back to Cathal. "Do you need me to lead this boat or not?"

"I do."

She spat in her left hand and extended it. "Then it is done."

166

"It is." Cathal spat in his hand and took hers. "Get your boat loaded so that we can set sail."

Cathal labored tirelessly, going from boat to boat to help with the loading. He saw that Maille was not standing and giving orders to others, but doing as much of the work of loading as she could with only one arm. He smiled. It had been wise to give her command.

When they were finally ready to sail, it was late with the sun already low on the horizon with dark clouds pressing down ominously. But, with not knowing what had happened when Ciarán found they had fled, Cathal felt any delay to be unwise. So they pushed off, put up the square sails and began to row towards the far, unknown shore. A chilling wind whipped around the currachs. Ronan frowned as he looked up at the sky. He muttered softly, but Cathal heard. "I do not like those clouds. By Manannán, they do not bode well."

III. ALBA

Chapter 27

Dawn crept slowly across the horizon. The sun painted the clouds that hung low in the sky with orange and red. Cathal watched as the breeze pushed the clouds across the sky. He sat in the sand, his forearms resting on his knees, and stared dully at the sea, the sea that he found himself hating. It had taken Maeve, a young woman from his currach, and likely his brother with all who were with him as well. Not far off the shore, the waves gently crashed against the Rock of Lugh and the Three Fairies. They were to have been the guides, the harbingers of a safe harbor. He cursed them for their capriciousness.

Cathal felt a hand on his shoulder. He turned and saw Aislinn, the breeze blowing a few, stray strands of hair across her face. She smiled. It was a sad smile.

"You stayed at your vigil all night?"

He nodded.

She pointed to the holed, leather-hulled boat that now rested on the beach about a hundred paces from them. "The currach has washed ashore. Perhaps that is a good sign."

Cathal shrugged. When he had seen it at first light, he had felt some hope. But it seemed that the damaged boat was all Manannán was willing to return.

She rubbed his shoulder. "I will stir the fire so that we can start breakfast."

Saying nothing, he turned back to the sea.

"The others are rising," she softly said. "They will be here soon. Will you help me?"

He slowly rose, stiff from sitting in the cold sand all night.

His thin, leather shoes creaked, hard and unforgiving after drying on his feet without being washed of the saltwater. He grabbed a log and tossed it on the embers. Since the first glimpse of the sun, he had let the fire die down, throwing green branches and damp wood on it to create a pillar of smoke. Now it was time to let his brother go and tend to those that lived. With a sigh, he turned to Aislinn.

She was looking past him, towards the sea, smiling. "Look."

Cathal turned and saw that something had come past the rocky point that sheltered the beach, the point that had taken Maeve's life. It was a boat. He started to run towards the water, but Aislinn grabbed his arm and turned him.

"Do not swim to it." Her eyes were pleading with him, knowing his mind. "Do not give Manannán another chance to claim you. They will land soon. Wait on the beach."

He started to say something, that he did not fear the sea, but her look caused him to stop. He nodded. The god of the sea proved last night that he was to be feared more than any man, any army. He slowly walked and waited on the beach where the waves lapped at his feet.

As they rounded the point and Connaire saw the other currachs, he felt a great relief. Lost in the dark and blown off course into a small cove, they had taken shelter there for the night. It had been a very small island with no trees big enough to give cover. Overturning the currach, they had huddled together under it and awaited the passing of the storm.

At first light, they had set sail, hoping to find the rest of the clann. Murchadh, the one of the crew who had some experience on the sea, had advised Connaire of the best course. It was away from the rising sun and back toward Eireann, but staying close to the islands.   Before long, they had spotted a thin column of smoke rising to the right and headed toward it.   Soon after, Murchadh saw the Rock of Lugh and the Three Fairies off the coast of an island. They knew they were in the right area.   Then Connaire saw the currachs on the shore and steered toward them.

As the boat neared the beach, he saw Cathal standing at water's edge with Aislinn holding his arm.   Others of the clann were heading across the sand toward the water.   When they reached land, Murchadh and several of the men dropped into the water and pulled the boat ashore.

As Connaire turned and slipped over the side, he felt strong hands grab his waist and lower him into the shallow water.   He turned and grinned at his brother.   "I thank you for your consideration, but I have been standing on my own for many years now."

Cathal turned red and stammered.   "I . . . I was worried that with your leg and . . . the sand can be treacherous, uh . . . slippery, I mean."

Connaire laughed.   "I am glad for any help you give me, Brother."

Aislinn rested her hand on Connaire's arm.   "He was worried.   That is all."

Cathal released Connaire.   He turned away.   "I have matters to attend to.   We must secure the damaged currach and see if it can be repaired."   He shook his head.   "We have much to do and little time.   I will see you both when we have breakfast."   He walked away, towards those that had started to pull the damaged currach up on the beach.

Connaire watched him go, bewildered.   "We are all safe. Why does he act as if he is in mourning?"

Aislinn sighed.   "We lost Maeve."

"What? How?"

"She was on the currach that hit the rocks. We would have lost Ronan as well, if not for your brother's quick action. He took it very hard." She looked around at the small groups that had gathered on the beach, looking unsure of what to do. "He is worried that he has led us into our destruction."

"He need have no worries." Connaire gave her a winning smile. "I will be beside him all the way, giving him my support."

As he turned to hobble away, Aislinn sighed. "I hope that will make the difference."

Connaire saw Ronan standing by the damaged currach, staring at the gaping hole in its side. He went to him, resting a hand on his friend's shoulder. They stood for a while, both staring at the currach and saying nothing.

Then Ronan shook his head and softly spoke. "I should have made sure we were safely on the beach before we started to unload."

"The sea was rough." Connaire tightened his grip on the smaller man's shoulder. "Manannán's realm was harsh last night. But you brought the rest through safely. And we still need you."

Ronan slowly shook his head. Then he suddenly struck the taut hides of the currach's side with his fist. "Manannán took her from me. But he will not stop us." He turned to face Connaire. Tears were in his eyes, but he did not weep. "We will repair this craft. We have hides, lard and pitch. We will need those, plus a needle to stitch the patch in place."

Although he wondered at the wisdom of voicing defiance of a god, Connaire saw hope in Ronan's words. Doing a task would keep his mind busy. "I will get the supplies and get help for the repair."

"No." Ronan's voice was firm, determined. "I will do it

alone."

"But what of pulling the hide taut while it is stitched? You cannot do that alone, can you?"

Ronan paused. "Perhaps not." He shook his head. "No, you are right. You can help me. But only you."

After they had gathered the supplies for the patch, they began their work. Ronan selected a hide that covered the hole nicely. He applied the pitch to one section and began to sew it with sinew. Some of the others had gathered to watch this, not having seen anyone work on a boat before, but Connaire shooed them away. He knew that Ronan would not like them watching while he worked. So the rest of the clann dragged the other two boats farther ashore before heading back to the encampment, leaving the two young men alone at their work.

Connaire was so intent at the repairing that he did not notice horsemen approaching until they were almost upon them. He stepped back from the boat. Four men, apparently warriors from the swords slung on their backs, rode to within several paces of them. They sat on their horses, staring grimly, and said nothing.

These men looked different from the people of Eireann. They wore shorter léines, with their legs sheathed in colored woolen cloth, but did not wear bratts. Two of the men had short, leather sleeveless shirts over their léines. All of them had long braids in front of their ears.

Connaire smiled, setting aside the pot of pitch he was holding, and stepped forward. One of the men marched his horse threateningly toward him. Connaire stood his ground.

The stranger finally spoke, his words understandable but odd sounding. "What are you doing on a beach of the Cenél nOegnusa?"

"We are from Eireann, across the sea--"

"I know where Eireann is. You have no right to be here."

The man turned his horse sideways, almost bumping Connaire who was forced to retreat a few steps. Connaire was unarmed, save for a short knife used for cutting the hide and making holes for stitching. Even if his leg were healed, he could not outrun horses to summon help. He would have to try to reason with them.

"We mean no insult. We were thrown here last night in the storm. Our currach was damaged. We need to repair it so that we can leave."

The man studied the boat.

"We could use that currach."

"I am sorry, but it is not for trade. We need it."

The man turned to Connaire with a cold smile. "I said nothing of trade. Dead men do not need a currach." He reached for his sword.

Ronan had been quiet, but suddenly yelled, "Connaire!"

As he turned to the voice, Connaire saw an oar flying through the air. It was as long as a man and he caught it by the handle, fighting to get control of it. Spinning back with a roar, he caught the rider just below his throat with the end of the oar. The man fell backwards off his horse and onto the sand. He landed awkwardly and Connaire was able to reach him and seize the rider's sword before the man could recover.

The other men had been taken by surprise and were just beginning to move toward Connaire when Ronan, screaming oaths, charged past Connaire with another oar. He swung the oar wildly, catching a horse squarely on a hind leg as the rider was trying to pull it out of the path of Ronan's weapon. The horse reared, then stumbled back in the soft sand. The rider was thrown off and, quick as a ferret, Ronan was on him. First he slammed the fallen rider across the back with the oar, dazing him. Then he pummeled the man about his head with clenched fists, before pulling the man's sword from its scabbard.

The other riders had drawn their swords and one had raised his to strike Ronan from behind. Connaire knew he could not reach him in time and yelled, "No!"

Suddenly an arrow appeared in the back of the man's shoulder. The rider uttered a sharp cry, dropped his sword and reached back at the arrow. Across the beach, several warriors were coming at a run, warriors of his clann. His brother was in the lead.

The two men still on their horses saw them, too. They turned their horses and, wildly kicking their flanks, rode away, one with his arm hanging limply at his side, the arrow still in his shoulder.

Ronan rose and lifted his sword over the stunned man at his feet. Connaire knew he was about to kill his fallen foe. He could not reach him in time to prevent it.

"Stop," he yelled. "We do not murder our fallen foes." Ronan looked to Connaire. His hands were shaking. He was a man wild with anger, driven beyond reason in his grief.

Connaire stretched out his hand. "He did not take Maeve from you. He is not Manannán."

For a moment the young sailor stood, sword raised over his foe. Then he slowly lowered it. Letting out a low, keening wail, he fell to his knees.

Cathal and the other warriors soon arrived, swords in hand. While a few of them roughly pulled the still-stunned enemy warriors to their feet, Cathal put his arm across his brother's shoulders.

"What happened? Who are they?"

"It seems we are in the lands of Cenél nOegnusa and they do not give hospitality to strangers. I am glad that you happened by."

"Aislinn was hunting and saw them approach. She

summoned the rest of us.   Luckily, she had her bow.   But I will say that you two are very formidable with oars."

Aislinn was kneeling by Ronan.   He was quiet now, but still shaking.   She smiled grimly at Connaire.   "I would not use my bow in an honorable battle, but there is no honor in four armed horsemen attacking two unarmed men on foot."

Cathal turned to the rider who Connaire had felled.   "Who are you and why did you attack my brother?"

The man jutted his chin forward defiantly.   "I am Aed, son of Oengus.   My father is the taoiseach of this island.   My father and brother will be back with many warriors.   You have invaded our lands and they will slaughter you."

Cathal smiled.   "From what I have seen, we only need oars to defeat them."   He turned to his warriors who held Aed.   "Bind these rude fellows and toss them in the cave.   Then take everything of value into it as well and post guards.   It seems we can expect to see more of this unfriendly crowd."

Connaire looked to the top of a rise in the direction the two riders had recently fled.   "I think they are here already."

At least five handcounts of riders had appeared at the crest, over twice their own number.

Connaire did a test swing with his newly-acquired sword and gave a short laugh.   "We may need more oars."

Chapter 28

Cathal was watching for them when riders started down the sandy slope towards them. Although he did not want to fight with the odds so against them, he saw no other option. To attempt to flee across the soft sand would place them scattered and fighting a running battle with poor footing against superior numbers of mounted warriors. They must stand and fight, hoping the other warriors in the clann would see riders and come to help, especially Tian, Cairbre and Gruagach. But he knew that was unlikely. Perhaps the boat could be of help.

"Form a line along the currach, with your back to it. It will limit the advantage of the horses and keep them from surrounding us."

Connaire prodded Aed, who now lay bound and glowering in the sand, with his foot. "What of this one? He and his friend might be stumbling blocks if we leave them here. Shall we toss them in the sea?"

Cathal smiled as he saw the fear enter the captives' eyes. They did not know his brother's odd sense of humor. "No, shove them under the currach. We can deal with them later." He shrugged. "Or those riders can, if we are dead."

Quickly the warriors lifted the overturned boat and shoved the prisoners under it. Then they formed a line in front of the boat, swords drawn and facing the approaching riders. Except for Aislinn. She notched an arrow on her bow and held it undrawn, but at ready.

As the riders neared, they slowed their horses to a walk. Some of the men had spears in hand, the rest drew their swords. Aislinn watched them, ready to take down any who would raise a spear to throw. They were dressed much as their companions who lay under the boat, but some had small shields that were decorated with paintings of animal heads, boars, wolves and one that was not recognizable. They fanned out, so that they enveloped the clann with a wall of horses and iron weapons. They silently sat on their horses, staring. Aislinn realized her hand was twitching, but not from fear. She wanted the waiting to end.

One of the riders rode forward, stopping in front of Aislinn, so close that she could see his green eyes. Cathal started to move towards him, but Aislinn shook her head. She could raise her bow and shoot him before he could get to her.

The rider was no taller than she, but wide with a body that looked to be of muscle rather than fat. His hair was black as the night sky, with a curling beard. When he spoke, he had the same odd sound to his words, but his voice was deep and mellow.

"So you are the one who put an arrow into the back of poor Brec."

"I did."

"That was not very honorable, was it? Now we shall have to kill you."

"When he and his three companions were going to slay two of my unarmed friends, it was most honorable. So kill us if you can. But you shall be the first to die." She brought her bow up slightly and drew back on the string, ready for his next move.

The man frowned, his face dark and angry. He turned and shouted. "Lonan. Come to us."

One of the warriors rode forward. He was a small man, short and thin. Aislinn thought he was one of the two who had fled, the one without her arrow.

The big man glared at the little man. "Is this true? And know that if you lie, I will twist off your gonads and stuff them down your throat."

He looked nervously about, as if seeking support from the others. They seemed to find other places to look.

Suddenly a voice came from under the boat. "She lies. They attacked us with spears."

Aislinn smiled. "If you look among us, you will see no spears. You will see only the oars that my two friends used to defend themselves from your warriors. They are now armed with the swords of your captured friends."

The stocky warrior looked around, studying the clann and their weapons. Suddenly he swung around and stuck his sword under Lonan's chin. His eyes narrowed. "I told you what I would do if you lied."

"But I did not lie." Lonan's voice was choked with fear and he had trouble speaking. "Aed lied. It was all his doing."

The warrior slowly lowered his sword, shaking his head. Then he sheathed it and turned back to Aislinn. "Once again, my brother has dishonored us. I am Oengus, son of Oengus. Sadly, Aed is my brother. You have my apology and assurance no harm will come to you for any of this."

Aislinn relaxed the tension on her bow. "We are sorry of this as well. We came only to find safety, not to do battle." She sighed. "And what of the one I shot? Brec, was it?"

Oengus shrugged. "He rode away to find the healer. It is in the hands of God. But if he dies, it will be no great loss. He is a coward and a discredit to this Cenél." He signaled to his warriors and they sheathed their swords and lowered their spears. "If you arrived during last night's storm, your sailing to our island has been rough. You must need food and drink."

Cathal came to Aislinn's side. "We do need fresh provisions. We will gladly give fair trade of goods."

Oengus lifted his hand. "No, you will be given proper hospitality. We are not all like my brother. We will return with meat and drink." He slowly shook his head, staring at the sand. "I am afraid I can only offer this for a short time. My brother has the ear of my father and I can only stave off confrontation for a few days."

Cathal nodded. "I understand such a brother very well. I left one behind. But we seem to have landed in the wrong place anyway. We are looking for the lands of Cenél Loairn. We thought this island to be part of those lands."

"You have landed on Île, not far from their lands. If you continue in your currach toward the rising sun and towards the colder lands, you will find them." Oengus spat on his hand and reached out with it to Cathal. "So I will protect you while you prepare to continue your voyage."

Cathal spat on his hand and grasped the outstretched hand of Oengus.

Aislinn unnotched her arrow. She felt this man was honorable. He was like the boar on his shield, short and powerful, but unlike the boar, in that he was not wild and brutal. She saw honesty in his eyes and she trusted him. He looked at her and seemed to sense it, giving her a smile.

"But what of your brother?" she asked.

"Kill him."

A shout of protest came from under the boat and Oengus laughed. "No, father likes him. Best keep him safe until you are ready to leave. Then release him. I will tell father that he is away hunting." He gave Lonan a menacing glare. "I am sure no one here will dispute that."

Aislinn stepped closer to the rider. "When we saw you and your men, we thought we were in a land with no men of honor. I am glad we were wrong."

Oengus, pulled his sheathed sword off and handed it to her. "We have no women warriors here. The church discourages it. But take this sword as my gift to you. I wish you God's protection, but you can use this if He does choose not to protect you."

Aislinn cocked her head. "The church?"

"The abbots, I should say. Christus's servants in Alba."

"Ah." This god had odd rules, ones that she could not follow. She reached up and took the sword. She could tell that it was a fine one. "Sad for you that you do not have the balance of women as your warriors. But I will take the sword with my thanks."

Without another word, Oengus and his warriors turned and rode away. Aed's voice could be heard screaming oaths against his brother until the clann's warriors pulled him from under the boat and gagged him with a piece of his own léine. His companion wisely kept silent.

As Aislinn stood watching Oengus and his warriors riding away across the beach, Cathal touched her shoulder.

"You seem to find this Oengus of great interest."

Aislinn could hear the jealousy in his voice. "He is a powerful warrior, a man of honor and courage." Then she smiled at Cathal. "Almost as honorable and courageous as you. Just not as fine to the eye."

With a laugh, she headed across the sand for their encampment.

Cathal hesitated for a moment, as if unsure of how to take what she had said. Then he hurried after her and put a possessive arm across her shoulder as they walked. She wrapped an arm around his waist and gave him a squeeze.

Chapter 29

A bright light was the first thing Cathal saw when he woke from a deep sleep. Blinking from the sunlight he tried to orient himself, he realized it was the sun creeping into the cave that had become their temporary home. No one else was in the cave. How long had he slept? He rolled to his hands and knees, then stiffly rose to his feet. He ached from sleeping so long on the hard, earthen floor. After shaking the sand from his bratt, given to him by Ronan, he wrapped it around his shoulders and walked slowly outside.

A fire smoldered near the mouth of the cave, almost dead. The time of morning meal must have long passed. A young girl was nearby, her back to him. She turned as he approached and smiled at him. He recognized her as Eavan, whom he had comforted on their voyage to this land. She walked up to him and handed him a bowl that was covered with another bowl.

"Aislinn said to give this to you when you awoke." She shrugged her shoulders. "I am afraid that the food is cold now. I can heat it for you if you wish."

Cathal stifled a yawn before he replied. "No, I am sure it will be fine. Where are the others?"

"They are preparing the currachs for us to leave."

"How long have I slept?"

"It is closer to midday than dawn. But Aislinn said to let you sleep, that you were very tired and needed your rest."

Thinking back to the night before, he remembered pulling Aislinn close to him as they lay together in the cave. He remembered reaching under her léine and resting his hand on her thigh. The next thing he remembered was waking. He gave a short laugh. Yes, he had been tired. Lifting the bowl off the top of the food, he found porridge and a large piece of salted cod. They were cold, but he ate ravenously. Mentally, he thanked Oengus for being true to his word and sending a sizable shipment of fish and grain, as well as ale.

After he had finished wiping the last bit of porridge from the bowl, he sighed and handed it to the girl.

"Thank you for the fine meal, Eavan. I am quite satisfied." He smiled at the girl and she giggled. "Now I must try to recover some of this lost morning. I will see what I can do to help us prepare to leave this fine island."

Eavan picked up another covered bowl and stepped close to Cathal. "I will walk with you. I am supposed to take food to our guests."

"Guests?" Then Cathal understood. "Ah, our unwilling guests. We should go without delay. I am sure that they are hungry."

"Aislinn said I should wait until you rose. Did I do wrong?"

He stroked her hair. "You will never do wrong if you obey Aislinn."

They walked together along the grassy hill toward the beach. Just before they reached the sand, Eavan turned to go over a small rise to where the prisoners were held. She waved to Cathal just before she crested the top and he strolled toward the currachs feeling rested and relaxed.

A scream pierced the air. It was Eavan. Cathal ran up the rise where she had gone. As he got to the top, he saw the girl halfway to where the prisoners had been kept, her plate of food held in front of her. A large rock partially blocked his sight, but he could see someone lying on the ground. Then he saw a man, sword in hand, running toward Eavan from behind the rock. It was Aed.

For a moment Cathal wondered how a prisoner who had been bound and guarded could be free and attacking the child, but he quickly drew his sword and ran to intercept Aed.

It seemed as though time had slowed. He saw the other warrior charging the girl, sword raised to strike and silence her. But he did not see Cathal. Putting every bit of strength he had into his dash, Cathal ran faster than he had ever run before. He knew that if he tripped the girl would die, but he did not have time to watch his footing. Only he could save the girl and he must risk all for that chance.

The smaller man was faster. Cathal could see he would never reach her in time. In desperation he yelled, "Eavan!"

Both Eavan and Aed turned to him. The girl acted first. She dove to the side, dropping the plate. Aed swung his sword at her, but missed and stepped on the plate. He stumbled, but recovered and reached for the girl. But Cathal had closed the gap.

Before Aed could react, Cathal swung his sword at Aed's sword arm. The honed iron blade sank into Aed's arm, biting into the bone. He screamed and dropped his sword. Blood spurted in a pulsing stream from the deep wound. Aed fell to his knees and clutched his arm.

Cathal dropped his sword and went to Eavan, making sure she had not been harmed. Then he went to his fallen opponent to see if he could stop the bleeding. But Aed grabbed his sword in his left hand and slashed out, slicing a shallow gash in Cathal's cheek before he could draw back.

Panting, he held his sword between himself and Cathal. Then he fell forward, landing on his face. Cathal knelt and tried to staunch the flow of blood, but could not. With a rasping gasp, Aed died.

With a sad shake of his head, Cathal went to the rock where

Aed had been held prisoner. The other captured warrior was still lying bound and immobile. The man who was to guard them, Murchadh, lay with his throat slit and a dark bruise on his forehead. Dark blood stained the earth under him. Cathal grabbed the prisoner by the front of his léine and held him suspended in the air.

"What happened?"

The other man gulped. "Your man fell asleep. Aed worked his way over to him and kicked him in the head. Then he used your guard's sword to cut his bonds. And kill your guard." There was a smell of fear, of urine, in the air. "I did none of this. It was Aed. Before he could escape, the girl screamed and he went after her."

Fighting the impulse to take revenge on this prisoner, Cathal set him down on the ground. This was a disaster. Two dead. One a good man. And he knew the elder Oengus would not forgive the death of the other. Or even if the younger Oengus would. They must prepare to leave. And prepare to fight.

Just past midday, the younger Oengus arrived with a number of his warriors. The currachs were loaded and ready. All of Cathal's clann were by them, armed and wary. Their captive was standing in the forefront, unbound. At his feet was Aed's body. Next to it was Murchadh's body. Oengus reined his horse to a stop, staring down at his brother.

"What is this? You have killed him." He looked to Cathal. "You have betrayed me."

Cathal shook his head. "I have not betrayed you. But I am responsible. A man who was no warrior, a fisherman, was on guard. Your brother killed him to escape. But that is not why he died."

"Then why? Why did you kill my little brother?"

Oengus' voice was choked.

"Because he was going to kill a girl, a child of but seven Samhains." Cathal motioned to Eavan, who came forward and clung to his thigh. She was shaking.

Oengus looked at the girl, then turned to the captive. "Aodh, is this true? And remember that deceit is the only thing I cannot forgive."

With eyes downcast, Aodh mutely nodded.

Cathal stepped closer to Oengus. "We will pay honor price for the death of your brother. We do not have great wealth, but we will pay."

Sadly shaking his head, Oengus said nothing for a moment. Then he cleared his throat. "You owe no honor price. I loved my brother, but he was wild and brutal. Leave now, before my father and the Cenél hear of this. I cannot protect you if they attack you." He paused, looking down at his brother's body. "And I must warn you that I will not try. I will give you the provisions we have brought you, but leave before more blood is shed."

Oengus dropped satchels on the beach and motioned his men to do likewise. Then he dismounted, threw his brother's body over his shoulder as if it were a feather and remounted. Without looking back, he rode away. His warriors followed, but some casting hostile glares before they left.

With a sigh, Cathal turned to his people. "Let us be gone from this cursed place before more die. Bury Murchadh and get these currachs in the sea."

Connaire touched his brother's arm. "Murchadh loved the sea. Let us bury him there, not in the cold earth."

Cathal studied his brother. Then he nodded. "We shall take him out to the sea and leave him in the place he loved." He closed his eyes and rubbed his temples. "And maybe Manannán will take kindly to it and let us pass safely."

Chapter 30

Working against the wind, the trio of currachs were powered by men and women of the clann, straining at their oars as they struggled toward what they all hoped would be a more hospitable shore. Cathal manned an oar, leaving the steering oar to Ronan. Although the sea was much calmer and the sky clearer than their first voyage, the warm sun and heavy work soon made the small boat as uncomfortable as a sweat house. When Eavan came by with a waterskin, he gladly pulled in his oar and drank.

The young girl looked anxiously toward the horizon. "How long will it be before we reach land again?"

Cathal lowered the waterskin and wiped his brow. "Not long, lass. Not like before. Ronan thinks we will be there for evening meal."

"Will the people there like us?"

He saw the fear in her eyes. "I am sure they will, child." If only he were. "Now take the water around. Many are thirsty."

Without another word, he slipped his oar back into the sea and began to row with all his strength.

As the sun moved across the sky, Cathal wondered if they would reach land by nightfall. They had endured a night on the tossing boats on their voyage before, but it had not been pleasant and he hoped they would not need to do it again. The wind had changed, letting them pull in their oars and rest while the sail was unfurled and pulled them along. Then he heard someone call, "Land ahead." He turned to look for shore, but heard Ronan call to them from his post in the rear.

"They are only islands, small ones. But we are close to mainland now." And he was right. They passed between two islands, one very small, and kept their course. There were more outcroppings of rocks, which they avoided, and a spit of land that Ronan steered the boat around.

At the next call of, "Land ahead," Ronan became excited. "That is it. Row now. We need to keep speed to maneuver."

As Cathal leaned into his oar, he saw his brother's currach following. With Murchadh dead, Connaire was guiding it. He gave a silent plea to Manannán to be merciful.

The landing was uneventful. The beach was covered with small rocks, polished smooth by the actions of the sea and as soon as the boat touched ground, the crew leaped off. Pulling it to land, they lifted it, so as to not grind the hide hull against the stones.

Having learned from their last landing, Cathal had the boats taken higher on shore before unloading. Then the boats and cargo were hauled to a rocky hollow in the forest above the shore.

That night, with a crude shelter made of the boats overturned and propped up to give some cover, they had a meal of fish stew with leeks and carrots, made from the supplies given to them by Oengus.

When he had finished, Cathal leaned on one arm and sighed. Aislinn, sitting next to him, gently stroked his back and spoke softly to him. "Be calm. We have safely made it here. All will be well. What troubles you?"

"It is nothing."

She leaned against him, resting her head on his shoulder. "Tell me. Fear of tomorrow?"

"No, not that."

"Then what? I want to know."

He sighed. "I am tired of fish. I miss a haunch of boar or a slab of beef."

Aislinn cuffed him on the back of his head, not very gently.

He grinned at her. "You did ask."

She laughed. "I did. Is there anything else you miss?"

"Yes." He slowly rose, then pulled her to her feet. "But that can be remedied."

He led her away from the fire, toward a bed he had prepared in the forest earlier. There were no clouds and the night promised to be dry. It was worth taking the risk of a storm to be alone for a night. Her smile showed him that Aislinn was of the same mind.

Tian gave a short laugh as he watched them leave. Leaning over to Gruagach, he whispered, "Does that make you feel like doing something amorous?"

Gruagach drew back and studied Tian for a moment. "Not with you."

Tian laughed so hard that he rolled on his side, tears streaming down his cheeks. Finally, he was able to sputter a few words amid his laughter. "You . . . you . . . . By Lugh, that was . . . a joke. Gruagach . . . my friend. That was a . . . joke. I have never heard you . . . tell a joke before. And a good one, no less."

Gruagach grinned. "Yes, it was, was it not?"

"Yes, it was." Taking a deep breath, Tian regained control of himself. "And I agree, not with you. There is another, however . . . ." He looked across the fire at Maille. She dropped her eyes when he looked at her. With an inward smile, he realized she had been watching him. He rose and brushed the dirt and leaves from his léine.

Then he walked to the center of the gathering and began to sing a song that had come into his mind, "Maille the Unconquerable."

Down along a wooded ridge with spear unslung and sword aloft
A warrior gallops through wooden maze

Down swiftly toward the battle haze
With pent up fury and eyes ablaze
Maille rides to join her taoiseach defending cattle, lands and crofts.

Winding through a trackless wood, bow and arrow at the ready
Maille stalks a great tusk boar
Through his heart her arrow tore
Thrashing and dying in his own gore
Her aim is true; and the relentless hunter's hand is steady.

Lying upon a homespun sheet, the maiden's charms are revealed
Gentle curve of hip and breast
Slender hands now come to rest
On the beating heart inside my chest
Maille smiles and kisses the love that will no longer be concealed.

When the last notes of Tian's song faded in the night, Maille rose and walked to the edge of the fire's light. As she reached it, she turned and smiled at Tian. Then she walked into the darkness.

Tian turned to Gruagach and grinned. "You are right, my friend. Not with you." Then he hurried after Maille.

Gruagach grunted and stared at the fire.

The next morning, Cathal called Tian, Gruagach and Cairbre to him.

"I need you to scout the area. We do not want any surprises as we had on Ìle."

Cairbre shook his head. "But are not these the lands of Ronan's mother, the lands of Cenél Loairn?"

"They are, as best we know. But we will take no further chances with the lives of this clann. Go and see the land. See where the nearest settlement is. See if it is friendly. If you have any doubts, stay hidden and watch. Then return here." He paused as Tian yawned several times. "Did you have trouble sleeping last night?"

"No, no trouble." Then Tian grinned. "Well, no trouble that I did not want."

Cathal sighed and looked skyward. "Then if you can keep your mind on the concerns of this clann, search the area and see if we are safe here."

Tian looked offended. "You know I have never let desires of my loins prevent me from my duty."

"No, no, you have not." Cathal slowly shook his head. "At least not so far. But make sure you are thorough and careful in this. It well could determine our fate here."

Cairbre leaned close to Cathal and spoke softly, but loud enough for the others to hear. "Do not worry. Gruagach and I will make sure that this task is done well."

"You and Gruagach?" Tian sputtered. "I will make sure that our assignment is fulfilled. What makes you two pig heads think that you are needed? I can do this alone, if need be."

While Tian spoke, Gruagach and Cairbre moved to his sides and lifted him by his arms. As they walked away, his feet dangling in the air, Tian started laughing. He gave a shake of his head in farewell.

"I go now, with my loyal servants, to do your bidding."

Having sent his scouts to their duties, Cathal organized the others to establish a settlement. Some hacked saplings into poles to support a shelter. Others foraged kindling and firewood, while the children searched for edible plants. Everyone had a job.

As Cathal helped carry hides to be used for a temporary shelter, he felt a tap on his shoulder and turned. It was Connaire, leaning on his crutch.

"Brother, I am of no use here."

Exhaling slowly, Cathal asked, "What do you want to do?"

"Much." Connaire gave a short laugh. "But I cannot."

"And what am I to do about that?"

"Nothing." Connaire brushed back his hair. "Nothing. If it is all right with you, I am going to check the forest behind us. It would not be wise to leave it unsurveyed."

For a moment Cathal almost told him of Tian's errand, but reconsidered. It would rid him of Connaire's hovering presence and do no harm.

"That would be a great help."

"It would? Then I will go now."

"Fine, fine."

As Connaire hobbled away, Cathal called to him. "Take care."

Connaire turned and smiled. "You need not worry. I shall be careful." He started to turn away, but added, "I may well be late, but I will take some dried fish for my evening meal."

"We will see you when you return."

Cathal went back to his work.

It was late, after evening meal when Tian, Gruagach and Cairbre returned. The latter two dropped wearily by the fire while Tian took Cathal aside to report.

"We saw a couple of warriors, but they did not see us. We followed them for some time and they met with several others."

Stroking his beard, Cathal considered this information. "Perhaps I am being too cautious. If we settle here, we will be neighbors. I will go tomorrow and take some gifts to introduce us."

Tian shook his head. "It would not be wise."

"Why? You said they did not see you. What makes you think they would be hostile?"

"I recognized one of the men in the second group. It was Bran."

A chill ran down Cathal's spine. Had he led his people to the hands of killers? Then he looked around.

"Where is Connaire?"

Blank looks were the only response. He turned back to Tian.

"Did you see my brother?"

Tian shrugged. "Why would I?"

"He also went to scout the area. He has not returned." Cathal grabbed Tian's shoulders. "Get the warriors together. We have to find him."

"It is dark and we are in a strange place." Tian shook his head and grabbed Cathal's shoulder. "It is hopeless to try tonight. We would only stumble through the darkness and some might be hurt. Let everyone rest and we will start at dawn."

For a moment Cathal tightly gripped Tian's shoulders, his eyes wide with fear. Then he realized it was not possible. He could not demand that the clann put themselves in peril for a vain hope. Either Connaire would survive the night or he would not. Nothing he or the clann could do would change that. With resignation, he released Tian.

"You are right. Get some food and rest. We will wait until tomorrow."

He turned and walked into the darkness, stopping not far away. He heard someone approaching and turned. It was Aislinn. Wordlessly, she comforted him, holding him tight. Tian must have told her of Connaire. Cathal stared into the starry sky.

Connaire, my brother, are you fated for tragedy?   Why does trouble haunt your steps?

Chapter 31

As the sun moved past midday, Connaire began to tire. He had intended to only go a short distance from the camp, but found himself fascinated by the lush foliage on the coastal hills and lost track of time and distance as he wandered inland from the coast. The forest was much denser than those around the lands of the clann in Eireann, with a variety of trees: hazel, alder, oak, birch, ling and a few elm and willow. He found berries in a small glen, with a most-welcome stream of cool water. But his leg was still not fully healed and walking with it bound in splints, balancing himself with his walking stick, was difficult work. When he realized how far he had wandered, the return trip was daunting and he decided to rest before starting back to the shore. He found a rock next to a tree and wearily sat on it, leaning back against the tree. The sun filtered through the leaves, pleasantly warming him in its soft light. His eyes drooped and he fell into a light sleep.

Waking with a start, Connaire sensed someone just behind him, to his right. With his sword slung at his side, he knew that he would never get it unsheathed in time if the person were hostile. Slowly he edged his hand to his dagger, hoping it would not be noticed. As soon as his hand settled on the haft, he drew it and turned to whoever was near him, blade pointed upward and ready.

It was a woman. A beautiful woman. She smiled wryly. Her voice was low and soft, like a comforting stream.

"Will you kill me quickly? I would hate to linger in pain."

Connaire sighed with relief and lowered his knife. "You startled me. I did not hear you come behind me."

"Since you were asleep, that does not surprise me. And I approached from your front." She looked down at his knife, still in his hand. "You can put that aside. If I had wanted to kill you, you would already be dead."

Recovering from his shock at her sudden appearance, Connaire studied her. She was not tall, of less than average height, but nicely proportioned. A bow was slung across her shoulder, its string dividing her léine between her prominent breasts. Her long, black hair hung loose, framing a face so white he wondered how she avoided the sun. But her eyes were what captured him. They were green, with a depth that seemed to swallow him. She stared at him with such an intensity that he felt impaled against the tree behind him. Her lips were thick and red, with a mocking half-smile playing on them. Connaire was speechless at her beauty.

Struggling to his feet, he sheathed his dagger. His good leg had fallen asleep from the hard seat he had chosen and he almost fell, steadying himself at the last moment with his stick.
She watched him as he almost pitched forward, not moving to help. Her expression reminded Connaire of a child watching a crippled insect: curious without compassion. He cleared his throat to speak, his voice starting with a croak.

"I, uh . . . ahem. I am Connaire. We . . . uh, my clann just arrived at the shore down there." He gestured towards where they had landed.

She said nothing.

Nervously, he continued. "We came from Eireann . . . . Well, not just now. We were on Ìle, but it did not go well . . . . Not the voyage. It was fine . . . . Not fine, really. We lost one of the clann. Not on the voyage, but the landing. Right after the landing, I mean."

Her silence remained unbroken, but her eyes held his with an unrelenting gaze. He wanted to turn away, but could not break the spell nor could he stop rambling.

"We are from across the sea. My father is Fergus, taoiseach

of our clann . . . . But we are not of his household now . . . . My name is Connaire."

As he was talking, her head suddenly cocked to one side. Her smile faded a moment, but quickly returned. But it seemed different, less amused and more thoughtful. She finally spoke.

"You already told me your name, Connaire son of Fergus. Mine is Deirdre."

"Is your settlement near? It cannot be safe for you to wander the woods alone."

She gave a short laugh. "I am more than capable of my own defense. I have my bow. And this." With a glint of light, a long, slim dagger appeared in her hand, poised beneath Connaire's chin. Then she gave another laugh and it disappeared, evidently to a sheath behind her back. "Yes, I live not far from here. My brother is the taoiseach of my clann." She raised her now-empty hand and gently caressed Connaire's cheek. "You interest me, Connaire son of Fergus."

Connaire took a half step back, but found himself against the tree that had been his backrest. Her eyes held his locked onto hers. She gently brushed his cheek with her hand. At her touch, he felt a warm flush wash across his face. He jerked as he felt her other hand between his legs, feeling for what he knew evinced his desire for her. Her smile widened when she felt him grow in her hand and she slowly rubbed him. He reached for her, starting to pull her close.

She stopped, her smile fading. "No. We do this as I wish or not at all. Agreed?"

He nodded, unable to speak.

"You may touch me anywhere but between my legs. You may not pull me close. You may not put your lips to mine. Understand?"

Again he nodded. He could easily pull her to him, force his way between her legs. He might even avoid her dagger. But that was not his way. He would never take a woman by force. And she seemed to know that. Her hand resumed its stroking, but her smile had been replaced with a look of determination.

It was not long before Connaire felt the approach of his climax. His breathing became more ragged, the blood pounded in his ears. His hands roamed across her body, rubbing her nipples into hardened tips and desperately kneading her buttocks. Yet his eyes never left hers, mesmerized by the intensity he saw there. Suddenly he moaned and spurted his release. His knees sagged and he would have fallen if it had not been for the tree behind him.

Deirdre wiped her hand on his léine. She ran the forefinger of her other hand across his lips. Her smile returned, one of triumph.

"You found that pleasurable, Connaire, son of Fergus." It was not a question. "I will be here on the day after the morrow. So will you."

Without another word, another touch, another look, she turned and disappeared into the woods.

Connaire sank down onto the rock where he had slept but a short time ago. He sat, recovering his strength and trying to understand the strange and enticing woman who had just disappeared. Who was she? Why had she done this? She had received no pleasure from him, had she? But he felt that in some way he could not comprehend, she had.

Looking down at his léine, he saw the damp stain. He felt an odd sense of shame and rose to find a stream to cleanse his clothes from the evidence of what had just happened. And he knew he would be back on the day after the morrow.

It was late when Connaire arrived back at the encampment

and he was cold from bathing in several streams on the way back. The Darkness had made it very difficult to find his way and only the stars in the clear sky and campfires of the clann had made it possible. Cathal rushed to him as he arrived and clamped his arm around his brother.

"Where have you been? We were worried."

Connaire shrugged off his brother's arm. His léine was still damp from his clothed bath and he did not want to explain. He was irritated at the thought of having to do so.

"Why should you worry? I am able to take care of myself. I am not your little brother any longer. I am just younger, not weaker." Even as he said it, Connaire knew it was not true, but it only made him angrier.

Cathal looked at his brother with a puzzled expression. "I know you are very capable. You proved that on the voyage here. But there are things about this place which you do not understand."

"But you do, oh, wise one?"

"Yes, I do." Cathal took a breath, trying to keep his temper in control. "Bran is in this land."

A quick shiver ran through Connaire, not just from his cold léine. "Bran is here? How do you know this?"

"Tian, Gruagach and Cairbre saw him. Did you see anyone while you were out there?"

For a moment, Connaire almost said that he had. Then he realized what Deirdre had said: her brother was the taoiseach, the chief of her clann. Could that be Bran? Could she be the sister of his clann's enemy? He would wait until he saw her again and ask. Until then, he must keep quiet.

"I saw nothing of this."

"You saw nothing of this? What does that mean?"

"I saw no one."

"No one?"

"Do you call me a liar?" Connaire felt his anger rise.

Cathal's face showed his confusion. "Of course you are not a liar. I was only asking."

Feeling suddenly drained, Connaire shook his head and rested his hand on Cathal's shoulder. "I am sorry, Brother. I am tired from my walk. It was most arduous and it has made me irritable. Forgive me."

"Of course. It is late and you are exhausted. Get some rest."

"I will."

As he walked toward his bed, Connaire was sure he could feel his brother's eyes boring into his back. He must be more careful in what he said.

Chapter 32

Having slept little that night, Connaire was relieved to see the sun rise. No longer would he have to pretend to himself that sleep would come. During the night he had resolved to tell Cathal that he might have met Bran's sister, then resolved to wait until he could ask Deirdre if she were Bran's sister, then resolved to . . . .

As dawn invaded his thoughts, Connaire had resolved nothing. He was the first to rise and stoke the cooking fire from the covered embers and sat studying it, as if it could help resolve his dilemma. Listlessly, he poked at the flames with a stick, glad to be alone for the moment.

"Brother, you are up early. Did you not sleep well?"

Connaire turned towards Cathal's voice. He was stretching, a smug smile on his lips. Did he know more than he was saying?

"I slept well enough." Connaire turned back to the fire. "Why do you ask?"

"No reason. It was a simple question. It is just that you often sleep late."

"And if I choose not to sleep late, why is that a concern of yours?" Connaire turned to glare at his brother.

"No concern." Cathal looked puzzled. "It was idle conversation." He shook his head. "I have to attend to the camp. I will talk with you later."

As his brother turned and walked away, Connaire watched him go with narrowed eyes. Was Cathal toying with him? Did he know something? Had his friends who had seen Bran been watching when he had been with Deirdre? Was he mocking him, that Deirdre had never allowed him to enter her, smug in his own nestling between Aislinn's thighs? Connaire spat into the fire. He would not be mocked. When he saw Deirdre again, they would couple as a man and a woman should.

As he left his brother, Cathal wondered what was causing Connaire's testiness. Had he done something to offend his brother? He could think of nothing. No, it must be irritation with his leg that was still healing. Yes, that must be it. As soon as his leg healed, he would be back to his normal self, cheerful and easy-going.

With that resolved in his mind, Cathal focused on the problem at hand: Bran. He saw Tian and motioned him over.

"We need to form a Cuirmtig as soon as possible. We need all the freemen and women to assemble to confront the danger from Bran and his followers."

Tian nodded. "We are a new clann now. I will summon all that should be in the Cuirmtig to meet." He paused, stroking his mustache. "I know what can be our temporary meeting place. At least for this first gathering."

"And where is that?"

"Not far inland. There are some hills we must cross, but we can be there well before midday. It would give all the clann a better feel for this land."

Cathal nodded. "It would be good to leave this coast for a little while. Get the clann together so that you can lead us to this place."

Cathal was eating his morning meal when Connaire approached. He still used his crutch, but seemed less dependent and moved more assuredly. He stopped in front of Cathal, his lips drawn and tight.

"What is this about forming a Cuirmtig to meet at some far place?"

"Far place?" Cathal shrugged. "It is but a short distance from here."

"It is far for someone who is crippled."

Cathal slowly shook his head. "You know you are not crippled."

Connaire waved a dismissive hand. "That is not the issue here. Why are you forming an Cuirmtig?"

"To deal with the problems we have encountered. Decisions must be made and we must acknowledge the fact that we are now our own clann. We need to form our own council."

"What problems? What decisions?"

"Bran?" Cathal raised an eyebrow. "Is he not a problem?"

Connaire dropped his eyes. "Is he? Perhaps we should wait before we do anything."

"The Cuirmtig will meet." No longer hungry, Cathal tossed the remainder of his meal into the fire and rose. "If you wish to attend, I will make sure you make it. If not, so be it."

But Connaire did go with the clann. Cathal observed that he moved very agilely along the low ridges and hills for one who claimed to be crippled. He refused any help and never met Cathal's eye. Not long after they descended into a valley, Tian indicated that they had arrived at their destination. Cathal was struck dumb with wonder. He felt Aislinn's hand on his arm and turned to her. She smiled.

"We have never seen such, have we?"

There was a clearing and in it were long, narrow stones, set upright in a ring of about three handcount of paces across. In the center was a stone cairn. Each of the standing stones was well over the height of a man.

Silently, in awe of this strange sight, the people of the clann wandered around, touching the stones. Who had placed them there? Why? Had the gods done this? Except for some circular designs on a few of the stones, nothing showed the hand of man.

After allowing for everyone to be amazed by the unusual setting, Tian mounted the cairn in the center of the ring. "My clann, we are a new clann in a new land and with a new taoiseach. Let us listen to him."

Cathal tore himself from wandering about the stones and walked to the center of the ring. "Clannsmen, we have arrived in this land and must now find our home. We have encountered a serious problem and must decide how to handle the matter."

"What is the problem?" It was Connaire.

"Bran. He is our problem."

"Do we know he is our problem? Has he attacked us?"

"Has he attacked us?" Cathal was aghast. His anger flared. "Of course he has attacked us. Have you forgotten?"

Tian stepped close to Cathal and nudged him. Cathal turned and saw him pointing to the edge of the stone ring. More than two handcounts of warriors were sitting on horseback, watching them. When they saw Tian pointing at them, they approached.

The men were dressed much like those on the island of Ìle, with woolen-clad legs and braided hair. But there were differences, exactly what, Cathal was not sure. They rode up to him and stopped, spears in hand, but not threatening. One of them, a big man with grey hair and beard, moved closer.

"You are in the lands of Cenél Loairn. Who are you?"

His tone was not hostile, but neither was it friendly. Cathal knew they were the intruders and kept his manner conciliatory. "We know we are on your land, but we come seeking refuge. Many here have kin in Cenél Loairn."

The grey-haired man considered this for a moment. "You

may remain in these lands until you present your request to Conall the Ri of Dál Riata. Bring two companions and come with us."

"We have no horses. We had to trade them when we came here."

"I will leave three of my warriors with your people, if you will give them hospitality. Then you can ride their horses."

"Hospitality is given. I expect the same to be given me and my people from yours."

Cathal spat on his palm and extended his hand. The other warrior paused, but then spat on his palm and took Cathal's hand.

"If any bother your people, they need only say Daigh has given you hospitality."

Cathal turned to Tian. "You and Connaire will go with me to meet the ri."

Connaire protested. "I am not ready to ride. Take another."

"You seem well enough to do what you want." Cathal sighed. "Very well. You stay here and act in my stead. I will take Cairbre."

In little time, Cathal and his companions were mounted and rode off with Daigh and his warriors. As he watched them go, Connaire felt an uneasy sense of betrayal. And he was the betrayer. But he had to be there on the next day to see Deirdre. Then he could find the truth and be done with her.

With difficulty, Connaire found the spot where he had met the woman who tormented his mind. Although his sense of direction was well developed from his days of hunting, this was new terrain and he had not been marking his trail before. This time he did, but it slowed his progress and he was later getting to the familiar tree and rock than he had expected.

She was not there.

With a heavy heart, Connaire sank on the rock by the tree. He was sure that he was alone, a fool to think she would meet him again. Suddenly, he heard her voice.

"If you make me wait again, I will not be here."

Spinning around, he saw her approaching from behind a tree. How had he not sensed her presence? She was very good at stalking prey.

"I, uh . . . I had trouble finding this place again."

"Then you had better mark your trail on the way back." Her tone was cool, disdainful. "I will not be at your beck and call."

He stood as she neared. When she was close enough, he took her shoulders and pulled her to him. Without even seeing her draw it, he felt her dagger at his throat. He dropped his hands to his side.

"I thought we had an agreement. Do we not?"

"Yes." His voice was muffled since he dared not open his mouth too wide for fear of impaling his jaw on her dagger.

"Good." She smiled. A cold smile.

Then he felt her hand on his crotch. And she began to rub him.

As before, she skillfully brought him to climax. This time the dagger did not leave his throat until she had finished. Then she sheathed it, ran her tongue across his lips and stepped back.

"I will be here on the day after next. So will you. If you bide by our agreement, you may touch me as before." Her smile faded. "I know you could force your way between my legs. I might be able to kill you first, but I might not. No matter what, it would be your last time with me."

Without even a glance back, she disappeared into the forest.

Connaire dropped to his stone seat. His léine again had a

spreading dampness in the front. He reached up and touched his throat. He felt blood. He realized he had not asked her about Bran. She had taken him on her terms and he knew, whatever he might tell himself, he would accept that.

He buried his head in his hands and wept.

Chapter 33

After another nearly sleepless night, Connaire was up before dawn and again stirred the cooking fire to life. It was a chill morning, with a thick fog moving in from the sea. He tossed several small logs on the fire when it had enough life and pulled his bratt close around him, hugging his legs. He was lost in thought, wondering how he had come to such a predicament, how he had come to deceive his family and friends, when he was jolted out of his reverie by a hand touching his shoulder. He jerked around to see Aislinn.

She looked at him quizzically. "Did I startle you?"

He shook his head. "No, of course not." Then he shrugged. "I was simply not aware you had crept up on me."

"Crept up on you?" She squeezed his shoulder. "What is wrong? Cathal and I have noticed that you are often angry of late. Is there something bothering you?"

"Only people prying into my affairs." He slipped away from her hand, stood abruptly and brushed the dirt from his clothing. "I must see to the others in this clann that Cathal has laid upon my shoulders."

As Connaire hobbled away on his crutch, he sensed Aislinn's eyes on his back.

When Cathal woke, at first he felt disoriented. He was in a strange house and his head ached. Then he remembered that he was in the house of the ri. He and his companions had ridden along the valley from the ring of stones until the sun was low on the horizon and a hill stood in front of them, rising steeply toward the cloudy sky. Cathal could see walls of stone and logs terraced on the side of the hill. He was glad he was entering as a guest rather than trying to attack the stronghold.

They dismounted and left the horses with a stableman in one of the buildings clustered at the base of the hill. Cathal, Tian and Cairbre followed Daigh and his men along a path that twisted its way up the hill. A guard standing above them where the path was carved deep into the stone of the hill nodded to Daigh as the party passed below him.

When they went through another made-made crevasse, they emerged on a flat area where there were a few, small buildings. Smoke curled from the yard in front of one and the sounds of a hammer pounding metal indicated a smith was at work nearby. Women bustled purposefully over the hard-packed earth, most carrying baskets or bundles, glancing curiously at Cathal and his companions. They said nothing to Cathal and his men, but nodded to Daigh as they passed. Cathal looked about in amazement both at such a hive of activity and the strong defenses. He caught Tian and Cairbre doing the same.

Tian lifted an eyebrow. "This must be how a ri lives. Poor fellow. So many in his household to feed."

Daigh looked back at him and laughed. "Yes, poor fellow. Still, he does have many responsibilities that I do not envy."

They continued their ascent until they came to a wall of stones piled high, with logs laid on top of them to give a greater height. As they passed through a gap in the wall, Cathal saw a large round house. A young man standing guard in front of it with a spear watched them warily.

Daigh stopped them. "Leave your weapons here. You are safe in the protection of Conall here."

Cathal, Tian and Cairbre slipped their swords and scabbards off and handed them to the guard, while Daigh and his men did the same. The guard placed them in a small shed by the doorway and allowed them to enter. Cathal glanced back to see the sun setting. He would never be able to return to the clann tonight.

Smoke from the cooking fire in the open area in the center gave the room a hazy, aromatic fog. The smoke filtered slowly through the thatched roof, but not before permeating the room with the smell of charred oak. Tables with men and women seated at their evening meal were scattered about, with noise of dogs fighting for scraps competing with many animated conversations. A large man seated behind the central table in a heavy, carved chair, the only one in a room of benches, beckoned to them. Daigh worked his way to him, followed closely by Cathal and his companions. When they reached the man, Daigh stepped forward.

"Conall, these men and their clann have come to us from Eireann. They seek refuge in these lands."

With that, he left Cathal and his men.

Conall leaned forward, resting his elbows on the table. He stared at the three men in silence, his eyes guarded. The man was older than Cathal, but not as old as Daigh, probably having seen six or more handcounts of Samhains. Although he was seated, he looked to be not as tall as Cathal, but at least as heavy. His face had the mien of a man who took pleasure in his food and drink. His auburn hair was long and neatly dressed, as was his beard.

Then Conall brushed back a small side braid of hair and smiled. He motioned to servants working tables and they brought a bench for the front of the table.

"Sit and sup with us, men of Eireann. Did know my lands there?"

Cathal sat and the others followed suit. A server poured a cup of mead for him and he drank heartily before responding.

"We come from those lands. That is why we seek to stay here."

Conall laughed. "So what did you do to force you to come here? Did you slay someone of importance?" He winked. "If you did, I hope it was an Uí Néill. They are a constant bother to my lands in Eireann."

Cathal smiled. "No, I left rather than kill my brother. It is a long tale and not worthy of telling. But I come from your lands in Eireann and would serve you here."

"Let us not talk of such things yet. The sun is almost down. Tonight we feast and drink. Then we shall drink again while I listen to your tale."

Tian gave a short laugh. "It might be best not to talk of serious matters when all parties are sober."

Conall snorted and kept his eyes on Cathal. "We can talk of your serious matters when your hound is restrained."

Tian glared at him. "This hound is never leashed."

Cathal placed his hand on Tian's arm. They needed this man's good will. He felt his friend relax, then Tian shrugged and smiled, addressing the ri.

"I thank you for your hospitality, Conall. Let us feast and pretend to be friends."

And they did feast. Cathal even persuaded Tian to sing, a tale of heroes, a tale of heroic deeds.

Tian smiled at Conall. "And who, my ri, might be your foes? I will sing a song of satire and ridicule them."

Conall laughed loudly and slapped the table, almost knocking over his cup of mead. He grinned at Cathal. "I think I will like this hound of yours." He turned to Tian. "Well, Brude of the Fortriu acts as though he is my overlord. Then the Cruithni have been a thorn in my buttocks for many years in Ulaidh. But now the Angles are becoming a problem, too."

Tian stroked his mustache thoughtfully, staring toward the

roof. Then he smiled. "Then it shall be 'The Mead Hall Song,' about the unready Angles who are attacked by the Fortriu."

Sitting in the great hall, drinking down the mead
Giggling with a wistful smile, recalling former deeds
"Do not bother us with worry, nor trouble us with needs,
We are sitting in the great hall, drowning in our mead."

The Fortriu were now coming from their northern land
The watch fires were all burning, the warning bells had rung
To beat their mighty army, we will turn out every hand
"We will need our brave men; Where are all the thanes?"

Sitting in the great hall, drinking down the mead
Giggling with a wistful smile, recalling former deeds
"Do not bother us with worry, nor trouble us with needs,
'We are sitting in the great hall, drowning in our mead."

The armies were now forming up across the battle plain
The Fortriu had some Cruithni with spears that were a gleam
"We need the gods to slow them down, ask them for some rain
So where are the druids? To sacrifice and sing"

Sitting in the great hall, drinking down the mead
Giggling with a wistful smile, recalling former deeds
"Do not bother us with worry, nor trouble us with needs,
'We are sitting in the great hall, drowning in our mead."

We are out here on the battlefield, fighting in the trees
They charge our left and then our right, we are pushed into a ring
The sky is hailing arrows and we are on our knees

"We need more men, quickly now, where is our mighty Ri!"

Sitting in the great hall, drinking down the mead
Giggling with a wistful smile, recalling former deeds
"Do not bother us with worry, nor trouble us with needs,
'We are sitting in the great hall, drowning in our mead."

While Tian sang, Cathal watched Conall nervously. This
song was not about the Angle king, but a barely-disguised satire of
their own ri. But Conall was enjoying his mead too much,
"giggling with a wistful smile," to understand. Then Conall joined
Tian on the third refrain and Cathal followed suit, both to sooth his
own edginess and to try to keep Conall distracted. Cathal also
joined Conall in his drinking to keep himself distracted. That was
why his head ached so that next morning.

Connaire was not in a good mood as he returned to the
encampment, having missed his morning meal. He had wandered
aimlessly in the forest after leaving Aislinn, but finally returned to
the clann. As he did, he was confronted by Maille.

She planted herself in front of him, eyes blazing with fury
like the Morrigan and holding a small, dark-haired man by the scruff
of his neck with her good arm. He did not attempt to free himself,
but stood trembling in her grasp. When she spoke, she spat her
words.

"I demand honor price from Gelbann."

Connaire realized the cowering man was Gelbann and
shrugged. "That is a matter for Cathal."

"You are acting in his stead."

With an exasperated shake of his head, he attempted to go
past her, but she blocked his way.

"Your brother entrusted you with the care of this clann. Did he err?"

Desperately, Connaire tried to think of a way to avoid this problem. "We need a brehon for matters of law."

"We have Fergal."

"He is not a brehon. Only in training."

Maille smiled coolly. "He is a glasaigne. It is strange that you would object when you claimed he was acceptable at that Dal not so long ago in Eireann. Do you change with the breeze?"

Angry at having been trapped so easily, he waved a dismissive hand. "Then summon Fergal and present your case."

"I have called him already." She looked around. "There he is."

Fergal was hurrying to where they stood. Others, curious at what was happening, were also gathering around.

Connaire rubbed his forehead. There was no avoiding this. When Fergal arrived, he took a breath. "What is your claim against Gelbann, Maille?

"This worm claims to have coupled with me."

"And this demands honor price?" He almost said that many had claimed such, but decided not to after seeing the fury in her eyes.

"Yes. The only one I have been with since our voyage is Tian. And before that . . . . Well, never with this turd."

Laughter rippled through the gathering crowd. But Connaire began to wonder why she had brought this to him rather than wait for Cathal. "Since you have had others, why do you think this demands honor price?"

"If I choose to lay with a man and he tells, that is between us. But this is a lie. He told many others that he has coupled with me, that he took me against a tree in the forest near our camp and that I

214

screamed in pleasure. I should make him scream when I shove my sword through his guts. I doubt that this mouse has the necessary equipment to even enter a woman."

Against a tree? Cannot enter a woman? Maille must have seen him with Deirdre and now brought this false charge against Gelbann to humiliate him. But Fergal was saying something.

"There is no precedent for this that I have learned." The brehon stroked his thin hair. "But I can see injury has been caused. By claiming to have coupled with Maille when he has not, Gelbann claims a greater standing for himself, one that would harm Maille's. Honor price should be due."

Connaire felt the eyes of everyone on him, taunting, laughing. How many knew? Well, they would not humiliate him. He looked around at those who waited for his decision. He stalled for time to think.

"What have you to say, Gelbann?"

The little man did not lift his head. When he started to speak, his voice cracked. "I meant no harm. People give me little respect, so I thought this might gain me some. I meant no harm. Do not let her kill me."

Connaire saw dampness on the front of Gelbann's léine and smelled urine. It reminded him of after his times with Deirdre. He hated the little man. But hated Maille even more.

"No honor price is due. This man has done nothing wrong. She is the one who has done wrong." Seeing the shocked look on those watching, he continued with spite in his voice. "I think Maille should pay honor price for false accusation, since she probably did spread her legs for Gelbann as she has for so many."

With a roar, Maille released the little man and reached for her sword with her left hand. Aislinn appeared at her side and grabbed her hand as it closed on the sword haft. She whispered something in the other woman's ear.   For a moment Maille stood, hand on her sword and glowering at Connaire.   Then she turned and stalked away.   Gelbann quickly scurried in the opposite direction. Those that had watched the proceedings turned and left as well, many of them muttering and shaking their heads.   Fergal stared at Connaire with a look of incomprehension for a moment before he shook his head and left.

With a sigh, Connaire walked over to Aislinn.   "I am glad you were there.   I would hate to have had to kill her."

"Kill her?"   She looked at him incredulously.   "I saved your life, you fool.   After what you just did, I am not sure why. Maybe because you once were an honorable man.   Maybe because you are Cathal's brother.   Fortunately, he should be back soon so that you can do nothing more to destroy this clann."

With that, she turned and stalked away in the direction Maille had gone.

Connaire stood watching as she left.

Chapter 34

It was not until midday that Conall finally was sober enough to listen as Cathal spoke of his clann's situation. Cathal was seated on a bench across from the ri, at the same table as the night before, but this time Cathal drank his mead sparingly. The talk had started with tales of great hunts and grand battles. Cathal had mainly listened.

Finally Conall rested his chin on his palm and sighed. "You are a morose one. You take my hospitality, but do not give any entertainment in return. What am I to do with you?"

Cathal held rein on his temper. He had tried several times to talk of why he was here, but bragging and drinking had held the fore. He placed his palms flat on the table to steady himself before he spoke.

"Although you have been generous with your hospitality, I have tried to tell you of why I came and you did not want to hear it. I have been here long and my people await my return. But more than that, they need a place they may settle and make their homes. They would be loyal clients for you and lend their swords when needed. We ask you to grant us lands to be our own."

"And why should I grant this to you?" He smiled as he said this, but Cathal saw a cunning in his eyes.

"There are over ten handcounts of us, including the children, with almost six handcounts of warriors and three currachs. We would oath our loyalty to you. We would make the land you gave us prosper."

The ri stroked his beard, then drank deeply of his mead. With a satisfied belch, he set his drinking cup on the table. "So you offer me men and currachs. Are these currachs with a handcount plus two benches?"

"They are."

"But you have only warriors for two of them. Not even that."

"My clann handled them well enough to get us here from Eireann. Even those that are not warriors can row. Often better than warriors."

The ri drummed his fingers on the table, his eyes on Cathal. "Why did you leave Eire?"

"Does it matter? We are here now. I would let the past die. It is not a tale to be told."

"You came to me. I will decide what is to be told."

Cathal considered turning and walking out, leaving this place. But there were others, others who depended upon him. For their sake, he would tell the tale.

"My father is the taoiseach of our clann. But he is now old and has lost his judgment. My brother--"

"I am older than you," interrupted the ri. "Would you turn on me as quickly as you did your father? Where is truth, honor and duty?"

Suddenly a deep, resonant voice came from behind Cathal. "Let him tell his story, Conall. You have asked him a question, so allow him to answer."

Cathal spun about and saw a tall man, taller even than Cathal, with a druidic tonsure standing behind him. The man wore a long garment, as long as a woman's léine, but of white wool. He was lean, almost gaunt, clean-shaven and his hair was streaked with gray. But the look of his eyes was what caught Cathal's attention. It was not the cold, piercing glare of the brehon Tairdelbach, but hypnotic nonetheless. Cathal felt entranced as if those eyes saw his thoughts as he saw the room around him. The room was silent.

Conall sighed, breaking the moment. "Colm Cille, will you interfere with everything I do while you are a guest within my house?"

"Only if you act unwisely or unfairly. Then I must."

The ri gave a disgruntled snort. "From how often you interrupt me, it seems that is everything I do."

The tall man smiled. "Not everything, but perhaps too much. That is why I must guide you."

"Very well. Cathal, continue and I will not say a word until you are finished."

He did not look pleased with being reprimanded, but Cathal pressed on with his story.

"My brother is no warrior and hates me because I am. I left because my brother was using my father, taking advantage of his mental weakness to attack me. When he convinced my father to take the woman to whom I am oathed for himself, I had to act. Rather than dispute my father's command and split the clann into fighting factions, I left. Originally, I planned to flee with my mate, but friends insisted on coming with us. We traded our livestock and what we could not carry for three currachs, as well as for weapons and jewelry to trade. Now we are here, seeking land from our ri."

When Cathal had started, the ri had seemed bored, yawning dramatically and motioning a servant for mead. When the tale reached the part about not disputing Fergus's command, he became interested, watching Cathal as he spoke. After Cathal finished, Conall drummed his fingers again on the table while he studied the narrator. Then he seemed to have arrived at a decision.

"Cathal, I dislike people who flee their clann. But I dislike people who cause fighting amongst their clannsmen more. You acted properly. I will grant you lands in return for your fealty."

"I thank you my--"

Conall held up his hand, stopping the gratitude. "There are conditions. One is the fealty to me. You said you have three currachs, which you say are handcount-and-two-benchers."

Cathal nodded. He felt uneasy.

"With the warriors you have, you can use one, maybe two of them. You also said you brought weapons. Are they well made?"

"They are. But these we brought to trade for livestock. We also will need other things to establish ourselves here. We have some grain, but may need more for planting. We might need more tools to build our homes. Without those, we might suffer from the weather or lack of food."

Conall smiled. "I am not unreasonable. I will give fair trade in horses and cattle, or grain and tools. You will be of no use to me if you starve or freeze to death."

Colm Cille chuckled. "He needs you as much as you need him, you see. Brude of the Fortriu and his men are constantly raiding, attacking weak points. He needs you, your warriors and your currachs. Remember that in your dealings."

"Enough of your meddling, old man." The ri glared at him. "I will be fair." He turned to Cathal. "Do you have enough slaves?"

Cathal shook his head. "We had few for our clann and could not afford the space to bring any."

"No matter. We have plenty from our raids on the lands of the Briotanachs. I will give you a few as a gesture of my good will." He turned to a tall, broad-shouldered, blond man standing behind him. "Oswald, go with Cathal and help him in his trading for what he needs. See that he is treated fairly or I will take your other ear. Then go with him to his clann and serve him."

Oswald looked at Cathal with a stare that was neither friendly nor hostile. Nor was it fearful. There was no emotion. Although the man's long hair covered most of the scar, Cathal noticed that he had only one ear. In battle when he was captured? Or a punishment for some minor infraction?

Conall gave a short wave of his hand. "Go now. Our business is finished and I have other matters to attend."

As he turned to go, Cathal remembered another problem. He turned back. "Ri Conall, there is a man in your lands who has done serious crimes to my clann. His name is Bran. I ask permission to deal with him."

"No." Conall's voice was firm. "Bran came to me as you did. He has proved himself in combat. You are unproven. Do not force me to choose."

"If you will allow me to explain--"

Conall rose and slammed his fist on the table. "I have given my answer. You presume too much. Stay away from Bran or feel my wrath."

Cathal felt a hand on his arm. It was Colm Cille. The old man was pulling him away. Cathal almost stayed to press his case, but realized that this must mean it was a hopeless cause. He turned and left, followed by Colm Cille and Oswald.

As soon as he got outside, Cathal turned to Colm Cille. "Who are you and what is your power over Conall? Are you a druid?"

The old man smiled. "I have no power but what God gives me. I am not a druid, but a follower of Christus."

"Christus?" Cathal noticed the same pendant on a chain around Colm Cille's neck that he had seen on Eoghan's druid. "Ah, of course. The new god."

"Not new, just new to you. He has always been here, even before the beginning of Eireann."

Cathal shook his head. "Gods, new or old, are a small part of my life. But I do thank you for your help. Is there anything I can do for you?"

"There may be a time. But for now just be fair to Oswald. He may be a slave, but he is a man. I must return to Conall to see that he does nothing foolish. I have little time here and must teach him much."

With that, he turned and went back into the round house. Cathal looked at Oswald. He was in a léine-like garment, worn and tattered, and his legs were wrapped in coarse wool. He had no bratt and was shivering in cold, damp wind, but his face was set and he said nothing.

Oswald guided Cathal to the traders. Cathal noticed he walked with a distinct limp, heavily favoring his left leg. Cathal stopped before a weaver's shed.

"Do you trade for these garments?"

"No, I give them to anyone who asks." He was a small, bald fat man who smiled snidely, a smile with but a few rotting teeth.

Cathal felt the quality of the bratts. "I would like two bratts, thick ones. Not these rags. And one broach."

The man looked Cathal over. "That will be costly."

Oswald stepped in front of Cathal. "No, it will not. You cheat people often and you will give a more than fair price or I will speak to Conall. He does not like you anyway, so he will welcome the news as a reason to thrash you."

The man went into his house, grumbling, but soon came back with the bratts and a broach of bronze.

"And how will you pay for this? With denarii?"

Cathal looked with incomprehension. Again, Oswald spoke. His accent was different than any Cathal had heard, harsh and guttural.

"You will receive payment from Conall when he receives goods from this man. You will wait until then."

The weaver opened his mouth as if to protest, but looked from Oswald to Cathal and said nothing.

As they walked away, Cathal handed one bratt and the broach to Oswald.

"Put this on."

Oswald stopped, holding the bratt in his hand.

"Why do you do this?"

"I need you to help me with this trading. If you are shivering, you look weak, even if you are not, and these traders seem to sense weakness." Then he smiled. "Besides, Colm Cille thinks I should treat you well and Colm Cille does not appear a man to offend."

Oswald mutely took the bratt and wrapped it over his shoulders. He grimly nodded a thanks, but said nothing.

As they walked among the craftsmen, Cathal thought of Colm Cille, White Dove. He looked more the falcon than the dove. He was an odd man. Still, he had been of great help. Perhaps he could return in kind someday.

Chapter 35

It was almost time for the evening meal before Cathal and his companions returned to the clann. As they approached the encampment, Cathal saw several warriors, all carrying spears, approaching with Gruagach's hulking form at the fore. Riding ahead with Tian and Cairbre, he made sure they were identified as friendly. With four handcounts of horses and fifteen handcounts of cattle, no doubt they made an impressive group. He could see the big man grin as they rode past on the way to the clann. When they arrived at the currachs and rude shelters that were their temporary home, Cathal slid off of his horse and was met by Aislinn. She embraced him and kissed him deeply.

Pulling back, Cathal looked at Aislinn curiously. "Why such a warm welcome?   It is not that I mind, but I have been away longer on hunts and in more danger in battle."

With a laugh, she gave him another quick kiss. "I know you can handle the wild boar and a hostile warrior, but the ri is . . . well, a different kind of animal.   But you must have done well. What will we have to give him for all that you have brought with you?"

"Not as much as you might think.   Oswald made sure the trades were in our favor."

"Oswald?"

"He is one of five, uh . . . slaves that the ri gave to me, but he has been a friend."   Cathal gestured toward the solemn, fair-haired man sitting on a horse nearby.   "The craftsmen and traders were in fear of him, I think."

Aislinn studied the man.   "And you, Oswald?   Do you think of Cathal as a friend."

"A slave has no friends. Only masters." He said it stoically.

Cathal cleared his throat, uncomfortable with the line of conversation. "Oswald, arrange for the men from the ri to take one of the currachs and the weapons and jewelry that we have traded. Then you and the other . . . servants join us for your meal."

After Oswald nodded and limped away, Aislinn looked at her mate oddly.

"I thought you never wanted slaves."

He shrugged uneasily. "They were a gift from Conall, the ri. He is not a man who likes to hear the word no. Besides, we will treat them better than they were treated by him." His father had never wanted slaves in the household, saying no chief had need to force loyalty and service. A good leader would find many willing to give them freely, without coercion. That was the Fergus he had admired and sadly remembered. Although some in the clann, including Aislinn's family, had slaves, most had agreed with Fergus. No doubt, Cathal mused, that would soon change. Ciarán loved slaves, willing or unwilling.

"Well, right now we do not need more to feed. We have little enough to eat for ourselves."

"I am sure they will be of great help."

She snorted. "Two little men and two weak women. They look like they might not survive the winter. This Oswald is the only one who might pull his own weight and I am not sure I trust him."

"You may be right." Cathal thoughtfully stroked his beard. "But you might be very wrong." He looked around. "Where is Connaire?"

"Probably hiding." She shook her head. "His only act in your stead was a disaster. He wrongly offended Maille. If I had not been there, she might have attacked him and I would not have faulted her if she had."

His eyes narrowed. "If she had attacked him, it would have been an attack on me and I am acting as taoiseach of this little clann. A taoiseach deserves respect."

"No one who does as he did deserves respect. If you had done so, you would have lost your standing. It was only because of their faith and trust in you and their expectation of your return that your brother was not ousted."

Taking a deep breath, Cathal pondered this news. Aislinn had always liked Connaire. "It is hard to believe that you would take the side of Maille over Connaire. I thought you disliked her greatly."

"I had no choice. Your brother was unjust."

He smiled. "Then perhaps Connaire helped the clann more than you think."

"Any more 'help' like that and there might not be a clann. You had best control your brother."

"I will, I will."

They started walking. He wrapped his arm across her shoulders and pulled her to him. At first she was tense and tried to pull away, but he held her fast. Then he felt her slowly relax and even lean against his shoulder. Connaire, Connaire, he thought, what has happened to you?

During the evening meal, Cathal watched the slaves. Two of the men and the women sat together, eyes downcast and hastily ate the meat they were given. Maille and Ronan had gone hunting and brought back two stags. Ronan said he did nothing more than help haul the kill back to camp. Cathal smiled when he heard that. No doubt Maille had imagined Connaire's face when she released the bowstring. Oswald had eaten quickly, silently devouring a goodly portion and belching afterwards.

Cathal went to the four slaves that were together, stood before them and smiled. "What are your names?"

One of the men looked up, eyes wide. Dressed in a long tunic, he was grey-haired and small. His voice quavered and his words were strange, almost unintelligible. He seemed to have trouble with his speech.

"I Aneirin," he said, tapping his chest. He pointed at a young woman, dark-haired and pretty, who looked away. "She Addfwyn, daughter of my brother." Then he indicated a youth who glared at Cathal. "He Cynfab, son of my brother." He gently rested his hand on a grey-haired woman who was silently weeping, head down. "She Rhedyn, my wife. I pray you, do not hurt her."

Cathal brushed back his hair. "I will not hurt any of you."

What sort of names were these? Why could this man not speak well? Was he without reason? This was going to be difficult.

"You speak strangely. Are you from near here?"

The man turned to the others and they spoke strange sounds, but some of them almost sounded like words Gaulish traders had spoken when they had come to the Fergus's clann to trade wine for hides, but not exactly.

Then Aneirin nodded and turned back to Cathal. "From far away. We speak not these words there. We speak words of the Cymry."

Cathal looked to Oswald. "What are they saying? What is this 'Cymry' and where are they from?" Then a thought struck him. "And where do you come from, Oswald? Your speech sounds strange and you look different from others here. How did you come to be with these people?"

A flicker of a smile touched Oswald's lips, but was quickly gone. "Cymry is how they call themselves. It means 'the people.' They come from the lands of Rheged and were taken in raids by Conall and his men. These men were not warriors, so they and their mates did not put up much of a fight. I was captured by Conall as well. I came from across the sea and was hired to protect these people." He shrugged. "I did not do it very well."

"The sea? You came from Eire?"

"I came from the sea that is towards the rising sun. This land is small. I came from a land across another sea, a land that is vast and powerful, Angeln. I am an Angle warrior." He looked down at the ground. "I was an Angle warrior. Now I am your slave."

What did this mean? Lands below with people who could hardly be understood, warriors from across another sea. It was too much to comprehend. He rubbed his brow. He looked to the one who called himself an Angle.

"Oswald, see that your . . . companions are situated for the night. Find them a place to sleep."

"And if I need anything for them?"

"Ask anyone you see. They will help you."

"No one listens to a slave."

"If anyone does not, tell them it is my order. Will that suffice?" Cathal could not hide his impatience.

Oswald nodded, gathered the others and left.

Aislinn walked up beside Cathal and took his arm. "I do not trust that one. He is a fearsome man."

He smiled at her. "And I am not?"

She did not smile in return. "Not in the way he is. You have a good heart."

"He is a warrior. I feel he is an honorable man."

She was silent for a time. Then she spoke under her breath. "I hope you are right. It would be very bad for us if you are wrong."

After the fire died, Cathal and Aislinn went to one of the rude sleeping shelters of limbs and hides that had been erected as temporary homes. Cathal stepped behind Aislinn and rubbed her shoulders. He could feel the tenseness there. Not what he had hoped to find on his return.

"What is wrong?"

"Did you speak with Connaire."

He paused, thinking. "I had planned to do so, but I do not think I saw him. Then I forgot about him when I talked with Oswald."

"I saw him. He was staying far from you. He knows he has not done well while you were away."

"I will speak with him first thing in the morning." He kept massaging her shoulders and neck. She relaxed a little and he felt encouraged. "And now would you welcome me back?"

Suddenly he felt her become tense. He looked up to see a form standing in front of them, outlined in the moonlight.

"Oswald?"

"Yes. I have done as you commanded. Would you like me to sleep here?"

"No! I have returned and want to be with my mate. Alone. Find somewhere else to sleep. Anywhere."

Oswald turned and started to leave, but Cathal called to him. "Oswald, I have something to ask you."

The Angle turned back and stood silently.

"You are a warrior. An Angle, whatever that is, but a warrior. I ask you as one warrior to another, would you harm us?"

There was silence. Then Oswald spoke softly.

"I do not plan to do so."

"Then I ask you to swear an oath, an oath on the honor of whatever god you prefer, that you will not harm us, any of us, in this clann."

Oswald said nothing.

"I ask you to swear this. I ask it not of a slave, but of a warrior."

Cathal thought he heard a laugh. A short, sad laugh.

"Very well, Cathal, as one warrior to another. I swear by Wōden that I will cause no harm to any in your clann unless someone tries to harm me. Is that satisfactory?"

"Yes. I could ask no more."

"Then I will find a place to sleep."

With that, he was gone.

Cathal placed his arm around Aislinn's waist.

"Do you feel safer?"

"Oh, much safer." The irony in her voice was obvious. "I will sleep well. But do not ask anything more than sleep."

She pulled away from his arm, lay down and pulled her bratt tightly around her. With a sigh, Cathal lay down next to her.

It was some time after dawn when Cathal woke to find Aislinn gone. He arose and went to the cooking fire. The slaves were already busy attending to preparing the morning meal. One woman was boiling the porridge in a cauldron while another was reheating venison from the night before on a spit. One man was restocking the woodpile while another was feeding wood into the fire. Cathal could not remember their strange-sounding names. Several of the clann sat and watched. Cathal glared at them.

"Do you have nothing to do?"

Gelbann was one of the ones sitting by the fire. He looked up at Cathal. "Is that not why you brought these slaves to us, to do the work?"

"I brought these . . . servants here because the ri insisted. But just because we have servants to help us does not mean we can grow fat and lazy. Either help them or find something else to do until the meal is ready."

With some soft grumbling, the watchers rose and left. Cathal shook his head and walked away from the clearing. These slaves seemed to be far more trouble than help. He felt someone touch his arm from behind. He turned to find Aislinn. She smiled at him.

"I should not have acted as I did last night. I was upset and part of it was what Connaire did while you were gone."

Cathal sighed. "I need to speak with him. Where is he?"

"He did not tell you?" She gave a short laugh. "At first light he took one of the horses and rode out. He said he had matters to attend to. I thought you had sent him on an errand."

"I knew nothing of this. Perhaps I can take overtake him. Which way did he go?"

"You would have difficulty finding him. It has been some time since he rode into the forest and no one knows where he was going. Wait until he returns."

Cathal looked to the forest. He could track his brother, but it would take time. If his brother hid his tracks by riding in streams and on rocky soil, it could take much time. Waiting for his return was wiser. "I suppose I must."

Aislinn pulled him back toward the cooking fire. "The morning meal should be ready. Have something to eat. You have much to do: a clann to lead. You are needed here."

As they neared the cooking fire, Oswald suddenly appeared at their side. Aislinn gave Cathal a startled look. Although Cathal had not been as much on his guard since they were in their own encampment, he was surprised that the big man had been able to approach so silently that they had been caught unawares. Slave or no, bad leg or no, Oswald still had the instincts of a warrior. Perhaps there was some justification to Aislinn's concern.

Chapter 36

Connaire was cautious on his ride. Because of his leg, he found he must ride slowly. Fearing that Cathal might follow him, he backtracked on his trail several times, using a stream to hide where he changed direction before finally heading for his rendezvous with Deirdre. He arrived halfway between dawn and midday. Resting on a rock near the now-familiar tree, he chewed on some cold venison he had packed in his pouch before leaving the camp. Staring at the ground as he ate without hunger, he wondered at how everything had gotten so strange. He was hiding from his own brother, lying to his family and friends. It did not rest easy on his heart.

Not long after midday, he heard a horse approaching. Then she appeared through the trees and slipped off of her mount and tied the reins to a tree. As she walked to him, she smiled. Or was it a smirk? He was not sure.

"Have I kept you waiting long?" Her voice was soft and low.

"Not long." He shrugged. "I just arrived myself."

"Of course you did." Her smile faded. "Have you become bored with me? Would you prefer we stopped meeting?"

"No, no." He rose awkwardly to his feet, having left his crutch at the camp. Using the tree to steady himself, he moved closer to her. "I would never become bored with you."

"Good." Her smiled returned. "I would like us to have more time together, to have more of each other."

"I would like that, too." He stepped towards her. "I would like to be with you much more." He paused. "I would like us to couple as a man and a woman should."

She stepped back. Her eyes turned cold. "I will not be used and cast aside by any man."

"I would never cast you aside." He reached out his hand to her, but she moved further away. He dropped his arm to his side. "I love you, Deirdre. I would oath with you, if you would have me."

She gave a short, humorless laugh. "That cannot be as long as there is enmity between your clann and mine, as long as you hate my brother."

"But he killed the children who herded our cattle. How can I not hate him? How can there be anything but hostility between our clanns?"

She turned away, but did not leave. "You know nothing of which you speak. There is much more than you understand. Bran is a kind man. There were others, ones that stayed with Eoghan, that were to blame. If you would talk to Bran, meet with him in parlay, you would know that I am right."

"I would do that." Yes, he would even meet with Bran to be with Deirdre. "But that would do no good. I do not speak for the clann."

She turned back to him and reached out to softly touch his cheek. He thought he saw tears in her eyes when she spoke. "Then have the person who does come. Have your brother meet with mine. There is a clearing near here, a short distance toward the morning sun. Have them meet alone, with no weapons. You and I will be the only others with them. Then I can be with you."

"I . . . I will try."

Her hand caressed the side of his face, then rested on the back of his neck. She stared into his eyes. "No, you will do it. Because that is the only way we can be together." Her hand fell to her side and her gaze to the earth. "Because if I mean so little to you that you will not do this for us, we shall never meet again."

"No, do not say that." He grabbed her shoulders and tried to pull her to him. "I will do it. I will bring my brother under parlay to meet your brother. We will find a way to reconcile our clanns."

Although she held back from him by keeping her palm against his chest, her smile returned. "I believe you. But we will wait until then. For now, I will give you pleasure, a greater pleasure than you have known."

One hand lifted his léine. Then he felt the gentle touch of her bare hand on him. Her nails softly scraped his hardened flesh. Her other hand suddenly cupped the sack between his legs, carefully kneading. He reached out to her, resting his hands on her breast, and closed his eyes, uttering a moan.

As she rode away, Deirdre could hardly suppress a laugh. It was going so well. She had been sure that Connaire could not resist her. Her skill at pleasuring men to control them had been honed by years of experience, learned to keep Bran's father from painfully coupling with her after her mother had died. She had been very young when her widowed mother had oathed to him and then her mother had died in childbirth before a full cycle of festivals had passed. A child of but ten Samhains must learn quickly how to cope or suffer. With a short laugh, she wondered if she should have thanked Bran's father for forcing her to acquire such a useful skill. Thanked him just before the youthful Bran had shoved a hot poker up his anus as he lay in alcoholic stupor after she had pleasured him. Bran had seen four more Samhains than she, but always obeyed her wishes.

Now she had only to convince Bran to follow her plan. He would agree, of course. He never could refuse her anything. He did love her, taking many beatings from his father for trying to save her. Then killing him in such a way. And she loved him. As much as she loved any man.

Yes, everything was perfect. By the setting of the sun tomorrow, her dream would be reality.

At evening meal, Cathal took his bowl of the thick stew that the new arrivals had prepared and found a log near the fire. With his flat barley cake, he scooped the meat and root vegetables and ate. It was very good and he sighed. Perhaps these servants were not bad for the clann. Aislinn soon joined him. When he saw Oswald with his bowl in hand, Cathal motioned him over.

"Sit by us."

Oswald hesitated, but then sat on the log.

Cathal studied the Angle. "Tell me, Oswald, why did you come from across a sea to fight for others?"

"For the Briotanachs?" He snorted. "They have much gold. We fight for the gold."

Aislinn shook her head. "You fight for gold? There is no honor in that."

"Do you not take cattle? Do you not take gold? Do you not take slaves? Why is there honor in that? We give our swords to protect those who cannot do so themselves." He shrugged. "If people give us gold willingly, why is that less honorable than taking it when they do not want to give it?"

Aislinn's face turned red. "Because to take gold to fight is . . . is . . . well, it is without honor."

Oswald's eye's narrowed. Cathal could sense his anger. This would come to no good end. "I can see that honor means something different to the Angles than to our people, but they hold honor as of great value. Just as we do. Oswald, you speak as we do, but the other . . . servants do not. Yet you come from a distant land and they live much nearer. Why is that?"

Oswald relaxed, then turned to his stew and barley cake. He spoke between bites. "People from different places often speak a different tongue. Some learn strange tongues quickly, others slowly. Or not at all. It is like any skill. Like weaving a basket, making jewelry or wielding a sword. I learn tongues quickly. I am known by my people as Oswald of many voices." He looked up from his bowl with a half smile. "I learn tongues almost as well as I silence them with my sword."

Cathal studied him, wondering if that was a threat, bragging or a statement of fact. But the Angle had turned to his bowl, eating noisily. He decided to let the claim rest.

"So how did you come to be a . . . servant?"

Oswald stopped eating for a moment, but then finished his meal before replying.

"I was taken while my pants were down. I was relieving myself when we were attacked." He gave a half smile. "I was defeated by a bout of the runs."

Cathal laughed. "I doubt that you would have been taken otherwise." He hesitated. "Is that when you gained your limp and lost your ear?"

The Angle studied his plate. "My limp, yes. My captor cut my hamstring so I could not run. But my ear, no. I was too slow in coming when Conall called. Because of my limp."

Aislinn gasped. "For nothing more than that?"

Oswald shrugged. "I am a slave. Perhaps I was fortunate. I think he meant to cleave my skull, but was too drunk to aim well."

Cathal was spared responding by the approach of another limping figure. It was Connaire.

On his ride back to the encampment, Connaire had thought of how his life had turned since meeting Deirdre. He had spoken untruthfully to his brother and acted without honor as chief of the clann. He resolved to make amends, to try to restore his honor and to avoid Deirdre. He knew that as long as he continued to see her she would hold him within her power. Breaking away from her was his only hope. Meeting with Cathal was the first step. When he entered the camp, he felt the eyes of the clann on him. Eyes that were no longer friendly. Silence greeted him as he made his way to his brother.

Cathal stood as Connaire approached. His face was cold, stony. With his heart pounding, Connaire stopped in front of him. His voice cracked as he spoke.

"Brother, I have come to tell you that I failed you." He dropped his eyes, unable to bear Cathal's stare. "You left me to act in your stead. It was a great honor and responsibility. I behaved foolishly and caused offense. In doing so I dishonored you. I have come to take whatever punishment you will mete out." He stopped, unable to continue. Then he raised his eyes to meet his brother's. "I ask only that you not send me from this clann, my family. But if you do, I will accept it as a just decision for the dishonor I have brought upon you."

Cathal shook his head slowly, sadness in his look. "I can forgive you anything you do to me. But you must go to the one you have wronged. Your fate will be her choice."

Connaire looked about him. The clann had gathered. Maille was standing by Tian and Connaire crutched over to them. Before he could say anything, Tian spoke.

"Boy, I would as soon you and I settle this with our swords. You are my friend's brother, but you have insulted the one to whom I am oathed."

Maille glared at Tian. "But it is I who he insulted and it is I who will decide this." She turned to Connaire. "You know that your offense would have cost you your life if not for Aislinn's hand."

"I do. And it would have been just. Now I will accept whatever fate you decide."

She hesitated, so he continued.

"You deserved honor price for an insult. I dismissed it for no valid reason and insulted you as well. I will gladly pay thrice, once for Gelbann's insult and two for mine."

The warrior woman studied him for a moment, eyes narrowed. Connaire's stomach churned, but he met her gaze unflinchingly. Then she spat on her palm and extended her hand. Connaire spat on his and grasped it.

She nodded. "Done."

Then she turned and left. Tian stared at him a moment, then gave a shrug and followed Maille.

Connaire sighed and his shoulders slumped with relief as he felt Cathal's arm drop across them.

"Well done, little brother. You have regained your honor." Connaire looked at him and saw his smile. "Now let us find you something to eat."

Chapter 37

Connaire sat on the familiar rock and waited for her. It was midday and the sunlight that filtered through the leaves of the trees warmed the afternoon. Unclasping his broach, he dropped his bratt on the leafy ground. Deirdre rode through the forest to him and dismounted. As she walked to him the diffused light played across her black hair and fair skin. A half-smile flickered across her lips.

As she neared him, he rose and reached for her. When his hands closed on her shoulders, she placed a cautioning hand on his chest, holding him back. This time he would not be stopped. He pulled her to him, then pressed his lips firmly against hers.

She struggled in his grasp, trying to break their kiss, but he held her tightly to him. Her breasts, soft and yielding, pressed against his chest. Slowly he ran his hand down her back to her buttocks, gently kneading them.

Gradually her squirming lessened, then stopped. Her lips yielded to his, her tongue searching his mouth. One of her arms was still trapped between them, but the other went around his neck, holding him to her. As if of one mind, they dropped to the leafy bed of the forest. When he pulled up her léine, she spread her legs. As he prepared to enter her, she whispered in his ear.

"Cathal. Oh, Cathal."

Connaire awoke with a jolt. He was in the shelter and it was night. He heard his brother and Aislinn, and knew they were coupling. In the roundhouse, he would have been far enough away to have ignored the sound, but in this tiny shelter he could hear everything plainly, too plainly. Even Aislinn when she whispered his brother's name in her throes of climax.

When they had finished, they became silent. Soon he heard their steady breathing and knew they were asleep. Connaire lay awake for a long time, aching with frustrated desire. Finally sleep overtook him, a fretful and tormented one.

Sometime before dawn Connaire awoke. After restlessly turning from side to side, he despaired of falling back asleep and rose, wrapping his bratt around him to ward off the early morning chill. The night was clear with a half-moon lighting the sky, so he had little trouble finding the fire pit. Stirring the banked embers to life, he threw a couple of small birch logs on the red coals. Soon the fire crackled to life.

He sat staring at the fire, occasionally throwing on more wood, until dawn began to glow in the sky. When the slaves stirred from their sleep and approached the fire to begin the morning meal preparation, he did not look up, continuing to study the flames as if they held the solution to his dilemma. But they did not.

With the dawn, Cathal woke and stretched contentedly. Aislinn still slept, so he quietly slipped out from the blankets and out of the shelter. He found his brother by the fire, staring at it. Walking quietly behind Connaire, Cathal rested his hand on his brother's shoulder. Giving a sudden start, Connaire spun around and frowned.

Cathal smiled. "Sorry to startle you. You are up early. Trouble sleeping?"

"Of course not." Connaire shook off his brother's hand and glared at him. "Why would you think that?"

Cathal shrugged, confused at this hostility. "I was merely asking. Why are you angry?"

"I am not angry." Connaire turned back to the fire and rubbed his forehead. "But you are right. I did not sleep well. Dreams. Odd dreams. They have made me irritable. Then you startled me. I am sorry to have reacted badly."

Cathal's smile returned. "Think nothing of it. I know how I feel after a bad night."

"Yours did not seem bad." Connaire shook his head. "I mean, you seem to have slept well. Anyway, I was wondering if you would like to ride with me after the morning meal."

"Ride with you? Where?"

"Nowhere. I mean, nowhere in particular. Just ride." Connaire paused. "Perhaps we could hunt."

Cathal almost said no; there was too much for him to do in camp. They needed to start on permanent houses while the weather was good, as well as corrals for the horses and cattle. He needed to organize a Cuirmtig. They needed to start being a clann. But Connaire seemed to be bothered by something and taking a little time alone with him might help. Besides, fresh game for meals was always welcome.

"We can leave after morning meal." Cathal dropped his hand back on his brother's shoulder. This time Connaire did not shrug it off as he stared at the fire. That must be a good sign.

As they rode into the forest, Connaire was silent. Several times Cathal tried to start a conversation, talking of the weather, what game they might find or which direction to ride. Only the last got anything other than non-committal, monosyllabic response. Connaire studied the sun.

"We should ride toward the sunrise." He paused. "I was in that area yesterday and saw tracks. Many of them. It must be a large herd of deer."

"But that is towards Bran's camp."

Connaire looked away and shrugged. "I am sure we will be in no danger."

He urged his horse ahead, not looking back. Riding was awkward since he was carrying his crutch in one hand and holding the reins with his other, his bow slung across his back. Carefully, he wove his way around the trees, moving toward the planned rendezvous. Soon he would have to tell Cathal the real reason for their trip: the meeting with Bran and Deirdre. If there could be an agreement between Bran and Cathal, it would be better for the clann. Some security could be attained. And he could have Deirdre. It would all be for the best for everyone.

As he neared the designated clearing, Cathal rode up to Connaire and grabbed his reins, pulling both horses to a halt. He silently pointed to a figure visible through the trees. Connarie could see enough of it to know it was Deirdre.

"That is Deirdre, a woman I met on one of my visits to this area of the forest. I want you to meet her."

Cathal eyed him suspiciously. "What is this about? This was all a ruse. There is no hunt, no herd of deer. You planned this meeting, but were untruthful to me. Why?"

"Because I feared that you would not come." Connaire studied his reins, keeping his eyes down. "You see, she is Bran's sister. We want you and Bran to meet, to see if the feud between our clanns can be peacefully resolved."

"You were right in thinking I would not come." Cathal spat on the ground. "The only way this feud can be resolved is with Bran's death."

"Bran has come to meet you, alone. Brother, do not refuse my request to at least talk with Bran." Connaire turned to look Cathal in the eyes. He heard the pleading tone of his own voice, but could not help it. He was desperate. "If you refuse, we will live our lives in this new land with no security. Fighting might start at any time and Bran's clann is larger. We have strong warriors and might well prevail, but at what cost? We could be so weakened that would be at the mercy of any others that might attack us. Take this chance. It is worth the risk."

Cathal's fixed stare held Connaire immobile. Then he slowly shook his head. "I will meet with him because it means so much to you. I hold no hope that Bran has changed. But I will meet him." He again spat on the ground. "I hope that she is worth it." With that, he urged his horse forward.

Connaire did not respond immediately, but then urged his horse after his brother's. This suddenly seemed wrong, a mistake that could have serious consequences. But before he could catch his brother, Cathal had reached Deirdre. She took his reins as he slid from his horse. She ignored Connaire when he arrived and he awkwardly slid from his horse, crutch in hand. As he hobbled over to his brother and the woman he wanted, he saw a clearing through the trees. There, seated on a fallen tree, was Bran.

Deirdre's brother smiled, the edges of his mouth lifting his bushy mustache that curled down along his chin into his beard. His shaggy black hair hung thick and loose, framing his large skull. His léine was tight on his wide chest. One hand rested on his knee while the other was on his bratt, which he had taken off and draped beside him on the log. He wore no sword, but a dagger was in his belt. He raised his hand from his knee in greeting as Cathal, Connaire and Deirdre came to the edge of the grassy clearing.

Connaire touched his brother's arm. "Perhaps this is not wise. I may have acted rashly in arranging this meeting."

Cathal smiled at him. "Perhaps. But I am here and your argument had merit. I do not fear Bran. I will take the chance of which you urged. And you can watch for any treachery for me."

Cathal had his spear in hand and planted it in the ground by the clearing. Then he pulled his sword from its scabbard and handed it to Connaire. Connaire held it in hand, while he grasped his crutch with the other. Then Cathal started to walk slowly across the clearing towards Bran.

Connaire looked at Deirdre, who was watching Cathal and Bran. "I hope this will resolve the feud between our clanns." He paused. "And I hope that now we can be oathed. I have done as you asked."

Deirdre did not turn to look at him as she spoke, her voice low and breathy. "Yes, you did. And now Bran will end our problems."

Connaire turned to follow her stare. Cathal was less than two paces from Bran when Bran rose from his seat. As he did, he reached under his bratt. His sword glinted in the sun as he pulled it from under its woolen hiding place.

Connaire momentarily did not react, stunned by Bran and Deirdre's duplicity. Then he raised Cathal's sword and headed into the clearing to aid his brother. As he did, Deirdre kicked his crutch from under him. He stumbled forward, falling hard. Keeping his grip on the sword, he was unable to catch himself and landed hard on his face. He felt Deirdre straddle his back and the point of her dagger at his throat. Her voice was soft, almost sensual, as she leaned close and spoke into his ear.

"Do not move. I can easily kill you before you can do anything. This fight is between Bran and your brother, but I cannot let you interfere."

From where he lay, Connaire could lift his head to see the clearing. As he did, he felt Deirdre's dagger prick his skin, reminding him that she could kill him before he could get to Bran. He knew he had to try, but he would have to wait until she relaxed her guard. With a sense of helplessness, he watched.

His brother had kept his dagger and quickly drawn it.

He crouched slightly, ready for Bran. Bran was heavier, but much of that was fat rather than muscle. Cathal was taller, with greater reach. Connaire had little doubt he was also more agile. Perhaps all was not lost and Cathal could survive the disaster of his gullible stupidity.

Chapter 38

When Bran stood with his sword in hand, Cathal reacted without pausing to think. Although he had not expected a hidden sword, such deceit was no surprise. Experience had shown Bran to be a man without honor. But had Connaire been aware of this plan? Had his own brother betrayed him as well? If not, why was he not coming to his aid? Or was he already dead?

Keeping his knees bent and dagger extended, he was ready for Bran's attack. Cathal knew that his only chance was to use his better speed to come in under Bran's guard. And his best chance would be after Bran made a heavy swing with his sword. But Bran seemed to have read his thoughts, confining himself to jabbing and short strokes. These Cathal was able to parry with his dagger, although not easily due to the sword's far greater length and weight. He needed to prod Bran into a rash move. And soon.

Then Cathal saw an opportunity. Becoming overconfident, Bran was slow to recover position after Cathal had deflected his sword downward. Cathal knew he would not have a chance to do any real damage before Bran could strike him with a back swing of his sword, but he jabbed at his enemy's forearm and drew back to a ready position before Bran could strike.

Bran roared as he looked down at his bleeding arm. The dagger's point had gone deep. By the way Bran could still move his arm, though, no serious damage had been done. Nonetheless, he had struck the first blow. And Bran reacted as Cathal had hoped. He swung his sword with all his might, aiming for Cathal's chest.

Cathal's plan almost worked too well. The speed of Bran's sword blade was so swift that he barely had time to throw himself to the ground to avoid it. He was able to land close to Bran. As his stocky foe turned his body from the force of his effort, Cathal took advantage of his momentary imbalance. Although not close enough to use his dagger, he was close enough to kick. Cathal drove his heel into Bran's knee. Lying on the grass, he could not get enough force to cause any real damage. All he could do was knock Bran off balance. Bran stumbled back and tripped over the log he had used as a seat. With a thud, he landed hard on his back.

Springing to his feet, Cathal leapt at his fallen foe. Bran had used his arms to try to break his fall and he was lying on the ground, propped up by his elbows, with his legs across the log. Although he still clutched his sword, there was no way Bran could raise it in time to defend himself. Cathal felt no mercy, for Bran was finally to receive justice.

From where he lay, Connaire witnessed it all. When Bran swung his sword at Cathal and his brother fell to the ground, he started to rise to come to his brother's aid. The dagger at his throat pressed harder, piercing his skin. He held back, for then he saw his brother kick at Bran's knee. The fall had been planned. Cathal was not only more capable physically than Bran, but tactically as well. But as his brother leapt toward the prone Bran, Connaire heard a twang of a bowstring. In an instant, the shaft of an arrow appeared in his brother's back, between his shoulders. Cathal sank to his knees. One hand vainly reached behind his back for the arrow.

With an anguished howl, Connaire pushed himself to his hands and knees, mindless of Deirdre's dagger. But Deirdre was no longer on his back and he struggled to his feet, grasping Cathal's sword. He saw Bran unhurriedly get off the ground and take a step to Cathal. Screaming, Connaire awkwardly stumbled toward Bran, hampered by his bad leg. Then he saw Bran swing his sword at his brother, who weakly tried to deflect it with his dagger. The sword dug into Cathal's arm and he dropped his dagger, falling on his side. Then Bran kicked Cathal's head and raised his sword to finish the killing. By that time, Connaire had reached them and positioned himself over his brother, sword at ready position.

Connaire glared at Bran, barely able to speak from through his rage. "Stop! Get back."

Bran laughed. It had an evil ring. He swung his sword. As it struck Connaire's blade, the force of the impact almost pulled the sword from his hand. Connaire barely had time to recover before Bran's sword again crashed into his, this time knocking it from his grasp.

Bran smirked. "Now stand aside, boy. You have no place here."

Connaire saw Cathal's dagger on the ground and snatched it, holding it in front of him.

Bran spat on the ground. "That did not save your brother and he was a far better warrior than you."

"That is true, but I will protect him as long as I draw breath."

"Then enjoy your last one."

As Bran brought back his sword to strike Connaire, Deirdre called out. "Hold!"

She was walking across the grass towards them, her dagger now sheathed. Her hair blew around her face and she reminded him of the Morrigan: lovely and deadly. Not to be trusted. He did not lower his dagger.

Bran turned to her and scowled. "If he stands in my path and tries to protect his brother, I will kill him."

"No, you will not." She stepped between Connaire and her brother, dwarfed by Bran, but not intimidated. "Connaire is to live. Cathal will die from his wounds. Leave him be." Then she turned to Connaire. She smiled at him, a smile that looked sad and almost wistful. "I am sorry it had to be like this. It is the only way we can have peace between our clans. And for us to be together."

Stunned, Connaire found it difficult to speak. The dagger in his hand drooped as he stared at the woman for whom he had betrayed his brother. "Together? What . . what are you saying? You tricked me into . . . into leading my brother to his death and you talk of . . . peace? Of us?"

She reached up and gently caressed his cheek. "It had to be. As long as your brother was alive, his hatred of my brother prevented us from being together, of peace between our clanns. Now you can be taoiseach and there will be peace."

"Peace?" Connaire brushed away her hand and rubbed his brow, trying to clear his thoughts. It seemed unreal, as if a nightmare. All this was a plan and he was a part of it, was to gain by it. This could not be happening. "Do you think that this will mean anything but war between our clanns? That all of us will not fight as long as life is in us to revenge this?"

Suddenly she grabbed his head, pulled him to her and kissed him. Her tongue slipped between has lips, probing his mouth. Taken by surprise, Connaire did not push her away. His dagger slipped from his hand. She grabbed his hand and pulled it under her léine, pressing it to the hidden thatch of hair between her legs. He felt her warm dampness and suddenly realized that she was excited by what had happened. By the fighting. By the killing.

Pulling back, he stared at her, aghast.

"You . . . you enjoyed this. You enjoyed the . . . . "

She put a finger to his lips. "I enjoyed knowing we can be together now. Take your brother's body back to your clann. He will die before you get there. Tell them you were attacked by raiders, that you fought to save him. They will believe you. After all, you were wounded." Her finger slipped from his lips to his neck. He flinched. Her dagger had cut him more than he realized. She brought her finger, red with his blood, to her lips and sucked on it, smiling.

"We are now of one blood."

His brother was dying because of him. Connaire dropped to his knees at Cathal's side. The shock of what had happened made him senseless, not tending to his own brother. With his dagger he tore a piece of his léine, tightly binding Cathal's slashed arm. The wound still bled, but it slowed greatly. Bending low, he put his cheek next to Cathal's mouth. He could feel a faint breath. Cathal was alive. He must get him to a healer.

Looking up, Connaire saw Bran and Deirdre were walking away, to their horses. She looked back at him for moment, smiled, and slipped onto her horse. Connaire turned back to Cathal, swallowing the bile that rose in his throat.

Connaire considered pulling the arrow from his brother's back, but a moan escaped Cathal's lips when he tried. He would take him to someone who was better at such a terrible task. Somehow, he was able to throw his brother over his shoulder as if he were a child and carry him to the horse. He did not think of it, but just did it. His weak leg ached. However, it had mended enough for the job. Slinging his unconscious brother over his horse's back, he climbed up behind him and rode towards the camp as rapidly as he dared, with his brother's body draped in front of him.

Chapter 39

Aislinn was working with several other men and women, weaving twigs as thick as a man's thumb into wattle panels. The clann needed shelters before winter and these would provide for communal round houses until ones could be made for individual families. Aislinn had never done such work, but everyone was doing whatever job was necessary to establish the clann in this new land. She was fighting to force a stubborn twig to weave between stakes driven into the ground when she saw Eavan running to them. The young girl grabbed Aislinn's hand and pulled her away from the wattling. She was so winded that she could barely speak.

"Aislinn, you must come quickly." Her breaths came in gasps, with words in between. "Cathal is hurt."

Cathal was hurt? He had been hunting with Connaire. Had there been an accident?

Aislinn sprinted to their shelter, quickly outdistancing Eavan. As she neared it, she saw a small crowd gathered outside of it. Pushing past them, she stooped to enter. She saw Tian and Gruagach kneeling beside someone lying on the ground. Maille, acting as a healer rather than a warrior, was there too. She was slowly pulling an arrow from the back of the person on the ground. It was Cathal.

Aislinn dropped to her knees beside her mate. She gently lifted his head and cradled it in her lap. She was not sure he was breathing until he uttered a soft moan as the arrow was pulled from his back. Maille carefully daubed some herbs on his back, then applied some spider webs to staunch the bleeding and wrapped a strip of cloth tightly around his back. Then she unwrapped a bloody rag from Cathal's sword arm, just below his shoulder.

Maille looked to the corner behind Aislinn. "It is well that you bound this arm. He might have lost all of his life's blood otherwise."

Aislinn turned and saw she was speaking to Connaire. He was sitting against the wall, legs crossed and his hands resting on his knees. His eyes stared, unfocused, straight ahead and tears slowly dripped from his chin. She glanced down to see the healer pouring strong ale on Cathal's arm where a gash that looked to be from a sharp blade was still bleeding. She looked back at Connaire.

"What happened? Were you attacked?"

He said nothing.

"Speak! What happened?"

He continued to mutely stare ahead.

Tian laid a hand on her arm. "I will talk to you about it shortly, after our healer has finished."

She nodded and turned back to Cathal. Maille had finished with his arm and was wrapping it with a clean cloth. She looked up at Aislinn.

"I have done what I can with the herbs of Dian Cécht." She gathered her bag of herbs and unused wrappings and stood. "I have given him a drought that will give him sleep soon."

Aislinn touched her hand. "What can I do to help him?"

The woman sadly shook her head. "There is nothing anyone can do now. Whether he lives or dies will be whether this turn of the wheel is done for him. Since we have no druid to tell us of what is to be Cathal's destiny, perhaps you should make an offering to Dagda, that he will spare Cathal and not send him to the land beyond the setting sun." With a sigh, Maille turned and left the shelter.

With Cathal's head still in her lap and her hand resting on his brow, Aislinn turned to Tian.

"Now tell me what has happened."

Tian shifted uneasily. He glanced at Connaire, then turned back to Aislinn.

"I do not know all that happened. Connaire was . . . . Well, he spoke wildly. I only know that Connaire feels responsible. There was a woman involved."

She turned to Connaire. She saw guilt in his eyes but his gaze did not waiver as he stared at nothing.

"Well? What was your part in this?"

Still he remained silent.

Aislinn gently laid Cathal's head on their bed. His breathing was raspy and irregular. She caressed the side of his face, remembering how he had looked that morning. She stood and went to Connaire, standing in front of him with her hands on her hips.

"Enough of this. Tell me what happened."

Connaire remained mute.

With all her strength, she slapped him in the cheek. The force of her blow knocked him on his side. He lay there, the print of her hand red on his face. Slowly, he began to speak, words mixed with choked sobs.

"I . . . I killed him. I killed Cathal."

Aislinn looked at him in disbelief and horror.

"You did this? You shot him in the back with an arrow and slashed him with a sword."

Connaire shook his head. "No, no. . . . I took him to Bran. I took him to his death. . . . . I did it for Deirdre."

Reaching down, Aislinn grabbed the front of Connaire's léine, pulling him up so his face was close to hers. Her voice shook with her fury. "You did what? By the paps of the Morrigan, how did you get him to go to Bran? And who is this Deirdre?"

"I . . . I tricked him. Deirdre said it would be safe . . . for the good of both clanns. It would bring peace between us."

Her hand was shaking with rage. "Who is this Deirdre?"

Connaire did not meet her eyes. "Bran's sister."

Releasing Connaire's léine and letting him drop to the ground, Aislinn stared in disbelief. "His sister? You did this for a woman who spread her legs with the Uí Néill to save her brother when we were chasing him. Did she spread her legs for you?"

Looking up at her, Connaire's stare held stunned horror. He shook his head slowly. Then he rose to his feet and started limping towards the doorway.

Aislinn grabbed his shoulder and spun him to face her, barely able to keep from striking him again. "Where are you going? To Deirdre?"

"No. I am going to kill Bran."

"You think you have a chance when he did this to Cathal? He will swat you like a gnat."

A small smile touched his lips. "Do you think I care?"

"He will not swat Gruagach and I so easily." It was Tian.

Connaire turned to him. "You do not need to do this for me."

"We do not do it for you." Tian's eyes were as cold as a winter's frost. "You have done nothing to merit our help."

"No." It was a voice, barely more than a hoarse whisper, from across the shelter. Cathal was awake. "No one . . . shall go after Bran."

Aislinn went to him, dropping to her knees. She took his hand and pressed it to her breast. With a gentle croon, she spoke to him. "Do not talk, my love. You must rest."

"I am dying." His voice was sure and final. "There are things that must be said." He groaned and shifted his wounded arm. "Bran will be ready. No more must die."

"Some must." Tian walked over to Cathal. "We cannot let this go unavenged."

"We can." Cathal stopped a moment. He coughed, grimacing as he did. "Go to Conall. Let the ri handle Bran."

Tian shook his head. "But if we do--"

Cathal held up his hand to stop Tian's protest while he coughed. "If we do, the clann will survive. We are too few to fight Bran." Another fit of coughing stopped him. He lay for a moment, laboriously breathing with eyes closed, but kept his hand up. Then he opened his eyes. "We have come a long distance to establish this clann. It must survive me." He turned to Connaire, who was standing back as far from Cathal as he could. "Come closer, Brother. There is much still to say and my strength is failing."

Eyes downcast, Connaire edged to his brother's side. Tears streamed down Connaire's face. Cathal smiled.

"I know you did not know what was to happen. You trusted her." Cathal glanced at Aislinn. "To love a woman is not wrong. It was your choice of a woman that was not wise." He sighed and closed his eyes, but kept his grip of Aislinn's hand.

They all remained silent, waiting. Finally Cathal roused and lifted his head. He looked at his brother.

"I want you to know, Brother, that all is forgiven. No one will hold this . . . mistake in judgment against you." He turned to Aislinn, then to Tian and Gruagach. "Now you tell Connaire the same. And swear to me that it will be true. All of you." Then his eyes closed and his head dropped back into Aislinn's lap. His breath was ragged and irregular.

They hesitated. Aislinn looked back at Tian and Gruagach. The big warrior shifted uneasily, his eyes going from Aislinn to Tian.

With a groan, Cathal opened his eyes and turned his gaze from Aislinn, to Tian, to Gruagach and back to Aislinn. "If I forgive my brother, then who are you to hold this against him, even if he was unwise? As your taoiseach for a short time and a friend for many years, I ask you to do this for me: forgive Connaire. He will punish himself far more than you could ever punish him. For my sake, for the sake of this young clann, I beg you to forgive him."

Although it was difficult to do so, Aislinn knew she must try for Cathal. It might be his last request and she could not deny him. "I will forgive Connaire as you have. It shall be as if it never was."

Tian spat on the ground, as if to rid himself of a foul taste. "As for Aislinn, it shall be for me. It is done."

Gruagach glared at Connaire, who stood facing the doorway with his head bowed and his shoulders shaking in silent weeping. He grimaced, then turned to Cathal. His voice was gruff. "I will forgive him. For you, my friend, for you."

Cathal managed a smile. "I take your promises as a sign of your friendship. Now I need to speak with Aislinn and Connaire alone." Seeing the hurt in Tian's and Gruagach's eyes, he reassured them. "This shall not take long and then I will welcome your return."

With reluctant glances back, the two warriors left the shelter.

Aislinn had tried not to weep, to keep as stoic as she had when her father had died. But her father had been old, had lived a good life, and was wracked by illness. Cathal was young and strong. And he was all she had left. With a sob, her tears began to course down her cheeks.

Cathal weakly squeezed Aislinn's hand and smiled at her.

"Do not weep for me. You have made my life happy. I could ask for nothing more." He looked up at his brother. "Connaire, come kneel by my side."

With obvious reluctance, Connaire dropped to his knees at Cathal's side, next to Aislinn. She moved away a little, so as not be touching him. Connaire kept his head bowed, eyes riveted to the ground.

"Connaire, my brother, I cannot lift my sword arm. Will you rest your hand on it?"

Mutely, Connaire complied.

Cathal's breathing seemed weaker to Aislinn. He closed his eyes again and she feared he was leaving her. But after a few moments he looked up at her and Connaire. "You two are the people I treasure most. I have something to ask, an oath I wish you to take. You may not like it, but it must be. Will you do it?"

Although he seemed to have trouble speaking, Connaire managed to croak his reply. "Anything you ask, I will swear."

Aislinn did not trust her voice and only nodded.

"Then swear to me that when I die, you will oath to each other, that you will take each other as mates."

Aislinn was stunned. Cathal was her only love. How could he suggest such a thing? Not only did she not love Connaire, he was responsible for what had happened to Cathal. To forgive is one thing, but she would never forget it. She would remember how he had betrayed Cathal until the day she died. She glanced at Connaire and sensed that he knew her thoughts. When he caught her look, he dropped his eyes.

"Brother, Aislinn and I cannot oath. She loves only you. There will never be that feeling between us."

With obvious difficulty, Cathal continued. "I do not expect you to love each other. That may come in time, but that is not why I ask this. This clann is very fragile now. They will have lost their taoiseach. And if some blame his brother, you Connaire, then it could cause this clann to fight among itself. That would give victory to Bran. But if Aislinn oaths with you, then it shows that you are not blamed and the clann will survive."

Aislinn caressed his cheek with her free hand. "I understand what you are trying to do but--"

Cathal touched her lips to quiet her.

"If you understand, then there is nothing more to say. Please, both of you, do as I bid. I love you both and I ask you to grant me this. Do it for me. Do it for the clann."

With a choked voice, Aislinn replied. "I swear that if you die, that I will oath with Connaire."

"Connaire?"

"I . . . I swear that if you die from this, I will . . . I will oath . . . to no woman but Aislinn."

Satisfied, Cathal closed his eyes. His ragged breathing became regular. The healer's drought had finally given him rest.

Aislinn glared at Connaire. In spite of her vow, she found it difficult even to have him near. She hated the very sight of him.

"Where are Cathal's dagger and sword?"

"I . . . I, uh, left them when I brought Cathal back."

"You left them? Fool. They will be trophies for Bran. I must have them for Cathal's grave."

"He left before we did. They are still there." He rose quickly. He seemed anxious to escape. "I will ride and get them."

"Do that." Then, unable to restrain herself from inflicting a verbal wound to the unscathed brother, she added her insult. "Just get the weapons.   Do not waste time coupling with your woman or your brother might be dead before you return."

Connaire quickly rose and hobbled out.   He could hear Tian's tenor voice singing.   It was a lament for his friend, Cathal.

In Tír na nÓg a warrior sleeps
Tired by his journey through watery deeps
From Donn's house, under western sea,
Brought by Manannán to bright company
Of warriors, maidens, and immortal gods
Cathal wakes to life in Tír na nÓg.

Cathal wakes, brave Fergus's son,
To bard's sweet lay of battles won.
Feast and rest, you've earned respite
From the tests and trials of warrior life.
From the wheel you now have earned a rest;
Farewell brave Cathal, Fergus's best.

Feast and rest 'til life reborn
By Danu's call and Dagda's horn
Then drinking deep from Connla's well
Clearing your mind of tales to tell.
But Danu's wheel has yet to turn;
Enjoy the rest that you have earned.

Mighty Danu has yet to assign
The turn of the wheel that is Cathal's time.
Feast and dance, make love and drink;
Into carefree sleep you will nightly sink.
For mortal life you will not yearn

'Til Danu's wheel begins to turn

Into mortal life will Danu send
Mighty Cathal back to the world of men

Aislinn sat, softly moaning while she gently rocked Cathal's head in her lap.

Chapter 40

Connaire had no memory of the ride when he arrived at the ill-fated meadow. His mind was numb, unwilling to comprehend what had happened, what he had caused. He rode into the clearing and dismounted by the log where Bran had sat in wait. Cathal's sword lay on the ground. Near it, Cathal's blood had soaked into the ground, leaving a dark stain. Connaire knelt and grasped the hilt of the sword. It was hot from lying in the sun and uncomfortable in his hand. He slipped it into his empty scabbard. Reaching down, he touched the blood-stained grass. While dry to the touch, it seemed still freshly spilt to Connaire and he choked back a sob.

Leading his horse by the reins, he hobbled to the edge of the meadow where Cathal's spear still stood where it had been planted. Nearby lay his own crutch, the emblem of his weakness. He pulled the spear from the ground, then turned and spat on his crutch. Without looking back, he pulled himself onto his horse and rode away.

As he arrived at the outskirts of the camp, Connaire saw Eavan, sitting on a rock with her head buried in her hands. Slipping off his horse, he went to her and knelt beside her, resting his hand on her shoulder.

"What is wrong, child."

She looked up at him, tears streaming down her face. "Have you not heard? Cathal is dead."

Connaire gasped. "Dead? I knew he was . . . injured. Are you sure that he has died?"

She nodded. "I was helping Maille gather wattling twigs. Tian came to us and told her."

The news hit Connaire like a sword-stroke and he fell to his knees beside the girl. She wrapped her arms around him and buried her head in his bratt, weeping. Connaire looked down at her, realizing that she knew nothing yet of his part in Cathal's death. He must deliver his brother's weapons to Aislinn. Perhaps she would use them on him. He almost hoped that she would.

Pulling himself away from the bereft girl, he stood. He felt numb, empty of all feeling and emotion, but needed to finish his task: the delivery of Cathal's sword and spear.

"I must go."

He turned his head as Eavan looked up at him, unable to meet her eyes. Quickly, he pulled himself on his horse. Seeing Oswald walking towards him, axe in hand, Connaire rode over to him.

"Is my brother dead?"

The Angle looked up at him. He studied Connaire a moment, his face betraying nothing. Then he shrugged.

"All I know was that I was told to leave and gather firewood." He paused, studying Connaire through narrowed eyes. "From what I heard, that should be no surprise to you."

Connaire's heart sank, the hopelessness of it all sweeping over him. Cathal was dead and as much by his hand as if he had stabbed his brother himself. The clann would know and hate him. He would oath to Aislinn, as he had promised his brother, but she would always hold him responsible for Cathal's death and despise him. Cathal had been wrong about this. As long as he was with the clann, he would be the cause of its ruin. The only chance it had would be to put Cathal's death behind it, and that would never happen as long as the person responsible was there, oathed to Cathal's mate and acting as taoiseach, the chief. No, the best thing for the clann would be for him to leave and never return. The time to do it was now, before his presence could cause more harm.

Connaire handed Cathal's spear to Oswald. The Angle questioningly raised an eyebrow, then took it. Slipping the sword and scabbard off, he handed them down as well. Oswald hesitated, then took them.

"Why do you give these to a slave? Do you not fear that I will use them to kill you and your people?"

Connaire shook his head. "If you wished to do that, the axe you carry would serve you better as a weapon than most men handle a sword. And I trust your oath to Cathal. Take these to Aislinn."

"And you? Are you afraid to stand before her and hand these to her?"

Dropping his eyes from Oswald's stare, Connaire sighed. "It would only do harm if I did." He took a deep breath. "Do you think me a coward?"

"Yes."

Connaire started to say something about the words of a slave, but stopped. Oswald's slavery was honorable compared to betraying a brother. "Then do this for Aislinn."

Connaire jerked the reins and turned his horse away from camp. He kicked its flanks and rode away at a gallop. As he did, he felt Oswald's stare boring into his back like the arrow that had pierced Cathal.

Evening was darkening the sky when Connaire saw some men in the distance. Not wanting to tire his horse, he soon slackened his pace. He had ridden steadily, stopping only to water and rest his horse periodically. After a time, he found himself on the coast and rode along the beach. When he saw the men, he considered turning away. But he wanted to put as much distance from the clann as possible, so he kept his course. If they were hostile, so much the better. He could at least die fighting.

As he neared, Connaire saw that the men had the distinctively druidic tonsure. There were four of them gathered by an overturned currach, tending a small fire. He thought about skirting their camp, but decided to talk to them. Because of Cathal's death, he wanted to ask them of land toward the setting sun, across the sea from Eireann, where the dead went before they returned to their new life. He wondered if he would see his brother when he returned, how long that might be, if he would recognize his brother if he saw him, if his brother would recognize him. Such questions had meant nothing to him before, but they suddenly had great import.

When he was but a stone's toss away, one of the druids saw him and walked to meet him. He was tall and lank, with speckles of grey in his brown hair. He wore a long woolen léine of white and an odd necklace. But his eyes were what drew Connaire. They were deep-set and hypnotic. They made Connaire uncomfortable, as if this druid somehow sensed how Connaire had caused the recent disaster. When the man spoke, his voice commanded attention with a deep, mellow resonance.

"Greetings, traveler. I am Colm Cille." He flashed a warm smile. "You look hungry. Come dine with us. Our fare is simple, just fish and coarse bread, but you are most welcome."

Connaire slipped from his horse, but hesitated, standing with the reins in his hand. "I am Connaire. I need to ask questions, if I might. My brother died and I want to know of the land toward the setting sun."

The man's smile flickered and his eyes looked sad. "I am sorry for your loss of your brother. I am most willing to talk of what happens after death, but it will not be what you expect. Your brother is not in a land across the sea."

Connaire was puzzled. "Is that not where he goes until he returns in another life?"

The man shook his head slowly. "You think I am a druid because of my hair, but I am not. I am a follower of the Christus and this is the tonsure of St. John the Beloved. But come, sit and sup with us, and I will tell you what I know of life after this one." Draping a long arm across Connaire's shoulder, he pulled him toward the other men.

Stumbling along beside Colm Cille, Connaire wondered about this god that was not of his clann. But who needed a new god? He should not have stopped. "I do appreciate your offer, but I must go."

"Why? You need to eat and what I say may be of comfort."

With a dismissive shake of his head, Connaire tried to pull away from Colm Cille. The tall man's grip, however, was stronger than it looked and Connaire was forced to keep walking to the fire. "You do not understand. You would not wish to share a meal with me."

Colm Cille looked at him with a raised eyebrow. "And why would I not? Any man is welcome to share whatever I have."

"Not a man who killed his own kinsman."

That did cause the tall man to pause. "And how did you come to kill your kinsman? Did he anger you and you struck him down?"

Connaire shook his head, averting his eyes. "I did not kill him with my own hand, but might as well have. What I did directly caused his death. My desire for a woman killed my taoiseach. I can never return to my clann."

The other man sighed. "You caused the death of one man, but my pride caused the death of armies. I, too, have left my clann. To atone for my sin, I have left my home in Eireann, never to see it again until I save as many lives as I caused to die."

Connaire raised his eyes to meet those of Colm Cille. There he saw both pain and compassion. Although he had no idea what this "sin" meant, he found this man to be compelling. "I will eat with you, if you will have me, and sleep in your camp. Tomorrow I must leave."

"We must leave in the morning as well. We sail to Ioua, where we have a community of followers of Christus. Where will you go?"

"Anywhere." Connaire shrugged. "As far as I can from my clann."

"Come with us. An extra pair of hands to pull an oar would be welcome. You can stay as long as you like and I will tell you my story, a story that shows how doing what we think is right may cause great injury. You may find some comfort in it."

Mulling over this offer, Connaire found himself tempted. He had nowhere to go. Although he did not care whether or not he lived, he found it impossible to kill himself. Dying by starvation was even worse. Going with these odd men until he could decide what he was to do had appeal.

Colm Cille took his arm and tugged him toward the fire. "Come. Meet my companions and then decide."

Connaire allowed himself to be led to the other men.

IV. EXILE

Chapter 41

As the light coming through the small window faded,
Connaire rubbed his eyes and leaned back in the hard wooden chair.
He had been struggling to understand the characters on the vellum
page and the break was welcome. Although the community had
candles made of beeswax, they were costly and none had been given
to him so that his studies must be done in daylight. His shoulders
were stiff from leaning over the book before him. He looked out
the window, watching the sun slip below a low hill as it painted the
clouds on the horizon in reds and purples. Then the bell that
summoned the men on the island to prayer sounded. With a sigh,
he stood and walked out the door. As he did, one of the men,
Brother Eochaidh, walked past, heading for the building with a cross
of wood in front.

Brother Eochaidh smiled at Connaire. "Will you be coming
to vespers?"

Connaire returned the smile. "You know that I will not, but
it was nice of you to ask."

"You could any time you wish. You do not have to believe
to stand and observe."

It was almost the same every time the brothers went to
prayer. They would encourage Connaire to attend and he would
refuse. But it did not bother Connaire. They had been kind and
accepting of him. Their way, however, was not his. With a wave
of his hand, he turned and walked toward the beach on the far side of
the isle.

When he had first arrived on Ioua, the isle of Colm Cille and
his companions, it had all seemed so strange. They were not

warriors, not even keeping any weapons, but their bravery was obvious. All of them wore the brown long woolen garment that he now wore. Although it was warm and protected the wearer from the cold wind that seemed ever-present on the isle, there was little else to commend it. None of the men wore torques, arm bands or any other ornamentation, except for a simple necklace with a cross. They spent their time working in the fields, copying strange characters from one sheet of vellum to another. Vellum was a fine leather made from the skin of a calf and stiffened. Such an odd material, but well suited for the brothers' purpose.

If not at work, they went to odd meetings that they called the Eucharist or ones called prayers. He had not understood them then and still did not. Yet, they had given him refuge and were teaching him to understand the strange markings they made and how they could convey thoughts and events.

As he crested the hill, Connaire gained a little more light. The sun was just touching the sea. Soon it would be dark. He knew the path well enough to navigate it with but a little starlight, but the half-moon was already dimly visible toward where the sun rose and he knew there would be no problem this night. He found a large stone and rested, remembering Colm Cille's story. Not long after they had landed there, the fascinating man had told him why he was there.

"Pride. It is a curse of men." The tall man's eyes had held Connaire transfixed, like twin spears pinning him to the wall of the room in which they sat. Anger had shone in them, but mixed with sadness. "Like the Apostle Paul, I am the greatest among sinners. Like he, I am the cause of suffering and death. Like him, I killed Christians."

Colm Cille had stopped speaking and had bowed his head. For a moment, Connaire had thought he heard the man sobbing. The warrior had been uneasy, not sure of what to do. Then the holy man had begun to speak again, his voice harsh and low.

"I am of the Uí Néill's. I am a cousin of the ri, descended from Niall of the Nine Hostages. In spite of my love of the Christus, it gave me great pride to say so. Great pride."

There had been a fire in the room to ward off the evening chill and Colm Cille had stirred it with a stick before continuing. The fire had not needed to be stirred.

"I studied under the holy Finnian. He thought of me as one of his twelve apostles of Eireann. Then he loaned me his psalter. I made a copy to keep, but he demanded I give it to him. I had done the work and I refused."

He had shaken his head. "No, I make it sound as though I had a right to refuse. I did not. God gives no rights, only gifts." He had paused, staring into the empty air. "So Finnian went to the Aird Ri, the highest voice in all of Eireann, and asked for a judgment. I spoke in defense of myself, but the ri decided that Finnian was right, saying, 'To every cow its calf and to every book its copy.'

"I did not agree and summoned my Uí Néill kinsmen to defend my right. A great battle was fought at Cúl Dreimhne and many, many men died, both my kinsmen and those who followed the Aird Ri. I sat on my horse, a man of God who did not bear a sword or spear, and watched men die for my pride."

Tears had streamed down Colm Cille's face. His voice had been choked. "In penance, I left my beloved country with twelve companions, never to return until I had saved the souls of as many men who died in that horrible battle. I caused the death of many for no good reason. So how can you say that you have done worse?"

Connaire had dropped his eyes to the fire. He had not trusted himself to look into Colm Cille's eyes. "Because the man whose death I caused was my own brother."

The holy man had laid his hand upon Connaire's shoulder. "God can forgive you if you will ask."

It had made no sense to Connaire then and still did not. It was his brother that he had wronged, as well as Aislinn and the clann. The gods did not expect him to beg forgiveness and they had no power to speak for those he had wronged. Just because Colm Cille and his followers thought all gods were but one, it changed nothing. He had nothing to ask this god of Colm Cille to forgive and there was nothing this god could do for him. He would live with what he had done as long as he drew breath. That was as it was. With a sigh of resignation, he stood and started back along the moonlit path. It was time for the evening meal.

The others had already gathered at the tables when he arrived. They were talking amongst themselves, but none were eating. Bowls of stew and slabs of bread were in front of them, untouched. When he went to his place on the bench across from Colm Cille, everyone turned to him. Although they did not look angry, he could tell they were not pleased. Uneasily, Connaire looked about him, then caught Colm Cille's eye. The holy man smiled.

"We were waiting until you arrived. We will give thanks to God for this food and dine as one."

Although he had never been the last to arrive for a meal before, Connaire was used to this odd ritual and stood with the others as they rose. Except for him, they all looked upward and Colm Cille's voice resonated in the small hall.

"For what we are about to receive, make us truly grateful. In the name of the Father, the Son and the Holy Ghost."

With that, all the others made the strange sign of a cross on their chests with their hands that Connaire had seen so often since arriving there, followed by a slow song about their god. Connaire studied his food, anxious to have this all end so they could eat. Soon it was so.

With gusto, Connaire began to eat. Although simple and of limited quantity, the food was good. He did miss his ale, but the community there drank water except for their Eucharist ritual, when they drank wine, and so-called feast days when they drank mead. And when they drank the wine in their ritual, they only took a small sip. Why bother? They would not even allow him to take that sip, claiming it was the blood of their god. But he could tell it was only wine. After a couple of times watching this, Connaire had stopped going to that ceremony.

Colm Cille had told him that drinking ale was not forbidden by their god, unless it was in excess, but that they had not yet had time to start brewing it. If they had spent less time doing worthless things like praying and going to odd ceremonies, Connaire was sure they would have had time to brew mead or ale.

As he was mulling over these thoughts while he ate, Connaire realized Colm Cille was studying him. His heavy eyebrows lifted as he smiled at the young warrior.

"So, how have your studies been progressing? Do you understand any of the writings yet?"

Connaire paused in his eating and shrugged. "Some. I get a few words, but many I do not understand. It is hard because I have to learn another tongue as well as the writing."

"Patience. You have learned more quickly than anyone I have ever known. I am amazed how quickly you are learning the language of Rome as well as its writing. You could become a great priest. If, of course, you wished to follow the Christus."

Connaire stopped scooping the stew into his mouth with the bread. "I am a warrior. Do not try to force this Christus on me."

The other man raised his hands in surrender. "I cannot do that even if I wanted to. You will choose as you will choose. I do, however, have something that might interest you. Brother Diarmuid is recording the tales of our people. At present, he is writing about Cú Chulainn in the *Táin bó Cuailnge*. You might enjoy working with him and learn more than by reading the Gospels of our Lord. It is a tale far more familiar to you, I am sure."

"You are recording that great cattle raid? Does it not refer to the Morrigan? She is a goddess, not your god, is she not? Does this tale not deny your Christus?"

Colm Cille slowly shook his head. "I do not know whether the gods of our people ever were or are now. They are no threat to God. If they ever existed or do exist, they were created by God and subject to him. But they are not God. The tales of our people must be preserved and, since none but the followers of Christus can do so with pen and ink, we must. They are part of us. Will you help Brother Diarmuid?"

Not sure what to think of this strange man and his stranger beliefs, Connaire shook his head. Then he nodded and the other man smiled.

Well, Connaire mused, you think you have me, but you do not. Your god is not for me. Why would I follow a god that is so weak that a handful of men can kill him? My gods are strong.

Chapter 42

As he labored beside Brother Diarmuid, bending low and swinging an iron sickle, Connaire's mind wandered. Such a task would have been beneath him when he had been in Eireann. He was a warrior, the son of the chief. But here, all were expected to do whatever task needed to be done. Even Colm Cille, the man who Connaire saw as the chief of this community, was helping with the harvest. Such lack of rank, along with the absence of women on the isle, was unnatural. A clann needed rank to maintain order and men needed women for obvious reasons. Although he enjoyed learning, the oddness of this group of men was beginning to wear upon him.

Lately he had been thinking more and more of his clann, wondering how they had fared since he had left. With Cathal dead, who had become chief? Had they gone to the ri to protest Bran's attack? Had the ri done anything?

Connaire's reverie was interrupted by the clanging of a bell. It was calling them to evening meal, followed by a time of prayer and singing to their god. At times, Colm Cille's deep voice dominated, intoning a chant he called *Altus Prosator*. Other times, the brothers played music on a three-pipe instrument while they sang songs written by some long-ago ri named David. Even though Connaire understood most of the words from the language of Rome, none of the singing made sense to him. There was nothing about heroic battles. Connaire was ready to eat, but would not be staying for the rest.

As he stood upright and stretched, someone grabbed his arm and pulled him toward the gathering hall where they would eat. It was Brother Diarmuid, someone Connaire had come to like since they had started working together on the tales of their people. He was a short man, with grey hair, a wide girth and a ready smile. He turned his smile on Connaire.

"So, my young friend, are you ready to feast after your labors in the field?"

Connaire returned the smile. "I am ready, but the meals here are not exactly feasts, are they?"

"Ah, but a feast should not mean overindulging. The Holy Scriptures speak against gluttony and drunkenness."

"And what of starvation? There are days when some of you here eat nothing. Starving yourself makes no sense."

The older man squeezed Connaire's arm. "Unless you follow Christus, you will not understand how fasting can focus one's mind on Him."

"You are saying I will never understand until I follow your god without understanding him." Connaire shrugged his shoulders. "Then I will never understand." He paused. "But you will be having a feast for Samhain, will you not?"

"No." Brother Diarmuid shook his head. "It is but another day."

Abruptly stopping and breaking free from Brother Diarmuid's grasp, Connaire stared at him. "No feast? But you do light bonfires to ward off those that lurk about that night, do you not?"

Brother Diarmuid slowed, but continued walking, speaking over his shoulder. "No, we do not. Although many followers of Christus still continue those ways of our people, here we do not."

"You do not fear the Otherworld, that those who dwell there will come across on that night to seize you? Do you fear nothing?"

"I fear many things, mainly my own weaknesses. Christus freed us from fear of the dead, giving us His protection. We do not need any druid to perform any rite to protect us." With a soft chuckle, Brother Diarmuid took Connaire's arm. "And I fear we will need protection if we keep the brothers waiting, standing here talking instead of going to evening meal."

Connaire allowed the stout brother to take control and accepted his guidance, at least physically.

Sitting at a work table with Brother Diarmuid, Connaire paused in his writing the *Táin bó Cuailnge*. It had been two days since Samhain. The brothers seemed to have survived without mishap.

Connaire had tended a small fire outside of his hut until dawn, shivering until the sun had streaked the clouds with bright purples and reds. It had just been the cold, he had told himself, but he had been relieved when Colm Cille's bell had summoned the brothers to the morning prayers and meal. This god of the brothers might not be as weak as he had thought if he protected them from the Otherworld without using bonfires on Samhain.

In Eireann, the druid Miach had conducted a rite of supplication while the bonfire roared. He had asked that the dwellers beneath the earth and the shades of their ancestors spare them on that night. The clann had feasted in their honor. What had Cathal's clann done, with no druid? Who would cast the yew rods to see what the future would bring? Had Cathal returned, seeking his brother who had fled his duties? Had he been angry? Would he find Connaire, hidden on this isle?

Abruptly, he was summoned from his thoughts by Brother Diarmuid's voice.

"You have stopped your work. Have you forgotten this part of the saga? It is where Ailill and Medb are gathering their army to invade Ulaidh."

"No, I have not forgotten." Connaire rubbed his eyes. Even using the candles, the light was dim in the late autumn sky in the late afternoon. "Why is it that my writing is simple while your pages have colorful and intricate decorations?"

Brother Diarmuid chuckled. "I know you do not yet understand, but we write the tales of our people to preserve them for those that come after us, but we copy the Holy Scripture not only to preserve them but as an act of worship. We honor our Lord by making them a thing of beauty."

"You are right that I do not understand. I do admire your dedication to your duties, but none of it makes any sense to me."

A voice resounded in the small hut from the doorway, the voice of Colm Cille. "The wisdom of man is folly to God. You must humble yourself before Him."

Connaire sighed. "And that I will not do. I can see that my presence here is not good for your clann. You are all of one mind and I am not. I need to leave."

"You are welcome here. I have told you that many times. If you do not believe in Him, that is between you and God. You have learned much. You read as well as most here and your skill in writing is even better. Each day you improve. Why must you leave the warmth and safety of this community?"

"Because I do not belong."

Connaire rose and walked to the door. Colm Cille stopped him, placing his hand on Connaire's chest.

"As long as you cannot forgive yourself for your brother's death, you will flee any who make you welcome. Your soul is tormented. God can change that."

Connaire turned, looking at the holy man. "Will your god bring my brother back to life, undo that which I have done?"

"He could. He can do anything. He brought Lazarus back from the dead. He Himself rose from the dead and promises we shall rise as well." Then Colm Cille sadly shook his head. "But, no, I do not think He will bring back your brother any more than He brought back to life all those men whose death I caused. I do not know why, but I accept it as His will."

"Then your god is worthless to me and you must accept that it is his will that I leave, for I shall in the morning." His words, Connaire realized, sounder harsher than he intended. He grasped Colm Cille's hand that still rested on his chest. "You have been kind to me, far kinder than I deserved. From what I have learned, you have followed what your god demands very well. But this community is for those who follow your god and, try as you may, I will always be an outsider. So, in the morning I will leave. However, I do so with a debt of hospitality that I can never repay."

Colm Cille dropped his hand. "You will do as God allows. What we have given, we have given because much more has been given to us. You owe us nothing. Go with our best wishes. And God's."

"Will you give me that good omen you call a blessing before I go, the sign of the cross?"

The holy man smiled. "Of course. I will send you away with God's blessing. Are you starting to believe?"

"No." Connaire shook his head. "But I do not know where I am going and need any help I can get."

Feeling Brother Diarmuid's hand on his shoulder, Connaire turned. In the brother's other hand was a silver cross on a thin strip of leather. Private possessions were minimal in the community, but most of the brothers wore a cross around their neck. Some were of simple wood, others of brass and a couple were of silver. The other silver one was worn by Colm Cille. Brother Diarmuid's was finely wrought, a gift the brother had said was from his mother. Connaire guessed that Diarmuid might even be the son of a ri, but Brother Diarmuid refused to speak of his earlier life.

With a smile, the brother offered the cross to Connaire. "Take this, my young friend. Let the cross of the Christus protect you on your travels."

"I . . . I could never take it. It is your only possession. I know it is your last tie to your family." Connaire shook his head. "And you know I do not follow your god."

"Earthly possessions mean nothing to me anymore. And I am now in the family of the Christus. He is my tie to them." Suddenly, before Connaire could react, the brother slipped the cross over his head. "You do not follow our Lord, but He can still protect you. A gift given by a friend should never be refused."

Fighting to show no emotion, Connaire mutely nodded his thanks. He cleared his throat, and returned Brother Diarmuid's smile. "I leave in the morning. I will remember your kindness and that of this community for all of my days."

Chapter 43

A drizzling rain filtered through the tree's leaves, soaking Connaire's hair as he hid behind the thick oak. He stood, his back pressed against the trunk, listening to the horsemen on the other side. They had stopped, talking amongst themselves in a strange language. He had drawn his sword, but knew he would have little chance if they discovered him. He had caught but a glimpse of them as they approached and knew there were more than a handcount of them, carrying spears and shields. They were so close he could smell their damp, sweaty horses. His only hope was that they would leave soon without realizing he was there. But they did not leave.

Slowly, careful to make no sound, Connaire slid down the tree trunk until he sat on the leaves. He rested the tip of his sword on the ground. As the sunlight through the trees began to fade, there was a crackling sound of a fire. From what they were doing, Connaire knew they were going to camp there. Pulling his bratt tight around him to ward off the evening chill, Connaire prepared for a long night.

For not the first time, Connaire wondered if he had been wise to leave the warmth and companionship of the brothers. Before he left they had provided him with warm clothing, including woolen trews, and food, oat cakes and salted beef. They even gave him a fine sword and dagger, ones of the brothers had once carried and said he would never use again. Then they had taken him across a narrow stretch of sea to the isle of Muile and had even arranged for his voyage with some merchants to the mainland of Alba. After that auspicious beginning, things had not gone well.

For many days now he had traveled in this strange, mountainous land. The mountains higher than any he had ever seen in Eireann, of gray stone with patches of low grass. They were too steep to easily climb, bare and forbidding. He had stayed in the valleys, keeping to what trees he could find for cover and for games. Soon his food had run out. With no bow, he had resorted to trapping hares with snares he fashioned from forest materials. But this day he had not caught any game and his hunger gnawed at him. Before long the smell of venison cooking on the fire wafted around the tree and tormented him. He wished he could seek hospitality with the horsemen, see if they would share their meal, but dared not. Not after what had happened but the day before.

Not finding a cave or other shelter the night before, Connaire had slept fitfully. When the morning came, he had continued his trek towards the rising sun, wearily plodding along a stream between two tall cliffs. He had not been watchful of his surroundings and suddenly found himself confronted by a horseman. He had a black, bushy beard and carried a spear and oddly-shaped, square shield. He menacingly lowered his spear so that it was pointed at Connaire's chest and spoke. What he said was incomprehensible.

Connaire shrugged, trying to show that he did not understand. The horsemen lowered his spear and galloped at him.

Connaire threw himself to the ground, to the side of the charging warrior. Pulling his sword from its scabbard as he rolled to his feet, Connaire stood ready.

The horseman charged again.

Connaire waited, timing his move. When the rider neared, Connaire leapt to the side of the horse away from the spear. The horseman tried to turn his mount, but it was too late. As the horse passed him, Connaire swung his sword at the rider's leg at the thigh. The blade bit deep into the flesh and bone. Blood spurted from the wound.

The warrior pulled his horse to face Connaire. But his face paled and his spear point drooped. Giving his horse free rein, the warrior rode away, leaning forward and dropping his shield as he rode.

By their appearance, these horsemen were of the same people as the one who had attacked him.

Several times, Connaire jerked awake just as he started to doze. He had no idea how long before dawn, but knew he must be awake before the other men rose in the morning. One might wander his way, perhaps looking for a place to relieve himself. Sleep could be fatal. But it was also relentless.

With a start, Connaire awakened. Several men stood around him in the light of dawn. All of them had spears pointed at him, with one spear's point touching his neck. Connaire sat motionless, fearing any movement would be his last. One of the men stepped closer and roughly kicked Connaire's sword from his hands. Then the man with the spear at his neck pulled the point away and motioned for him to rise. Slowly, stiff from his damp, uncomfortable rest and wary of the brandished spear, Connaire rose.

A large, black-haired man with a trim beard that jutted forward came close to Connaire, looking at him through narrowed eyes. He spoke, but the words were odd and made no sense to Connaire. Fearing that a shrug might be an insult to these men, he decided to try to communicate in his own tongue.

"I am Connaire. I am from Eireann, but now live in Dál Riata. I come meaning no harm and only want passage through your land."

With a quick shake of his head, the other man turned to his companions and spoke in his strange tongue. Then he turned back to Connaire and said something.

Connaire shook his head. "I do not understand you."

As he started to raise his hands to try to communicate with the men, one of them struck the side of his head with the shaft of a spear. Falling to the ground, Connaire managed to land on all fours. His ears rang and the ground seemed to spin before his eye. He shook his head, trying to clear his vision. Then he was roughly grabbed and pulled to his feet.

The man who had spoken to him seemed to be the leader. He had taken Connaire's sword from the ground and was studying it. He said something to the men holding the young warrior and they pulled him to the tree behind him, pinning him there. The leader brought back the sword to a ready position.

Connaire steeled himself for the blow to come, one that would be a killing strike. He wanted to close his eyes, not see it coming, but looked into the eyes of the man who meant to kill him. He saw no mercy there, only anger.

Suddenly the man's eyes changed. Doubt flickered in them. He was looking at Connaire's chest. When Connaire had fallen to his hands and knees, the silver cross he wore around his neck had slipped from under his léine and now hung openly on his chest.

The leader lowered his sword, pointed to the cross and said something.

Connaire knew there might be an opportunity here, but what? Unable to converse with this man, how could he discover why this cross stayed his execution. Perhaps they were followers of Christus.

"This cross was given to me by Brother Diarmuid." Connaire saw no flicker of recognition in the other man's eyes. "I was with him and Colm Cille on the isle of Ioua."

That got visible a reaction, a questioning look from the leader. He momentarily considered claiming to be a follower of the Christus, but his life was not worth such deception. He decided to add something. "They are friends of mine."

With a gesture of his hand, the leader spoke to his men. Connaire was turned and his face shoved against the tree. He felt his hands bound behind him. Then the men pulled him over to their campsite.

Although their fire had burned to embers, some venison remained in a spit by it. Connaire caught the leader's eye. He nodded toward the meat. The man studied him for a moment. Then he laughed and said something to the other men. They laughed too, but one of them took a chunk from the spit. He smiled coldly at Connaire, then shoved it in his mouth.

Connaire gagged, dropping the meat. Desperate, he dropped to his knees and picked it up with his mouth. It was too big to eat in one piece, so he gnawed off part, allowing the rest to drop, and hungrily chewed it. He repeated this a couple of times, trying to ignore the gritty dirt as he ate, while the men broke camp. He had barely finished the venison when the riders threw their blankets on their horses and began to mount. One of them placed a cord over Connaire's neck and mounted his horse. Then they began to ride, Connaire stumbling behind like a leashed dog.

Chapter 44

As the morning waned and the sun warmed the air, Connaire struggled to keep pace with the riders as they rode along a stream. For a time, he succeeded, since their gait was slow. But his injured leg was not fully recovered and began to ache. After a time, the pain worsened and his slight limp became more pronounced. His foot struck a large stone and he fell. With his hands bound, he landed hard on his chest and face, knocking the wind out of him and painfully scraping the skin from his cheeks and forehead on the coarse gravel.

The rider, feeling the tug of the cord, stopped and turned. The cord was tight on Connaire's neck, choking him. The other man relaxed the tension so that Connaire could breathe. As soon as Connaire struggled to his knees, his captor kicked his horse ahead. Connaire tried to rise to his feet, but was again pulled to the ground. The cord was taut on his neck, dragging him a short distance, when Connaire heard a yell and the rider halted.

Lying on the ground, Connaire's chest heaved as he tried to regain his breath. His neck ached and his face burned from the pain of many scrapes. Spitting dirt and blood, he decided that he probably would not survive the journey to wherever they were going and began to hope for a quick death.

Footsteps approached and Connaire looked up to see the leader. Two other men came with him and he motioned for them to get Connaire to his feet. Grabbing his arms, they jerked him upright.

The leader said something. When Connaire did not respond, one of the men at his side took his tether and started to walk, pulling Connaire after him. Connaire painfully limped behind him.

Again the leader spoke.   Then someone hit him the back of his head and he fell forward, landing on his bruised face.   Before he could react, his feet were bound together.   Two men lifted him and took him to a horse, carrying him by his legs and shoulders.   The leader mounted the horse and, with a heave, the men tossed Connaire across the horse in front of him.   Connaire landed hard on his ribs, sending a bolt of pain though his body.   The rider pushed Connaire so that he rested on his stomach on the backbone of the horse.   Without a word, the other men mounted and they continued their ride.

Bouncing along on his belly on the back of a horse, hands and feet bound, was not much better than being dragged by his neck. Before long it felt like he was being hit in the stomach every time the horse's back rose and fell.   Hazel and alder branches periodically slapped his battered face.   His head began to pound from the blood rushing to it.   Finally, mercifully, he lost consciousness.

When he came to, Connaire realized it was midday.   They stopped for the men to eat and he was lying on his side on the ground, his hands and feet still bound.   When the leader came over to him, Connaire used his tongue to indicate his thirst.   For a moment, the man just stared at the young warrior.   Then he said something and one of the riders brought a waterskin.   The man poured water from the skin down Connaire's face, laughing as he lapped wildly at the stream.

Seeing one of the men relieving himself by a tree, Connaire used his head to indicate that he needed to do so as well.   One man released his bonds while another stood close, holding a sword. After massaging his wrists and ankles a moment, he tried to rise but could not.   After several attempts, the man who had released him helped him to stand and walk to a tree.   After he had finished, the man bound Connaire's hands behind him, but not as tightly. Then they put him on the horse, but riding upright behind the leader this time.

Connaire realized they would not kill him yet. As long as he survived, he might find a way to escape. As he awkwardly balanced on the horse, they continued their journey.

After several days, days of cruelty that seemed to last forever, the men showed the anticipation that comes with the end of a journey. The sun was low in the sky as their trail began to rise abruptly. Looking ahead, Connaire could see an enclosure high on a hill, an enclosure like none he had ever seen before. It was vast, hundreds of paces across. The walls of enormous logs, covered with what looked to be tar. Their trail ended at a gate. It was closed and the heads of several men were visible above the walls at each side of it.

When they arrived at the gate, Connaire could see that they were over the height of two men and walls stood the height of three. With such walls, such a place must be impregnable and Connaire despaired of ever escaping.

The gate opened. They rode through. Once inside, the leader shoved Connaire off the horse and he fell heavily to the ground. The rider said something to his men and they grabbed Connaire, pushing him into a windowless building. They bound his ankles and left, shutting the door as they did.

Connaire lay on the cold, hard-packed earth, with almost every part of his body aching. For a while, he tried to loosen his bonds, but they were too tight. All he succeeded in doing was to rub the flesh from his wrist and ankles, causing them to bleed. He closed his eyes, awaiting his death.

After a time that seemed forever, he heard the door open. Straining his neck to see the doorway, he saw a short, portly man enter.   Night had fallen, but the man carried a candle.   Although the light was dim, Connaire recognized the tonsure of a druid, also worn by the brothers on Ioua.   Was he one of these strangers or from Ioua?   Only one way to know.

"Do you understand me?"

The man knelt beside him.   "Of course I understand you.   Are you alright?"

Connaire almost laughed, but the pain made that impossible.   "I have been beaten, dragged by my neck and am bound so tightly I cannot feel my hands and feet.   Other than that, I am quite well."

"Sorry.   That was a stupid question."   The man cut his bonds.

Although his limbs were now free, they were useless.   Connaire rolled onto his back and flexed his fingers.   The man took one of his hands and began to massage it gently.   Connaire stopped him by resting his other hand on top.

"Are they going to kill me?"

Taking Connaire's hand off of his, the man continued his massaging.   "No.   At least I hope not.   You killed the cousin of the man who brought you here.   You would be dead now if you were not a follower of the Christus."

"But I am not."

"Drust, the man who brought you here, said that you wear the cross."   The man lowered his candle so that it lit Connaire's chest.   He gasped.   "It is Brother Diarmuid's.   How did you get it?   Did you steal it?"

Connaire struggled to rise, but settled on resting on one elbow.   "I will not take that as an insult as I should, but I did not steal it.   Brother Diarmuid gave it to me when I left Ioua."

"But it is his most valued possession."

"He told me that earthly possessions do not matter. He wanted me to have it." Connaire swallowed with difficulty. "I am no thief, but I am so thirsty that I would steal water."

"Of course, of course. Where is my mind?" The man patted Connaire's hand. "I will return shortly."

Dropping back onto the ground, Connaire fell into an exhausted sleep, a sleep that was more of a stupor than a repose. He woke to find the man from before gently washing his face. Disoriented, Connaire shook his head, trying to clear his thoughts.

"Where am I?" But he remembered before the answer came. "Have I been asleep long? What is to happen to me?"

"You are at Craig Padraig, the stronghold of the Fortriu. Rest a while. You will need your strength. You will be brought before Brude, the Ri of the Fortriu. Drust wants you to be executed for killing his cousin."

"That must be the horseman who attacked me. I only defended myself. I tried to talk to him, but he charged me. What else could I do?"

The man picked up the waterskin and put it to Connaire's mouth. "Drink some water first. Then we will talk."

Connaire drank greedily, almost choking. He stopped to take a breath.

The man with him set the skin aside. "I will tell Brude what you have told me. He knows Drust's cousin, as he knows Drust. But Brude's sister is married to Drust's brother, and he tolerates those men for that reason. Brude loves his sister and might kill you to keep her happy."

"Whatever happens to me, I thank you for your kindness." Connaire closed his eyes, drawing upon his waning strength. "If I am to die, let my name not be forgotten. I am Connaire, son of Fergus."

"I am Brother Padraig, named for the saint who brought the message of the Christus to Eireann."

Connaire opened his eyes. "I am glad that you are here. Might I have more water?"

"Of course. But drink slowly this time." As the brother brought the waterskin to Connaire's lips, he sighed. "I must warn you, however, that I cannot take your side when you appear before Brude. I am to act as translator and advisor. If I go past that and help you, all Colm Cille's efforts to bring these people to following the Christus might be lost. And it would only hurt your chances of surviving."

When he finished drinking, Connaire smiled at Padraig. "Do as honor and duty demands. You must, and I ask nothing more."

Padraig sighed again. "At least I can make you more presentable. We can replace those." He gestured to Connaire's clothes, which were torn and bloody. Then he poured water on a cloth. "And, although I can do nothing for your bruises and scrapes, I can at least wipe the dirt and blood from your face."

Chapter 45

Night was falling before a guard came to summon Connaire. Padraig had cleaned his abrasions and provided a change of clothing. Now he wore a léine and trews that had obviously been made for a shorter, stockier man, perhaps the man who now stood before him. He was barrel chested, with brown hair and beard, and wore a long, blue cloak that covered almost all of his body. In one hand he had a sword and in the other a torch.

Padraig had departed earlier, so Connaire tried to comprehend the other's strange tongue, but could not. Then the man poked him with his sword, forcing him out the door. In the darkness, little of the walled settlement was visible. Clouds covered the stars, making the guard's torch behind him the only guiding light. People surrounded scattered fires to ward off the chill in the air, but were too far away to light Connaire's path. By the not-too-gentle prodding of the sword, the guard directed Connaire to a large, dark building.

Once inside the door, he found a crowded hall where two large fires lit the cavernous wooden interior with a smoky light. Music from two of the triple-piped instruments like the Bothers had played and a drum beat in rhythm competed with the voices of those gathered in the room, mostly losing. There were rows of tables and benches where men and women noisily feasted and drank, while cooks turned spits of roasting carcasses. The tantalizing aroma of sizzling beef and pork filled the hall, causing Connaire's growling stomach to make him aware that he had not eaten a decent meal for days. A man was waving to him by one of the fires and, recognizing him as Padraig, he edged towards him.

When he met him, the brother took his arm and led him to a long table, set apart from the others and with a bench on only one side.   Large, copper platters of savory meat and cups of drink were on the table.   A large man, with greying hair, sat in the center.   He wore a heavy red cloak, draped across his shoulders and pinned by a large, ornate broach.   A thick, gold torque circled his neck.   His arms were bare, powerful and covered with intricate, colorful designs.   His dark eyes narrowed as he looked Connaire up and down.   There was no warmth there.

But what made Connaire's heart sink was the man next to him.   He was the leader of his captors, Drust.   And he was smiling, but there was no warmth in his eyes.

Standing close at Connaire's side, Padraig spoke softly into his ear.   "This is the ri, Brude.   I will translate for you, but be wary of traps.   I will try to warn you of any I hear.   I hope that--"

Harshly, Brude interrupted the brother.   He seemed angry. Padraig nodded and turned to Connaire.

"I am to only translate what he says.   That is mainly what I will do."

Brude again spoke to Padraig, who then turned to Connaire. "Why did you murder Drust's cousin?"

Connaire shook his head.   "I did not murder him.   He attacked me and I defended myself.   I did not understand him and he took that as an offense.   Then Drust and his men took me as I slept."

Padraig relayed the information to Brude.   When he did, Drust's face darkened and he said something to the ri.   Brude stroked his beard, then spoke to Padraig for translation.   This became the pattern of the conversation.

"He asks why he should believe you."

"Ask him if he saw the body.   I was on foot and that man charged me on horseback with a spear.   I sidestepped and struck his leg with my sword.   How could that be murder?"

Again Drust said something to the ri.

"Drust says that you lie, that you are without honor. His cousin was a great warrior and you must have ambushed him to steal his horse."

Connaire's anger swelled in him like a wave. "Tell the ri that I will meet Drust in combat right now to see who lies."

Padraig looked at him dubiously. "You are in no condition to fight Drust. You are weakened from your captive--"

"Tell him!" Connaire knew the brother was right. He was so weakened that he was having trouble standing and his body ached. "I ask you, Brother, just tell him."

With a shake of his head, Padraig turned back to the ri and spoke. Drust rose, his face twisted in a cold grin. The ri pushed him back onto the bench. He studied Connaire a moment, then replied. The brother was taken aback.

"He asks if you are a friend of Colm Cille, a follower of his Christus. Think carefully, because that cross around your neck was all that brought you here alive. The Fortriu often fight with Dál Riata and consider them deadly enemies. Since Colm Cille came here, however, Brude has commanded that none of our followers are to be killed without the ri's permission. He does not follow Christus himself, but has great respect for us because of Colm Cille."

"Tell him I am a friend of Colm Cille, but I do not follow the Christus. I follow the gods of my ancestors."

"I do not think that wise. Just say that you are a friend and leave it at that."

"In the name of your god, I ask you to tell him exactly what I said."

Padraig sighed, sadness in his eyes, and spoke to the ri. Drust laughed and took a drink from his cup. Brude silently stared at Connaire, drumming his fingers on the table. Then he spoke. Drust rose from the bench, angrily saying something to the ri. A short, hostile exchange followed, but ended when Brude stood, towering over Drust. The smaller man mumbled something and sank to the bench, but his eyes still flashed defiance. The ri motioned to Padraig to continue.

"The ri says that your truthful answer, knowing that I warned you, has saved you. A man without honor would have lied to save his life." Padraig smiled. "But Drust was not pleased with this and said that the ri was weak. Brude told him that he was not so weak that he could not kill anyone who insulted him. Drust said that he had not meant to insult him and asked for forgiveness."

Brude motioned to a servant, who brought a bench and placed it in front of the table. Then he motioned for Connaire to sit and have some of the meat on one of the platters. With a last stormy glare at Connaire, Drust rose and shoved his way out of the hall.

Padraig grinned and nodded to Connaire. "Eat. Brude welcomes you to his table."

Stunned at his good fortune, Connaire sat on the bench and tore a chunk of beef from a haunch sitting before him. Like the starving man he was, he quickly devoured it, then ripped another piece of the meat.

The ri continued his questioning of Connaire through Padraig and, between bites, Connaire replied.

"Why do you wander through our lands alone? Do you have no family, no people?"

Connaire considered not replying. No, to be truthful in disgrace was necessary. "I have left my clann because I caused the death of the taoiseach. I can never return. I have no one now. I am alone."

"Where will you go?"

"I do not know. But I must keep traveling."

The ri studied him. "I like you. You have great courage, even enough to be truthful when you speak to me. No man would lie about being the cause of his own taoiseach's death. I will give you food and a horse to help you on your way." Then he laughed. "And clothing that will fit you."

Connaire stopped eating in mid-bite. How could his fortune have suddenly changed so much for the better? "I thank you for your kindness and your hospitality. I do not know how I can ever repay you."

Brude cocked his head to one side. "I know you are from Dál Riata. Do not return there. I have battled with them often. We even slew Gabran, the uncle of their ri, in a battle some time ago. We will battle again and I would hate to have to kill such an honorable warrior as you."

"I am not as honorable as you think." Connaire sadly shook his head. "I wish that I were. Although I intend never to return to the lands of my clann, I know not where the gods and my fate may take me. I can make no oath in that matter."

"I can respect that." Brude studied him. "But if we do meet in battle, remember this day."

"I will. That I can swear."

Just before sunrise the next morning, as Connaire was rising, Padraig hurried into his lodgings. By the light of a candle the brother held, Connaire saw he carried fresh clothes, as promised by Brude. Padraig looked anxiously to the door, wiping sweat from the side of his round face.

"Make haste and dress quickly. You must leave immediately, slip out the gate and flee. You are in great danger. Drust wants to take you to the drowning pool."

Connaire yawned and stretched. "The drowning pool? What is that?"

"It is where the Fortriu take those they execute. It is in a sacred cavern not far away, a dark pool where they drown them."

Connaire sat up. "But do I not have the protection of the Ri? Does his word carry no weight with his warriors?"

"Only as long as his warriors accept his command." The stout brother was breathing rapidly. "We just heard of a raid that happened last evening, a raid by Conall's men. It is a violation of the truce between the Fortriu and Dál Riata, a truce I witnessed. You are of Dál Riata. Brude will protect you if he can, but he will not kill his own men to do so."

"If he will not honor his word, no matter what the cost, then he is without honor." Connaire spat on the ground.

Padraig placed a hand on Connaire's shoulder. "For any ri, duty sometimes comes before honor. But do not judge too harshly. There may be a time when you find difficult choices make you do things which you wish you did not do."

Remembrance of how he had betrayed his brother, how he had fled his clann rather than fulfill his oath to his brother, cut into him like the sharp edge of a sword and he winced. "Yes, I have no right to make such a judgment." He began to dress quickly in the dim light. "I am grateful that you sneaked in to bring me clothes and warn me. I hope you know of some way out of here. I have never seen such a huge, formidable place."

"Brude will shortly send for the guard at the sunrise gate. It is raining, so the guard will be glad for the chance to escape the storm. Just as the sky begins to lighten, you can escape. I have tethered a horse behind a large boulder between two alders at the bottom of the hill."

Connaire was taken aback. "Brude is helping me escape?"

Padraig smiled. "He is keeping his word as far as he can. There is risk in this for him, but for some reason he has taken a liking to you. Take this." He handed Connaire the sword Drust had taken from him. "And go with God."

"Thank you, Brother. You have been a great friend."

Padraig shoved him out the door. "Time for chatter is gone. Hurry."

A heavy rain fell, driving any people or dogs that might be about to shelter. The drumming of the rain muffled the sound of his steps as Connaire wove his way among the scattered buildings. The first muted glimmer of the dawn was barely visible through the dark clouds as he headed toward the gate. He hoped Padraig's god was with him as well as all the gods of his ancestors. He could use all the help he could get.

Chapter 46

A steady drizzle sifted through the leaves of the large oaks that towered above Connaire. He wished he could find shelter rather than standing motionless, his back pressed against the rough trunk, but the men riding past not far away made that impossible. They were out of sight, but he heard them talking loudly and their dogs barking. His bratt was wrapped over his horse's eyes and he gently stroked its muzzle to sooth the animal.

"Easy now, Bús Deataigh," he whispered to his horse. "We would not want these fellows to find us."

There had been distant thunder and lightning not long before and he feared that his mount would betray his hiding if it occurred again.

Although his escape had gone well, he had soon been pursued. At first, he had put some distance between himself and his pursuers, riding Bús Deataigh, his Cloud of Smoke. The black mare had been swift and unseen by their pursuers, inspiring Connaire to give her that name. But two days ago she had stepped on a sharp stone and bruised her sole. To ride her any farther might permanently lame her, so Connaire had been forced to walk Bús Deataigh to give the bruise a chance to heal. It had slowed him greatly and allowed those who followed to close the gap. He could have left his horse behind and struck out on foot, probably making better time, but the abandoned horse would have betrayed his route and the fact that he was on foot. Besides, as soon as his mount recovered he would be able to travel much faster. His leg, still not fully recovered from the break, ached as he pressed ahead.

Since his flight from the fort, it had rained steadily, sometimes a drizzle and other times a downpour, making him miserable. Footing on the mud and wet rocks was treacherous, made worse by his limp. The only good Connaire saw in the weather was that it washed way his tracks. Although those following him had dogs, he knew they could not catch his scent in the rain, making any noise he might accidentally make his main enemy. He must move stealthily or be caught. And make sure Bús Deataigh made no noise as well.

When he no longer heard the voices and barks, Connaire pulled his bratt off his horse's face and continued his trek toward the setting sun, but adjusted his route to keep far away from those he had just heard on his trail. Using the bratt to shield his head from the unceasing rain helped some, but the wool's natural water-shedding ability had been overtaxed. Padraig had given him one of the Fortriu sleeved cloaks as well, but it, too, was soaked and cold, chilling him. He wished he could build a fire to warm and dry himself, but dared not.

The terrain was rugged and inhospitable, with steep, craggy mountains above thick forests and raging streams. Connaire stayed to the forests, using them for cover if he needed to hide. At times that took him far off course. As the sun set and the evening sky darkened behind its gray clouds, Connaire looked for some shelter.

In the distance he heard the howling of a wolf and unsheathed his sword. Bús Deataigh pulled skittishly against the reins he held firmly in hand, her eyes wide. Another reason to keep his horse. Even lame, she would warn him if wolves approached while he slept.

As the starless night fell, Connaire took shelter in a cleft between two rocks that had a slight overhang. He hobbled Bús Deataigh and pulled his meager meal from a satchel slung across her back. Again he thanked the gods for Padraig, who had left provisions with the waiting horse. He had consumed the dried meat and cheese in the first three days and for the last three had subsisted on oat cakes wrapped in waxed cloth in an ineffective attempt to keep them dry. At least finding drinking water had not been a problem. When he finished, he huddled as far under the overhang as possible and wrapped his bratt tightly around him. Sleeping on cold, wet rock would normally be almost impossible, but Connaire was so exhausted that he soon drifted into dreamless sleep.

With a start, Connaire awoke. There was a light. Sunlight. Even though the sun had not yet crested the mountains, its light painted the scattered clouds with oranges and reds. Rime crusted the ground and his bratt. As he brushed back his hair, he found it there as well. He stood and shook his bratt, trying to get rid of some of the rain it had absorbed. At least the night had not been cold enough to freeze it around him. Wrapping it around himself again before all the warmth from his body was gone from the wool, he walked slowly over to his horse. He freed her from the hobble and allowed her to graze on the meager grass while he sat on a rock and chewed on an oat cake.

With little more than one cake left, Connaire knew his situation was dire. The coast must be near, but then what? Would he find anyone there? If he did, would they be hostile? But what other choice was there? Turn and fight against a band of well-fed, angry warriors? No, he had to press on, to see if there might be some glimmer of hope when he reached the shore.

Rising slowly, his body aching from the night on the cold rock, Connaire limped to his horse and took its reins in hand. Unlike him, she seemed to be walking normally. Tomorrow he would ride. Too soon and Bús Deataigh could be lamed. Better to walk one more day. He was shivering, his teeth chattering. Setting as fast and steady a pace as his leg would allow, Connaire hoped the exertion would warm him. If not, at least it might kill him and end this misery.

By midday, his pace had slowed. As the day warmed a little, cold was less of a problem than pain and exhaustion. By following a rushing stream, he was able to avoid climbing any mountains as well as keep his course towards the sea. At least he hoped the stream would eventually get there. Keeping his head down, watching where he stepped, he worked his way along the rocky bank of the stream. When he looked up, he saw something in the distance down the glen. It looked like a stretch of sandy beach.

Stepping up the pace, he stumbled along the streamside toward his goal. As he got closer he realized that the beach was on the far side of the stream. Not only that, but another stream came into the one he was following just ahead, making it bigger and deeper. He would have to cross it there if he were to reach the beach.

The water did not appear deep, maybe thigh high, but fast-moving and cold. The rocky bottom would likely be slick. He would have to be very careful not to lose his footing. Taking a deep breath, he stepped down into the water. As he carefully edged into the stream, he gasped from the shock of the near-freezing water. He tugged at Bús Deataigh's reins to have her follow, but she balked. Nervous of the rushing water, she pulled her head back and neighed. Although they had not been together long, Connaire had developed some rapport with her. Stroking her head, he spoke softly, coaxingly to her. Reluctantly, Bús Deataigh allowed herself to be led into the swift-moving stream.

As they neared the midpoint, Connaire stumbled on the slippery rocks. He tried to regain his footing, but the current was too strong. As his feet were knocked from under him by the churning water, he clung to the reins of his horse. She stood, legs straight, holding him from being swept downstream. Connaire tried to pull himself up with the reins, but found he did not have the strength. As the stream raged around him, he bobbed helplessly at the end of the reins like bait at the end of a fishing line. He gulped mouthfuls of water as he tried to breathe. The water tugged at him, pulling him from his lifeline. Its icy coldness was sapping his last vestiges of energy and numbing his hands. He did not know how much longer he could hold onto the reins. If he released his hold, the current would sweep him along to where the other stream converged, to be battered to death on the rocks or drown. But he was too weakened to regain his foothold.

Slowly, with great care, Bús Deataigh started toward the far shore of the stream, pulling Connaire along. A couple of times she faltered and Connaire feared that she would fall into the stream as well. Finally, they reached the far bank. Connaire crawled out of the water and collapsed. Bús Deataigh walked a short distance farther and found a patch of grass to graze.

Connaire lay on the rocky bank, gasping. Slowly some of his strength returned and he began to feel the chill of his wet clothes. He realized he would have to find someplace he could build a fire and get food or he might die from cold, weakness and fatigue. With great effort he got to his hands and knees, then stood. He staggered to his horse, clutching her around the neck to keep from falling. Reaching into the satchel, he found the last of the oat cakes. He broke off a piece and gave it to Bús Deataigh, then ate the rest. If he did not find refuge soon, half of an oak cake would not make any difference and she deserved a reward.

After a couple of failed attempts, he climbed onto the back of his horse. He rode down a rocky slope to the sandy beach. It was not the sea, however, because he could see there was an opposite shore. It was a large lake, larger than any he had ever seen or could even have imagined. But it was not the sea. Had he failed again?

Looking toward the far end of the beach he saw what appeared to be a stone wall. To see it from such a distance, it must be very wide and tall. People must be there. Whether they were friendly or not, he would ride to the wall.

He rode slowly. Although the stiff breeze along the lake painfully cut through his soaking wet clothes, he did not want to push Bús Deataigh too hard in case the injury had not healed and, in his condition, did not know if he could keep his seat at a faster pace. As he neared the wall, he realized it was an enclosure of stone, like an enormous, roofless round house. It must be the height of five or six men and more than twenty paces wide. Although he had seen low walls of stacked stone, the size and precision of the stacking of these stones was beyond comprehension. He was so amazed by the marvelous structure ahead that he almost did not hear the danger behind.

It was the baying of the hounds that caught his attention. He turned to see at least a hand count of men in pursuit, galloping along the beach behind him. He kicked his horse's sides, heading for the stone building, if for no other reason than he did not wish to stand and die before he reached it. Bús Deataigh was true, putting her heart into the effort. He leaned low, his head close to his horse's ear, calling encouragement into her ear. Then her gait changed, becoming slower and uneven. Her leg had not fully recovered and the injury returned in the strain of the chase. Still she tried, giving the run her all. But when Connaire glanced back, he saw his enemies were closing in on him.

Suddenly Bús Deataigh stumbled, her front legs collapsing as she nosed into the sand. Connaire was thrown over her neck. He tried to roll with the fall, but landed hard and sprawled face down. As he lay on his stomach in the damp sand, he felt a sharp pain in his shoulder and his whole body ached. But he knew his pursuers would spear him where he lay if he did not stand. Slowly he got to his knees. One arm hurt so much that it was useless, but it was not his sword arm. Drawing his sword and using it as a staff, he stood to face his attackers. His vision was blurred, making it difficult to focus on them. Spitting sand and blood, he tried to hold his sword in the ready position, but the tip kept dropping to the ground. Bús Deataigh was thrashing about in the sand near him, neighing wildly and vainly attempting to rise.

The riders were almost upon him. He could see their spears raised for the kill. He was having trouble staying on his feet. In his condition he could not have taken one of the riders, much less the number that were in front of him. He knew he had no chance against them. Hopefully, death would be swift.

Connaire thought he heard a sharp noise, but he was so dazed that he could not be sure. Was it the twang of a bowstring? Then another. And one more. He realized the three lead riders had fallen from their saddles. Were those arrows in their throats? One of the remaining ones yelled and kept coming, but there was another twang and he fell from his horse. The last one turned to flee, but a final twang brought him down.

Through his mental haze, Connaire realized that archers must have saved him. He turned to see two of them. They looked like women. No, a woman and a lass. He tried to walk to them, but fell to his knees. His horse lay on her side nearby, exhausted, sides heaving and sweaty, eyes wide with pain and fright. He dropped his sword and reached toward her, trying to speak comfort to her, but only managed a croaking sound.

Then darkness came over him and he knew nothing.

Chapter 47

Smoke. He smelled smoke. With a groan, Connaire opened his eyes. Every bone in his body ached. He had no energy to rise. When he tried to move his arm, a pain shot through his shoulder and he moaned. Where was he?

He was inside a building, lying on a straw mattress and covered with heavy pelts. Although the light of a hearth fire in the center of the room was hazy, he could see the curved wall next to him was of stone. A black dog, the largest he had ever seen, was curled next to his bed. Turning to the fire, he saw one of the archers from the beach. She was the lass, the smaller one. When she saw him looking at her, she picked up a cup and walked to him. He realized he was very thirsty.

She knelt beside him and lifted his head, putting the cup to his lips. Greedily, he gulped the water, barely pausing for a breath. She lowered his head to the bed and he lay panting. She placed a cool hand on his brow and smiled at him.

He tried to speak, but a coughing fit stopped him. After a moment he tried again. His voice was a hoarse croaking. "Who are you?"

She said nothing. Did she understand him? Did she speak in the tongue of the Fortriu? He tried to remember how they had spoken in the fort of Brude, but had not been there long enough to learn any words. The effort of that tired him. He closed his eyes to rest for a moment.

The next thing Connaire knew he felt as if he were lying in a fire. It was dark and the heat was oppressive. Desperately he struggled to throw off the furs on top of him. They weighed upon him like a stone. Try as he might, he could not get them off and the heat beneath them rose so that he felt he was being roasted alive.

Frantically, he fought the covers until he finally threw them off of the bed. He lay, gasping for breath in the welcome cold air.

Suddenly he felt a hand on his chest. From the dim light of the dying embers of the hearth fire, he could see two dark forms. A hand rested on his brow. Its coolness gave some relief. Then he heard a voice, female but strong.

"You have a bad fever, worse than before. Brid, get him some water."

One of the shadows left, but soon returned. He felt his head lifted and a cup at his lips. Cold water. He drank it all. Then he sank back onto the bed.

"Brid will stay with you and cool your fever with a damp cloth."

Soon he felt the relief of a cool, wet cloth on his brow. He closed his eyes.

It was cold. Connaire opened his eyes. It was still dark, with only faint outlines visible from the dying embers of the hearth fire. He was shivering. His bed was damp, soaked with sweat. How long had he been asleep? Vaguely, he remembered waking, feverish and sweating. Sometimes it had been light, other times not. How many times had he awakened? He remembered someone always had been there when he did. The dog? Yes, but also the lass. She had given him water, cooling water. And broth. Yes, beef broth. Where was she?

Connaire tried to rise. He had no strength. He fell back on the bed and pain stabbed his shoulder like a dagger, causing him to cry out. In an instant, someone was at his side, hand on his brow. He could not see anything but a dark shape, a shadow, but he knew who it was. In the recesses of his unconscious memory, he recognized her touch. It was the lass.

"Brid? That's your name, is it not?"

She said nothing, gently caressing his brow.

He was violently shaking, his teeth chattering. "I am cold."

She was gone for a moment, but soon returned, threw off his sweat-soaked cover and replaced it with a warm, dry fur. Then she crawled next to him, her body giving him her heat through her thin garment. He sighed and relaxed in the comfort of her. Sleep came quickly.

It was light, or at least the hearth fire was burning brightly. Connaire was alone in his bed. Had she been a dream, a delusion born of his illness? No, she had been next to him. The child had been there for him through it all and had saved him with her very life's warmth.

Looking around, Connaire saw that, except for the massive dog curled beside his bed, he was alone. His bed lay in an alcove, which was one of several off of the central room. The stone wall next to him rose higher than a man to a rough-hewn plank ceiling over the alcove, with wooden walls on two sides. He estimated the far wall to be three handcounts of paces from the one by him. He could not see the ceiling of the central room and the smoke from the hearth fire in the middle of it rose unobstructed. What sort of house was this? It was nothing like the round houses of Eireann with their wattle and daub walls and conical thatch roofs.

Connaire wanted to see more of this strange house. He tossed off the woolen blanket that covered him, swinging his legs over the side of the bed. As he tried to rise, the pain in his shoulder caused him to double over and he sat back on the bed with a low grunt. The dog by his bed rose and looked at him curiously. His back was as high as a man's waist and looked as heavy as one. Then he sat by Connaire's bed and rested his massive head with drooping jowls on Connaire's chest, staring at him with sad, pleading eyes.   Using his good arm, Connaire rubbed him behind the ears.

"So you are awake."

The voice came from another, hidden alcove.   He heard footsteps and a woman slowly walked into sight.   At first she reminded him of Aislinn and Maille, warrior women whose bodies were conditioned by training and exercise, but there was a difference.   She was older, taller, more powerful and her face was harder, colder.   In some ways, she seemed to be the female version of Cathal, but a Cathal without mercy.   Her clothes were those of a warrior: trews, a short léine and a tight vest that accentuated her ample breasts.   Her long, brown hair with streaks of gray hung loose around her angular face.   Her expression was neutral, neither hostile not friendly.

"You have caused me problems, my young refugee.   We had to kill those who pursued you.   All of them.   And bury them before any of their companions heard of it.   I live in uneasy peace with the Fortriu.   Now I have killed a handcount of their warriors. What did you do to them?"

Connaire realized he was naked and cleared his throat.   He wished he had some water.

"I killed one of them when he attacked me without reason. I thank you for your help and am sorry to have been of so much trouble.   If I might borrow some clothes I will leave now so that I am of no further bother."

As he said that, Connaire rolled off of the bed, onto his knees, and rose shakily to his feet, grabbing the blanket from the bed as a makeshift garment.   As pain in his shoulder struck him, he dropped the blanket, leaving himself completely exposed.   The woman looked at him with her head cocked to one side and smiled.

"You have grit, I will say that. What is wrong with your arm?"

Connaire grimaced. "I do not know. I cannot use it after I fell from Bús Dea-- my horse."

The woman took his arm in one hand and prodded his shoulder with the other. "Your shoulder has been pulled from its socket. I will repair it."

"How is she? My horse, I mean."

"Your horse is dead. I had to kill it. Broken leg."

Tears formed at the corners of Connaire's eyes. It was just the prodding, he told himself.

She paused, glancing down at the dog that was sitting close to the young warrior. "I mourn your horse with you. You seem to have a way with animals. Even Cú Chulainn likes you, and he normally does not like men."

"Your dog has the name of a hero?"

"I am going to fix your shoulder. Sit on the bed and drink this." She handed him a cup of golden liquid.

Connaire sank to the bed and took a swig from the cup. He gagged, spitting it back into the cup. It was mead, strong mead.

"Drink it all. You will need it."

Connaire emptied the cup.

She placed his injured arm tight along his body, then bent it at the elbow.

"Keep your upper arm close to you and do not fight me."

She grasped his wrist and turned his forearm until it rested on his chest, then slowly rotated his forearm away from his body until it pulled painfully.

Connaire gritted his teeth, determined not to cry out. When she brought his arm back to his chest and again rotated it out from his body, it brought tears to his eyes, but he remained silent.

Suddenly there was a popping sound and the pain eased. Connaire breathed a sigh of relief.

A flicker of a smile crept across her lips, but quickly faded. "Done."

Connaire flexed his fingers and moved his arm. The pain was almost gone. He started to rise from the bed, but felt faint and sat back down. Then he tried again, rising more slowly, and was able to stand, albeit shakily. Clutching the blanket around him, he faced the woman who stood in front of him. He smiled at her, but she did not return the gesture.

Taking a deep breath, he unflinchingly held her gaze. "You have restored my arm. I am grateful. I do thank you for all you have done and, as I said before, I am sorry to have been such a bother. If I might rest a little while to regain my strength and borrow some clothes, I will leave before I cause you any more trouble. But I would like to know who it is to whom I owe my very life."

She gave a short laugh. "I am Scáthach. I would gladly let you leave but as long as I can do this-" She shoved his chest, sharply but not with great force, and he fell back onto the bed. "You would not make it far from here and my daughter would drag you back like the cur that is licking your hand. She has a fondness for wounded animals."

The dog had gone to him when he had fallen onto the bed and was washing Connaire's hand with his tongue. Connaire patted his head and looked up to the woman who called herself Scáthach.

"You have a dog named for one of Eire's greatest warriors and claim the name of the woman who trained him? Why?"

"Because I am descended from them both. The *Táin bó Cúailnge* tells of Cú Chulainn and his son by Aife, but not of his daughter with Scáthach. It is from her womb that I find my ancestors." She studied him a moment with a raised eyebrow. "But that is not important now. You are hungry."

It was not a question, but a statement of fact. Connaire realized he was not just hungry, but famished. He nodded.

"My daughter has prepared a beef stew for you. Stay there while I get you a bowl." She gave a short chuckle, obviously knowing he was not able to leave, and walked away.

Exhausted, Connaire fell back on the bed. Although the sharp pain in his shoulder was gone, every other part of his body ached. Cú Chulainn sat by him and licked his cheek. Connaire did not have the energy to stop the dog's tongue-bath. He closed his eyes to rest for a moment.

When he opened his eyes, Connaire sensed that time had passed. Although where he lay looked much the same, the fire seemed different, burning more brightly. The dog was curled beside the bed, asleep. His thirst and his hunger were dominant.

He swung his legs off the bed and a rose to a sitting position. Everything spun in front of him and it was all he could do to not fall back. Slowly, the spinning stopped and he cautiously rose to his feet. He took a few faltering steps, leaning against the wooden wall for support. Then he stepped on Cú Chulainn's tail.

With a yelp, the dog sprang to his feet, bumping into Connaire. Falling backward, he sat down hard on the bed. As he did, his arm struck a small table that had been placed by his bed, knocking it over. A large, wooden bowl of savory-smelling stew spilled on the ground. The hound forgot his injured tail and began lapping the stew.

Connaire looked up to see Scáthach grimly standing by the divider wall, arms folded across her chest. "You certainly are trouble." Then a trace of a smile crossed her lips. "But if you are quick, you might get some of the stew before Cú Chulainn finishes it."

Connaire eyed the hound, who was ravenously attacking the stew on the floor with his tongue. He almost was hungry enough to contest the dog's right to it. "I would, but I don't think I could best Cú Chulainn in my present condition."

Scáthach laughed. "Even your best would not be good enough. I have seen Cú Chulainn take down a full-antlered stag by himself and hold off a pack of determined wolves that wanted the meat until we could reach him. We had to shoot several before they would leave. Let Cú Chulainn have his fill. Brid is getting you another bowl, anyway."

Within moments, the lass appeared around the corner with a steaming bowl of stew. The hound had finished the spilled bowl and eyed the fresh batch as he licked his chops. Brid whistled sharply and Cú Chulainn meekly curled at Connaire's feet. She sat on the bed and handed the warrior the bowl with a couple of oat cakes.

Connaire greedily scooped the stew into his mouth with the oat cakes, quickly consuming all that was in the bowl. While he ate, Brid gently daubed the scrapes and cuts on his face with an ointment from a small jar, managing to do so in spite of the fact that he never slowed his eating while she did. After he finished the stew, she took each of his hands in turn and applied the ointment to their wounds.

Connaire smiled at her and took one of her hands in his. "Thank you. You are very kind and a fine healer."

She returned his smile, then she took his bowl and silently left. Connaire followed her with his eyes. Then he turned to Scáthach.

"She does not say much. Is she shy?"

"Brid cannot speak.   I do not know why.   She can hear and commands animals like Cú Chulainn and her horse with a whistle or a look."   Scáthach shook her head.   "She lets her wishes known to them better than I can with words."

The lass returned with a waterskin, which she quickly handed to Connaire.   Turning to her mother, she made several quick movements with her hands.   Scáthach sighed.

"It seems the troubles you cause continue.   Several Fortriu warriors are approaching."

Connaire struggled to his feet.   "I will meet them.   You have saved my life and I do appreciate it, but you have no need to do more."

The woman stepped closer and gave Connaire a quick shove, knocking him back on the bed.   "You are too weak to even walk out to meet them.   I will convince them we have not seen you.   They fear me enough not to question me too closely.   Besides, Brid would not allow you to die at their hands."   She rolled her eyes.   "As I said, she gets attached to strays.   That is how we acquired Cú Chulainn."

The two women left, accompanied by the hound.   Connaire tried to rise, but found he did not have enough strength left to even stand.   Resting his forehead in his hands, he silently pleaded with the gods, including Colm Cille's, to not allow any more lives to be lost because of him.

Chapter 48

After a short time, there were voices below, those of Scáthach and at least two men. Connaire could not understand what they were saying, words that sounded like those he had heard in Brude's fort. He looked around for his sword, but could not see it. With great difficulty, he managed to rise, leaning against the wooden divider. Slowly, he staggered a few steps toward the center of the house, using the wall to keep from falling. He must find his sword.

Suddenly Brid came around the divider. She rushed to his side, taking his arm to support him. She put a finger to his lips, signaling him to silence. After she had guided him back to the bed, she pulled the fur cover from it and laid it underneath. She motioned for him to get under the bed and lie on the fur. With her help, Connaire crawled into the low space. Then she placed a woolen blanket over the bed so that it hid him, leaving a little gap for him to be able to watch the room. She left for a moment, but then returned and shoved the rest of his clothes and his dagger to him.

Brid whistled sharply and Cú Chulainn trotted into Connaire's room. She made some hand gestures to the hound, who came over to the bed and lay down by the bed. He nosed under the blanket, licking Connaire's face before three sharp whistles of different pitches from Brid commanded the dog's attention. Cú Chulainn lay in front of the blanket, watching the hearth.

Brid walked to the end of the divider and leaned against the wall where Connaire's quarters opened to the central hearth. Then Connaire saw his sword was propped against the wall behind Brid. She must have placed it there, close at hand.

The voices grew louder and approached the hearth. There were two, no three. Wait, there were a full handcount of warriors.

A couple of them had swords, the others had war axes slung across their backs. Two of the axemen were wearing trews with no léine. They were powerful-looking men with strange designs covering their bodies, like those he had seen on the arms of some of the men with Brude.

Scáthach came into Connaire's view. She carried a jug and cups, which she distributed to the men and filled from the jug. Then they all sat on their haunches, talking in the strange tongue. With feigned nonchalance, one man rose and strolled around the house. From his hiding place, Connaire could see the man looking around. He disappeared from view and shortly Connaire heard his tread above him. He realized that there must be another area above the ceiling as well as below the floor.

Another man rose and strolled around the house. Brid's hand slowly crept toward his sword a couple of times, then pulled back. He gripped his dagger, determined to somehow rush to her aid if she were attacked. But after a while, the roamers returned to the hearth. The other men drained their cups and rose. After speaking to Scáthach, they nodded to Brid and they left.

Connaire started to crawl from under the bed, but he saw Brid motion for him to stay. After but a moment, one of the warriors with the markings returned. He went to the hearth, stooping to pick up something. As he did, he slowly glanced around the room. Connaire felt as though he was peering under the bed, directly at him. When the warrior stood, he sauntered towards Brid, smiling and saying something. Her hand edged toward the sword, but Cú Chulainn's growl halted the man in his tracks. The large hound stood and inched forward, head lowered and stiff-legged. The low rumbling in his throat grew louder.

The man reached for the axe slung on his back. Scáthach grabbed his wrist from behind and said something Connaire could not understand. Then she said a few more words.

For a moment they stood there. The warrior turned his head to look at Scáthach. He spoke and she released his wrist. He eyed her coldly for a moment, then turned and left.

Brid quickly came to Connaire's bed and lifted the blanket. She helped him crawl from under it and climb into bed. As soon as he was lying down, Cú Chulainn started to lick his face.

Scáthach sighed. "You seem to have won over my household. I will let you stay while your conquests nurse you to health."

Connaire pushed the hound's face away. "What did they say? They seemed suspicious."

"They asked me if I had seen you, if you had killed their friends." She gave a short laugh. "I told them that I had seen no man kill their companions."

Connaire laughed at the ruse. "That is no lie, but did they suspect the truth?"

"I am sure they felt something was amiss." She smirked. "But they knew better than to claim that I lied. So I sent Brid to hide you, then I invited them inside so that they could look around."

"How did you tell her to hide me without them hearing?"

"I will show you."

Scáthach made several odd gestures with her hand. Brid made some with hers. Scáthach laughed. "I asked Brid if you were any trouble. She said you were standing when she found you, but as weak as a baby. And just as easy to handle."

Connaire reddened. "I am not fully recovered, but I was ready to come to your aid if the Fortriu had made trouble."

This time Scáthach's laugh was a roar. It continued so long that tears ran down her cheeks. Brid was trying not to laugh, but was having trouble not doing so.

Connaire was insulted. He wanted to stand and walk out of the house, but feared falling on his face. "I am a warrior. Perhaps I might not be at my best right now, but with a handcount of them against two women, or a woman and a lass, my help in a fight would matter."

Brid sat on his bed and gently touched his cheek. He could see in her face that she was sorry for the slight from her mother.

"Boy, how old are you?"

Connaire turned to Scáthach. "I am no boy. Next Samhain will be three handcounts plus three for me."

"By then, Brid will have seen four handcounts."

Connaire vaguely recalled when she had lain close to him to keep him warm, the feel of her breasts against his back. Small and firm, with nipples that pressed into his skin. In his delirium, he had almost forgotten. "Even so, two women against a handcount of strong warriors?"

Scáthach frowned. "Do not misjudge us. Those warriors were no match for the two of us. In fact, not for either of us alone. And they knew it. That is why they pretended to believe I had not seen you. That and the hound. When I told the last warrior that Cú Chulainn hated all men, he believed me." She shrugged. "Until you fell into our lives, that was true."

"What if they had found me? I suppose you will say that they would have ignored me because of their great fear of you?" Connaire knew his voice betrayed his disbelief, but did not care. It was insult for insult.

"No, they would have died bravely." She turned and started to walk away. "And Brid would have had to clean the floors. After all, you are her charge and I make her clean up the mess after her pets."

Before Scáthach could leave, Brid had flown from the bed and grabbed her arm. She spun the bigger woman around and made gesture with her hands so rapidly they seemed a blur to Connaire. Scáthach must have understood because her hands were moving almost as fast. After a few moments, Scáthach sighed and nodded. She turned to Connaire,

"My daughter wishes me to train you as a warrior. I have agreed to do so after you have regained your strength."

Connaire was offended that she thought him not a trained warrior. "What if I do not want your training?"

"Then you are a fool. If you think those five would have feared you any more than those Brid and I killed on the beach to save you, then you do not need me." She crossed her arms, staring at him. "Decide now, for I have little patience with fools."

Connaire considered her offer. His pride urged him to reject it. What did he need to learn from this woman? But his pride had cost Cathal his life. Then he saw the pleading in Brid's eyes. Staying a while longer might not be so bad.

"I accept your offer. I thank you for it." He smiled. "And I will try to heal quickly so I can begin my lessons."

"Good. The faster we start, the sooner we can finish and you can leave."

Brid pulled her arm and scowled at her.

Scáthach grimaced. "And I apologize for comparing you to a pet." Then she turned and, as she walked away, muttering a bit too loudly, "It was an insult to Cú Chulainn."

Brid stamped her foot, but let her mother leave. Then she returned to Connaire's side and sat on the bed. She reached over and gently stroked his cheek.

Connaire rested his hand on hers and looked into her eyes. "You have been very kind. I do appreciate it."

He realized he was feeling more than gratitude. Knowing that she was not a lass, but a woman, an elfin woman, changed how he viewed her. He realized that she was desirable, that he was attracted to her, that he wanted her.

She leaned over him and their lips met. He wrapped his hand behind her neck and caressed it. It felt so wonderful that he almost wept. Then he remembered and he pulled away.

"I . . . I cannot . . . ." He saw the hurt in her eyes. And it pained him to see it. "I am promised to another and cannot." He fought back tears of frustration, of sadness. "She hates me, but I have promised to oath with her. I cannot break that promise. I have already caused so much pain. I do not ask you to understand. I do not know if I do. But it must be."

Brid smiled sadly at him, a tear escaping the edge of her eye. Then she placed a kiss on his forehead and left.

Connaire lay, staring at the wood ceiling, mentally cursing the whims of fate that had finally brought him a woman who he could love and might even love him, only to be denied.

Chapter 49

Connaire awakened with a jolt. As had been the pattern for the last few weeks, Scáthach's rough shaking had ripped him from his dreams. She was gone before he was fully awake, leaving him to struggle from his bed alone. It was cold and dark. He yawned and swung his legs over the side of the bed. Cú Chulainn grunted as his heel bumped the dog's ribs, but did not move from his curled rest.

With a shake of his head, Connaire began to dress. How long had he been there? It must be halfway between Samhain and Imbolc, the time of the shortest days of the year. Definitely the coldest, he decided as he shivered through dressing.

Grabbing the wooden sword Scáthach had given him as soon as he could walk again, Connaire stumbled out of his sleeping quarters, heading toward the stairs. He saw that Brid was tending the fire, feeding kindling to the glowing embers. By the time he and Scáthach returned, she would have oatmeal porridge bubbling in the cauldron. His stomach was growling already, but morning meal would have to wait until Scáthach had pounded him with her wooden sword for a while.

Brid looked up at him and smiled at him in the dim firelight, as she did every morning since his training had begun. He smiled in return. Could she see in his eyes that he ached for her? Probably not. With a sad shake of his head, he turned and walked to the staircase.

It had been a surprise to Connaire to find that this house, called a broch, had two stone walls, one inside the other. In the narrow space between them was a stone staircase. He had realized quickly that the partial roof above his sleeping quarters was also a floor of another level. Although his father's roundhouse had not had that, it was not unknown in Eireann. But the room below had been a surprise. He had never heard of a house with three levels. The creaky wood floor of his quarters was the ceiling of a room that stored goods and housed animals in the winter, which also had the only entry door for the house. This morning he was going to the top level, as he did every morning, for the first training of the day.

Scáthach was sitting on her haunches, chin resting on her practice sword, watching him as he stepped out of the staircase. Flickering torches lit the room.

"You are moving slowly, boy. Not sleep well?"

Connaire gave a short laugh. "As well as my bruised body would allow."

She shrugged. "Then stop my sword before it hits you." She stood and slowly swung her sword around her head, loosening her muscles. "Ready?"

Connaire went to ready position, his sword in front of him. As quickly as a ferret, she struck. Her sword came across at chest level and Connaire parried. Before she could swing again, Connaire attacked. She countered his sword's blow and came back at him, the arc of her sword aimed at his head. Connaire blocked it just before it met his skull. This back and forth action continued without a hit until the young warrior saw an opportunity.

Scáthach's guard had dropped momentarily after he had thwarted her latest attack. She had stepped back, her sword lowered slightly. Connaire lunged forward, his sword in motion. But before it could connect, her sword came up, striking his elbow. His arm went numb and he dropped his weapon. Then she struck him hard across his side, knocking the wind from him. He dropped to his knees, clutching his bruised side with his other arm.

As he knelt on the floor, gasping, he felt her gently tap his shoulder with her sword.

"You are doing better, but still fall for my traps. I wanted you to do what you did. In battle, you would be dead. Rest a moment and we will continue."

As he took slow, deep breaths with his eyes closed, Connaire focused on controlling the pain. Scáthach had taught him how to do so while he was still weak, in bed. She had told him to control the pain or it would control him. And she had been right. It still hurt, but it would not stop him. Taking one more deep breath, he opened his eyes and slowly rose.

Scáthach was again resting on her haunches, watching him. "Are you ready?"

Connaire nodded, bringing his sword to ready position.

Like an arrow from the bow, the warrior woman came at him. Again there was a furious exchange of blows, all parried, all answered in kind. Then, as Scáthach swung her sword, head high, at Connaire, he deflected it up. Before she could recover, Connaire angled his sword down, striking her in the ribs. She staggered back, but attempted a counter blow with a wide arc down towards Connaire's side. He easily deflected it and again angled his wooden blade toward her. This time he struck her hip. Her leg collapsed and she fell on her side with a groan.

For a moment Connaire felt the exhilaration of victory. He had finally landed his first blow. No first two blows. And the mighty Scáthach was down. Then he saw her struggling to her feet, a woman old enough to be his own mother that he had knocked to the ground. He dropped his sword and grabbed her arm.

Scáthach shook off his help, her face twisted in anger and in pain. "You were lucky. Do not think that makes you better than I at swordplay." Then she paused. The pain was still in her face, but the anger lessened. "I should not have said that. No, you were not lucky. You did well."

"I . . . I did not mean to hurt you."

Anger returned to her eyes. "Then you are a fool. I meant to hurt you. Never worry about hurting your opponent, whoever it may be. Always fight to win, to kill if it is actual combat. Otherwise stick to herding cattle." She turned and limped towards the stairs. "Brid will have morning meal ready. I am hungry. You must be as well. You have earned your meal this morning. Come."

As he watched her, Connaire fought the urge to run to her and help her walk. Then he smiled. He had realized earlier that he loved Scáthach, not as a lover but as a mother. Like the mother he had never known. Now he realized that she had some affection for him, too.

After following Scáthach down the darkened staircase to the living area, Connaire wanted to help her. Even in the faint light, he could see she was having trouble walking. Had he struck her that hard? But when they reached the level ground of the main floor, she seemed to recover, walking with but a slight limp. As they approached the cooking fire, Brid looked up. Seeing her mother's gait, she raised a questioning eyebrow.

Scáthach sat carefully on a nearby bench. With a low sigh, she closed her eyes. "He is finally becoming a warrior, daughter. He had his first hit this morning. Two, in fact. Reward him with an extra serving of porridge."

Connaire glanced at Brid, not knowing what to say. He had hurt her mother. "I am sorry. I did not mean--"

"Stop!" Scáthach pulled herself to her feet. "If you wish to be a warrior, act like one."

She grabbed a steaming bowl from Brid's hands and hobbled to her sleeping area. Brid ladled another bowl of porridge from the pot and handed it to Connaire. As he took it, her hand gently glided over his.   He pretended not to notice, but a tingling lingered.   He kept his eyes on his bowl, afraid what he might betray if he looked at her.

Scáthach's voice interrupted.   "When you both have finished your porridge and pawing each other, Brid, take him outside and teach him how to use a bow properly.   If he keeps apologizing when he makes a decent strike with his sword, it may be his only hope."

Chapter 50

A freezing wind cut across Connaire's face as he struggled through the knee-deep snow. The light dimmed as the afternoon sun was setting, although hidden behind the storm clouds. By narrowing his eyes to mere slits, he kept the sleety snow out of them, but his cheeks and lips were exposed to the winter's blast. His armload of firewood prevented him from pulling his cloak up to block the wind. Lately he had stopped scraping off his beard with a sharpened shell, finding the facial hair gave some protection, but not enough. He glanced back at Brid, struggling behind him with her arms full of split logs. He was amazed at the strength she carried in her small frame. Then another gust of frigid wind forced him to concentrate on keeping his footing on the snow-covered path to the stone tower.

As soon as he got into the shelter of the lower level of the tower, he dropped his load and turned to help Brid. But she was only a few steps behind him and was inside before he could act. She dropped her load of wood by his and rubbed her hands together. Connaire closed the door, barring it against the chilling gusts. That had been the last load of the wood that Scáthach's tenants had delivered to the short wall that surrounded the tower. Now they could regain some of the warmth they had lost in their task.

Connaire took Brid's hands in his, massaging them back to life. Brid looked up at him and smiled. He felt his hands begin to heat as well, but was not sure if it was from the rubbing. She reached up and gently touched his cheek, now covered by a winter's beard.

One of the sheep kept in the lower quarters of the tower during the winter months nudged Connaire's leg, pushing between Brid and him. She was the only black sheep in the small flock and was named Dubh for that reason. She also had a peculiarly obsessive fondness for Connaire. The ewe seemed to sense the feelings between Brid and him and was determined to keep them apart.

Brid laughed. She made hand signs. Connaire had learned enough of them since he had arrived to understand what she was saying. *Your lover wants you.*

He reached down and patted Dubh's bulging side.

"Another has already been there," he told Brid. He glanced at the ram who was eyeing him suspiciously. "And I think I know who."

Brid laughed again. It was a pleasing sound.

From the floor above came Scáthach's voice, her words with a slight slur from mead. "The fire will die before you bring up the wood. It would be a poor way to honor Imbolc on this festival night."

With a shrug and wry grin, Brid pulled away and loaded her arms with wood. Connaire followed suit and they both carefully climbed the irregular stone stairs to the next level.

Connaire and Brid dropped the firewood near the hearth. Scáthach was seated on a stool near it, a cup in one hand. Her other arm was strapped to her body by strips of cloth. A jug of mead was set close by. Steam from a cauldron bubbling over the fire filled the air with the savory smell of mutton stew.

Brid went to the pot and stirred the contents with a wooden spoon. She sampled it, frowning. She picked up a small pot of herbs and added some, stirring them in the mixture.

Scáthach belched, then laughed and waved her cup. "I have started the feast without you two. I was afraid you might be humping in the animal shelter below. After all, it is Brid's festival. The goddess Brid, I mean, not my daughter." She took a deep drink from her cup before continuing. "My daughter's name is really Scáthach too, you know. Scáthach nic Scáthach: Scáthach the daughter of Scáthach."

Connaire was taken aback. "But you always call her Brid."

She shrugged. "I started doing it when she showed her talent as a healer. Brid is the goddess of healing, so I called her that as a joke. Since she liked it, now that is what I call her." Her look darkened. "But you have no right to do so. You should call her Scáthach."

Connaire bridled at her tone. It was not up to her. "I will call your daughter by what name she wishes, not what you wish."

Scáthach rose unsteadily to her feet. She staggered sideways and Connaire caught her. Angrily, she pulled away, almost falling before Brid steadied her. She glared at Connaire, drinking again from her cup, spilling some mead on the front of her léine as she did. When she spoke, she was having trouble with her words, speaking slowly and indistinctly.

"You would not speak to me so if I had not injured my arm on the stairs, you scurrilous whelp. Just because I had a little mead and fell down the steps, you think you can speak to me however you wish. You are like Brid's father. Worthless and unfaithful. You will hurt her like he did me."

Her words stung. There was truth in them. He had walked away from his duty, from his oath, from his promise. He had betrayed his brother and his clann. He turned away and started toward his sleeping quarters. Brid grabbed his arm, pulling him back. Her mother continued her rant.

"Do you know what happened to her father, that handsome bastard who was going to leave me after humping me? Leave me and his own daughter."

Brid's grip tightened on Connaire's arm, silently begging him not to say anything. Scáthach lifted the cup to her lips, but found it empty and turned it upside down. Then she sat awkwardly on the stool and grabbed the jug of mead, overfilling her cup. Mead sloshed over the floor, leaving a damp stain on the straw covering the wood. She took a swig, then set the cup on the floor with exaggerated care and rubbed her eyes before continuing.

"I killed him. I stuck him with my sword like I would a wild boar. I spilled his stinking guts on the ground."

She began to weep. With tears streaming down her cheeks, she uttered a low moan. "I killed him. I had to do it."

Brid came to Scáthach's side, pulling her mother's head to her breast. Scáthach clutched her daughter to her with her good arm, burying her head in her stomach as she sobbed. After a time, the sobs quieted. Scáthach's breathing was slow and deep. She was asleep.

With her hand motions, Brid let Connaire know that she needed him to help. They carried Scáthach to her sleeping quarters and laid her in her bed. Tenderly, Brid covered her mother and brushed her hair from her face. Then she took Connaire's hand and led him back to the hearth.

After Brid had dished him a bowl of stew and they were silently eating, Connaire's mind drifted to remembrances of past Imbolcs, of when the clann had feasted in the hope of an early spring and an end of winter. In Eireann, the winters had not been as cold and severe as here, but the promise of spring was always welcome. What was his clann doing on this Imbolc? Were they still together?

With a jolt, Connaire felt Brid's hand on his. He realized he had been far off and she had known it. Her eyes were studying him, trying to read his thoughts. He smiled and patted her hand.

After a moment, she smiled in return. She took the empty stew bowl from his hand and gave him a cup of mead.

Connaire had some questions. He knew enough of the Brid's language of the hands and of gestures to ask them.

Did your mother kill your father?

Yes. She has said so many times.

Did you see it happen?

No. I was a baby.

She seems sad about it.

Brid slowly nodded her head. *She is. She loved him. Her temper is strong. When she drinks too much mead, she cannot control it. Then she is always sorry. But it is too late.*

They stayed by the fire for some time. Occasionally, they would converse in the language of the hands, but mainly they were just together. After a time, the fire burned low and the chill of the night crept over them. Connaire stood and started toward his sleeping quarters. Brid walked with him.

Connaire sat on his bed and Brid sat next to him. She leaned her head against his shoulder and took his hand in both of hers. Gently she rested his hand on her thigh, covering it with hers. Connaire gently began to message the top of her leg, slowly moving higher. One of her hands slipped up his chest and along the back of his neck, pulling him close. Their lips met and their kiss was long and deep.

Tears welled in the corners of Connaire's eyes. This woman, the woman he had come to love in but a short time, he had betrayed before he ever knew her. He pulled away.

"I . . . I cannot. I have promised my brother, as he lay dying, that I would oath no one but his oath-mate after his death." He shook his head. "If I could go back and change it all, I would. But I caused my brother's death and it is my duty to obey his wish.

I ask that you accept this as I must.   It would be false to you to couple with you when I cannot oath with you."   He looked into her eyes.   "Forgive me.   You deserve a man who can give you his heart as well as his body."

He could see her sadness, but she managed a small smile. She held him tightly to her.   He wrapped his arms around her. They lay back on the bed and she tugged the coverings over them. They lay there together, clutching each other, until sleep took them.

Chapter 51

When she opened her eyes, Scáthach knew it was not going to be a good morning. Her vision was blurry and her head felt as though it were being trampled by horses. A herd of them.

She rolled off of her bed and shakily rose. The pain was worse. Good. It would remind her of the dangers of too much mead. But then she had had many such reminders. Maybe this one would work.

Clutching a blanket around her, Scáthach stumbled to the hearth fire. Some porridge was bubbling in the bottom of a pot set near the flickering blaze. She grabbed a bowl and ladled a healthy portion. One swallow of the oat porridge brought such nausea that she nearly retched.

She set the bowl on the floor. Better something to soothe the stomach first. As she reached for the jug of mead, she heard footsteps on the stairs. Quickly she picked up the bowl.

Brid came into the room. She smiled at Scáthach and spoke to her with her hands.

How are you?

Scáthach gave a dismissive wave. *I have been worse. Where is your friend?*

He is doing the routine you gave him: carrying a heavy stone as he walks along the wall.

Scáthach shrugged. *At least he does as he is told.*

Brid stamped her foot. *Mother, why do you torment him? He is a good man.*

No man is good. Our very line is from Cú Chulainn, who abandoned your ancestress.

As she knelt in front of her mother, there were tears in Brid's eyes. *You know I love you, but do not do this to me. I love him and I know he loves me. Do not turn him away.*

With a shake of her head, Scáthach shakily rose. *You know nothing of anything outside of our broch. I will not make him turn away. He will do so of his own will.*

Brid grabbed her hand, holding tightly as she spoke with her other one. *Then let him decide. Promise me that.*

He will. Trust me.

Perhaps. But until then, do not push him from us.

Scáthach shrugged. *If you wish. But do not say I did not warn you.*

Her mother tried to pull away, but Brid held tight to her hand. *Promise me. Give me your word that you will not force Connaire away.*

With a sigh, Scáthach nodded. *I promise that I will not try to force your Connaire away.*

Promise you will help me to win him.

Scáthach jerked her hand back. *That is foolish. He has other plans. He will never choose to stay here.*

Promise.

Rubbing her brow with her free hand, Scáthach considered. If she refused, she probably would lose her daughter. If she agreed, the young warrior might leave despite anything she did. But if he stayed, then her daughter would stay as well. Stay as long as she was alive. Perhaps Connaire might be persuaded to stay. To keep her daughter, she would endure him.

I promise. I will do everything I can do to keep your young man here with you.

Brid stood and embraced her mother. No words of the hands or spoken were needed. Her mother was good to her word.

Scáthach stared at the wall behind her daughter.

What have I done? He will hurt her. I know he will.

Then she slowly exhaled.

At least I will be here for her.

Connaire struggled to keep his footing on the low wall around the broch. The stone he carried seemed to grow in weight with every turn he made of the wall. He was glad that it was a low wall because more than once he had lost his balance and thrown the stone to one side as he fell on the other when his foot slipped on the icy stones. Yet he was able to last much longer now than he had in days before. He was more powerful and more agile. With a wry smile, he acknowledged to himself that the lessons were working. He was much stronger and a better warrior than ever before. Perhaps even Cathal's equal. If Cathal had still been alive.

With his mind on keeping his balance and his brother, Connaire was taken unawares when Brid touched the back of his leg. With a grunt, he flung the stone away and fell towards her, landing in the hard snow. As he lay there, she dropped on top of him, grinning impishly.

"You have ruined my training, you know."

She nodded.

"Your mother will be angry with me."

She shook her head.

"Yes she will." Then he sighed. "I do not think she likes me. If not for you, she would have turned me out long ago."

Brid touched her forefinger to his lips, indicating that she wished to speak with the hands. He had come to understand that often she preferred him to speak in the same manner as she did.

Your mother will be angry.

She shrugged. *I can handle my mother.*

He hesitated. *Why does she hate me?*

It is not you. I think she likes you very much. She fears losing me. And she does not trust you. She was hurt by my father. To her, you are he.

Gently he brushed back a wisp of hair that had fallen in front of her eyes. *You know that she has nothing to fear.*

With an angry shake of her head, she stood and turned away. Fighting snow and stiff muscles, he struggled to his feet. Brid walked hurriedly away, entering the broch's low door.

Connaire stood, watching her go. Mentally, he called to her.

I would do anything for you, Brid. I would gladly die for you. I love you. I just cannot make love to you.

When Scáthach saw Brid rush into the main room and into her sleeping area, she knew something was wrong. Should she go to her? Her mother had died when she was much younger than Brid, so she was not sure what a mother should do. I understand a sword much better than I do people, she thought. A sword is useful and consistent.

Until of late, Brid had been more like a sword. That young warrior was at fault. She would talk to Brid, then confront Connaire. He would either leave or die.

Brid was lying on her bed, staring at the ceiling. There were tears in her eyes.

"Are you alright?" Stupid question. Of course she was not.

Brid merely nodded.

"Did Connaire do something that hurt you?" Scáthach spat on the floor. "I will teach him that he does not insult a daughter of Scáthach."

Her daughter grabbed her hand. Her eyes were pleading. Then she released her mother and spoke the words of the hands. *He did nothing. It is I who hurt myself.*

How?

I love him. I know that he cannot return my love, but I still love him

Scáthach cocked her head. *He is the one who caused this.*

No. I did it. Brid gave her a hard look. *Do not harm him. If you do, you will lose me forever. Do you understand?*

I understand. Scáthach shrugged. *So be it.*

Brid turned away, facing the wall.

Scáthach stood, unsure what to do. Then she went to her sleeping quarters. Reaching under her bed, she pulled out a small pottery jar. With a thumb and forefinger she drew out a pinch of ground herbs and leaves. For a moment she rolled it around, then dropped it into the jar.

"You brought me nothing but pain. Perhaps you might bring my daughter happiness. Perhaps, perhaps not."

Then she shoved the jar as far under her bed as she could reach.

Chapter 52

With the passing days, Connaire felt his muscles grow, harden. His skill with sword, spear and bow increased. Although he seldom won with sword against Scáthach or with bow against Brid, his strength gave him an edge with the spear. His throws could outdistance the others and his accuracy was such that Scáthach finally gave him a grudging compliment. After he had solidly hit his mark while she had underthrown by a handcount or more paces, she turned and studied him a moment before speaking.

"I have taught you well. If you have a spear with you, you can kill your foe before he gets close enough to use his sword." Then she smiled wryly. "And judging from your swordplay, that might be a good idea."

But Connaire knew this was high praise from the warrior woman. He also knew he was closing the gap between her ability with a sword and his own. She was better at planning her moves, more skillful in her strokes, but he had more power and was quicker in reacting to her attack. And the more he practiced, the more his planning and skill improved. Although she still scored more hits on him with their wooden swords than he did on her, Connaire felt that soon would change. Plus, the power of his hits were far more telling. Although he tried to pull his stroke if he knew it would strike her, if he were too obvious she would fly into a rage. Either she would furiously attack him, swinging her sword with a fury worthy of the Morrigan, or angrily stomp back to the broch for a night of drunken ranting.

On nights like that she would sit by the fire, drinking mead and yelling to the walls about the perfidy of men. Sometimes she rose on her wobbly legs and stagger around the hearth, ranting about how warriors no longer were willing to do what was necessary to excel. The words might vary, but the theme was always the same.

"Once this house was filled with warriors, men and women who were willing to train, to work to be the best. Now fewer and fewer women are warriors and those that are, like the men, want to ride around the countryside and hunt instead of honing their skills."

She would shake her head and drink more mead. "Now instead of a household of fine warriors, I train a clumsy boy, a clumsy boy without any wealth."

Then she would glare at Connaire. "I train him for nothing because of my besotted daughter. He is as worthless as her father, Earc: fine looks with no depth. Bright flames and nothing more. If not for my tenants, I would starve and freeze without wood for a hearth fire."

With a sigh, she would collapse on her stool by the fire, looking into the flames as if they had an answer. "I have but a single oaf for a student and a lovesick fool for a daughter. Why do I continue to live?"

On those nights, Connaire would stay in his sleeping area, sitting silently on his bed until the storm had passed. Brid would often sit on the bed next to him, leaning against his shoulder with her eyes closed. At first, he tried to sit stoically next her, not reacting to her closeness. Then he found himself wrapping his arm across her shoulders, holding her to him. He would close his eyes, lean his cheek on her hair, and try to pretend that there was some future, some hope for them. But he could not. In the back of his mind, he could never forget that they were doomed to not be with each other.

Then, when Scáthach finally collapsed on the floor, Brid and Connaire would carry her to her bed.

An unseasonable warm spell melted the snow and ice. The sun shone. It was more like a couple of moon-phase cycles after Beltane than a moon-phase cycle before. Instead of training in the smoky confines of the broch's upper floor, they could return to the clean air of the outdoors. Scáthach's mood lightened with the sky and her mead drinking lessened. Night brought conversation instead of rants.

After finishing her evening meal, Scáthach emitted an appreciative belch and took a sip of her mead. She gave Connaire a sidelong glance. "You wonder why only Brid and I live in this broch and how we came to be here, do you not? And why my tenants faithfully bring foodstuff and firewood to us?"

Connaire shrugged. "It is not my business. I am a guest."

"But you do wonder, do you not?"

"It is true, I have wondered. But it is not a guest's place to ask such questions."

She smiled, a warm smile. "And I will reward you for your restraint. I will tell you."

After refilling her mead cup, she continued. "I do not know who built this broch, but my grandmother told me that it has been the home of the Scáthachs since before memory. We trained warriors from Eireann and they rewarded us handsomely. We acquired lands and tenants who stayed with us because we could protect them. We were the best warriors ever and our trainees would fight by our side if we were attacked. All feared and respected the house of Scáthach."

She sipped her mead and studied Connaire for a moment before continuing. "Scáthach would choose her mate from her warriors. When you live so close for so long, you know who you want and all of the young men would want the Scáthach. Then he would stay, helping to train the newcomers. Until Earc."

With a sigh, she closed her eyes and rubbed them. "I was attracted to him, but knew he would never stay. But he . . . tricked me into sleeping with him. He was a great healer and had a potion that addled the mind. My heart was lost to him and Brid was writhing in my belly when he told me he was leaving. So I killed him."

Silence descended on the room. Scáthach stared at the fire. Connaire stirred uneasily. Brid rested her hand on his, as if urging him to silence. But he had to ask.

"Did you still love him?"

Scáthach nodded. "But, for me, love was less important than honor."

Connaire closed his eyes, fighting the memory of Deirdre and his brother's death. If only he had used that as his guide then. He was only dimly aware of Brid's hand slipping from his.

The next day they all walked along the beach a ways from the broch. The loch shimmered in the winter sun with an entrancing beauty. A hawk soared high, searching for prey. Cú Chulainn chased any bird that dared to land on the sand within his sight. Connaire felt relaxed, enjoying the break from his training routine. He thought of how pleasant it would be to stay here, to be with Brid in this land of towering mountains and vast lochs until he passed to the lands towards the setting sun. But Scáthach broke his reverie.

"Are you ready?"

He turned and found her standing with one of the practice swords at ready and another proffered to him. With a sigh, he took it and went to the ready position. Brid sat in the sand to watch, looking resignedly at him. Cú Chulainn returned from a failed attempt to capture his prey and lay with his head resting on his paw, watching. It would be another day of defending himself from the violent attacks of the warrior woman.

But when they engaged swords, he was surprised. She was moving more slowly than normal, almost in a dance. True, it was a dance of battle, but she did not seem intent on striking the first blow. Instead she was letting him see her moves, how she was able to parry a blow into a strike. She was laying bare the finesse and fluidity of motion that made her such an exceptional swordswoman. For Connaire, it was an epiphany, a moment when he understood how to bring his strength together with Scáthach's skill and grace.

They continued to battle, but without the ferocious intensity they normally had. Connaire found that he was enjoying the fight rather than desperately trying for a strike. It seemed to go on forever. Finally, without either making a strike, they stopped without either acknowledging defeat and leaned breathlessly on their swords. Then they both began to laugh.

Connaire was laughing so hard that he sank to his knees in the damp sand. He looked to Brid and saw her laughing as well. Then her eyes widened and she rose to her feet. The hound stood, baring his teeth with a low growl, his hackles up.

Riding towards them were more than a handcount of men. They were between them and the broch, between them and real weapons. All they had were two wooden swords.

Scáthach had seen them as well. She raised a cautioning hand. "Let me deal with them."

As they rode up and reined their horses to a halt, Connaire's heart sank. They were well-armed Fortriu warriors. And at the fore was Drust. When he saw Connaire, Drust smiled coldly.

"So this is the hole that you scurried into. I have been looking for you."

With a start, Connaire realized Drust was speaking the language of Eireann. During the time the Fortriu had held him captive, Connaire had believed Drust did not understand his words. Before Connaire could speak, Scáthach stepped in front of him.

"What business do you have with this boy?"

"Boy? This 'boy' murdered my kinsman." Drust spat on the sand. "Now I will kill him for it,"

"Not here. You can do with him as you will, but not here. I gave him hospitality and his blood cannot be shed here." She turned to Connaire and winked. "You will have to take him off of my lands before you kill him."

Drust glared angrily at her, but nodded to his men. Two dismounted and walked towards Connaire, swords drawn. Four stayed on their horses. Scáthach stepped aside as they approached. The hound growled as they walked past him, but Brid gave a low whistle and he did not move.

As the men passed by her, Scáthach suddenly swung her wooden sword upward, catching one of the warriors in the throat. With a gurgle of bloody foam, he sank to his knees.

Connaire swung at the second warrior, but he was able to deflect Connaire's practice blade with his iron sword and went to ready position. Connaire knew wood had no chance against metal. He made an awkward thrust at the Fortriu and, as he had hoped, the other confidently batted it away. As he did, he was exposed. The wooden sword was light and Connaire dipped it under the other warrior's blade and lunged at his exposed neck with all his might. Although only pointed wood, the sword sank deep into his throat. With a surprised stare, he staggered back, dropped his sword and fell to the ground, blood spurting from the wound. Quickly Connaire grabbed the iron sword.

As the two warriors had dismounted to take Connaire, Brid had assessed the men on the horses. She trusted her mother and Connaire to handle the first two. If not, all would be lost anyway. The warrior on horseback nearest her was focused on Connaire, holding his spear loosely at his side. When she saw her mother swing her wooden sword, Brid leapt at the spear and pulled it from the warrior's grasp. He turned to her, pulling his sword from its scabbard. She plunged the spear into his chest. As he fell to the sand, she grabbed his sword and sprang onto his horse.

One of the remaining warriors, who had seen half of their number quickly fall to two wooden swords, turned his horse and headed away at a gallop. Brid kicked her horse into pursuit. Although normally a man on his own horse would have the advantage, Brid knew she would catch him. She was much lighter and her rapport with animals gave her the edge. Dropping the reins, she gripped the horse's mane and gently stroked its neck. It seemed to understand, increasing its pace so that they were soon next to the warrior.

When he saw her ride up to him, the warrior drew his blade. His eyes were wide with fear. He swung wildly and would have struck Brid if she had not slid down the horse's side. She was clinging tightly to the horse's mane with one hand as her horse galloped along the beach, gripping her sword with the other. Swinging low, she sliced through the warrior's side. He dropped his sword and tried to staunch the gush of blood. Then he slipped off of his horse and fell to the ground.

As Connaire rose with the iron sword in his hand, the warrior next to Drust turned and rode away. Brid was pursuing the other warrior in a different direction. Connaire knew the fleeing warrior must be stopped or Brude would return with an army of warriors. Scáthach and Brid would die for helping him. He saw the spear in the body of the warrior on the ground and rushed to it. Pulling it from the body, he took careful aim at the fleeing Fortriu and flung it with all his might. He saw the spear strike true and the man fell. His horse slowed, then turned and went back to nose the body of its owner.

There was only one man left: Drust. At the moment all the others had attacked, the massive hound had leapt at that Fortriu warrior and, grabbing his leg, pulled him from his horse. Before Drust could draw his sword, Cú Chulainn was at his neck. It took both his hands and all his strength to keep the hound from tearing into his throat.

When all the other warriors had been defeated, Scáthach called to Cú Chulainn. The hound stood over Drust, but stopped his attack. Scáthach stood at ready, near enough to kill Drust should he try to draw his sword. Brid was riding back at full gallop. Connaire edged slowly forward, sword in hand. Drust gave a short, humorless laugh as he lay on the sand.

"So now the four of you will kill me?"

Scáthach inched closer. "As you would have killed Connaire with your men? Perhaps we should. But, no, that will not happen."

"You will let me leave?"

Scáthach smiled the smile of a wolf. "No, but we will give you a chance. We will let you fight Connaire."

Connaire took a sharp breath. Drust looked at Connaire, evaluating.

"And if I win?"

Scáthach glanced at Connaire. "You will not."

Drust glanced at Connaire. "But if I do?"

"Then you live."

"Then I accept." Drust laughed again. "What choice do I have?"

Scáthach eyed him coldly. "None." She turned to Connaire. "Do not lose. If he lives, it will not go well for Brid and me."

Connaire nodded. His training was at an end.

Chapter 53

Scáthach stood to one side, sword in one hand and reins of the horses in her other. She looked relaxed, but Connaire knew she was like a cat watching a mouse. Her sword even twitched periodically like the tail of a cat. Cú Chulainn lay near her, staring at Drust and uttering a low growl from time to time. Drust was swinging his sword from side to side, glaring at Connaire. Brid was at Connaire's side.

Connaire spoke to her with the words of the hands.

Drust speaks the tongue of Eireann and Dál Riata, yet pretended not to with me before. Why?

He does not want anyone to know.

Then why did he do so with your mother?

She taught him to speak it. When she taught him to fight. He learned both well.

Connaire was taken aback. *He was taught by your mother? I did not know she trained the Fortriu.*

Brid shrugged. *Few come to learn anymore. We must eat.* Then she touched his cheek. *But never has she had any warrior who learned as well as you. And today she showed you things she has never shown anyone but me.*

But am I better than Drust? Then he hesitated. *I have only killed one man and that was but a short time ago. I had no choice.*

You have no choice now. If Drust lives, we will not be safe. The Fortriu may not kill us, but they will certainly drive us from our home. Mother has placed great faith in you.

I will not let you down. He just hoped that he could make good on his promise.

Connaire turned to Drust, slowly swinging his sword to loosen the tension between his shoulders. Drust gave a short laugh, as if to say that he would make short work of him. Connaire glanced back at Brid before going to ready position.

Without warning, Drust flung himself to the attack. Not having been ready, Connaire found himself on the defensive, parrying without replying. A moment's doubt flickered across his mind, worry that he would fail Brid and Scáthach rather than concern for himself. He felt stronger than Drust, but feared he lacked the skill and experience.

Drust swung sideways and Connaire awkwardly parried. As Drust's blade slid down his own, it clipped his forearm. He stepped back as he blocked a head blow and tripped on a branch lying on the beach. His guard dropped as he tried to break his fall and Drust stepped forward for the kill.

Knowing he had no chance to avoid the coming sword stroke, Connaire kicked hard at Drust's knee, catching him in midstride. Caught by surprise, he staggered back. Connaire rolled over and was on his feet with sword at ready by the time Drust recovered his balance.

At that point, Connaire caught a glimpse of Scáthach, her sword sheathed and her arms crossed. She was looking away in disgust. He realized she knew he could do better. Taking a breath, he calmed himself, clearing his mind of everything but the fight and focusing on allowing his training to guide his movements.

Again Drust flew at him with a fury. This time, Connaire reacted instinctively, following his training. With his body responding to the attack almost unconsciously, he began to see the method of Drust's attack. The blows were not random, but followed a certain pattern, using Connaire's counter blows as an indicator of any weakness. But how Drust reacted to that weakness had a pattern in itself. Then Connaire knew he could beat the Fortriu warrior.

Every time Drust swung his sword, Connaire's met it and turned it aside. At first, Connaire merely parried without a reply. He was learning. Then he began his own attack, using his skill rather than strength. He gave no force to his blows, using them as tests of how Drust would counter. But his moves were fast and relentless.

Drust was parrying, but increasingly frantically. He no longer tried to attack Connaire, only trying to keep himself from being hit. Sometimes Connaire scored a hit, but without causing serious injury. Although Connaire bled some from the hit to his arm, Drust bled a little from each of a number of cuts to his arms and torso.

Connaire felt a certain rhythm of movement, much like what Scáthach had shown him earlier. Then he began to add more force to his blows. He could see that Drust was barely able to deflect the strokes of his sword. And he saw something else: fear and panic in Drust's eyes. The Fortriu knew he was doomed.

Their swordplay had led them up and down the beach. At times they neared the spectators. Suddenly, when they were close to Brid, Drust spun around and put his swordpoint at the neck of the startled woman. Drust was panting heavily as he spoke.

"If I die, so does she. Drop your sword and come here."

For a moment, Connaire considered the odds. He knew he could not strike Drust before he killed Brid, but the Fortriu must know he would die anyway. However, Drust also had realized he would soon be dead if the fight continued. Dead, no matter what. So he had acted in desperation. Connaire realized this was a way for Drust to kill him before he died. If he dropped his sword and went to Drust, the Fortriu would kill him. He had no doubt Brid and Scáthach would soon exact revenge. Then let it be so. He would gladly sacrifice his life to save Brid.

"I will drop my sword, but if you harm her in any way, I will hunt you through every life we have. I promise you that."

Drust gave a short laugh. "I would beat you every time, but I will not harm her if you do as I say. You have my word."

Connaire spat on the sand, but said nothing. He could hear the low rumble of Cú Chulainn's growl. Scáthach must be keeping him from attacking, for it would mean Brid's death. He dropped his sword in the sand. He could see Brid's hand saying, *No, no, no, no.* Still watching for any opening, he stepped forward.

As soon as he was close enough, Drust pulled his sword from Brid's neck and swung it at Connaire. He started do dive to the side, but knew he would not avoid the blade. Then he heard a thud and turned to see Drust with a spear through his chest.

Scáthach walked slowly over to them. "You are not the only one who can throw a spear, boy."

Drust was lying on the ground, clutching the spear in his chest. Blood flowed from the wound and some trickled from the side of his mouth. Scáthach whistled for the hound who came quickly to them.

"Cú Chulainn. Piss."

The dog lifted his leg and shot a yellow stream on the dying man. Scáthach knelt beside him.

"No one threatens my daughter and lives, you coward." She grabbed a handful of sand and shoved it into Drust's mouth. "You are not even worth finishing off."

They stood and watched as Drust died. He choked on the sand as his life's blood soaked into the sand. With a final spasm, he was gone.   Brid had wanted to go to him with her dagger, to help him die quickly, mercifully, but Scáthach held her back.

Connaire stood and watched Drust's slow death.   If not for what he had done to Brid, he would have made his death quick. However, he found that he felt the same as Scáthach about how Drust should die.   He would let no one harm Brid.

When Drust was finally dead, Scáthach sighed.   "Now we have to clean up this mess before any other Fortriu come calling."

Chapter 54

The weather changed and a sleety rain was pounding on them as they finished burying the Fortriu warriors. It had been a miserable task, muddy and cold. They had worked in silence as they dug ditches for the bodies, dumped them in and shoveled the dirt back.

Scáthach pondered the changes that must surely come to her and her daughter's life. She knew that the Fortriu had never totally accepted that she had no part in the disappearance of the warriors that had been pursuing Connaire when he had stumbled into their lives. Even if they were fortunate enough to have had Drust keep silent about where he was going, Scáthach had little doubt that she and her daughter would be suspect. Brude was losing too many trained warriors for any other explanations. Such men did not just disappear. All they could do was delay the inevitable.

She sighed and rested on her spade. "We need to kill the Fortriu horses. If they are not found, Brude might think Dál Riatan raiders killed them and stole the horses."

Brid stopped her work, glaring at her mother. She violently shook her head.

"Brid, you have to understand." Scáthach's tone was pleading, cajoling. "I am sure that one of the reasons we have been suspected in the last incident is that you would not allow me to slit the throats of those horses. A handcount of warriors do not just fall off their mounts and die in the forest. And it definitely would not happen twice." She paused. "Or would you rather Brude and his men descend upon us and we all die?"

In spite of the rain, Scáthach could see her daughter's tears. What if her daughter refused? What then? How far would Brid go to protect the horses? Then Connaire went to her and wrapped his arm across the young woman's shoulders.

"I know how you feel about killing for no reason, but we must. We will all die if Brude comes with an army."

For a moment, Scáthach was not sure how Brid would react. But then she turned and wrapped her arms around Connaire and buried her head in his chest.

Scáthach spit on the ground. It was not really about the horses. It was all the killing. The girl had no stomach for it. However great her skills with a bow and with a sword, she always had a problem killing. She would never be a real warrior. Tossing her spade to the ground, she picked up her sword and went to the tethered horses. They seemed to sense her intent and she could see the fear in their eyes as they whinnied and pulled against the ropes that held them.

She glanced over to Brid and Connaire. Her daughter's eyes were turned away, but Connaire was watching. He called to her.

"Just do it quickly."

Scáthach shook her head. He was almost as weak as her daughter. With a smooth stroke, she sliced through the neck of the first horse. Moving with dispatch, she slit the throats of two more horses before they could react. Blood spurted and panic spread through the remaining horses. Their wild neighs filled the air and they madly reared and pawed at her with their hooves.

Wiping the blood from her face, Scáthach considered her next move. She was glad that, unlike most warriors, she kept a keen edge on her blade. It was better to risk having your sword stuck in an opponent's bone than not have it draw blood. When one of the horses dropped its forelegs to the ground and raised its head, she was able to move closer and slit its throat. The last horse stood shaking, its eyes wide, its breathing ragged.

Then Scáthach felt a hand grab her arm. She turned to see Brid holding her, tears flowing. Glancing over to Connaire, she saw him standing with fists clenched. And she saw Cú Chulainn, her hound, huddled behind him. Betrayed by her own dog.

"Fine. I will let this one live. He will be the cause of our ruin."

Throwing down her sword, she pulled her arm free and went to her spade. Angrily grabbing it, she began to toss mud into the air. Without a word, Brid and Connaire picked up their spades and began to dig.

Night fell quickly in the winter months. By the time they had buried the horses, it was dark. Cautiously, they worked their way back to the broch. With no moonlight and no torches, it was a slow journey for such a short distance. Scáthach could hear the horse, led by Brid. No doubt she was being guided by Connaire and the cursed hound was with them. Only she was alone.

When she reached the door, Scáthach flung it open and stumbled up the stairs to the living quarters. As she stirred the embers on the hearth to life, she considered the future. It was not good.

The Fortriu would soon be looking for their lost warriors. They would come to the broch and find the horse. It was Drust's horse. No matter how Brude felt about Drust, he had been kin and a warrior in his household. He would be avenged. They would all be lost. Unless . . . .

If Connaire would take Brid and return to his people, they would be saved. Scáthach knew Brude would never let her escape, but it was different with her daughter. And he did not know Connaire was alive, much less harbored in their broch.

There might be a chance if Connaire would take Brid. She would gladly die to save her daughter. There was a problem. Connaire seemed unwilling to take Brid with him.

This was puzzling. She could see by the way they acted that they were attracted to each other. Yet she was fairly certain they had not coupled. What else was necessary? She had coupled with a number of men that had mattered little to her, Drust included. She remembered how he had taken his pleasure and immediately went to sleep. Little cause for mourning him, she thought with a shrug.

But what of Connaire and Brid? They must be lacking in animal desires. There was only one answer.

Scáthach went to her sleeping quarters and retrieved the earthenware jar from under her bed. Whatever it contained would change that. The time Brid's father had used it on her and the few times she had used it on men had proved its power. She smiled when she thought of those times. She had even used it again herself and had enjoyed the result. Yes, this would solve the problem. She quickly stashed it under her bed as she heard Connaire and Brid coming up the stairs.

Connaire wearily shook his head. "I am so tired I am almost willing to forget evening meal and go to bed."

Scáthach slowly walked out of her sleeping area. "With all that blood and mud all over you?"

Connaire looked down at his blood-stained, begrimed léine. "I, uh . . . I do need a bath."

"I will start the bathwater fire." She smiled at him. "Have Brid reheat what was left from the midday meal while I am gone."

Connaire stared after her as she left. He turned to Brid and spoke in the language of hands.

Does that seem odd to you?

Brid shrugged. *I do not know any more what is odd. At least she is not angry with us for saving the horse.*

Connaire considered this. *That is true. Considering that it was Drust's horse, I am amazed. She might have held the horse responsible for its master.*

That is true. Brid paused. *Why is she acting this way?*

Chapter 55

Scáthach sighed as she soaked in her hot bath. Normally she and Brid bathed together in the large wooden tub. Although she had often told Connaire he could join them, he had balked at the idea. She knew why. He was a young man who had the urge to couple and did not want his obvious desire to show when he was in the tub, unclad, with them. Instead he had the cooler, dirtied water of a servant.

With a smile she remembered the young men who had come to learn of war from her and whom she had also taught how to make love. It had been a long time since her last one, too long. She thought back to how she had even considered having Connaire. But watching Brid hover over him had let her know that her daughter's desire for him was greater. So she had sacrificed her own pleasure for her daughter's. And the foolish girl had done nothing.

As she rose from her bath, Scáthach groaned. Of late, her body ached after a fight. Looking down at her taut stomach and muscular thighs, her body looked much the same as it had before Brid's birth. A warrior woman's body. But she felt her nine handcounts of Samhains at times like this, when her body chided her for acting as though she were as young as her daughter. She sensed that this turn of the wheel was nearing an end and she had to do everything she could to protect her daughter. And she would.

With a quick twist, Scáthach wrung much of the water from her hair. After using the drying cloths and hanging them close to the fire, she threw a fur robe over her shoulders and left the bath house.

While Scáthach had been gone, Connaire and Brid had restocked the firewood and stoked the fire that heated a beef stew. As he sat close to her in front of the roaring blaze, Connaire could feel Brid shaking. Was it the killing of the men or the killing of the horses? Or both? He did not ask. He hoped it was the horses.

He had seen strong men cry over the body of a slain mount while their comrades lay dead on the field. It was the way of a warrior. They knew that men and women would have another turn of the wheel after their journey towards the setting sun. Let the filidh make songs to remember the fallen; the warrior was born to fight. He put his arm across her shoulders and pulled her to him. She leaned against his chest and her shaking stopped. He ached with love and desire.

Then he heard Scáthach's footsteps on the stairs and she breezed into the room. Her robe was wrapped around her and her damp hair hung loose. Somehow, she looked younger, more vital.

"Keeping each other warm, are we?" She smirked at him as she picked up a jug of mead. "You had better go to the bath house before the water is cold."

"Have you already bathed?" As he said it, Connaire realized how foolish it sounded. Of course she had already bathed. "What I mean is, why did you not wait for Brid?"

She strode into her sleeping area, lost to Connaire's view. "As soon as the water was hot I needed to get rid of the filth. You can bathe with Brid."

"But. . . ." Connaire could not think of what to say. They had been living in the same house, seeing each other's bodies on occasion. That had been difficult enough. Being alone, unclothed and close to Brid was too much. "I will wait until Brid has bathed."

Scáthach returned to the hearth and sat on a stool, her robe gaping open. She held the mead jug in one hand and two cups in her other. "You must like cold, dirty water. What do you think, Brid?"

Brid looked up at Connaire. She shook her head and spoke in the language of the hands.

You are tired and begrimed. You must not wait. Bathe with me.

Connaire shook his head. *I dare not.*

I will not attack you. She smiled. *I promise.*

"Enough of this." Scáthach poured mead into the two cups and proffered them to the young warrior and her daughter. "You both stink. Drink this to warm you and go bathe yourselves."

Connaire reluctantly took the cup and drank the mead. It tasted a little odd, but warmed and relaxed him. When he finished, he put out his cup for more and Scáthach refilled it. He noticed that Brid did the same. They both downed their mead quickly. Then she took his hand and they headed to the bath shed that adjoined the broch. As they did, Connaire glanced back to see Scáthach smiling. It looked odd. He realized that he had never seen her smile so broadly before.

After they left, Scáthach went back to her sleeping area. She shoved the small jar back under her bed and picked up a different jug of mead and a cup that sat on the floor nearby. After filling the cup, she sat on her bed and took a long drink.

As she lay back on her bed, she wondered how soon the drought would take effect. Brid's father had never told her how much he had used on her, but when Scáthach had used it since then, a pinch had more than sufficed. Not expecting Connaire and Brid to have two cups, she had heavily dosed their jug of mead with the potion.   Taking her jug of mead with her, Scáthach moved close to the fire to dry her hair.   As she combed her fingers through her long tresses in the warmth of the fire, she chuckled.   At least now she could be sure that the boy would couple with Brid and take her away from the danger of Fortriu revenge.

When they entered the bath house, the fire dimly lit the room through the smoke as it filtered through the thatch roof. Steam from a large iron cauldron of water made the air damp as well as smoky.   Brid began to scoop buckets-full of water from the cauldron into the bathing tub.

Connaire found watching her stimulating, so much so that he could barely resist grabbing her and tearing off her clothes. Then she turned to him and slowly undressed.   Mesmerized, Connaire was almost unaware that he was doing the same.

The dark thatch between her legs held his gaze.   Then he glanced down and saw that he was rock-hard with desire.   His mind was in a fog, almost as if he were dreaming, as he picked her up and slipped her into the tub.   Quickly, he climbed in himself and pulled her to him.   He could feel her nipples hard against his chest as their lips met.

Grabbing her buttocks, he lifted her and slowly entered her. She softly gasped and then pressed her lips to his again.   She began to rock against him with a steadily increasing intensity. Suddenly she stopped, clenching him tightly and softly whimpering.   With a cry, he felt powerful spasms wrack his body.

Barely keeping their heads above water, they clung to each other.   When Connaire regained his senses, he realized he was still hard and inside her.   Then she began to move up and down on him again.

From her alcoholic stupor, Scáthach heard them when they finally came up the stairs. They were not trying to be quiet, moaning and bumping into furniture and walls. They must still be feeling the effects of the potion.

Then she remembered the dosed mead was still by the fire. She had to tell them not to drink any more. Who knew what too much of the draught might cause? She tried to rise, but her head spun wildly. As she fell back on her bed, she knocked over a mead jug. Nothing spilled. It was empty. She sighed. At least she had not grabbed the wrong jug when she went to bed.

When she heard the sounds of a jug clinking against cups, she again tried to rise. But, figuring that it was probably too late to stop them anyway, she abandoned her efforts and went back to sleep.

Her dreams were filled with thumpings and groans.

Chapter 56

Scáthach woke to a mouth that tasted like it was full of wool and a head that felt like someone was beating it with a rock. A large rock. Reluctantly she opened her eyes. By the light of the fire on the hearth she knew it must be morning. So much the worse. A little more sleep might help. With a groan, she pushed herself up and swung her legs out of bed. Her hands were shaking. She vowed to herself that she would not drink so much mead again. Too often, mornings began this way.

As she sat on the edge of her bed, still wrapped only in the fur robe she had worn from her bath the night before, Scáthach desperately felt the need to relieve herself. When she struggled to her feet, she felt her gorge rise and staggered toward the stairs, unsure whether she would make it outside. She saw Brid and Connaire standing by the hearth as she rushed by, but was more concerned with safely making it out of the door than them.

After she had heeded nature's call, Scáthach entered the low door of the broch. Shoving her way past the cattle, she went to the barrel of mead stored there. A pitcher hung on a peg above it and she grabbed it. Perhaps a little mead would help her steady her hand. She lifted the lid and filled the pitcher. Without a cup, she had to drink from the pitcher, taking a deep swig. And then another. It was time to face her daughter and explain why she had drugged the mead.

With a sigh, she slowly climbed the steps to the living area. As she did, Connaire was descending. She tried to manage a smile of greeting, but he brushed past her without a word, a bundle slung on his back.

When she reached the top, Scáthach saw Brid, standing by the hearth with tears streaming down her cheeks. Then her daughter quickly turned away, as if to hide her emotions.

"What has he done?" Scáthach spun Brid around to face her, gripping her shoulders. "Has he hurt you?"

Brid's hands spoke quickly, the anger flashing in her eyes. *Him hurt me? After what you did, you can accuse him of hurting me?*

Scáthach took a drink from the pitcher, then sighed. "I did it for you. I thought he was the type of man who would stay with you if you coupled. I though him honorable and committed to duty."

Honorable? What would you know about honor? Brid spat on the floor. *Yes, your potion worked and we coupled like dogs.*

Scáthach chuckled. Then she grimaced, for even that caused her head to throb so badly that she put her hand to her forehead to stop it. She spoke through gritted teeth.

"Then why are you angry? You should thank me. What is bothering you?"

He promised his dying brother that he would oath to no other than his brother's mate. Now he knows he must return to her and be true to that promise. Brid shook her head. *Because of last night, he feels he must leave now or he will never keep that promise.*

"He is no better than your father." The warrior woman flung the pitcher at the hearth, shattering it and sending rivulets of mead across the floor. She stalked into her sleeping area and grabbed her sword and scabbard from where it hung on the wall, unsheathing it. This man was like them all, a dog after a bitch in heat, wanting to couple and then leave.   But this dog would not leave alive.

As Scáthach strode toward the stairs, her daughter grabbed her sword arm and pleaded with her free hand.

No.   You cannot do this.

With a powerful shove, her mother knocked Brid backward.   Scáthach saw her slip on the mead-dampened floor and land on the hearth stones.   Oblivious of the thud as her daughter's head struck the stone, she continued on her way.

Connaire had put a bridle on Drust's horse and slung a satchel of food across its back when he saw Scáthach coming toward him, sword in hand.   It had begun to rain heavily, drenching him and making the ground muddy.   Cú Chulainn was close by his side, no doubt sensing that he was leaving.

She called to him, her voice filled with anger.   "Stand and face me, boy.   Do not try to hide behind the horse you are stealing."

Connaire shook his head.   He had wished to avoid such a confrontation.

"I will not fight you, Scáthach.   I am taking this horse because you feared its presence would betray you to Brude.   I have done nothing dishonorable to you, but I must leave to keep my word to my brother."

She grabbed the reins from his hand and stood, sword in hand, in front of him.   Her eyes were wild, reminding Connaire of the legendary Cú Chulainn in battle rage.

"Nothing dishonorable?   You coupled with my daughter and now run away?   You have brought the wrath of the Fortriu upon us and leave us to die?   You are a worthless coward and will not leave here alive.   Draw your sword or I will slay you like the viper that you are."

For a moment Connaire considered letting her do just that. But if he died, he could never fulfill his promise to his brother. Slowly, he drew his sword, swearing to himself and the gods that he would not use it to harm her. He saw the hound back away behind him, confusion in its eyes. Which master would he protect?

Scáthach's attack was quick and savage. With no attempt at defending herself, she swung her sword in wide, powerful swaths, one after another. Although Connaire had no trouble blocking them, the shear intensity of her sword strokes drove him back. If he missed a parry, he knew he would be severely wounded. She would show no mercy.

The rain was so heavy that it was blinding and the ground was slick with mud. As he stepped back, Connaire heard a yelp. Realizing he had stepped on the hound's foot, he tried to sidestep and slipped in the mud. He fell to the ground with a bone-jarring thump.

Momentarily dazed, Connaire barely had time to raise his sword as he saw Scáthach lunging at him. Then she lurched as she slipped in the mud, falling towards him. He tried to turn his sword away, but she landed on him before he could. His sword was deep in her body.

Brid lay on the floor of the broch, stunned by her fall. She rolled onto her stomach and pushed herself up. The room spun around her. She tried to stand, but sank to her knees. For a while she stayed there until her head cleared enough that she felt she could rise. As she stumbled towards the stairs, fear knotted her stomach.

Once she reached the door out of the broch, she saw a scene through the driving rain that filled her with dread. Her mother lay on the ground, a sword in her chest.   Connaire knelt beside her, his hands covering his eyes.   Cú Chulainn lay by Scáthach, licking her face.

Brid rushed to her mother.   Scáthach's eyes were closed. Kneeling, Brid felt her mother's heart.   It was still beating.   She was alive.

Grabbing Connaire's léine, she shook him.

He dropped his hands to his side and looked at her, tears in his eyes.   "I killed her.   I killed your mother."   He looked skyward, weeping.   "Kill me.   Please.   I bring nothing but woe to all who help me."

Brid pulled his head down so that he was looking at her.
She is not dead.   Help me take her to her bed.
"I am not worthy to live."

Brid slapped him.
To save my mother I need your help.   Help me.

Connaire nodded dazedly.   The two of them lifted Scáthach and carried her inside.   Cú Chulainn silently followed.

As they laid her on her bed, Scáthach groaned.   Brid grabbed a couple of jars from her sleeping area.   One had a mixture of moss and spider webs that should slow the flow of blood.   The other had an herb that relieved pain.   As Connaire watched, she slowly removed the sword and applied the moss. Blood oozed from the wound, but slowly.   Brid sighed.   Perhaps she could heal her mother.   Then she noticed the bubbles.

Scáthach opened her eyes.   Her chest hurt.   She could not seem to catch her breath, taking short, shallow gulps of air.   Her daughter and Connaire were there.   Then she remembered.   She had trouble speaking,

"I have been foolish.   I ask that you let it be forgotten."

Both of them nodded.   Although Brid physically could not speak, Scáthach saw from Connaire's face that he could not as well.

"A warrior does not weep, lad."

It hurt to speak.   She was still alive, but having trouble breathing.   Something was very wrong.   She looked into Brid's eyes.

"I am dying, daughter, am I not?"

Brid slowly nodded.   There was no reason to lie.   As a warrior who had seen many battle wounds, Scáthach would know hers was fatal.   None survived such an injury as hers.   When Scáthach took Brid's hand and squeezed it, she started.   Although she knew her mother loved her, Brid's upbringing had been as a warrior and sentimentality was shunned.   Her mother's unfamiliar maternalism brought home to her that her mother would soon be gone forever.

Brid uttered a low moan and wept.

Chapter 57

Cú Chulainn stood, looking confusedly from one person to another. When Brid moaned, he went to her, but she ignored him. Then he sat by Scáthach's bed and rested his chin on her leg. She weakly rested her hand on his head. His sad eyes studied her, but he seemed to sense something was gravely wrong and did nothing more.

For a moment Scáthach lay with her eyes closed, with only the sound of her rapid, rasping breathing. Her chest hurt so much that even that was a struggle. But there was still much to be done before she died, so she forced herself to open her eyes and, with great effort, spoke.

"My daughter, I am thirsty. Get me some cool water from the well."

Connaire stepped close. "I will go. You need her here to try to heal you."

"No!" She winced in pain from the effort and continued more softly. "I am dying, boy, and she can do nothing to stop that . . . . I want her to go. Will you do that for me, my child?"

Brid nodded, incomprehension in her eyes. She pulled her hand from her mother's, picked up an empty jug and hurried to the door.

As soon as Brid had left the room, Scáthach turned to Connaire. "There is little time and I have little strength left, so let me speak without interrupting. I need for you to take Brid after I die and-"

He knelt by her bed, eyes downcast. "I cannot. I am so sorry that I did this to you, but I--"

She reached out and grabbed his arm with her waning strength. "Can you not be quiet in my last moments and listen?

You did nothing. I was trying to kill you and fell on your sword. A drunken, clumsy fool." She closed her eyes a moment in pain, but quickly continued. "That is not what I want to tell you. You must take Brid with you." She held up her hand to stop him from speaking, grimacing from the effort.

"I know you will not break your promise to your brother and I do not ask that you oath with her. Not even that you couple, although you are both fools not to. Take her into your household as you would a kinswoman in need."

"But why?" He shook his head. "Would she not prefer to stay here, in her home?"

"Brude will be here soon with his warriors. He is no fool. I am sure he suspected what happened to those pursuing you, but ignored it out of friendship to me." A flicker of a smile crossed her lips. "Perhaps he fondly remembered when we coupled."

Connaire pulled back. "You and Brude?"

She waved her hand as if shooing a fly. "One of many and of little matter to me. But what does matter is that you killed Drust, his kinsman, and he must act. I am sure he knows Drust was headed here and when he does not return to the Fortriu, Brude will come with many more men. Even if I were still with you, there would be no hope." A spasm of pain shot through her chest and she gritted her teeth.

Connaire dropped to his knees beside her. "I will take her from here. I will find a safe place for her to live. It would only make her miserable if she were with me when I am oathed to another."

Scáthach grabbed his arm. "No. She can speak to no one but you after I am dead. Others think her stupid because she cannot speak words. She will be more alone than you can imagine. You must do this for me. I have trained you with nothing demanded from you in return. You owe me this."

Connaire lowered his eyes. "I will do as you ask. I do owe you a great debt, but I do this for Brid. She will be protected and loved as long as I live."

Scáthach heard the sound of Brid coming up the stairs and dropped her hand to the bed. She closed her eyes to rest a moment, muttering to herself. "You are a fool, boy, not to oath her. An honorable fool, perhaps, but still a fool."

When Brid returned to see Connaire kneeling beside her mother, she feared that she had already died and rushed to her bed. When she heard her mother breathing, she was only slightly relieved. Her breathing was slow, with crackling and wheezing. Her end was near. She opened her eyes.

"I have been talking with Connaire. He is going to take you with him as one of his household."

Brid shook her head violently, sending her tears flying. She would not take the sop of being in his household while he was oathed to another woman. Then she felt his arm across her shoulder and heard his choked words.

"I . . . I know I have no right to ask you, but I want you to be with me . . . . I do love you, as you must know. I want to be with you . . . . Even if it is as a sister. A beloved sister . . . . Will you go with me?"

With a feeling of emptiness, Brid nodded. Even if she could never have him as she wished, it was better to be with him than not. Better than being alone.

Her mother took her hand. Her words were slow and raspy. "You have pleased me, daughter. He will be good to you." She cleared her throat, then turned her head and spat blood on the bed beside her. "It will not be long now."

Connaire touched Scáthach's hand. "You will travel to the land towards the setting sun until you return in your new life. I hope that I meet you again."

She gave a short laugh that ended in a choking sound. Her voice was nothing more than a whisper. "If you believe that, boy, you are even a greater fool than I thought. This is all there is."

It looked as though Connaire was going to say something, but did not. Brid was glad. It would only upset Scáthach if he argued about it.

Her mother tugged her hand and she leaned closer. She could hardly understand her mother's words. "I am cold . . . . Get a pelt to cover me."

Brid took a pelt from the foot of the bed and started to pull it over her mother. Uttering a low gurgling sound, Scáthach fell silent, her eyes staring sightlessly at the ceiling.

Brid's inhuman howl, like that of a wounded animal, pierced the air. Cú Chulainn lifted his head and joined her, making an eerie banshee-like wail. Connaire pulled her to his chest, gently stroking her back, quieting her. For a short time, she leaned against him, shaking. Suddenly she pulled away, rose and stumbled to the stairs.

Taken by surprise, Connaire did not immediately react. Then he got to his feet and ran after her. Brid was driving the cattle with a stick from the bottom level of the broch, out into the rainy yard. He went to her and stood in front of her.

"What are you doing?"

She pushed him away and continued to drive the cattle out of the door. He stepped back in front of her.

"We need to pack and leave soon. We will bury your mother first, but we need to leave as quickly as possible. Your mother told me that she is sure that Brude will be here before long with his warriors. They will want revenge for Drust and his companions. We must leave."

With a shake of her head, she pushed him aside again. But he grabbed her arm and turned her to face him. Then he lifted her chin until she was forced to meet his eyes. Tears were in hers. With his other hand he spoke in the silent language.

You will come with me if I have to carry you.

Angrily, she shook her head.

If you do not, then I will stay and we will both die when Brude comes. Is that what you want?

You have no place here now. Go to your dead brother's wife.

Only if you go with me. It is you I love and I will die rather than see harm come to you.

She sighed. Then she shook her head, slowly this time, and spoke with her hands.

Very well, I will go with you. First I will give these animals to our tenants . . . my tenants. Then I will burn this place. After that, I will go. She looked about her. *There is only sadness and death here now.*

Burn the broch? Why? It will act like a signal fire to Brude.

Because I must. My mother did not believe in the gods or a next life. She did not want to lie in the cold ground. Let me finish this and I will go with you.

Connaire picked up a thick stick from the floor. "Then we will do this together."

She smiled at him, a sad smile. But it was a smile and Connaire felt his heart lift to see it. And he set to work.

After the animals were safely out, Brid carried wood and straw up the stairs to the living area. Connaire followed and found her making a pile next to the hearth. Cú Chulainn lay by Scáthach's bed, as if standing guard. They made several trips and created a huge pile, enough for a great bonfire. Then Brid told him that she was going to get the tenants to take the livestock and left.

Connaire began to load leather bags with what they would need for their trip. They would only have three horses, Scáthach's, Brid's, and Drust's, with only one to be used for goods. Things like the valuable cooking cauldron were too heavy to take. Extra weapons, however, were a necessity. When he took the first load down to the horses, Brid was there and a few men were driving the cattle away. They glumly looked back at Connaire, but said nothing. He turned to Brid.

"What did you tell them? They do not seem glad to be getting the cattle."

The truth. My mother died in an accident. She was their protector as my ancestors were protectors of their ancestors. They fear what will happen to them now. She shrugged. *But there is nothing I can do. And that is painful for me as well as them.*

"I have packed everything I thought we could take. See if I missed anything."

They went up the stairs. She looked around, picking up an item or two. He noticed she studiously avoided going near her mother's sleeping area or even looking in that direction. Then she turned to him.

We are ready.   Take Cú Chulainn and meet me at the horses.   I will start the fire.

He reached out and touched her cheek.   "Take care you do not come to harm."

She nodded and looked away.

Connaire went to the hound.   He slipped a braided leather loop over the dog's head and pulled him along as he went down the stairs.   Cú Chulainn howled as they went out the door.   They stood in the rain and waited.

It seemed like Brid was taking too long.   Connaire could see by the smoke filtering though the thatched roof far above him that the bonfire was burning.   Just as he was ready to go back in to find her, Brid appeared at the doorway.   In one hand she carried a torch and in the other a leather bag.   She stuck the torch in the ground at the doorway, just out of the rain, and then handed Connaire the bag.   It was surprisingly heavy.   She gathered some wood and straw, putting it just inside the door.   Then she set the torch to it, dropping it on the burning pile.

Without looking at Connaire, she took the bag from his hand, lashed it to the pack horse and mounted her own.   She finally looked up at him, the rain hiding the tears he knew were flowing.   She gave him a quick nod and he freed the hound before mounting his horse.   They set off along the beach, heading he knew not where.   He glanced back and saw Cú Chulainn standing by the doorway, perhaps wanting to go back inside to Scáthach, but unable to get past the fire.   He whistled.   The hound hesitated.   When Brid whistled, he turned and followed.

Smoke and flames, rising like a bonfire in the dismal sky, were visible for some distance as they rode.

Chapter 58

They rode steadily through the day, stopping only to eat hastily or to water the horses. Heavy rain persisted and cast a steady pall on their journey. Brid was at the fore, since she knew the land. They stayed along the coastline of the loch as long as they could. Its damp, firm sand gave good footing for the horses and it was easier than winding through the forest. They needed to put distance between them and the broch before Brude and his warriors could find them. Brude would be tracking them.

Finally, they were forced to take a route through the trackless forest. Slowly, they worked their way through the dense woods. Low branches clawed at them, making their passage painful, but the canopy filtered the rain.

When the evening grew so dark that continuing was a danger, Connaire pulled his horse to a halt beside a rocky overhang. He dismounted and Brid followed suit. As she began to unload the pack horse, Connaire grabbed an axe. He whistled for Cú Chulainn to go with him, but the hound refused, staying close to Brid. Connaire shrugged and went to look for dry firewood.

After stumbling through undergrowth for some time in his vain search for any wood not soaked, Connaire was forced to resign himself to a night without a fire. He supposed it would not matter that much. After all, they had nothing to cook and it would be difficult in this rain to keep the embers smoldering at night to stir to life in the morning.

As he turned to retrace his steps, he found a new problem. He was unsure of his trail. He had marked his trail, notching trees with his axe as he went, but could not see any of them in the dark. Normally his sense of direction would have guided him, but the darkened forest, the steady rain, his meandering path and his exhaustion all worked against him. He walked slowly in the direction that felt right, feeling the trunks of the trees he passed in hopes of finding one of his notches. Then something in the distance caught his eye. It was a faint flicker of a fire.

Whose fire was it? It was too far away to be Brid and she would not have had time to kindle such a flame. Was it from Brude and his warriors? Was it from some other travelers? In this region, it was unlikely that they would be friendly. He had to find Brid, warn her. Be there with her.

He pushed ahead, slipping on the wet leaves, branches scratching his face and hands. Panic welled inside him. Was he even going in the right direction? What if Brid, worried about him, tried to follow his trail and they passed each other in the darkness?

In his haste, Connaire caught his foot on a root and he pitched forwards, falling hard against an oak tree and striking his head on the trunk. Momentarily dazed, he clutched the tree to keep from falling to the ground. Then he felt something, a gash in the trunk. It was one he had made. He had been going in the right direction. As he pushed away from the tree, he realized it had a trunk that split into two. He had only marked one tree like that, not far from Bird. He knew where he was.

When Connaire reached their camp, he saw Brid bent over, placing wood on a small fire. She had erected a cow hide shelter close to the rocky overhang, using it to protect the entrance. He rushed to her, pulling the wood from her hands and kicked dirt on the fire.

He was sore and tired, his breath ragged. He held her to his chest. "I had to stop you. We are not alone in this forest. I saw another fire. They would see ours."

Brid took his hands and placed them on hers, then began to speak with them. It took a moment, but he began to understand what she was saying.

I saw no fire.

Connaire looked around. He did not see it either. Then he realized why. "The rocks in front of our shelter hide it."

Then they hide us as well. Help me build our fire again.

Fortunately, the embers were still hot and Brid had made a small pile of dry kindling.

Once the fire was going, Brid touched his face. *What happened? You look like you have been fighting.* A small smile crept across her lips. *And lost.*

With the sleeve of her léine, already damp from the rain, she gently wiped the blood from his cuts. He turned his head and almost raised his hand to stop her, but did not. He liked her touch.

"I could not find any dry wood and . . . ." He gave a short, self-conscious laugh. "Well, I lost my trail in the darkness and it took some time to find it. That is when I saw the fire." He looked quizzically at her. "Where did you find dry wood?"

After I set up the shelter, I went hunting. I found a tree fallen across a gully nearby. I was able to get under it and find enough dry wood for the fire.

Connaire gave a short laugh. "And I wasted my time going the wrong way. Too bad you did not find any game. I am so hungry I would eat it raw."

Brid reached behind a rock and brought up the carcass of a large hare by its ears. *If you will clean it, I will cook it.* She gave him a smile. *Unless you prefer it raw.*

Connaire shook his head as he took the hare. "No, I will be glad to clean it. But the way this night has gone, I might cut off my own hand."

She rested her hand on his a moment. *Be careful. I may need that hand.*

The hare was large enough for them to have their fill, including Cú Chulainn. After they had eaten and banked the coals on the fire, they crawled into the shelter. Connaire and Brid lay on a bed of leaves with a blanket over it and another on top of them, the hound curled at their feet. It was a cold night and Connaire pulled close to Brid to keep her warm. She was turned away from him as he nestled close to her. He wrapped his arm around her and she clutched it to her chest. He could feel her shaking and realized it was not from the cold. She was silently weeping.

Scáthach had not only been her mother, but her only real companion since birth. She had been the only one with whom Brid could talk. Until Connaire had come along. He had taken away her entire world. He could never be her mate, but he would protect her and be her companion as long as they both lived. By the gods, he made this his solemn oath. As binding as the one he had given his brother that prevented him from being the mate of the woman he loved.

Connaire woke with the dawn. The rain had stopped and sunlight filtered through the branches. He yawned and stretched. Brid was already up. The fire was blazing and she was starting to take down the shelter before Connaire was even out of it. He stood, stretching again.

"Why do you hurry?"

She stopped her work and turned to him. *We must leave. The rain has stopped and Brude will be on our trail.*

He looked at her quizzically. "He has probably been on it already. Why are you so suddenly afraid?"

376

I am not afraid, but I know the Fortriu. I know their hounds. They can track a mouse that is three days away. They will track us. We must leave.

Connaire nodded and started to tie their leather satchels on the pack horse. If Brid feared the hounds of Fortriu, then he should too. Soon they were packed and on their horses.

Connaire had planned to head in the direction they had been going the day before, but realized he had no idea where they were going. This was a hostile land. He needed friends.

"Brid, where is the sea?"

A loch?

"Yes, in a way. The greatest one. The one that seems to go forever." How could she not know of the sea? "You must have seen it before."

Why?

"Because there we might find safety. If we can find a currach to take us across, my people are there."

She looked at him uneasily. *Is there no other way?*

"Not if we are to escape from Brude."

She shook her head. Sadness was in her eyes. She pointed away from the rising sun. *It is there.*

It was also the direction where Connaire had seen the fire the night before. There was no choice. The sea was their only hope. He turned his horse and kicked its sides. He glanced back to see Brid follow with the hound beside her.

Throughout the morning, they rode without stop. At first it was slow, working their way through the dense forest, but then they found a track heading in the right direction. Their pace quickened. About midday, Brid pulled dried beef and oatcakes from a satchel and they ate while they rode. Finally, they crested a rise and, stretching out across the horizon, was the sea.

Connaire breathed a sigh of relief. They would reach the water. He chuckled softly. They only had to find a currach. Only. He wondered how many days they would have to ride down the coast to find someone with a currach. And whether the Fortriu hounds would find them first.

He looked back at Brid. She was staring at the hound. Cú Chulainn stood facing where they had come. His stance was tense, his hackles raised.

Connaire looked back at Brid. She looked up at Connaire and spoke quickly with her hands.

They are coming. Listen. You can hear their hounds.

"Ride for the sea."

She hesitated.

This time he yelled as loudly as he could. "Ride for the sea. We are not going to sit here and let them kill us. We have to try."

She shook her head. *We are finished. It is easier to die here than to be run down like the hare we had last night. Let us stand and fight.*

Connaire turned his horse and rode back to her. He grabbed her arm and held it tightly.

"We are not dead yet. I will do everything I can to keep you alive. I do not care about myself, but I will not give up on saving you. If I have to, I will throw you on my horse and carry you."

Tears welled in her eyes. She leaned over and kissed him on the lips. Then she pulled away and kicked her horse to a gallop, heading towards the sea. Connaire kicked his horse's sides and followed.

As they cleared the forest onto a pebbly beach, Brid stopped and stared down the coastline. Connaire saw about a handcount of dismounted men with their horses not far from them. They were loading a currach. He almost laughed out loud. The gods had smiled on them.

They rode towards the men and, as they neared them, Connaire could see that there was only one warrior among them. He was a young man, a Fortriu by the patterns on his skin, and he pulled his sword as Connaire and Brid neared. All the others were holy men by the crosses they wore, followers of the Christus. Then one of the men, who had been facing away and loading the boat, turned around. The man seemed startled, then waved and smiled at Connaire. He called out in a loud voice.

"Connaire, my prayers were answered. God has kept you safe and now sends you back to my care."

Connaire smiled. Whether the old gods or the new god, it did not matter. Somehow, he was back with his previous savior from the Fortriu's. It was Brother Padraig.

Chapter 59

The young warrior stood uneasily, sword in hand, his eyes darting back and forth from Connaire to Padraig. The monk spoke to the man and a short conversation ensued, which Connaire could not understand. Then he felt Brid touch his arm and turned. She spoke to him in the language of the hands, awkwardly because she had drawn her sword.

Be on guard. He is a Fortriu. He may know that Brude and a band of warriors are looking for you and that they suspected my mother and I of helping you, of killing their warriors.

Connaire sadly shook his head. "Will I be forced to kill again, this time a lad for whom I have no anger?"

Let me do it for you. Then his blood will not be on your hands.

"Sheath your sword. I am the one who began all this by betraying my brother. I will not have you kill for me again."

The young man ended his conversation with Padraig, although the holy man continued to speak in a pleading voice. The Fortriu walked slowly toward Connaire, his sword in ready position, cocked to one side and slightly raised. His intent was clear.

Connaire slipped off his horse, threw off his bratt and drew his sword. He saw fear in the young man's eyes, but no hesitation. The lad must know that he had little chance against a warrior of Connaire's stature. He was nearly a head shorter and did not have Connaire's hardened muscles. But honor will make a man do that which he knows will cause his own death. The young warrior was ready to die. He was almost within sword's reach and the combat would begin.

Connaire sighed. This would not be combat. It would be like slaughtering a young animal, a pup that attacked. How could the Morrigan allow such a travesty of warfare? But if he were to see Brid to safety, he had no choice. He would make it as swift and as painless as possible. He raised his sword.

Suddenly, moving far more swiftly than Connaire would have expected possible for the stout little man, Padraig rushed forward. He grabbed the Fortriu's sword arm. With a sudden wrench, he pulled the sword out of the surprised youth's hand and flung it into the water. The young man struck Padraig in the face and he fell hard to the ground, sitting in the sand with blood flowing from his nose.

Connaire sheathed his sword and lunged at the young man, grabbed the front of his léine with one hand and lifted him from the ground. The smaller warrior tried vainly to break Connaire's grip with one hand while he swung wildly with the other, but Connaire's face was beyond his reach.

Connaire's voice shook with rage as he spoke. "No warrior strikes a holy man. Let us see how you like your nose broken, boy."

"No, Connaire. Let him be." Brother Padraig's tone was stern, though muffled by his injury. "I acted as I did to prevent bloodshed. He is just a lad. Besides, he is Ciniod, Brude's son. You do not want to incur his wrath."

Connaire slowly lowered the young warrior until his feet touched the ground, still tightly clenching the front of his léine and keeping him at arm's length. "Tell him, Brother, that I have already killed his cousin, Drust, so his father already is after me. I will release him, but if he does anything to offend me, I will kill him with my bare hands."

"You killed Drust? Why?" Connaire heard the horror in the monk's voice.

"Because he tried to kill me." Connaire paused, glancing down at Brother Padraig. "It was a fair fight, although Drust tried to make it otherwise."

Brother Padraig spoke to Ciniod in the language of the Fortriu. Connaire thought he understood a few words this time, ones about swords and honor. Then Ciniod said something to Brother Padraig and he replied. The young man stopped struggling, going almost limp. Connaire released his grip on Ciniod's léine and the Fortriu stepped back, hands hanging at his sides.

Connaire relaxed a little. "What you said seems to have worked. What did he ask you?"

"When I told him you had killed Drust in single combat, he asked if you might have ambushed him."

"And your reply?"

"That you are a truthful man. I also told him that his father would not want him to needlessly throw away his own life by attacking you." The monk paused, studying Connaire. "Drust was well known as one of the Fortriu's most able warriors."

Connaire shrugged. "There will always be one better. Any warrior who forgets that is a fool."

He felt a hand touch his arm and turned to see Brid had come behind him.

Will these druids help? The hounds are closer.

Now that he was no longer distracted by Ciniod, Connaire heard the baying of the hounds. They were closer. Brother Padraig had risen from the ground and was brushing the sand from the back of his clothes and daubing at his bleeding nose with his sleeve.

"Brother Padraig, Brude and his warriors will be here soon. Will you take us with you?"

Padraig looked at him dubiously. "It is not a problem to take you, but we cannot take her."

"Why? I am the one who killed Drust, not her."

Padraig sadly shook his head. "We are sailing to the holy isle of Ioua. Women are not allowed there."

Connaire rested his hand on the small monk's shoulder, gripping it tightly. "When I was on Ioua, I learned the meaning of letters from Brother Eochaidh. I copied them onto new vellum for him, the writings of your Christus. He spoke of loving everyone, man or woman."

Padraig nodded. "It is true. And Saint Paul wrote than in Christus there is no male or female. But we have taken a vow of chastity. We allow no women, so as not to be tempted."

Connaire roughly shook Padraig's shoulder, almost knocking him from his feet. "I am not asking you to couple with her. I am asking you to save her life. If you do not save her, Brude will have her taken to the drowning cave. Is that how you show the love of Christus? By leaving someone He loves to die?"

Padraig softly chuckled. "Well said, my friend. If you ever choose to follow the Christus, you will be a fine spokesman. Though Colm Cille may have my hide for it, you both are most welcome."

"And the hound?"

Cú Chulainn was pacing the beach, hackles up, and growling every time he heard the hounds baying.

"The hound, too. All of you." He smiled wryly. "But I may have you explain to Colm Cille. You are far more eloquent that I."

Connaire turned and went to Brid.

"We will be safe. Brother Padraig will take us all."

You go. I will stay here.

"What? Brude will kill you. Or capture you and take you to the cave where they drown their enemies. You told me that you have horrible dreams of dying that way."

I do. She reached up and touched his cheek. *I greatly fear the water. I have never learned to swim. A bath is as much water as I ever want to be in. I cannot go with you. I cannot go in that little boat and sail across the sea. I cannot. Leave me. The Fortriu will not take me alive, take me to their drowning place.*

The hounds were nearing. He could hear them clearly now. There was no time. He shook his head. "Very well. I will do as you wish. Help me unload the horses and put what I need on the boat."

She nodded, went to the pack horse and began to untie the leather straps. Connaire looked to Padraig. He signaled the holy man to follow him. With a puzzled look on his face, Padraig complied.

Connaire went behind Brid, then grabbed her wrists and pulled them behind her back. The hound seemed torn between Brid and his new master, so Connaire whistled the command to fetch a stick and the hound ran off before Brid could countermand him. As she frantically struggled in his grip, he turned to Padraig.

"Take a strap and bind her hands."

Brid tried to twist away and to kick him. Padraig undid a strap that bound a satchel to the horse and tied Brid's wrist.

Connaire shook his head. "Tighter. She is very strong and determined to die."

Connaire watched as Padraig tightened the knot. He grimaced as he saw the leather bite into Brid's wrists, but knew it was necessary. Then he pushed her to the ground and tied her ankles with another strap that the brother gave him. He picked her up and flung her over his shoulder, holding her tightly, and walked to the currach. As gently as he could, he laid her writhing body in the bottom of the boat. As he did, Connaire barely escaped being kicked in the face by her bound feet as he stepped back.

While the brothers finished loading their goods on the currach, Connaire took the weapons from the pack horse and carried them to the boat. Brother Padraig stopped him with a gentle but firm hand on his chest.

"You will not need those on Ioua."

"I know, Brother, but I will not always be on Ioua."

Padraig shook his head. "It is a place of peace. No weapons."

"Then I will leave these in your care until I leave."

"No." As short as he was, Brother Padraig towered over Connaire. "Leave them."

Connaire opened his arms and dropped them in the water. "As you wish, Padraig. But I will take my own sword and Brid's as well as her bow. Nothing more."

Padraig sighed. "Very well. But you will leave them in your quarters and never carry them while you are on the isle."

"Agreed."

Connaire went to Brid's horse. There was a heavy satchel strapped to it, one that Brid held of great value, so he untied it and carried it to the currach. He carefully placed it on the boards along the keel.

The hound had returned with a large stick in his mouth, so Connaire tried to pull him to the boat. Cú Chulainn's legs were planted, his tail tucked between his legs. He must fear the water as much as his mistress.

Connaire shook his head. "I do not have time for this."

He grabbed the big hound around its middle and carried it to the currach, flinging it inside. The brothers were already aboard, so Connaire pushed the leather-hulled boat off the shore and into the sea.

Suddenly, Ciniod sprinted from where he had been standing toward the shallow water where Connaire had dropped the weapons. From the corner of his eye, Connaire saw him and turned, wading back to the shore. The young warrior was almost to the water when Connaire stepped in front of him. He spread his arms wide and roared like an angry bear. Ciniod fell back, landing hard on the sand.

Connaire pointed his finger at the young man and yelled. "Stay! If you move I will have to kill you. I am tired of killing. I do not want to kill you, but I will if you force me."

Ciniod stayed, his eyes wide. Connaire could see the damp patch on the front of his léine that showed that he had pissed himself. He could fear. Good.

Connaire turned and waded back to the currach, pushing it farther into the sea. Then, with the brothers helping him, he climbed onto the boat. He grabbed a pair of oars and rowed. The breeze was with them, so one of the brothers hoisted the leather sail while a couple of others grabbed oars.

As he rowed, Connaire saw a large company of warriors ride to the beach they had just left. He saw one, who he was sure was Brude, dismount and go to the lad, who was now sitting in the sand, head bowed.

Then Brude stood. They were still close enough to shore that a well-thrown spear might reach them. An arrow surely would. Or, since the currach was heavy-laden, some of the warriors might be able swim to them. But instead, Brude waved, as if to say a thank you for sparing his son.

Connaire paused but a moment in his rowing to wave in reply. It was the honor of warriors, enemies or not.

V. RETURN

Chapter 60

When the sail filled with the wind and pulled the small boat, the men shipped their oars and relaxed, rubbing their hands. Connaire worked his way along the currach to Brid, lying on her side on the bottom boards. She was shaking, eyes closed and jaw clenched. The hound was curled by her. Connaire knelt in front of her and loosened the leather straps binding her ankles.

Without warning, Brid kicked back, striking a glancing blow in Connaire's crotch. With a groan, he clutched his groin and sank to his knees. After several gasping breaths, he was able to speak.

"You may hate me for putting you on this currach, but I could not leave you to die." He took another deep breath. "I love you, Brid. I will die with you, if that is to be, but I will never leave you."

Tears formed in the corners of her eyes and trickle down her cheeks, eyes still clamped shut.

"Will you let me free you?"

She nodded.

Cautiously, Connaire finished untying Brid. She curled into a ball for a moment, her body shaking. Then she reached out a hand and grabbed Connaire's léine. She pulled him close and wrapped both her arms around him. He could feel her silent sobs. Cú Chulainn licked his face and he pushed the hound away. He whispered into Brid's ear.

"Are you feeling better? I know you fear the sea, but I am here and will not let anything happen to you."

Brid pulled back far enough to look in his eyes. She silently mouthed the words, I love you.

Connaire smiled. "Then you will not kick me again?"

She shook her head, freeing her hands so that she could speak to him.

I am sorry that I hurt you. She looked to her side and shuddered. *But I do fear the water.*

"I will keep you safe. I promise." He smiled. "And if this boat sank, I am a good swimmer."

The fear he saw in Brid's eyes made Connaire regret his words. "I did not mean that I think this boat is in danger of sinking. I came from Eireann on a boat like this without a problem. I am sure that the brothers are better sailors than I."

Cú Chulainn shoved in between them, shoving his nose in Connaire's face. Like his mistress, he was quivering.

Connaire shook his head. "It seems your hound fears the seas as much as you do." He gently pushed Cú Chulainn away. "But I must see if I can help the brothers."

As he crouched and moved slowly toward Brother Padraig, Connaire glanced back at Brid. She was clutching the hound to her breast. Perhaps in time they would become less fearful of the sea. But then, perhaps not.

The hound and Brid stayed huddled together throughout the voyage.

It was late in the day when the currach landed on the isle. The sun had sunk low in the sky, painting the streaks of low clouds in pinks and purples. As the boat hit the sandy beach, the brothers hopped into the water and pulled it ashore. It ground onto the beach and Connaire slipped over the side, quickly reaching up for Brid. She hesitantly threw her leg over the side. Connaire grabbed her waist and lifted her. Then he gently set her on the shore. She turned to him and smiled, the first for some time. He smiled in return.

"See? You have made it safely to dry land, just as I promised."

She touched his lips with a finger. *You promised to save me if we sank. We did not.*

He laughed. "You are right. Nonetheless, we are safe."

Connaire ducked as the hound leapt over him from the currach. Then he turned to see men approaching, the brothers from Ioua. At the fore was Colm Cille.

When the leader of the religious community arrived, he embraced Connaire.

"It is good to see you again, my son."

Brother Padraig cleared his throat. Colm Cille pulled back and looked at him, his thick eyebrow arched.

"Is there something bothering you, Brother?"

"Um, I just wanted you to know of all of our passengers."

Colm Cille looked around until his gaze fell on Brid. He turned to Padraig. "A woman? What have you done?"

Connaire stepped between the two men. "I am the one who insisted. If I had not, she and I would be dead now." Cú Chulainn was shoving his wet nose onto Connaire's leg, holding a piece of driftwood in his mouth. "And the hound, too. We would all have been killed by the Fortriu."

"You and your hound are welcome. But your woman must go to the isle of Eilean nam Ban."

Connaire shook his head. "Brid must remain with me."

The holy man studied Connaire askance. "The isle is very near. She will be with other women."

"She must remain with me."

Colm Cille shook his head. "You bring the unexpected to our community. Like it or not, my friend, I believe you bring the will of God. She may stay with you, but you may not couple with her while you are here."

"Agreed."

"Do I have your word?"

Connaire spat in his palm and pressed it to Colm Cille's.

Colm Cille smiled. "You word is sufficient. I do not need your oath." Then he turned and walked away.

Connaire looked at Brother Padraig. The little man shifted his weight from one leg to another.

Connaire chuckled. "Why are you nervous, my friend?"

"You do not understand what you have done. Colm Cille has often said that where there is a cow there is a woman, and where there is a woman there is mischief. That is why all cows and women are on Eilean nam Ban. You have forced him to go against this. He will blame me."

Connaire grinned. "I think that you do not understand your leader as well as I do. While he may be called a dove, he has the heart of a warrior. Only weak men try to blame others for their decisions. Colm Cille is not weak."

The little brother wiped his brow with his sleeve. "I hope that you are correct. I have seen Colm Cille in righteous anger and it is a fearsome sight."

"Trust me. I do understand the man." Connaire paused, thinking of the tale that Colm Cille had shared on his last visit to the isle. "We have regrets in common that shall haunt us as long as we live. We have both caused the deaths of those we loved."

The monk looked up into Connaire's eyes, but did not ask the question Connaire feared. Gratefully, the warrior stretched his arm across Padraig's shoulders and pulled him to his side. Then he wrapped his other arm around Brid, hugging her close.

Brother Padraig began to chuckle. Then Connaire felt Brid's silent laugh. Like a billowing wave, his laughter rolled out of him. Once again, he had escaped death. This time it did not cost him the one he loved. Perhaps this god of these monks did have some plan for him.

With the hound following, they walked, half stumbled, to the community of the brothers.

Connaire awoke in a sweat. It was still dark. He rose from his stiff, wooden bed and stretched his aching muscles. Keeping as quiet as he could, he edged his way to the door of the hut. He did not want to wake Brid, but needed the cold, brisk air outside. As he slipped out, Cú Chulainn pushed his way past him. In the moonlight, Connaire saw the hound find a tree and lift his leg. He sighed. Would that he could so easily relieve himself of his own nightly torments.

What did these dreams mean? He understood dreaming of lying between Brid's legs. His hardness from that nighttime reverie made him wish he could slip into her bed when he went back inside. Even though frustrating, that part of the dream was not as disturbing as what followed. Brid had become Scáthach, first as a living person. He had tried desperately to pull away, but then she became a skeleton, clutching him tightly with her arms and legs of bone, and continued to pound against him in a macabre imitation of coupling until it drew his seed from him. Its skull grinned in horrific triumph. He had almost cried out in agony when it had happened, waking as the scream rose in his throat.

Druids said dreams were messages from the gods. If so, what was the message? That they were angry because he had killed Scáthach?   Or was it because he had allowed Deirdre to use his desire for her to lead his own brother to his death?   All Connaire knew was that dreams like that one of Scáthach would drive him crazy if they continued.   There were no druids on Ioua, but there was Colm Cille.   He would talk to him.   Perhaps the monk would be able to tell him why his nights were so tormented.

Connaire quietly opened the door and went back into the hut.   He carefully inched towards Brid's bed.   He knelt beside it and rested his hand close to her.   His tears trickled down his cheeks.   If the god of Colm Cille existed, he must be cruel.   No loving god would make a man endure the pain of loving someone so much and never again having her.   Not only that, he was destined to take as his mate a woman he did not love, while the one he loved would be only a part of his household, like a sister.

He stayed there for some time, until his knees ached from kneeling.   Then he crawled back into his own bed, but sleep did not come.   He feared the return of the dreams that haunted his nights.

Finally, the morning light filtered into the hut.   Wearily, Connaire rolled off of his bed.   Brid sat up in her bed, stretching. She opened the door, letting in the sunlight.   She turned to him and smiled.   Connaire brushed back his thick hair with his fingers and smiled back.

At least she did not know the torments of his mind, of his horrific dreams.   They were too sickening.   No matter what, she must never know those.

Brid motioned him to follow as she left the hut to wash before the morning meal with the brothers.   Connaire sighed, hesitating a moment, then followed.

Chapter 61

In the darkening hut, Connaire set his pen on the table,
rubbed his hands together. He glanced down at the hound, curled
in a corner, softly snoring. The work day was almost over. He
knew from his last sojourn on the isle that, as the days grew longer,
the brothers ended their labors with the setting sun. Precious
candles were saved until the seasons would again be short.

Connaire closed his eyes and gently massaged them with
his fingertips. With a sigh, he dropped his hands to the table. He
turned to Brid, sitting next to him. She was intent upon her work,
pen in hand and her tongue curling on the side of her upper lip.

Connaire was proud that she had taken so aptly to copying
the brothers' holy books, but part of him wished she had not done
so with such speed. Colm Cille had once said Connaire had a
natural talent for learning to understand the writings of their god.
Brid had learned more quickly and now showed a better hand in
copying. Connaire was torn between happiness that she had such
a talent and wishing that she had not done quite as well as he.

She looked up at him and smiled. Then she took a small
scrap of vellum and wrote on it. Connaire slowly deciphered the
words. "You appear to be a badger."

For a moment Connaire was not sure what she meant, but
then looked down at his ink-stained pen hand and remembered that
he had rubbed his eyes. He must have left a black stain.

He started to try to wipe his eye with his other hand, but
Brid laid her hand on his and stopped him. Looking down, he saw
that both his hands were covered with ink. She took a damp cloth
they kept near for removing errors in their copying and daubed
around his eyes.

He let her minister to his stain, but soon tired of it and pulled away.

"Enough. Let it be. If I look like a badger, it must be the will of the brothers' God."

Brid gave him a bemused shrug and smiled. She spoke to him with her hands. *I like badgers. Brave fighters.*

"You need to be careful of how you speak of fighting here. The brothers are against it."

Does not their Apostle Paul say, "I have fought the good fight?" And was not the writer of their Psalms a warrior-king?

Connaire laughed. "The brothers may rue ever having taught you to understand their writings."

I like the brothers, but I do not understand them. Why do these men not wish to couple? Are they missing what a man needs to do so?

He shook his head. "That is not why. They feel that their god wants them to not be distracted in following him by coupling. They seem to still want to, which is why they allow no women or girls here." He paused, then grinned. "Except for you, but that is only because I demanded you stay with me. I am sure many of the brothers have had thoughts of coupling since you arrived. I have seen many of them walking with an odd bulge in the front of their robes. They will have to make their robes bigger in the front if you are here much longer."

You are making a joke.

"No, I have seen it. I even saw one brother couple with a knothole out of frustration after you walked by him."

She laughed. *Did he start a new branch?* Then she grew serious, studying his face and cocking her head to one side. *Have you had thoughts of coupling with me?*

Connaire reddened. "I have. You know I have. But I pledged to my brother to take Aislinn as my mate. We will never be mates and it will only make it more difficult when I oath to Aislinn."

She gently rested her hand on his. *I was wrong to ask that. I know you must keep your pledge.* Connaire saw a tear in the corner of her eye as she continued. *As I know you love me.*

Connaire rose and walked from the hut. The setting sun painted the cloud-streaked sky with bright oranges and purples, but to Connaire it was ugly, an omen of worsening times in his life. And in Brid's life. He must return to the clann and she come with him. No longer would they be together as lovers. Even though they had not been able to couple again, they were lovers.

As he stood, staring at the horizon, Brid came to his side, slipping her arm around his. He had to tell her.

"It has been almost three cycles of the moon and Beltane has passed. I must go to my clann. I cannot avoid it any longer." He took a deep breath and slowly exhaled. "Then I will have to oath with Aislinn. I am sorry."

Brid stepped back, her hands barely visible in the twilight. *You must keep your promise. I will not go.*

He grabbed her wrist. "You must come. I will not abandon you." He paused, knowing he could not promise much to her. "You will be a respected member of my household."

She pulled her hand away and continued. *I will go to the isle of the women. The bothers will take me after you leave.*

"You cannot go there. They cannot talk the words of the hands with you. Brother Eochaidh says that he does not think any of them can write words. You will be completely alone." He paused, thinking desperately for more reasons. "Besides, they are not warriors. None of them. They could not understand you, even if you found a way to speak to them."

It had grown too dark to see if she replied in the language of the hands, but when he felt her touch his arm, he knew she had not. She was waiting.

He swallowed hard. "I want you to come with me. I do not want to ever be away from you."

She gripped his arm tightly, then released it and went back into the hut. He knew that meant she would come with him. But should she? He could never have her as his mate. She would have to watch him oath to, even couple with Aislinn. The thought nauseated him. Maybe it would be better for her to stay with the women on Eilean nam Ban.

No. She would live her days in misery, a life of isolation. There was only one solution. She must return with him to the clann. He would find her a suitable mate. Maybe not one worthy of her, but at least one who would see her worth. A warrior, like her. Yes, perhaps Cairbre would do. He was a good man, a noble warrior who would value one such as Brid.

As Connaire stood in thought, Brid came from the hut and took his arm. Cú Chulainn followed at their heels as they walked to the small hall where the brothers dined. He knew that the only way he could show his love for her was to do as she was doing for him: give her to another. His heart ached, but Connaire felt that at least he finally saw the only honorable course to take. Following the honorable course was seldom easy.

When they entered the low-ceilinged wooden hall, the brothers were seated on their long benches at their tables, food already before them. They were waiting for Brid and Connaire so that they could say a blessing on the food. A small table and bench were off in one corner, reserved for the two visitors. Kind as they had been, the brothers would not go so far as to have a woman sit at their table.

As soon as soon as Brid and Connaire were seated, Brother Padraig read a Psalm and Colm Cille gave his evening meal prayer. Although the food was not overly-abundant, it was enough and there was always a bowl for Cú Chulainn. The hound had slowly become the favorite of the holy community, often fed scraps from the table by the brothers. He still normally stayed close to Brid, but on occasion visited the brothers when he felt ignored. The community had no dogs, not needing them for hunting or warning of impending attack. Since Cú Chulainn had been with them, however, Connaire wondered if this might change.

He wondered what other changes their visit might bring to the community. In warmer weather, Brid shed her trews and wore only her léine. He had noticed that some of the brothers cast furtive glances at Brid's shapely legs as she walked by. They had sacrificed the pleasures of women for their god. Perhaps leaving the isle might help keep the brothers from remembering too well what they had sacrificed.

After the meal, Connaire went to Colm Cille.

"Brid and I would like to leave your isle tomorrow. I need to return to my clann."

The holy man solemnly studied him from under his thick, grey eyebrows.

"I have enjoyed having you here, but it is time for you to leave. The presence of your companion is most disruptive."
Then Colm Cille smiled. "God has a purpose for you, my young warrior. He has shown me I need to allow Him to control this isle. Now He will use you with your clann."

He glanced down at Cú Chulainn, who had seated himself on the brother's foot and was looking longingly up at him. He leaned down and rubbed him behind his ears. "Like this hound, the hound of Heaven will pursue you until you tire. Then He will have you follow Him as I have. Your torments will lessen and you will see how all things work in His will."

Connaire shook his head. "If this god thinks I will follow him because all that has happened is his will, then he is gravely mistaken. I led my brother to his death. I killed Brid's mother. I must live the rest of my life with the women I love close by, but denied me. This is his will? He is a very cruel god. I will leave him here on this isle with you."

Colm Cille gently rested his hand on Connaire's arm. "I know what trials you are enduring. But He will see you through them, if you let him."

"You know nothing of me. You only know that this god of yours has helped you in some way." Connaire spat on the dirt. "But, for me, he is nothing but a cruel hoaxer."

Connaire turned and walked to his hut, shaking with rage.

The next morning Brother Padraig came to Connaire's hut before morning meal. Connaire had not slept much, haunted by his dreams, and was standing outside in the morning chill. He did not have his bratt around him, feeling a certain cleansing in enduring the cold.

The stout brother had obviously been in a hurry to get to Connaire, as he was panting and rested a moment before speaking.

"Connaire, Colm Cille has told me that you are leaving us. He has a currach ready to take you to your clann. He asks that you come to morning meal and then be ready to depart." He paused to catch his breath. Connaire thought he saw a tear in the little man's eye. "I will miss you, my friend. I feel as though I have seen you grow from a frightened youth to a confident warrior."

Connaire draped an arm across the brother's shoulders. "You have, my friend. You have. I am now a true warrior."

But confident? Will I ever be truly confident?

Connaire called back to the hut. "Brid, pack our belongings. We leave after morning meal."

The sky was overcast and a slight drizzle dampened the air. All of their things were loaded into the currach. Brid reluctantly allowed Connaire to help her into the boat, then squatted on the deck planks, clutching her knees to her chest. Connaire grabbed the hound and dropped him into the boat. Cú Chulainn crawled over to Brid and pushed his head into her arms. She hugged him close to her. A few of the brothers climbed in to man the oars. They were ready to depart.

Connaire turned to Colm Cille.

"I am sorry if I offended you by what I said about your god, Brother. You are a good man and have done nothing but good to us. Your hospitality has been most honorable."

The holy man smiled. "You have not offended me. And God has heard much worse." Colm Cille came closer. "I may see you again soon, Connaire, son of Fergus. I am to see Aedán made the Ri of Dál Riata."

"Is Conall dead?"

"Yes, he died in battle." Colm Cille chuckled sadly. "At least he did not drown in his wine. I did not want Aedán to be ri, but an angel commanded me three times to support him and I had to obey. I will be there when he is made ri."

Colm Cille rested his hand on the gunwale of the boat. "Be safe and go with God on your voyage."

Connaire started to say that he had no need of Colm Cille's cruel god, but did not. He merely nodded and silently climbed into the currach. The brothers on shore pushed the boat off the sand, and Connaire and the brothers on board took up their oars.

Chapter 62

The sun sat low on the horizon, barely visible under the heavy-hanging clouds. There was a chill in the air, foreboding a coming storm. Connaire found some comfort in seeing that coastline was near when he glanced over his shoulder, pulling hard on his oar. They should be on shore before the storm broke.

As the hull ground onto the gravel beach, the rowers shipped their oars and dropped over the side of the boat. They used the waves to help bring the boat ashore, tugging it farther up the shore each time a wave lifted the hull.

As Connaire helped the brothers pull the currach out of the sea, Cú Chulainn leapt out of the boat, barely clearing Connaire's head as he sought the safety of land. The hound was followed by Brid, jumping over the side after him.

As soon as the boat was safely on the beach, Connaire turned to Brid and the hound. Brid was kneeling beside Cú Chulainn, stroking his side as he looked up gratefully and lapped her face with his broad tongue. Connaire grinned, seeing his companions united in their hatred of the sea.

Once the craft was unloaded, the brothers began to prepare camp for the night. Connaire and Brid shouldered their goods. Since the currach had landed in the area where he had left this shore about a full cycle of the festivals ago, he knew where his clann should be. Now that he had started his journey, Connaire was anxious to finish it. They bade the brothers farewell and set off along the beach with their meager belongings carried in satchels slung over their shoulders. With no horses, the journey would take more than a day.

Connaire glanced at the sky, with a prayer to Manannán that he keep the storm at sea. They trod the shoreline until it became too dark to see the way in the cloudy twilight, then moved inland to find some shelter among the trees.

With the coming of night, they built a small fire, even though they would not need it for cooking. Since there had been no time for hunting, their evening meal would be dried fish. Still, the flames gave a certain comfort, a feeling of hearth and security even if there were none. They huddled together under their bratts with the hound curled close to them, adding his warmth to theirs. Although the storm did not come, the air was chill for that time of the year and Connaire wished they had been able to carry a hide shelter with them. Such a heavy load was not possible without a pack horse.

With the dawn, they rose. A mist lay heavy across the land, dripping from the canopy of leaves above. To avoid that, they stayed on the treeless shore, meandering along the waterline.

It was almost midday when Connaire noticed horsemen approaching in the distance, coming at a gallop along the beach. He glanced back at Brid. She saw them too. The fog had lifted enough that he could see that two men were in the lead, pursued by almost two handcounts of warriors. As they neared, he could see the two being pursued were Dál Riatans and the pursuers looked to be Fortriu.

Although this was not his battle, Connaire dropped his parcels and unsheathed his sword. Without looking back, he knew Brid had followed his lead.

The first horseman passed him almost without looking. Connaire could see the panic in his eyes. The second horseman pulled up next to him.

"You stand as though you are one of my kinsmen, ready to do battle."

Connaire nodded. "And you flee as one who wishes to avoid it."

"You shame me." The man on the horse was broad-shouldered, with fair hair and beard, his eyes deep green. He drew his sword. "I do not know you, warrior, but I hope to, if we survive. Will you stand with me?"

Connaire smiled. "Have I not stood before you did? And you have a horse that will carry you away if this fight goes badly."

The warrior laughed. "You are bold. I swear this to you, brave one. I will not leave you. If you die, so do I. And, if we live, you shall be rewarded for your courage."

Connaire pointed back to where the warrior had come from. "Now is not the time for words."

The enemy horsemen were upon them. One, brandishing a spear overhead, charged Connaire. As he drew near, he stabbed at Connaire. Dropping his sword, Connaire grabbed the spear and pulled the tip to the ground. As the point buried itself in the rocks, the enemy warrior was pulled from his horse by the spear he held in his grasp. Connaire used the warrior's own speed to launch him through the air as he still clutched his spear, landing awkwardly, headfirst on the rocky beach.

Connaire barely had time to pull the spear from the ground before another warrior was upon him, brandishing his own spear. Connaire hurled his captured spear, sinking it deep in the warrior's chest. The man dropped his weapon and grabbed the spear with both hands, falling backwards from his horse.

Another warrior, sword raised high, was riding at Connaire. With no weapon, he could only dive to one side. But he knew it was only a momentary salvation. As he lay on the ground, he saw his own sword on the ground, too far away to reach in time. The warrior turned and rode directly at him, swinging his sword in a slow, downward arc. If the sword did not get him, the horse's hooves would.

Suddenly Connaire saw an arrow appear in the neck of the warrior. Brid. He scrambled to his sword, grabbed it and held it at the ready position as he looked for his next foe.

The two men he had killed lay on the ground. The man Brid had just shot and another one with an arrow in his neck lay dead. Cú Chulainn stood over the body of one more warrior, blood dripping from the hound's teeth. The warrior they had saved had also killed one of his pursuers. The rest, now outnumbered, turned and rode away at a gallop.

The man on horseback rode over to Connaire. "You have stood by me and saved my life, but I do not know who you are."

Connaire sheathed his sword. "I am Connaire, son of Fergus. My clann has given allegiance to Conall, the Ri of Dál Riata."

"Ah, but Conall is dead."

"I know. We will follow the next ri."

The man laughed. "If not for you, who knows who would be the next ri? I am Aedán mac Gabrán. I am on my way to Dun Ad to become the Ri of Dál Riata."

"You are Aedán?" Connaire was dumbfounded. "Where are the warriors to guard you?"

Aedán rubbed the back of his neck. "Mostly dead. Except for him." He indicated the rider who had been with him, now slowly riding back, sword in hand.

Connaire mirthlessly chuckled. "I can see why he survived."

Aedán sighed. "Yes, he was at the fore of our escape. But you were at the fore of our defense." He nodded at Cú Chulainn and Brid. "You, your hound and your daughter."

Connaire felt his anger rise and he fought to keep it in check. "She is not my daughter. If not for a promise, she would be my mate."

Aedán studied them both for a moment. "I can see now that I am mistaken. You both have put me in your debt. I must go now to Dun Ad, but would like you to be there as my guests when I become ri. It will be on the day after the morrow."

Connaire nodded. "If it is possible, we will be there."

"And bring your hound." Aiden gestured at Cú Chulainn. "He is worth a handcount of warriors. What do you call him?"

"Cú Chulainn."

Aedán smiled. "Well named. I hope to see you on the morrow."

Then he turned and rode to his companion. Connaire could see from his angry gestures that Aedán was not pleased with his companion.

Brid touched Connaire's arm as he watched them ride away. She motioned to the horses, now riderless, standing nearby.

He shrugged. "At least now we shall ride."

She smiled and nodded.

After burying the fallen warriors under piles of stones, they set off to find Connaire's people. By midday they reached the place where he had last seen his clann. It was exactly where he remembered, but not as he had expected. Connaire dismounted and walked slowly into the clearing.

The wind brushed the grass. A few houses, not finished, dotted the area. Wicker walls, half complete, made hollow circles. But there was not a person, not even a cow to be seen. The hound patrolled the area, wandering around the empty shells of the houses, sniffing. They were alone.

Connaire stood, staring at nothing.   Had they returned to
Eire?   Had Bran's warriors driven them away or, worse yet, killed
so many that the rest had fled?   Where were they?

Then Brid touched his arm.   Dazed, he turned to her and
she spoke with her hands.

They are gone.

Connaire nodded.

Do you know where?

He shook his head, unable to think of anything to say.

We must go.

He said nothing.

*We must go.   Let us go to Dun Ad.   Aedán has invited us.
He will give us hospitality.*

Connaire looked at her.   All that had driven him, all that he
had felt he must do, was gone.   His clann was gone.   He was
alone.   Except for Brid, he was alone.   She was all that he had
left.   He grabbed her, pulled her close, and buried his head in her
hair.   He spoke softly.

"We will go to Dun Ad."

They had nowhere else to go.

Chapter 63

First they rode back to where they had saved Aedán from his pursuers. It was dusk, but he could still see the mounds of stone. Although it was time to make camp, this place was not a welcome one. The shades of the warriors might still be lurking, not yet on their journey to the island of the dead towards the setting sun. So they continued to ride until darkness had fallen, then rode a short distance into the forest to find a bed of fallen leaves.

They were tired, exhausted both from a day of fighting and riding, but also from the disappointment of finding the clann gone. They made no fire, but ate some dried fish and wrapped themselves together in their bratts to fight the chill night. He lay on his side, facing away from her, and she snuggled close to his back. It was how they had often slept since they had left her home.

Connaire felt Brid's hand creep up his leg, gently brushing him. He felt himself harden. He started to push her hand away, remembering his promise to his brother. A promise for the good of the clann. But was there a clann any longer? Aislinn was gone. With her went any obligation, for his promise to oath to her was no longer possible. Now his only clann was Brid. And the hound that was curled up against them.

He turned to Brid and slipped one hand between her legs as the other cupped her breast. She was wet, wanting him. Kissing her with a long, desperate kiss, he pulled one of her legs across his hip and slowly entered her. They began to couple, tentatively at first, but soon frantically. She began to whimper, then bit his shoulder. As she did, he lost himself to their coupling, throbbing inside her.

They lay together, holding each other tightly, as he felt himself shrivel. He carefully stroked her hair as he whispered into her ear.

"I oath to you, Scáthach nic Scáthach, not for a year, but forever. I will die before I will ever leave you or turn away from coupling again. I will be yours as completely as a slave. I hope that you will oath to me, but my love does not depend on that."

Brid pulled back. For a moment Connaire was unsure of how she felt about his oath. There was no light to see her face, to see if she would accept or reject his oath. But then he felt her take his hand and write letters on it. They were the letters of the brothers, the letters they had written on the parchments. He had to concentrate on what she was saying, at times having her repeat a letter. But finally he understood.

I oath to you, Connaire mac Fergus. You own my heart as you would own a horse, a sword or a bratt. I will die before I leave you. I would die if you left me.

When she finished, Connaire grabbed her hand and held it tightly.

"You will never have cause to worry about my love for you."

They fell asleep with arms and legs still intertwined.

Connaire awoke to water dripping on his face. The dim light of the early-morning sun was almost lost under the heavy, gray clouds. A drizzling rain filtered through the trees that he and Brid had used for cover.

Brid was awake, unmoving in his arms, watching him. She smiled. Connaire returned her smile, gently touching her face.

"You are my mate, Brid. I can now give myself to you completely."

She freed her hands and spoke to him. *I gave myself to you long ago.* She brushed the rain from her face. *We must find shelter and food soon or we will not be mates for long.*

Connaire laughed. "You are right. Now that you are my clann, we must go to Dun Ad and offer ourselves in service to Aedán. Perhaps he will bring us into his clann."

They rose, shook the water from their bratts before putting them around their shoulders and mounted the horses. As they rode onto the rocky shore, Connaire whistled and Cú Chulainn bounded from the forest.

Connaire studied the direction the two men had ridden the day before. Then he turned to Brid. "There is a problem. We know Dun Ad is this way, but we have no idea exactly where it is. I suppose we should try to follow their trail as much as we can."

She gave a shrug, as if to say she did not have a better plan.

Until well past midday they rode without stopping. The hound loped along beside them, periodically glancing up with a baleful look that told of his desire to rest. But, fearing being caught without shelter as the drizzle turned to heavy rain, they did not slacken their pace until finally they had to dismount to rest their horses and eat a meal of dried fish. Their last one. He had not expected to find his clann gone.

Connaire studied the shoreline ahead. He had once bragged to Ciarán that he could track a mouse through a meadow. But horses left no trail on the rocky coast. He had been watching where the forest met the beach. Unless there was a worn path he doubted that he would detect where Aedán and his companion had entered the woods. Two men left little trace and the drizzle could hide much. Still, he looked for the broken twig, the mashed leaf, anything that might show that riders had been that way.

With a sigh of frustration, he mounted his horse. He glanced back to make sure Brid had followed suit, then kicked his horse's sides. He prayed to the gods, including Colm Cille's, that he would find the way to Dun Ad.

When they reached the place where the brothers had landed them ashore the day before, Connaire saw a currach on the beach. Several men, wearing the long, white tunics of the brothers from the isle of Ioua, were around it. One was a man who looked like the tall figure of Colm Cille. He glanced back at Brid, who looked at him with equal perplexity, then urged his horse to a gallop.

Arriving at the boat, Connaire saw that it was indeed the holy man and others from his isle who stood on the shore. He smiled at Connaire and, making the sign of the cross of Christus, hailed him.

"Connaire, we meet again so soon. I expected you to be with your clann."

Connaire dismounted and raised his hand in greeting. "And I did not expect you to be here."

"I said that I would be here to anoint Aedán as Samuel anointed David, to be the new ri. He shall be God's agent on this earth."

Connaire could not suppress a grin. "Did Samuel not also anoint Saul? And did not Saul fail your god?"

For a moment, Colm Cille seemed taken aback. Then he smiled. "I often underestimate you, Connaire. You could well have been a brother, with your quick mind and reading of the Holy Scriptures. You might have well been my heir to God's mission in Dál Riata." He paused. "And still might be, since you have been following a life of abstinence."

Connaire could not keep from laughing, glancing back at Brid, who still sat on her horse. She shook with suppressed mirth.

Turning back to the holy man, he had to wait a moment before he could speak.

"I am afraid that I am no longer abstinent. I am now oathed to Brid and we coupled last night."

Colm Cille was momentarily nonplussed. He stroked his chin, thinking. "That is how it should be. The Apostle Paul said that it is better to oath to your beloved than to burn with passion. But what of your promise to your brother?"

"When I went to where I left them, there was nothing. My clann is gone." He shook his head. "No, not gone, but changed. Brid is my clann."

The hound nudged his hand. Connaire looked down. "I am corrected. Brid and Cú Chulainn are my clann."

"A small clann, my friend. We are on our way to Dun Ad. The ri might be willing to help you and your new clann. Will you join us?"

Connaire could not resist a soft chuckle. "Indeed he might be willing to help us, as we helped him."

Colm Cille lifted one eyebrow as he studied Connaire. "You helped the Ri?"

Connaire shrugged. "He seemed to have been momentarily without friends. At least loyal friends. We befriended him."

A wry grin momentarily slipped across Brid's lips.

The holy man cocked his head. "There is always more that you do not say than you do say."

Connaire shrugged. "So we go to Dun Ad?"

"We go to Dun Ad."

Chapter 64

By the time their small party neared Dun Ad, the drizzle had ceased and dusk was near. The two warriors had ridden their horses slowly as to not outpace the brothers, who were on foot. The fort stood alone on a hill in a marshy plain, starkly outlined against the cloudy sky. Connaire pulled his horse to a halt and studied it. Temporary, cowhide shelters surrounded the hill to house the warriors and craftsmen who had gathered for the entrusting of Dál Riata to the new ri. A narrow trail wove its way in and out of large rocks to the top, where logs were stacked as a high wall. Smoke plumes from a number of fires wove their way to the skies. The fort's dominance of the lands around it made it more impressive than Scáthach's broch. Brid and the hound stayed at his side, but the brothers had not stopped. Colm Cille slowed and turned, but Connaire motioned for him to continue. He was not ready to enter the fort.

Connaire felt that when he reached the top of the hill, his life would be changed. As when the brothers ended their writing and decorating one page and turned to another, part of his life would end and it would change forever. He would be admitting that his clann was gone, that the friends and family with whom he had fled had ceased to exist. All that he was by birth and kinship would be over. Like a rogue warrior who had been cast out by his own people, he would have lost his heritage. And he had been the cause.

With a sigh, he glanced at Brid. She eyed him warily. He realized that she must sense his sadness. She, too, had lost all that had been her life: her home and her mother. Yet she had never shown despair. He brought his horse close to hers, leaned over

and reached out to her.   She grabbed his hand and squeezed it.
Then she released his hand and they rode toward the fort.

As they neared the shelters in the shadow of the hill,
Connaire could see the bustle of activity as people laughed and
chatted, traded goods and livestock.   They had churned the
meadow into a muddy quagmire.   Several smiths worked to one
side, melting, molding and beating metal.   One man was
bargaining with a smith holding a bronze torque.   Nearby was a
large corral of horses and they rode to it.

Connaire and Brid left their newly acquired mounts in the
corral and, with Brid taking the satchel she had saved from the
broch, they hiked up the path to Dun Ad with the hound at their
heels.   Along the trail, spearmen stood on rocky perches, spaced at
wide intervals.   They did not even look at the three of them as they
passed.   Connaire realized that they were a show of prestige by
Áedán rather than any protection.   No enemy was anywhere to be
seen.

At the top of the trail, a tall, burly warrior with a thick beard
and bushy eyebrows glared at him.   His long hair had streaks of
much grey in the black.

He barred their way with his spear.

"You must be aire forgaill to enter.   The ri is to be
consecrated with his tuaths and there is no room for such as you."

Connaire bristled.   "I am taoiseach of my clann.   Step
aside."

The big man laughed and pointed at the bronze torque
around Connaire's neck.   "You are Aire Désa, at best.   What is
your clann?"

"MacFergus."

"I have never heard of such a clann.   Where are your
warriors?"

"They stand before you. Tell Áedán that we are here. He asked us to come."

The guard laughed. "Tell Áedán that Connaire is here with his clann of a child and a cur?"

Connaire's jaw clenched. "Tell him that Connaire is here with his mate and Cú Chulainn."

"Cú Chulainn? Is this a jest?" He snorted. "Perhaps I should toss you down the hill with the rest of the rabble."

Connaire and Brid swiftly drew their swords and the hound stood with forelegs spread and teeth bared. Connaire glared at him. "It was no jest. Do as I asked."

"I am not at your biding. My duty is to keep out who are not worthy to enter." The guard lifted his spear, pointing it at Connaire's chest. "Like you."

With the speed of a wildcat, Connaire grabbed the spear from the guard's grasp and brought his sword to the man's throat. "I could kill you easily for the insult to my honor, but I will not. Go to Áedán. Tell him what I have said. If he refuses us entry, we will leave without argument. If you do not do this, I will kill you and Áedán will pay the honor price. He owes me."

The man's voice was choked, just above a whisper. "But I cannot leave this place without a guard."

"We will guard it. No one will pass."

The guard nodded and Connaire released him. He backed away, turned and hurried off.

As soon as the guard left, Brid reached up and removed the bronze torque from Connaire's neck. Then she pulled a golden one, well crafted, from the satchel she carried and started to put it around his neck.

Connaire held up his hand to stop her. "Such a torque is for a ri, not me." He smiled. "Besides, I am sure Áedán's is not so fine and I would not want him to think I was claiming his status."

Brid shrugged, then pulled a silver one from the satchel. It was so finely wrought that Connaire was speechless. It was a twisting band that ended with two snarling wolves' heads with bared fangs and protruding tongues, almost meeting. This time she pushed his protesting hand away, pulled the heads apart and slipped it around his neck. Then she bent the torque so it would stay safely around his neck. Next she brought out two arm bands of equal quality and workmanship with the same wolfish theme and put them on his sword arm. Finally, she reached into the bag and produced a wonderfully-made broach, with two similar wolves' heads, and replaced the one securing his bratt.

She touched her finger to his lips, then spoke with her hands. *A taoiseach must look a taoiseach.*

Connaire smiled. "Even if his clann is so small?"

She returned his smile and nodded.

At that point, two warriors, carrying cups of ale, approached the entrance. Their garments were coarse and their torques of poorly-made bronze. Both were powerfully built men, one tall and the other shorter, but with the shoulders of a bull.

Connaire stepped in front of them. The tall one spoke carefully, but some words showed he had drunk too much from his cup. "We want to see the consecration. Stand aside."

Connaire smiled. "I am sorry, but you must wait until the guard returns. We are to let no one enter until he returns."

The tall warrior leaned close, his breath heavy with ale. "You will stop me?"

Then he started to draw his sword.

Connaire did not want to kill the man. So he swung his fist into the man's belly. Hard. The man grunted and staggered back, but was able to tug his sword from its scabbard. Before he could use it, Connaire stepped forward, driving his fist into the man's face. He could hear the sound of breaking teeth and saw the blood spurt from his mouth. The tall man fell, landing hard on his back.

The other man started to draw his sword, but Brid quickly had her sword at his neck and the hound was ready to leap. He wisely took his hand away from the hilt.

Connaire shook his head disgustedly. "Take your friend and go back down the path. Take this and trade it for more ale." He tossed the bullish man the bronze torque Brid had taken from his neck.

As the two men staggered away, the taller supported by the shorter, Connaire turned to see Áedán and the guard watching.

Áedán gave a short laugh and shook his head. "I need to keep you away from our kinsmen. You need to keep your anger for the Fortriu."

"I am sorry to have hurt him. But at least these warriors walked away." Connaire grinned. "Or one did."

"Keary told me he should have challenged you." Áedán nodded toward the guard. "That would have been most foolish."

Then Áedán stepped forward and embraced Connaire. "I need warriors like you, Connaire of clann MacFergus." He stepped back. "But you must leave your weapons with Keary so that you do not kill any of my guests. Then you may enter, taoiseach of the small but fierce MacFergus clann."

When Connaire and Brid had left their swords and Brid's bow with the guard, Áedán led them away. "Come with me. I have someone I wish you to meet."

As they wove their way through the crowd of nobility, Áedán would pause to speak to one or another. When he did, he would introduce Connaire and Brid as the most valiant warriors in all Dál Riata.   Then he would kneel beside the hound and cradle its jowls in his hands and add that they were the most valiant in the land, "save for the heroic Cú Chulainn."

The hound loved it.

Finally they came to a large round house and entered.   As Connaire's eyes adapted to the dim firelight, he saw a person near the center of the room who brought dread to his heart.   Profiled by the fire, as she talked to someone next to her, was Aislinn, the woman he had sworn to his dying brother that he would oath.

Chapter 65

Connaire stood as unmoving as a stone, staring. His mouth went dry in panic. Before him was the reason he had fled his clann. He had been prepared to fulfill his promise to his brother, but had been relieved when he thought it was no longer possible. It had given him new hope, a chance to have the woman he loved as his mate. Suddenly, like an egg dropped upon a stone hearth, all was shattered and ruined. He was numb, unable to think.

Connaire was brought out of his stupor by Brid's grip tightening on his arm. He turned to her. She gave him a questioning look, asking what was bothering him. Fortunately, she had not realized exactly where he was staring.

Connaire shook his head. "It is nothing. Just the fire caught my eye." He smiled at her. "I think I saw Colm Cille across the room. Let us greet him."

Áedán was deep in conversation and did not seem to notice when they moved away. As they wove their way through the people, Connaire felt pangs of guilt that he had not told Brid the truth. He was just not ready to confront the dilemma before him. He had felt that as long as he took no other mate, he had not broken his promise to his brother. And it was only when he felt that Aislinn was gone that he had oathed to Brid. Now Aislinn was here. One oath would be broken, either to Cathal or to Brid.

More by chance than by actual plan, they did find Colm Cille standing with a few of the brothers. Colm Cille saw Connaire and Brid approaching and welcomed him with a smile.

"You decided to come to the anointing of our new ri. I am glad to see you. Have you learned anything of your clann?"

Connaire shrugged. "When we arrived where they had been, it was abandoned. Houses were unfinished and no one had been there for some time. As I told you before, they are gone."

"So you have lost your clann. Have you asked Áedán if he knows anything of them?"

Connaire shifted uneasily on his feet. "I have not. He has many matters of greater importance that are demanding his attention. I will speak of it later with him."

The holy man lifted one bushy eyebrow. "There is more here than what you say."

Connaire cast a fleeting glance at Brid and Colm Cille's eyes flashed with understanding. He turned to one of the brothers, a short, lean man with graying hair. "Caoimhin, you remember Brid, who stayed with us a time on our isle?"

Caoimhin nodded, giving Brid a quick smile.

"I brought the Gospel of Mark we completed to show Áedán. Would you show it to her? She did some of the fine scripting and I am sure would like to see the finished work."

"I would be glad to do so." The little man spoke with a low, soft voice and nodded to Brid. "Come with me, child."

Brid looked dubiously at Connaire, but he merely shrugged. The brother gently took her arm and she allowed him to lead her away.

Colm Cille turned to Connaire, his deep-set eyes boring into the young warrior. "Tell me."

Connaire sighed. "As you know, I returned here to oath to my brother's mate, Aislinn. I accepted that I would never oath to Brid, the only one I will ever love. But I found my clann had gone, I knew not where."

The holy man nodded.

"Now I find that Aislinn, the mate of my dead brother, is not only alive, but here."

"Ah. And you have since oathed to Brid. Now you find you must break one oath or another."

Connaire nodded.

Colm Cille draped his arm across Connaire's shoulders. "I understand that this is difficult for you. You find yourself torn between loyalty to your dead brother and loyalty to Brid, both for whom you have great love. You wonder what is the honorable course in this situation, where you must dishonor one or the other. Is that the case?"

Again, Connaire could only nod.

Colm Cille stroked his chin. "Perhaps I can help. Do you love Aislinn or she you?"

Connaire shook his head. "I imagine that she despises me as the cause of my brother's death."

Colm Cille softly grunted. "But you and Brid love each other."

"You know that we do."

"Then you must keep your oath to the living. God considers all oaths binding, but you will cause more harm by breaking the one to Brid than the one to your brother. He is no longer here, but she is. God will forgive slighting the dead more readily than hurting the living."

Connaire turned to look in Colm Cille's eyes. A knot welled in his throat and he had difficulty speaking. Finally he was able to choke out a couple of words.

"Thank you."

At that moment, Brid and Caoimhin returned. She cocked her head with a look of curiosity.

Connaire sluffed Colm Cille's arm from his shoulder. He took Brid's arm and led her from the building.

Standing in the cooling night air, he wrapped his arms around Brid and pulled her close. He hugged her tightly, his eyes closed. For a moment, she was stiff, not understanding Connaire's sudden embrace, but slowly relaxed and returned his hug.

He took a deep breath. "Brid, when we came into the house, I saw someone I never expected to see again. It was Aislinn."

He felt her muscles tense.

"But it will change nothing. I have oathed to you and that will endure. I broke my promise to my brother, but I will never break my oath to you. You are my love."

He felt her slowly relax. Then she pulled his mouth to hers and kissed him. He returned her kiss fervently. Then he reluctantly pulled back.

"I must go and see Aislinn. I need to tell her of . . . you. And that I will not oath with her. Honor requires it."

He paused.

"And I must know what has happened to the clann. You can wait here and I will return as quickly as I can."

In the dim light from the doorway, he could see her violently shake her head. She spoke with her hands, but it was too dark. Connaire held up his hands to show that he did not understand. Brid stamped her foot angrily, showing her frustration. Then she simply pointed to herself, to him and to the door.

He understood. She would go with him.

They entered the warmth of the crowded round house and worked their way through the smoky air towards the fire. Aislinn was still there.

Brid motioned with her head toward Aislinn. The question in her eyes was, is that your brother's mate?

He nodded.

Brid pointed at Aislinn. Connaire nodded again. "Yes, that is Aislinn."

Brid shook her head with exasperation. She patted her stomach and pointed at Aislinn.

Then Connaire looked lower and saw. There was no doubt that Aislinn was with child. Whose child?

"Do you know Aislinn?"

It was Áedán. He was standing close by them and studying them with curiosity.

"I, ah . . . . Yes, I know her. She was my brother's wife."

A heavy hand fell on Connaire's shoulder from behind. "Is your brother's wife."

Connaire turned around. It was Cathal.

Chapter 66

Tears welled in Connaire's eyes. His brother was alive.
He reached out to pull Cathal close, but his brother stepped back.

"So you have come to claim her? You cannot. As you
can see, in spite of your stupidity, I did not die."

Connaire was stunned. For a moment he could not speak,
staring at his brother. "You think I came back here to oath with
Aislinn? How can you believe that?"

Cathal leaned close, the smell of ale strongly on his breath.
"If you would lead me into a trap meant to kill me, why would I
not?"

Stepping back, Connaire stared at his brother. He had
changed. His face was fuller, weaker. Although he was still tall
and broad-shouldered, his stomach hung over his belt. His silver
torque was tight around his neck. In his hand, Cathal clutched a
large cup that slopped ale as he gestured. This was not the Cathal
that Connaire remembered.

"Connaire! You have returned." It was Aislinn.

Connaire turned as she rushed to him. Aislinn wrapped
her arms around him, pulling him tight to her rounded belly and
hugged him. Then she pulled back as she studied him.

"You have changed from a boy to a warrior. Áedán told
me of how you saved him."

"I . . . ." Connaire glanced at Brid, who stood awkwardly a
half a pace away. "Brid and I merely gave him some assistance.
I am sure he would have been safe without us."

Aislinn laughed. "From what Áedán said, he would have
surely been killed by Brude's men if you had not been there." She
looked over at Brid and smiled. "And this is Brid, the one who
helped you?"

Connaire realized that Áedán had quietly slipped away, evidently to tell Aislinn that Connaire was there and the story of their meeting. "Yes, this is Brid." Connaire reached over and pulled her to him, hugging her tightly to his side and smiling at her. "She has saved me a number of times. She is my mate."

Connaire could see the surprise register in her eyes. "Your mate?" Thankfully, she said nothing about Brid looking like a child. "I am so pleased for both of you." She took one of Brid's hands. "I am so pleased that Connaire has found someone like you."

Brid smiled, then looked to Connaire with pleading eyes.

How could he forget to warn Aislinn? "Brid cannot speak. I mean Brid cannot speak words."

Aislinn looked puzzled. "Cannot speak words?"

"She can speak with a language of the hands, but only she, her mother . . who is now dead, and I can also speak that language."

"A language of the hands." Aislinn shrugged. "I have never heard of such. Perhaps you can teach me so that I can speak to Brid."

Cathal belched and looked down at his cup. "I have had enough of this talk. My cup is empty and I need more ale."

He walked unsteadily away. Connaire could see the sadness in Aislinn's eyes that followed him.

"What has happened to my brother? And what has happened to the clann?"

Aislinn sighed. "The clann has survived. So has Cathal, as you can see. The healer did well. She gave him back his life. Since he recovered, though, he has little strength in his sword arm. He can barely even hold his sword. Although he tries with his other hand, he has little skill with it."

Watching his brother as he wove his way through the crowd for more ale, Connaire realized that Cathal did not hold his cup with his sword hand, which he had tucked in his belt. While the arrow had not killed his brother, it had taken away his arm. He was no longer a great warrior.

He turned back to Aislinn. "Then who is taoiseach?"

Aislinn turned away a moment before she spoke.

"Cathal is still taoiseach."

Connaire was taken aback. "But his arm is crippled. Is that good for the clann?"

"Gruagach and Tian will not allow anyone to speak of a new taoiseach unless Cathal wishes it." Aislinn sadly shook her head. "While I admire their love of Cathal, I fear it will doom our clann. No clann should be led by a blemished taoiseach."

"And what has become of my brother? My brother is a fat drunkard and I am the cause. What can I do?"

Aislinn looked back at him. "When Cathal was wounded, it was because you were foolish. But he did not die and he makes his own choices now. Cathal himself chose to become bitter. That is not your fault. Since he cannot hold a sword, he decided to cling to a cup." She cleared her throat, as though her words were being torn from her heart. "Even worse, he has decided not to step down and have the clann chose a new taoiseach. By his decision, he will ruin the clann as he has himself. I have lost the Cathal I loved."

Connaire watched tears slowly trickle down her cheeks. Aislinn's shoulders shook. He stood awkwardly, trying to decide what he should do. He glanced back at Brid, but her bewildered expression gave him little hope of help from her.

Fortunately Cú Chulainn knew exactly what to do. He gently nuzzled Aislinn's hand. She jerked as his cold nose touched her skin, but then rested her hand on his head. Regaining her composure, she looked down at her comforter and took a deep breath before speaking.

"This must be the famous Cú Chulainn that Áedán says so richly deserves his name." She rubbed the hound behind his ears and the dog rolled his eyes up at her in delight. She turned to Connaire. "But you must have a tale of your own. You left a boy, but have returned a man." She smiled, reached past him and patted Brid's shoulder. "And you have a fine mate. I want to hear all of how you found her."

"I will tell you of my travels, but first tell me of the clann. What has happened? When I left, you were building houses on our new land. The land is abandoned and the houses unfinished. When I found them, I feared disaster. Since I thought my brother had died, I did not know if Bran had attacked you, the clann had gone back to Eireann or what."

Aislinn sighed. "Yes, much has happened since you left. Before I start, I must sit. My back pains me."

They found a bench against the wall and Connaire had little trouble persuading one of the occupants to give Aislinn his place. His presence was all that was necessary. Aislinn sat on the bench and uttered a soft groan. Then she smiled at Connaire.

"Bearing a child is more difficult than fighting a battle. Be glad you will never experience it."

She paused, staring at the fire in the center of the room.

"Cathal exacted a promise from Tian, Cairbre and Gruagach that they would not seek revenge on Bran. He feared our small numbers would fare poorly against Bran's clann. Instead, they went to the ri and lodged a claim for honor price. For a time, Conall did nothing. I think he had lost his courage after Brude defeated him some time ago."

Aislinn sadly shook her head.

"In time, Cathal was paid an honor price for his wound, a generous one. Conall's warriors collected it. Twenty cows. And after that time Cathal and Conall were often together. They became friends and soon friends of the cup, drinking and talking of deeds rather than doing them. Conall is now dead, but Cathal and his cup are still keeping close company."

Connaire gently laid his hand on Aislinn's shoulder. "I am sorry that I was not here. I should have been. I failed in my duty to you, to my brother and to the clann."

She rested her hand on his. "But now you are with your people again. And we need you."

"I will not leave again. But where did the clann go?"

Aislinn chuckled. "To an island."

Connaire cocked his head. "An island? You have left the shore? Where is it?"

She smiled enigmatically. "It is not far from here. I will show you. Help me stand and we will go to it."

Connaire helped her rise, holding her gently under her arm. "But must we not stay for the consecration of the Ri?"

"It will not be until midday on the morrow. You can return, but I am afraid that I will not have strength enough to do so."

She squinted as she peered through the smoky haze, looking in all directions. Then gave a disgusted grunt. "Your brother is near the door, sitting on the floor. Would you bring him as we go?"

Connaire saw where she had been looking. Cathal was sprawled on the ground, leaning on the wall and his head awkwardly resting on his shoulder. A cup lay on its side next to him, staining the dirt. Drink had taken Cathal. Those near him would glance down and shake their heads in disgust. A warrior should never lose control of himself in this way.

Connaire walked over to Cathal and leaned down. He pulled his brother across his shoulder and slowly stood. Cathal was heavy. Then he, Aislinn, Brid and the hound walked from the gray, smoky round house into the chilly, star-filled night. The cup lay where it had fallen on the dirt.

Chapter 67

The guard at the entrance to the fort stopped them as they approached. By the light of the fire close to him, Connaire could see a wariness in his face. He eyed Cathal's limp body slung over Connaire's shoulder.

"Is this another you have decided to keep from the consecration on the morrow?"

Connaire grinned. "No, this is my brother. He . . . has taken ill and I must take him to his home." He nodded back at Aislinn. "His mate has asked me to do so."

The guard suddenly seemed to notice Aislinn. "I am so sorry, Aislinn. I did not recognize his . . . ." He glanced nervously at Cathal's rump. "I did not recognize Cathal from this vantage."

Aislinn chuckled. "No, he usually makes it out on his own legs or stays the night. But his brother has returned from a long journey and we want to return home. Might we have a torch to light our way down and find our horses?"

"Of course." He grabbed one of the torches stuck in the earth by the fire, lit it and handed it to Aislinn. "Go with God."

Connaire snorted loudly, but muttered softly. "Or with the gods."

The guard pretended not to have heard.

After they carefully navigated down the steep path to the base of the hill, they found their horses in the corral. Connaire doused the torch in the dirt and stuck it in the ground at the base of the hill. After he laid Cathal across the back of his horse, he saw Aislinn studying her horse. Being so close to having her child, it was difficult for her to mount and Connaire stepped close to offer her a step of his clasped hands.

She turned to him and glared. "I am still a warrior. I can manage this."

Connaire slowly stepped back, dropping his hands. Then he turned and slipped onto his horse.

He watched as Aislinn made a few unsuccessful attempts to mount her horse. No doubt the long day and late hour had tired her, but he feared offending her again by making the same offer. He was not sure what to do when Brid stepped close behind Aislinn.

Brid touched Aislinn's arm. Aislinn quickly turned, obviously ready for Connaire. When she saw Brid, she seemed confused. Then Brid smiled at her. No words. She helped Aislinn onto her horse, then quickly mounted her own.

Connaire sat a moment, wondering what made Brid's help acceptable. Then he shrugged. What did it matter? He held the reins of his brother's horse, ready to ride.

"Lead us to your island, my sister. I hope it is not too far, for I fear neither my brother nor I can make a long ride this late."

"If that is the only fear you have, then you are fortunate, my brother. We do not have far to go."

It was too dark to see, but Connaire was sure that she was laughing at him. He followed as she led them along a path away from the fort, toward a full moon that lit their path. A fortunate turn.

After they left the plain surrounding Dun Ad, they wove their way through a forest. Connaire was so tired that he lost direction, trusting Aislinn to lead them safely to her island. But it seemed to him that they were heading inland, away from the sea.

Connaire was dozing to the slow, methodical sway of his horse when a sudden jolt awoke him. They were at the edge of the forest. Aislinn had stopped and his horse had as well. He glanced behind him momentarily, seeing his brother still lying across his horse and Brid a shadowy form in the rear. The hound was beside her.

Turning back, the moon lit the vista before him. A clear area stretched down to a lake. In the lake was a small island: an island that was a palisaded fort. It was a crannog, an island built by men. On it was a large house surrounded by a wooden wall and the only way onto it was by a bridge that could be raised. Connaire had heard tales of such places on Eireann, but never seen one. How had the clann, small as it was, built it in so short a time?

Aislinn turned, but he could not see her expression in the dim moonlight.

"Our island. Welcome home, Brother."

"But how did you build it so quickly?"

She sighed. "It is late. I will tell you all in the morning."

Then she turned and rode ahead. Connaire followed, glancing back to be sure that Brid was behind him.

When they reached the causeway from the mainland to the island, Connaire pulled his horse to a stop. Aislinn, already on the log bridge, turned to him.

"What is the problem? We are here, your home."

Connaire studied the wooden path across the water dubiously. "Are you certain it will bear the weight of all of us? It is only wood."

She laughed. "It has borne my weight, which has become great, as well as men like Gruagach. You need not fear whether it will bear yours or not."

Then she turned and rode on.

432

For a moment he hesitated, but then Connaire followed. If the causeway collapsed under him, so be it. He would not show fear, especially when Aislinn had none. He kicked the flanks of his horse, urging it on.

As he rode across the causeway, he glanced back at Brid and the hound. They were slowly following. Crossing the wooden bridge must not seem very frightening now that they had crossed water in a small boat.

They passed through the opening of the stake palisade. A large roundhouse dominated the island. Off to the side was a corral, with several horses. They dismounted and secured their mounts inside it. The island seemed to be of wood and stone, but oddly springy as he walked.

Aislinn gently touched Cathal. Connaire thought he saw a tear gleam in the moonlight.

"Brother, help me take him to his bed. We will have to go up a ladder and be most quiet. We do not wish to wake the others in the house. Then take the sleeping area to your sword hand of the door. No one is there."

Connaire nodded and threw his brother across his shoulder, this time more ready for his weight, and followed Aislinn into the house.

It was a full three handcount of paces across and a dim light shone from the dying fire in the center hearth. With effort, Connaire followed Aislinn up a ladder to the next floor, where their sleeping area was. He laid Cathal on his bed, only knowing by a couple of snorts that he was alive and still unconscious. In the darkness, he felt Aislinn's hand touch his in thanks before he quietly descended the ladder. No doubt there were others in the household, but asleep.

Brid and Cú Chulainn were waiting for him. He leaned close to her and softly spoke, knowing that she could not see his hands well in the faint light.

"We will sleep now. In the morning, I will have to meet those I left behind, left dishonorably."

Brid grabbed his shoulders and turned him toward the fire. Two men stood, swords in hand. Even in the shadowy light, Connaire knew who they were: Gruagach and Tian. The shorter one, Tian, spoke.

"Who are you? I would know before I kill you."

"I am Connaire."

There was silence for a moment.

Then Tian continued. "Have you not done enough harm to this clann?"

Coldness crept into Connaire's heart. It was not the coldness of fear, but the knowledge that he might have to kill again. "I have not returned to cause further harm. I have come back to my clann."

"But your clann might rather you die."

"That is not your decision. In the morning, let the clann decide if they want me to stay or to leave."

"You arrogant pup, Gruagach and I will decide if you will even live until the dawn."

Connaire heard the soft murmur of Brid's bow being drawn and a low growl from the hound. Reluctantly, he drew his sword. Although he was fond of the men before him, he had to protect the ones he loved. He had no doubt that Tian and Gruagach would die, but this was not how he wanted to return to his clann.

434

Chapter 68

"If you harm them, you will answer to me. The laws of hospitality protect them."

Aislinn's voice come from above. By the dim glow of embers on the hearth, Connaire watched her carefully descend the ladder. Tian and Gruagach had turned when she spoke. Tian spat on the ground.

"You would give hospitality to this cur who would kill his own brother? Your mate?"

"He did not try to kill Cathal, as you well know." She stepped between Connaire and his antagonists. A sword hung loosely in her hand, a warning. "He was a foolish boy, blinded by love. But you would dishonor me by breaking hospitality. You are foolish, but no boy."

Gruagach took a step forward, only to be blocked by Aislinn. She raised her sword. "Will you kill me too? That is the only way you will reach Connaire."

The powerful warrior glowered at Connaire. "You hide behind a woman with child? You are the same coward who abandoned his clann. You have no stomach for a fight."

Connaire hesitated a moment, stung by the challenge. Then he sheathed his sword. "I will fight you in the morning at any place you wish, except for this house. I will not dishonor the hospitality that has been given."

Tian cocked his head. "How can you claim hospitality when this is your clann, even though abandoned?"

"It is not my clann unless the aire will allow me to return. I did abandon it in its time of need. I cannot return unless they allow me." He reached down to calm the hound, who still stood with hackles raised. "If the clann wishes me to leave, I will. And if either one or both of you wish to seek revenge once I am beyond the law, I will meet you then. But if you shed blood now, you have less honor than I did when I fled."

Slowly, Tian sheathed his sword, then motioned for Gruagach to do the same. "Until the morning, then."

The two turned away from the fire and disappeared into the darkness. Aislinn came close to Connaire and laid her hand on his arm.

"I am sorry that this happened in my house. There is much anger in those two. It will not be easy in the morning when the aire meet. Tian speaks well and has no love of you."

Connaire shook his head. "Perhaps it would be best if we left."

"Again?" Aislinn's voice had a steely edge and she dropped her hand. "I thought you had changed, but you still flee any trouble." She turned toward the ladder.

"No." He quickly grabbed her arm. "I would gladly stay and fight any who would try to keep me away. But is that the best for the clann? I have already done so much damage."

She stopped, but did not turn back to him, her head bowed. "Know this, my mate's brother. If you leave, this clann will not survive. It will die. You must become taoiseach if it is to continue."

Connaire gasped. "Become taoiseach? But what of my brother? He is taoiseach and you are his mate. Are you not betraying him?"

"By remaining its taoiseach, Cathal is betraying this clann." She sighed. "I love him better than my own life. But now I am with child and I must think of my child. And the clann, with all its children. You are the only one related closely enough to be taoiseach instead of Cathal. There is no one else of his Derbfhine here."

"I cannot take my brother's place. I would rather leave than does that to him."

She half turned, so that he saw her profile in the glow from the hearth. There was a glint of a tear. "If you go, do so before dawn. And do not return."

With a quick tug, Aislinn pulled away from his grip and, dropping her sword on the floor, went to the ladder and slowly climbed up.

For some time Connaire stood staring after her, numbed. Her words cut him more deeply than if she had struck him with a sharpened sword. He wanted to turn and flee, take Brid and the hound and never turn back. On the morrow, the situation would only worsen. Now was the last chance to avoid it. He remembered all those times of his childhood with Cathal. Times when Cathal had been with him, taught him, even protected him. How could he turn upon this brother?

He was jolted back to the moment by Brid's hand touching his shoulder. He turned to her. It was too dark to see her expression, but he did not need to. He pulled her close to him, hugging her tightly to his breast. They stood that way for a moment. Then he stepped back.

"We must rest. It has been a long journey. And it may not be over." Closing his eyes, he rubbed his forehead. "It might be best for us to leave before dawn."

Brid pulled his hand down from his forehead to her cheek. He opened his eyes. She held it there and, with her other hand, touched his chest, then hers. He understood. They were bonded together. She would go where he went. Then she led him to a sleeping area.

She lay with her head on his chest, an arm across his neck. By her soft breathing, he could tell she was asleep. They had not coupled. His mind was too troubled and she seemed to understand.

He was torn. Would it be better to leave or stay? Which would be best for the clann, for his brother, for Aislinn, and for Brid? He would gladly die for them, but what good would his death do? Living is sometimes the hardest choice. If he left, would that not save his brother's place as chief? But was that really the best choice or merely the easiest? Still, how could he betray his brother again?

Throughout the night, he struggled with these questions. Just before dawn, he rose. Brid woke and he motioned for her to go with him. The hound, who had made many grunts and growls in its sleep, awoke too and followed.

Aislinn awkwardly backed down the ladder and went to the hearth. There she stirred the fire to life. As its flames climbed she could see the sleeping area where Connaire should have been. Empty. She bit back angry tears. She moved the smaller cauldron over the fire, poured water into it and added several handfuls of ground oats. Then she heeded the urging of her bladder and went outside.

Once outside, she saw a sky of orange, red and yellow, painted by the first rays of the sun streaking across the clouds. It crept slowly above the horizon, sending warming rays into the chill morning. Arching her back, she massaged her aching muscles as she watched the dawn. Connaire had fled and, once again, she must try and keep the fragmenting clann together. She shivered, pulling her bratt closer around her body, and glanced at the corral.

Slowly, she walked over to it. Connaire's and Brid's mounts were still there.

Cautiously, Aislinn walked around the house. Although some planks gave with the weight of her step, they made no noise. Then she saw them. Connaire and Brid were on the far side of the entrance of the house, facing each other. Their hands were making odd motions, evidently the language Connaire had spoken about earlier. First one, then the other, would make odd gestures. Finally Brid put her arms around Connaire's waist and hugged him tightly to herself. Connaire returned the embrace.

Feeling as though she had improperly intruded, Aislinn slipped back around the house and went across the causeway to heed her bladder's demand before she went back inside.

It was some time before the rest of the household stirred. Finally, they gathered at the hearth. Tian and Maille sat by the fire and Gruagach stood near them. Although Maille acted as though nothing were amiss, both men seemed to have found something interesting on the floor and never lifted their eyes from it.

Aislinn stifled a chuckle.

"Gruagach, Cathal seems to having trouble waking again this morning. Porridge will be ready soon. Will you fetch him?"

The big man grunted and went up the ladder. Cathal's angry voice pierced the air, followed by Gruagach's rumble. Finally, Cathal half-stumbled down the ladder, followed by Gruagach. Cathal eyed everyone gathered, then slowly smiled.

"So where is my brother? Gone?"

Tian shrugged. "So it would seem."

Aislinn noted that there was no triumph in his voice. Could it be that he had hoped that Connaire would stay and restore the clann?

"Well, good riddance." Cathal filled a cup with strong ale, took a heavy swig, and edged close to the cauldron. "I am starved."

Aislinn scooped a bowl of the bubbling porridge and handed it to him. At that moment, Connaire, Brid and the hound came through the door. Cathal dropped his bowl and it shattered on the stone hearth, splattering porridge over the floor.

Aislinn took another bowl and filled it with porridge and handed it to her mate with a look of sublime innocence.

"Would you like honey and butter with this one?"

Chapter 69

Conversation was limited during the morning meal. Aislinn introduced Maille to Brid and explained that Brid could not speak. She told of how Connaire had surprisingly appeared at Dun Ad and how he and Brid had saved Áedán. Then Maille and Aislinn chatted about the consecration of the ri that would begin just before midday. Both seemed oblivious to the tension in the air, but Connaire was sure they were not. They were warriors.

He glanced at the others as he ate. Cathal intently studied his porridge as he stirred it and took a bite every so often, never looking at anyone else. His cup of ale sat on the floor, untouched. Gruagach and Tian quietly finished their porridge, then exchanged glances and left the house.

Brid smiled at Connaire when their eyes met and spoke her love in her look.

Cathal set his porridge down by the cauldron and abruptly stood. He studied Connaire a moment, then spoke in a hoarse rasp, charged with emotion.

"We need to speak, Brother. Alone. I will wait outside."

Then he turned and walked out of the house.

Connaire sighed. He did not want to have a confrontation with his brother, but feared it was inevitable. As he rose, Brid took his hand. Her eyes held the question: should she come in case the three others were waiting together outside? He shook his head. He knew that was not his brother's way. He trusted Cathal's honor.

Connaire squinted as he left the house. Although a cover of clouds was high overhead, they had lifted enough to the east for the sun to peek through. But not enough to give warmth. The morning chill was worsened by a light drizzle. He saw Cathal standing by the wall at the edge of the crannog, facing away from the sun. He was alone.

Connaire walked over to Cathal and stood next to him. They both silently looked out over the lake, staring at the trees on the far edge. In that moment, Connaire felt like he was with the brother he had loved and admired for all his life and not the man who had become a lover of the cup, who valued his drink more than his clann.

After some time, Cathal turned to Connaire. "You are responsible for my arm."

Connaire silently nodded, not turning to face his brother.

"You reneged on your promise to me when you rode away. You thought I was dead and abandoned your duty to me and to the clann."

Connaire nodded.

"Returning now does not alter any of that. What you have done will never be forgotten."

Connaire nodded.

"There are those in the clann who want you turned out, sent outside of the law."

Connaire nodded.

Cathal grabbed Connaire with his good hand and turned him, fire in his eyes. "Can you not speak? What is your defense?"

Connaire's voice cracked with emotion. "I have none."

"But you have returned. For how long?"

"For as long as you and the clann will allow. I have nowhere else to go and no other people than this clann." He paused. "And I have no other brother that I love."

Cathal gripped him fiercely, his fingers digging into Connaire's shoulder. "I wanted to hate you. I almost succeeded.

But last night I knew I could not and it angered me. I was speaking through the cup when I spoke the words I did. When I saw you this morning, I tried again and failed. You are the brother I love." He shook Connaire roughly. "But do not ever abandon me or this clann again."

Connaire spoke just above a whisper, his voice shaking. "I would gladly die first."

Cathal pulled Connaire close, embracing him with his arm. Connaire wrapped his brother in his arms. Tears formed in his eyes. He was home.

Then Tian's words of the night before hit him. He pulled back.

"Will the aire refuse me? Tian has said that they will meet and I will be turned away from the clann that I abandoned."

Cathal snorted. "You have no worry. Aislinn and I will speak for you. Tian will say nothing against you. I will see to that. I am still the taoiseach." He smiled wryly. "For a while longer, at least."

"For a while longer?"

Cathal shrugged. "A taoiseach needs to lead his clann into battle. My withered sword arm cannot do that. I know it. Tian and Gruagach have prevented anyone of speaking of this disfigurement, one that harms the clann." He softly sighed. "Having you return reminds me of the man I once was, a man with honor. Now you are here and I know there will be those who would have you be taoiseach."

"Brother, I did not return to do you more harm. You are also my taoiseach and my sword is at your-"

Cathal held up his hand. "Say no more of this. I am not questioning your loyalty. What matters now is to have you restored to the clann. I will talk to Tian about your return and then we will ride to Dun Ad."

Connaire merely nodded, not knowing what to say.

Then he saw a man approaching, limping. It was Oswald, the Angle slave. He had a sword sheathed at his side and a dagger in his belt.

The only way a slave would be armed is if he had stolen the weapons. The only reason an armed slave would confront his master was if he meant to kill him.

Connaire was unarmed. So was his brother. He knew he could outrun the Angle, but what if the armed slave went inside the house? He would catch the women unaware. They were all warriors themselves, but would not expect such an attack. The big Angle might well wound or kill some of them before they could reach their weapons. The only thing he could do was to rush Oswald, with the vain hope of grabbing him before he could draw his sword, and yell to warn those in the house.

Just as he started to move, he felt Cathal's hand on his shoulder.

"Connaire, you remember Oswald the Angle?"

Connaire turned to his brother, confused by his lack of alarm. "Your slave? Do you not see that he is armed?"

"Ah. Yes. Much has changed while you were away, my brother. Oswald is now a warrior of this clann."

Chapter 70

Although it was not unknown for a slave to be freed, even to become a part of the clann, Connaire had never known one to become a warrior of that clann. He turned to Cathal with a questioning look.

Cathal shrugged. "We have lost a handcount of our people since you left, including you. They returned to Eireann, to our father and his clann. Since Dál Riata is a kingdom of two lands, it was easy for them to find a boat going back."

He sighed and laid his arm across Connaire's shoulders. "I have not been the taoiseach I should have been. I blamed you for everything, even though you were not the problem. Seeing you again has brought me back to my duties. Now come meet Oswald as a warrior of our clann."

Reluctantly, Connaire allowed Cathal to lead him to Oswald. The Angle's face was expressionless. His cold eyes held Connaire's.

"So you have returned."

"I have."

Oswald spat on the ground. "Have you found your backbone?"

Connaire stepped close to the Angle. He was slightly taller, but the former slave was broader and armed. "I have."

Cathal slipped between them and turned to Oswald. "Are we not glad that my brother has returned to his clann?"

"That will be up to the assembly of the aire, will it not? I have just returned and must see to other matters."

With a threat hanging in the air, Oswald turned and limped away.

Cathal slowly exhaled. "My brother, I fear that my battle might be harder than I expected."

"You have not made Oswald an aire, have you?"

"No, he is not a noble, but a warrior and a member of my household."

Connaire was stunned. "You have made your slave a member of your household?"

Cathal turned to him, his eyes flashing anger. "You abandoned my household. Do not judge me for whom I have included."

"It is just that it is not our way. A slave should not--"

Cathal shoved his brother, staggering him. "You speak of our way? You are not even a part of this clann and you are telling me what I can and cannot do?"

Connaire bowed his head. "You are right. What reason do I have to criticize you? I do not even have a standing in the clann anymore."

Cathal sighed and rested his hand on Connaire's shoulder. "I am sorry, my brother. I should not have said that. I still have anger that will take time to overcome. The anger is more for myself than for you. Have patience with me." He glanced at the sun across the lake. "We will talk more when we return from Dun Ad. Now it is time to ride to see the consecration of the ri."

They walked to the house, together.

Their party arrived at Dun Ad halfway between dawn and midday. There were two handcounts of them, including Tian, Maille, and Gruagach. At the base of the hill, a forest of tents had been raised and hawkers sold everything from food and drink to jewelry and weapons, as well as horses and saddlery. Due to the large crowd expected, only Connaire, Brid, Cathal and Aislinn were allowed entrance to the fort, followed by the hound.

A monk sat by the gate with a list of those permitted to enter, backed by two burly guards. Connaire recognized Brother Diarmuid, who had taught him to write. The short, plump man greeted him with a warm smile.

"Connaire. It is good to see you again." He turned to Brid. "And how is my best pupil?"

Putting an arm around Brid's shoulders and pulling her close, Connaire returned the smile. "We are oathed now, Brother. She is my mate."

Brother Diarmuid's eyes widened with delight. "This is wonderful. God be with you both."

Connaire reached over and pulled Cathal closer. "And this is my brother, Cathal, and his mate, Aislinn."

"Your brother?" The monk cocked his head. "But I thought he was--"

Cathal laughed loudly. "No, as you can see, I am very much alive. And glad that Connaire has returned to his clann."

With a bemused chuckle, Brother Diarmuid motioned for them to enter. "I must hear more of this tale. But others are impatiently waiting, so it will have to be later."

Once inside the walls of the fort, Connaire and his companions found a noisy, milling crowd of men and women. There was a feeling of festivity, like an oenach. Like a large fair. The aroma of roasting cows and pigs filled the air. Despite the guards at the gate, hawkers pressed their wares on anyone who would listen and even on those who would not. Ale and mead flowed freely, courtesy of Áedán. Jugglers wandered through the crowd, mesmerizing onlookers with their skill. Acrobats walked on their hands or did flips in scarce open spaces.

Connaire felt a hand on his shoulder and turned to see Áedán, smiling broadly.

"Welcome, my friend. If not for you, this might have been a funeral instead of a consecration. Come with me."

The Ri-to-be started to weave his way through the masses, then paused and looked back. "Bring your brother and both your mates."

They followed Áedán, stopping when he had to greet or speak with various well-wishers. Finally, they reached the great hall, the round house where they had been the night before. Guards flanked the door. When they went inside, the darker, quieter surroundings were a welcome relief. Áedán motioned to a servant, who brought cups and a pitcher. He smiled at his guests.

"I think you will enjoy this wine. It arrived from Gaul a few days ago and is said to be of the highest quality. It has not been diluted with water, so be cautious."

As soon as Áedán had finished his cup, he handed it back to the servant.

"I must go and make myself visible. Enjoy your wine. Have as much as you want." He winked. "But be sure you are sober enough to see my consecration."

After he left, the servant came around with more wine, first to Connaire, then to Brid and Aislinn. None of them took more. Finally he came to Cathal. He studied his empty cup for a moment, then held up a hand to signify that he had had enough. He took a deep breath.

"We had better go outside and find a place to see the consecration."

Connaire draped his arm across his brother's shoulders. "I am glad you refused the second cup."

Cathal shrugged. "The ri asked us to be sober for his consecration." He gave his brother a wry grin. "But nothing was said about afterwards."

As they left the great hall, Connaire suddenly stopped. His heart beat wildly as he stared ahead. Two people, a man and a woman. A dark–haired man of medium height and a shapely woman with raven hair. Was the man who he thought it was? And was he with whom he thought he was with?

Connaire felt Cathal's hand on his shoulder.

"What is it, brother? You look as though you have seen a shade from the other world."

It took a moment for him to speak. "I. . . I thought I saw . . . It looked like Ciarán."

"Ah. Yes. Father sent him here to fetch Aislinn or never return. He came to us, but the aire refused to let him remain with the clann. So he went to Bran and was welcomed."

Connaire turned to his brother.

"And was that Deirdre with him?"

Cathal nodded.

"By the paps of the Morrigan, there has never been a better match. A vole and an adder. They will be trouble for us."

"Yes, brother, they will. But as soon as the aire return you to the clann, they will be your problem.

Connaire looked at him questioningly.

Cathal grinned. "Soon I will step down as taoiseach. It will not happen today, but there will be a day when it must happen. You know this as well as I do. I would be surprised if Aislinn has not already spoken of this to you. She knows that it would be best for me and for the clann." He chuckled. "But your eyes betray you. She has already spoken with you, has she not?"

Chapter 71

Before the dumbfounded Connaire could reply, Cathal grabbed his arm and pulled him toward the top of a rise in the fort. "Let us go to the place of the Ri's consecration. All the taoiseachs of the clanns will be there, so we should be there early."

People were milling around the area and Cathal shouldered his way past them. Connaire, Aislinn, Brid, and the hound followed close behind. At the top of the rise was a large stone, mostly embedded in the ground. Carved into the exposed top was a footprint.

Cathal pointed to the print.

"After Áedán is consecrated by Colm Cille, he will step into the footprint as the first in the land. Then the other taoiseachs will follow, showing that they will follow him. The greatest taoiseachs will be first to follow. I will be the last to do so, since I am the taoiseach of the smallest clann."

Cathal then pointed to a bowl carved in a stone rising from the ground, several paces back. "This is water from a sacred well. It has been sacred since before the new faith was in this land, but now has been blessed by Colm Cille."

Connaire cocked his head. "Blessed? Was it not already sacred?"

With a shrug, Cathal dismissed Connaire's question. "I leave such worries as that to holy men. Besides, we have all been baptized into the new faith. The whole clann."

Connaire slowly shook his head. "Much has changed while I have been away. So tell me of your embracing the new faith."

Cathal pursed his lips and slowly exhaled. "I am not a holy man. The brother who came to us told us of a god who was also a man, who was three persons in one god-"

"Yes, yes, I know of all that. I was on the isle of the brothers, Ioua, for about a season. But how did you come to follow the new faith?"

"That is a tale in itself." The older brother thoughtfully stroked his chin. "You see, after Conall's death there were some who opposed having a son of Gabran, Conall's brother, becoming the next ri. Dondchad was a son of Conall and fought for Cenél nGabráin. I was a friend of Dondchad and stood with him." He smiled ruefully. "At least as well as a one-armed warrior might. We fought a battle about who would be the next ri. Dondchad was killed, but Áedán, a son of Gabran, will become our ri. His followers are of the new faith, so our clann is now, too."

"But does it not require that you worship only this new god, this Christus? Has the clann forsaken the gods of our people?"

Cathal shifted uneasily from one foot to another. "Some have. Others still follow the old traditions. They have just added another god."

Aislinn stepped close to Cathal, giving him a dark look. "Those of us who have embraced the new faith are sad for them, for they have a foot in both camps and are loyal to neither." Then she smiled at Connaire. "That is why I was able to forgive you before you returned and welcome you home. Did you not learn much of the faith from your time with the brothers? But you decided not to follow it?"

"I did learn much." Connaire nodded thoughtfully. "They are good men but I could not follow their faith."

"Why?"

"Because . . . ." Connaire stopped. The main reason for his reluctance to even consider the new faith was that any god that would allow him to love a woman as much as he loved Brid while never being able to oath with her was not worth following. The gods of the old way did not claim to be fair, but the Christus was supposed to love mankind.

He swallowed. Now Brid was his mate. He was saved the problem of answering by the deep drones of several horns, signaling that the consecration was about to begin.

The crowds had gathered around them. Having been early, they were close to the fore. There were a few in front of them, but Connaire's height gave him an advantage. Brid was not so fortunate. A large man with finely woven clothing and a gold torque was right in front of her, gesturing as he talked to his companions on either side of him. Connaire hoisted her like a child and set her on his shoulder. She gasped in surprise, then wrapped her arm around the back of his head, gently caressing his cheek.

Warriors forced a path through the crowd, followed by the Ri-to-be and Colm Cille. Áedán, wearing a bratt woven of many colors and gold jewelry, strode purposefully to the rock. Colm Cille was behind him, carrying a shepherd's staff and a silver cup. They stopped by the basin carved in the stone and the holy man dipped the cup into the water. When the horns stopped, he slowly poured the water on the top of Áedán's head. Colm Cille's voice rose like the loudest of the horns, piercing the air with a deep resonance.

"As Samuel anointed David to be king of Israel, I anoint you to be Ri of Dál Riata. Be as fair, as wise and as brave as David. Love God as he did. Lead your people as he did." He raised his hand and lowered it, then moved it from side to side.

"May the Lord bless you, and keep you. May the Lord make his face shine upon you, and be gracious to you. May the Lord lift up his countenance upon you, and give you peace. May the Lord smile upon you and this land, in the name of the Father, the Son and the Holy Ghost."

Connaire noticed that a number of those present made a similar sign on their chests, the same sign of the cross of the Christus he had seen the brothers do on Ioua.

A chant rose from the crowd, starting with a few voices, then growing to a roar. "Áe-dán! Áe-dán! Áe-dán!"

The Ri smiled and waved to the crowd. Then he took off his shoe and stepped forward, placing his foot in the stone depression that matched it. A line of chiefs followed him, stepping into the footprint.

Just before Cathal was Bran. He wore a silver chain around his neck and his thick, black hair was pulled back into a silver ring. His bratt was held across his wide shoulders with a silver broach. He saw Connaire and smiled. He pointed skyward with his middle finger, then slowly curled it, an insult that signified a wilting male member.

Connaire's eyes narrowed. He traced his forefinger across his throat. Bran's smile faded. The threat was understood. He spat on the ground at Cathal's feet as he stepped out of the stone footprint.

As the last chief stepped off the footprint, the sound of horns and drums suddenly filled the air. With the ceremony of allegiance over, the crowd surged toward the roasting boar and mead, pulling Connaire, Brid still on his shoulder, with them. Suddenly he found himself next to Ciarán and Deirdre.

Chapter 72

Ciarán smiled, a fox confronting his prey.

"Brother, I heard that you had fled. So now you have scurried back to Cathal like a frightened kitten."

Slowly, deliberately, Connaire took Brid from her roost on his shoulder and set her on her feet. Then, just as he started towards Ciarán, Brid stepped in front of him. She spoke one word in the language of the hands: *hospitality.*

Connaire understood. They were all there under the Rí's hospitality. Any violation of that and the Rí would punish him.

Clenching his fists at his side, he stepped close to his oldest brother and spoke with barely-controlled anger. "What has happened between Cathal and me is between us. I am with my clann now and will remain. I would suggest you scurry back to Father before you are skewered like a rat in the grain house. This kitten is now a tomcat with fangs."

Ciarán stepped back, fear flickering in his eyes. He bumped into Deirdre, who stopped his retreat. She studied Connaire a moment, then laughed, a cold, cruel laugh.

"My, but the little boy thinks he is a man now. Some parts have grown large, but what of hidden ones? Are they still a boy's size?" She smirked at Brid. "Perhaps that is why you prefer a little girl to a woman."

Brid moved so quickly that Connaire barely saw it happen. With her fingers rigidly together, she struck Deirdre just below the rib cage. He recognized it as a move Scáthach had taught him, the breath-taker.

Deirdre staggered back, then fell to her knees, gasping. Eyes wide, she clutched her chest as she fought for breath. People around them turned to see what was happening. Brid stood next to Connaire, holding his arm like a frightened child.

Ciarán stared at Brid. Before he could speak, Connaire smiled and firmly grasped his arm.

"Brother, you must see to your friend. She seems to be choking." His eyes narrowed. "We can continue our discussion on the long road home."

Ciarán glanced around. No one seemed to have seen what had happened. Who would believe a young woman, a girl had done that? The threat about the long road home was obvious. He forced a smile. "Yes, I will help her. You and your . . . friend go enjoy the feast."

As Connaire turned to walk away, Ciarán spoke under his breath. "But we will continue this discussion later. Only then I will have the final word."

Connaire smiled. Ciarán had not realized his muttering was heard.

After wandering for a time through a crowd that was growing steadily more raucous, Connaire and Brid found Cathal and Aislinn at a table with other celebrants. Platters of meat and pitchers of mead were generously laid out on the table and the revelers were making full use of them. Both Cathal and Aislinn held chunks of roasted meat and had smears of grease on their faces. Cathal grinned and motioned for Connaire and Brid to have a seat at the bench across from them.

"Where have you been? I feared all the boars in Dál Riata would be devoured before you joined us."

Connaire gave a half smile. "Having a little conversation with our brother and his companion."

Cathal grew serious. "And?"

Connaire shrugged. "Ciarán is the same, a little man with a large mouth. And Deirdre . . . . Well, let us say that Brid took the wind out of her sail."

Aislinn looked puzzled. "What does that mean?"

Brid gave her an ingenuous smile, sat on the bench and grabbed a joint of boar.

Connaire joined her and heard a grunt as his foot hit something soft under the table. He looked under and saw the hound had been gnawing on a rib bone. Cú Chulainn raised his lip in a silent snarl, then went back to his feast.

The younger brother shook his head. "Roasted boar. A hero's fare. He will be spoiled forever."

Revelry continued through the day. Jugglers and acrobats performed, moving from table to table so that all could see. In the center of it all, musicians blew their horns and banged their drums as loudly as they could to be heard above the din of mead-loosened voices and laughter. Dancers, many from the crowd of well-wishers, frolicked more wildly as the day wore on. Servers kept the platters of meat and pitchers of mead full to overflowing.

Connaire and Cathal had their share of food and drink. As the sun moved lower on the horizon, they found everything much more humorous. When a passing buxom woman reached suggestively across Connaire's shoulder to take his cup and drink from it, both he and his brother roared with laughter. At that moment, Brid stood and staggered from the table, stepping heavily on the woman's foot. As the woman howled with pain and limped away, Connaire gave Brid a stern look.

"Do not break hospitality."

With an artless look, she touched her hand to her chest and held it up in the air as if to say, "Who, me?"

Connaire sighed. Although the mead affected his judgment, he knew it was time to stop drinking. He reached across the table and grabbed Cathal's hand as he was raising his cup to his lips.

"Brother, the day is growing late. We must leave."

Cathal looked at him quizzically. "Leave? But we have just begun to enjoy the feast."

"No, we must leave before someone . . ." Connaire glanced at Brid who seemed to have found her cup very interesting and was studying it intently. "breaks hospitality and we have to pay honor price."

"Someone?" Cathal seemed confused. "You mean me? I have done nothing but eat and drink."

"Yes, we both have done a lot of that. But now we must leave."

Cathal exhaled disgustedly. "Very well. We will go."

He rose, cup in hand. Connaire saw a silent thanks in Aislinn's eyes as she helped him walk towards the gate.

At the base of Dun Ad's hill, the festivities were still in full swing. It was twilight and torches had already been lit, but the milling crowds ebbed and flowed like a dark sea. With difficulty, they found the rest of their party, Oswald, Tian, Maille and Gruagach. After finally locating their mounts in the corral, they were ready to leave.

Brid touched his arm to get his attention and spoke in the language of the hands. *Where is Cú Chulainn?*

Connaire looked around, realizing he had not seen the hound since they had been at their table. He turned to the others.

"You go home. I must go back to the fort and get the hound. I will follow soon."

Aislinn shook her head. "No, we will wait and go together."

Connaire pointed to his brother who was dozing in his saddle. "If you do not go now, he will fall off his horse." He glanced at the other four, who had obviously enjoyed the free-flowing mead. "And they will not be far behind. Go now. We will follow shortly."

Aislinn looked around at her companions. She shrugged and mounted her horse. "You will probably catch us on the trail."

Brid stood next to him as they rode away. He started to insist she go with them, but decided not to when he saw the look in her eye. She was not in the mood for arguing.

Finding the hound was easy. He was asleep under the table where they had left him. Connaire marveled that the dog that woke at the smallest sound when they were at home at night could sleep through such noise.

For part of the ride home, they had the company of others returning to their homes after the consecration. Finally, the two of them and the hound split off on the trail that led to their crannog. Night had fallen. The moon slipped in and out of the clouds, its light flickering intermittently through the trees.

Suddenly the hound halted in front of them and growled, his front feet spread and hackles up. Several dark forms, a handcount or more, blocked the trail. As the moon slipped out from the clouds Connaire recognized Bran and Deirdre, with a few warriors behind them. And standing to the side was Ciarán, his bow at his side.

Chapter 73

Connaire slipped from his horse, drawing his sword. He glanced back and saw Brid had already dismounted, an arrow notched in her bow. After soothing his nervous mount by gently stroking his flank, he stepped forward.

"Bran, why do you block our path?"

"Your path? I did not realize that you owned it." The stocky man opened his arms wide. "I thought it was free for any to use. My friends and I are just journeying home on it."

"We are not boys playing a game of hurling. You have your men behind you with drawn swords and Ciarán tries to conceal his bow." Connaire glanced from side to side. "And where is your archer who will shoot me when I begin to best you, as happened with my brother?"

Just as he finished, Connaire heard the twang of a bowstring, quickly followed by another. Then came two short, sharp cries, and the sound of heavy objects falling through the trees. Connaire smiled. Brid must have spotted two hidden archers. They were threats no longer.

With a clunk, Ciarán dropped his bow to the ground. Connaire quickly glanced back at Brid and saw she had her bow drawn, aiming at Deirdre. For a moment, he was surprised, since Deirdre posed no threat. But then he understood.

"Bran, if you have any other ambushers ready, have them stand down. If I am struck by an arrow, your sister will die. And you can judge the accuracy of my archer by the two men you just lost."

Bran made a chopping motion with his hand, then took a step towards Connaire, his hand on the hilt of his sword. "Tell your companion to turn her bow. My sister is no danger to you and no hidden archer lies in wait for you. This fight is between the two of us."

For a moment, Connaire stood, head cocked, listening. Bran's hand motion had tipped him. There was one more in the trees. Then he heard it. The snap of a branch. He gave several short whistles.

Cú Chulainn slowly rose and backed away. Then the hound loped into the forest. In a short time, sharp screams pierced the night, with the sounds of desperate thrashing in the underbrush. Then silence. The hound returned and sat next to Connaire, panting heavily. When he glanced down, the dog's bloody mouth showed that his battle was won.

"My hound seems to have found some game tonight." He looked to Bran's warriors who stood across the path. "There will be no more tricks. I will fight Bran in single combat. If any of you make any move to intervene, you will die."

One of the warriors sheathed his sword and backed away. The others hesitated, then followed suit. Ciarán turned and ran after them. There was only Bran, Deirdre, Connaire, Brid and Cú Chulainn, standing on the moonlit path.

Bran looked around. "You seem to have frightened everyone away. Now it is you, your Morrigan, and your hound from the Otherworld against me and my sister. Hardly fair."

"Fair?" Connaire laughed without humor. "This, from the man who had my brother shot in the back, then attacked him and left him to die? "Fair' is not a word you should use." He spat in the dirt. "Yet I would not act as you have done. Yours was the hand that started this, yours will be the hand to end it. Leave if you wish, and we will meet again another time."

Bran hesitated, then turned and started to walk away. Connaire glanced down as he sheathed his sword. As he looked up, Bran was charging him, arms outstretched. Before Connaire could react, he had his thick arms around him, locking his hands and pinning the younger warrior's arms to his side. With bear-like strength, Bran lifted Connaire from the ground, squeezing the breath from him.

Connaire vainly struggled to free his arms. Then he heard a low growl. Gasping, he ordered the hound back. "Cú Chulainn. No! Stay."

Perhaps the growl caused Bran to ease his grasp, but Connaire was able to spread the big man's arms enough to slip down a little. Enough that he could pound his forehead sharply against Bran's nose.

Pain shot through Connaire's head, but he felt Bran's grasp loosen. With a cry, he was able to break free and fell to the ground. Kneeling and still dazed, he saw Bran staggering back and shaking his head, his nose bleeding. If he recovered first, Connaire knew the big man would keep the fight close, using his size and weight to his advantage. Connaire rolled away, getting as much distance as he could.

Rising to his knees, Connaire saw that Bran had recovered and was glaring angrily at him. Connaire rose unsteadily to his feet, drawing his sword. He gave a short laugh.

"Fool that I am, I should have known not to trust your honor. This time I will be ready."

Bran spat. "To win is what matters. Your warrior's honor is but a myth: a tale for children. And only the living can have children to tell the myths. You will not."

Breathing deeply and steadily, Connaire felt his strength returning. He exhaled slowly.

"Then let the myth be decided here."

Like two wolves, they circled, warily eyeing each other. Several times Bran struck, but each time Connaire easily parried his thrust. Connaire let Bran attack, learning more of his opponent with every attempt Bran made to penetrate his defense. His training under Scáthach made it child's play. And Bran began to realize it. Even in the dim light of the moon, Connaire saw fear grow in Bran's eyes.

Desperately, Bran swung his sword. Connaire met some blows and let others fly past. Although he knew he was a far better swordsman, he knew that Bran was like a wild bear, dangerous to underestimate. If he tried to end the duel too quickly, Bran might well find an opportunity to strike a lucky blow. Better to let him wear himself down. Like the hound pursuing the bear, he allowed Bran's fury to exhaust him.

Bran stepped back, resting his hands on his knees as he tried to regain his breath. Connaire felt a sense of sadness. Too many lives had been lost, too many had died for no reason.

"Bran, if you will lay down your sword and submit to the judgment of Áedán's brehon, this will end now. If not, I will kill you."

Bran raised his head, panting. "You insolent whelp. I have been toying with you up to now. But that is over."

With a roar, Bran charged, stumbling and wildly swinging his sword. Connaire thought he might fall before reaching him. As the big man closed in, he suddenly seemed to have found his footing and thrust accurately at Connaire's chest. Surprised by the feint, Connaire barely deflected Bran's sword in time to prevent a serious wound as it sliced a thin gash in his arm. A trickle of blood dripped from it. Painful, but not serious.

Connaire would not be duped again. The time for toying was over. He was ready when Bran swung again. Judging the moment, Connaire batted away his sword and lunged forward. His sword sank deep into Bran's chest. The big man fell to his knees, dropping his sword. He stared dazedly at the blade deep in his chest, blood trickling from the side of his mouth. Then, like a tree felled by an ax, he fell forward onto Connaire's sword.

With a wail like a *bean sídhe* of death, Deirdre ran at Connaire with her dagger raised high. Before she reached him, Brid leapt forward with her sword at the woman's throat.

Connaire stayed her hand. "Enough death. Let her drop her knife and mourn her brother."

With a moan, Deirdre let her dagger slip from her fingers. After a questioning look to Connaire, Brid lowered her blade. Deidre fell to her knees, crawling to Bran. She lifted his head to her lap, rocking and keening.

Connaire rested his arm across Brid's shoulders. She looked up at him and gently caressed his cheek. He thought he saw the glint of a tear in the moonlight. She carefully wrapped a strip of cloth she tore from her léine around his wound. He leaned down and gently kissed her. She wrapped her arms around his neck, pulling him close.

He softly whispered in her ear. "I love you, my elf. You have saved my life again. Now let us go home."

Brid pulled back a little. She smiled through her tears and nodded, talking with her hands. *Yes, home.*

Chapter 74

Connaire woke with a start. Brid, her head upon his chest, jerked awake from his movement. He smelled the fire in the hearth. It was morning and the morning meal was cooking.

Brid stretched, back arched cat-like, and smiled at him. When they had arrived at the crannog after their battle with Bran and his cohorts, all the others had gone to bed. Connaire could hear the snores and wheezes of those who had indulged heavily in the free food and drink at Áedán's consecration. Although he was sure that Aislinn at least had heard them enter, she had said nothing.

He and Brid had bathed quickly in the frigid lake that surrounded the artificial island, forcing the hound to join them to wash off the blood. Brid had applied herbs to his wound, then bound it before they gone to bed. Naked, they nestled close to each other for warmth.

Connaire had grown hard with desire. The rough, wool blanket rubbing his body, still tingling from the cold water, had heightened the stimulation of Brid's bare skin against his. With the excitement of battle and the exhilaration of surviving rushing through his body, he was desperate to enter her. She seemed to sense his need and climbed on top of him, locking her mouth to his. Their coupling had been fast and urgent, both of them reaching their moment of release quickly. Then they collapsed, panting and clutching each other tightly. The next thing Connaire knew, it was morning.

Brid rose and dressed. Connaire slowly stroked the inside of her thigh until she pushed his hand away and pulled on her woolen trews. After giving him a quick kiss, she left their sleeping area. With a sigh, Connaire rose and dressed.

When he stepped out into the center hall, it was empty. There was a cauldron on the hearth by the fire and he went to it. Although it was almost empty, there was enough porridge in it for Brid and him. Everyone else must have eaten. How late had he slept? Taking a pottery basin, he went out to get some water to wash his face.

It looked like the clann had gathered on the decking outside the house. Cathal was seated in a chair and all the others were standing, some with half smiles and some with grim sternness. Fergal, the clann's counselor, stood by Cathal's sword arm. Brid was kneeling by Cú Chulainn, gently stroking his head. Her hard, cold glare went from face to face. It was a meeting of the Cuirmtig. They had come to decide his fate with the clann.

Aislinn walked up to him and gently touched his arm. "You have not had your morning meal yet, have you? You and Brid come with me and I will heat the porridge for you."

Connaire looked down at her. "I seem to have lost my appetite."

"Nonsense." Her touch became a strong grip. "You both will come with me." She smiled up at him. "And bring Cú Chulainn as well."

"We have been waiting for some time now while Connaire slept. It is time this matter was settled." It was Tian.

Cathal turned to him, his eyes flashing with anger. "I am still taoiseach and I will say when we will begin. You summoned the Cuirmtig without asking me and now demand my brother suffer this in hunger?" He glanced around at all those gathered. "We will wait. And any that do not wish to do so are free to leave."

Tian started to say something, but stopped. Instead he shook his head and turned to look out over the lake. Gruagach stood at his side with a confused look on his face. Connaire stifled a chuckle. Aislinn might be with child and his brother might have a lamed arm, but both were still formidable foes. He allowed Aislinn to lead him away.

Once inside the house, Connaire and Brid sat at the table while Aislinn reheated the porridge and spoke of what had happened while they slept that morning.

"Cathal had thought this would not happen. He has spoken with many in the clann and told them he did not feel you had deserted him or the clann. They seemed satisfied."

She sadly shook her head as she ladled porridge into two bowls and handed them to Connaire and Brid. Then she sat on a stool, arching her back and rubbing it before she continued.

"But Tian has been angry all morning. After seeing Bran last night, it was as though it had all just happened. I think that he wanted revenge for Cathal and the clann and, because he could not break hospitality and do so, has made you the target of his anger. He has gone to any who would listen and roused them to demand the Cuirmtig meet to decide if you will remain with us. I cannot remember when I have seen Cathal so angry. I feared that he would challenge Tian to a fight when he heard of it."

Connaire closed his eyes and rubbed his temples. "It is my fault for returning. I should go now, before I bring more trouble to this clann."

Aislinn stiffly rose from her stool and stood over Connaire.

"I am only going to say this to you one more time. Cathal loves you, probably more than he does me. It hurt him more that you left than the wounds from Bran. He became a drunken weakling. Not so much in strength as in will. Now he is the man I oathed to, strong and determined. Allow him to be your brother again."

She turned and faced the fire. Her voice was brittle, ready

to break.

"If you leave, never let me see you again. I will kill you myself if I do."

Connaire felt as though a dagger had been driven into his heart. He stood and went to her, wrapping his arms around her from behind and pulling her tightly to his breast.

"I only would leave to help you and Cathal. I will stay until I am driven out at the point of a sword. Even then, I will die before I will ever abandon you and Cathal again."

He could feel her shudder as she released her pent-up emotions. She was weeping, but he knew it was with relief.

Aislinn pulled away and turned to him. Her eyes were moist, but she was in control of herself again. "Finish your porridge and let us return to your brother. He needs you as much as you need him."

When they walked outside, Connaire saw the clann had divided into two groups. One group surrounded Tian, listening to him as he spoke grandly and gestured wildly. The other group was with Cathal, who stood and chatted with them with a smile. He showed no hesitation or uneasiness, exuding confidence in his very manner. He was a leader again.

When Cathal saw Connaire, he sat in his chair and motioned for his brother to join him. Connaire walked over to him, feeling every eye on him as he did. Some were muttering unhappily. Fergal stepped forward and rapped his staff on the wooden deck. The crowd became silent.

Fergal spoke in a strong, firm voice. "The Cuirmtig has been summoned by Tian on the charge that Connaire, brother of Cathal, has no standing in this clann. It is claimed that he broke his oath to this clann, fled the clann in cowardice and is no longer under the protection or law of this clann. He should be driven from us and can be killed without honor price. He should be outside the laws of our people."

Fergal stepped back to stand by Cathal. For a moment, Cathal said nothing as he thoughtfully rubbed his bearded chin. Then he looked to Tian.

"Are these the charges you bring against my brother? Have they been stated correctly?"

Tian moved to the center of the open area in front of Cathal. He stood erect, defiant. "I bring these charges against a man named Connaire, not against your brother. He broke his oath after leading the taoiseach of this clann into a cowardly ambush by our enemies where he almost died from-"

"Stop!" Cathal rose from his chair, glaring at Tian. "Connaire is my brother and you will not say otherwise. I asked you if these charges are correct. Nothing more. You will make no speeches, but answer my question."

Tian mutely nodded, obviously unprepared for Cathal's anger.

Cathal sat back into his chair. "Then the charge of breaking his oath is to be forgotten since the only oath given was to me and to Aislinn." He glanced at Aislinn. "If that is agreeable to you, of course."

Aislinn smiled and nodded.

Tian stepped closer to Cathal, waving his hands as he spoke. "You do not have the right to dismiss my charge in such a manner. I will be heard."

Fergal banged his heavy staff with a resounding thud. "I have the right and I do agree with Cathal. You cannot bring a charge of breaking an oath unless it was made to you. A relative can do so if the one who received the oath is dead, but that still gives you no right in this matter."

Cathal sat back in his chair, drumming his fingers on his thigh. "Now as to the charge of cowardice, I can attest that Connaire was no coward."

Tian looked shocked. "But he led you into an ambush. You admit that, do you not?"

Cathal leaned forward in his chair. "I can attest that he unwisely believed a woman of no honor. That may be stupidity, but it is not cowardice. He even stood over me with my sword in hand to keep Bran from finishing the kill. He was a stripling lad then, but that is not the action of a coward. If anything, it was foolhardy bravery."

Tian was so upset that he sputtered, his usual eloquence gone. "He did abandon this clann at a time of crisis. Even you cannot deny that."

Before Cathal could answer, a warrior of the clann pushed his way in front of Tian. "Sir, some of the ri's warriors are here, demanding entrance."

Cathal looked surprised. "The ri's warriors? Demanding entrance?" He lifted one hand in acquiescence. "Let them enter."

Two handcounts of warriors, one carrying the ri's banner, came across the bridge to the crannog. A mountain of a man as big as Gruagach, stopped in front of Cathal. "I am Treasach, commander of the ri's guard. I am here at the command of Áedán, Ri of Dál Riata. I am to take a man known as Connaire, a woman known as Brid and a . . ." The warrior seemed embarrassed. "And a hound known as Cú Chulainn to Dun Ad."

"To Dun Ad?" Cathal stood with a confused expression. "Why?"

"To answer the charge of the murder of Bran and three of his warriors."

"Bran is dead?"

The ri's warrior nodded. "His sister and your own brother have accused these three of murder. I am to take them to answer for this charge." He looked around. "Are the accused here?"

Connaire shrugged his shoulders and raised his hand. "I am here. My mate, Brid, is here too."

Treasach turned to him. "And the hound? Is he muzzled so we can take him."

Connaire chuckled. "No, he is licking the hand of one of your men."

The commander spun around to see Cú Chulainn being petted by one of his warriors. He turned back to Connaire and sighed. "The ri has said that if you will swear that you will come without problem, we will not bind you. Do you swear this?"

Connaire smiled wryly. "While some might not trust my oath, it seems the ri does. You have my word." He pointed to Brid and Cú Chulainn. "And that of my mate and our hound."

Treasach nodded solemnly. "The ri sent horses for you. Come with me."

After the guards left with their prisoners, everyone stood in numbed silence.

Then Tian spoke.

"Are we going to just stand here? We cannot do nothing while Ciarán and that she-wolf sister of Bran do this. Connaire and Brid need us. To the horses." Then he paused and glanced nervously at Cathal. "If that is the command of our taoiseach, of course."

Cathal grinned. "Well said, my friend. It is my command."

As the clann rushed to saddle their horses, Cathal felt a

calmness that he had not felt in some time. He knew that his brother had not murdered Bran. Bran must have tried to ambush Connaire and died in the attack. He also felt Áedán was a wise, fair man and would see the real character of Deirdre and Ciarán. No doubt it was greatly because Ciarán and Bran's sister were making the charges that the clann had rallied behind Connaire, but there would no longer be any threat of exile.

Chapter 75

Connaire, Brid and the hound stood in front of the ri, who was flanked by several of his personal guards. Treasach and his men were the only ones carrying weapons in the crowded hall, filled with many who had traveled far for the revelries the night before and stayed to see the hearing of the charges. Their mutterings made a steady, droning sound, not unlike a hive of bees. Of the three prisoners, only the hound seemed pleased to be there. He sat and looked around, slowly panting, with a dog's friendly grin.

The ri sat in his chair with his brehon at his sword hand. On his other side stood Deirdre and Ciarán, with the warriors who had fled the night before huddled behind them. Stretched out in the open space between the ri and the prisoners were the bloody bodies of Bran and his three men, two with arrows still in them. A fire burned in the center hearth and guards holding torches stood around the edges of the hall, the flames giving a grim, smoky light.

The brehon pounded the heavy staff he carried on the floor several times and the crowed quieted.

Áedán shifted in his chair. "It has been requested . . ." He paused a moment. "Rather insistently requested to bring the three accused, Connaire, Brid and Cú Chulainn, to judgment for the charge of murder. I will now have Gaeth, my brehon, conduct this hearing and determine the validity of this charge. If they are found guilty, I will impose the sentence."

Deirdre, her eyes narrowed in hate and her hands clenched at her sides, stepped towards the ri, to be stopped by the hand of a beefy guard. She quickly glanced at the prisoners. Her voice shook with anger as she spoke. "What is there to question? The bodies of my brother, one of your taoiseachs, lies dead with those who tried to defend him. Pass sentence now and be done with it."

An audible gasp rose as one from the audience.

Gaeth vigorously pounded his staff, then motioned for the guard to push her back. His voice was tense, barely restrained. "You think you can order the ri? Your audacity does you no good. We are a people of laws and they will be followed. Since you have already stated your charge, now explain what happened and then the accused will speak. If you cannot abide by the way of the law, leave now before I fine you and fine you heavily."

Deirdre stepped back, her chin raised defiantly. "I only ask justice for my poor brother." She pointed at Connaire. "I will tell you how he murdered Bran last night. And how that . . . that thing who is his companion and their beast killed my brother's warriors."

She paused dramatically, looking around.

"Many of you here know me. Some know me very well."

Connaire saw a smile flicker across her lips. She looked meaningfully at Connaire, then at Áedán with a seductive air.

Connaire felt a sense of dread wash over him. Had she seduced the ri as well?

But Áedán's face showed no emotion. Several men muttered amongst each other. Probably her lovers, Connaire thought.

Gaeth pounded his staff, glaring at the crowd. "We will have silence or I will have everyone ejected but the accusers, the accused and the witnesses." He turned to Deirdre. "Who you know, as you state it, has no bearing on these charges. Proceed."

Momentarily taken aback, she hesitated. Then she continued. "I must protest. It has everything to do with Bran's murder. You see, I once was very close to Connaire, but he was never able to couple with me. When I grew tired of his inadequacies and rejected him, he fled his clann in disgrace. Now he has returned and when I spurned him at the consecration, my brother had to protect me from his anger. That is why he killed my brother, so that he could force himself on me."

Connaire started to protest, but the brehon pounded his staff again. "Keep quiet, Connaire. You will have your chance to speak. Remain silent now or suffer a fine."

Nearly to the point of blind rage, only Brid's hand on his arm calmed Connaire. Then he felt another hand on his shoulder. He turned to see Cathal with Fergal at his side. Cathal smiled and gave a short nod before one of the guards pushed him back. Connaire took a deep breath as he turned back to his accuser. His clann had come to stand with him.

With a confident smirk, Deirdre pursued her tale. "When we were riding home last night, three of our men, the ones here, had ridden ahead to scout the trail. Suddenly, two of the warriors still with us were struck by arrows, ambushed from high in the trees. When they fell from their horses, the last man riding with us leapt from his horse to seek out the archer. That beast leapt upon him and savagely tore out his throat."

She pointed at the hound, who was resting his head against the leg of a guard who was scratching him behind the ears. Realizing Deirdre was pointing his way, the guard pulled his hand away. But Cú Chulainn kept nudging it until the guard folded his arms, staring straight ahead.

Deirdre glared at the guard. Everyone had turned when she had pointed, to see the "savage beast." Most were snickering and some were even laughing out loud. She waited to speak until after Gaeth had once more pounded for silence.

"Bran bravely slid from his horse to help his companion when Connaire stepped from behind a tree and stabbed him before my poor brother even had a chance to draw his sword. While this was happening, I had been calling to our other three warriors, who came at a gallop. Hearing our warriors approach, those murderers fled into the woods. It was too dark to follow them and they would have the advantage of cover for another ambush, so we took our dead and returned home.

"I stand now demanding justice for my people. I saw my brother murdered before my eyes, a brother who I dearly loved. No longer will I hear his laughing voice, feel his kind touch. He is lost to me forever."

She stood with her hands clasped in front of her, head high and tears streaming down her cheeks.

This time Gaeth did not need to pound his staff, for the hall was silent when she finished speaking. He leaned on his staff, studying Deirdre with a piercing gaze. She met it without flinching, her eyes moist. Then he turned to Ciarán.

"Is this what happened?"

Ciarán kept his eyes from meeting his brother's as he nodded.

"I need to hear you state that this is what happened."

"It is." Ciarán spoke in a harsh croak.

"Do you have anything to add?"

"No."

The brehon glanced at the three warriors behind Deirdre and Ciarán. "Do you concur with this account?"

They grunted their barely-audible agreement.

The brehon turned to Connaire. "Did you murder Bran? And did your companion kill two of his men? And did your hound kill the other?"

Connaire took a deep breath and exhaled slowly. "I did kill Bran, but in combat. My two companions did kill the others, but because they were going to kill us. The rest of this tale is false as well."

Deirdre started to step forward, only to meet the hand of the guard again. "You lie! You could never have bested my brother in fair combat. Everyone here knows the prowess of my brother with a sword."

Connaire spat on the ground. "Bran never fought a fair fight in his life."

Gaeth pounded his staff with such force that it audibly cracked. "I will have no such outburst here." He sighed as he studied his split staff, then turned and nodded to Connaire. "You may now tell your account of the events."

Before Connaire could speak, Fergal stepped in front of him. "Brehon Gaeth, I would speak for Connaire."

The old man lifted an eyebrow. "Why should I allow you to speak for him? Do you have legal standing?"

"I did complete my first course of studies as a glasaigne and sat under Brehon Seanan for over two handcounts of season cycles. I only stopped my studies to come here with my taoiseach and now serve as his counsel."

"Seanan is a respected teacher. You may speak for Connaire, but he will still have to answer any question I put to him."

Fergal gave a half bow. "Of course."

The short, somewhat pudgy young counselor walked over to the bodies on the floor. He slowly edged around them, stroking his sparse beard. A few times he crouched to take a better look, even opening the hands of the dead warriors. Connaire thought he heard him humming, but it was so soft that he could not be sure. Finally Fergal returned to stand by Connaire.

"I would like to ask some questions of Bran's sister, Brehon

476

Gaeth."

Gaeth nodded.

Fergal clasped his hands behind his back and walked over to Deirdre. "As I entered this hall, I heard you say that you rejected Connaire because he was unable to couple. Yet he is now oathed to Brid. This would--"

Deirdre interrupted with a voice filled with spite. "She is no woman. She is so short and her paps are so small that I doubt she can even take a man between her legs. She must have come from a sídhe on some Samhain, when the portal to her fairy mound was open."

Brid pushed in front of Fergal. She tapped her breast, made the known hand sign for coupling and pointed to Connaire. Then she pointed to Deirdre, made the same hand sign and pointed to Deirdre again. The meaning was clear: Connaire coupled with Brid and Deirdre coupled with herself. Those who could see began to laugh as Brid stood, legs slightly apart and knees bent, ready for a fight.

Fergal quickly pulled Brid away as the brehon pounded his staff on the floor, with it giving a hollow, rattling sound. His stern glare pinned Deirdre. "You have had your say, now remain quiet until the question is finished. For your insult, you shall pay one hide."

Deirdre stamped her foot. "For that? I only said what everyone is thinking. She is no real woman."

"Make it two hides. Fergal, find another question."

Fergal raised his hands in resignation. "Of course. Deirdre, let us talk of this claimed ambush. You say Connaire attacked you on the pathway to your settlement, yet we saw blood on the way here from our crannog that would indicate the struggle was there."

Deirdre shrugged her shoulders. "I know nothing of blood on your trail."

Fergal leaned forward. "Then if the ri goes with us as we take the path to your settlement, you will show us where your valiant warriors fell and bled? Their blood will still be there."

She hesitated. "Perhaps we accidentally took the wrong fork in the dark last night."

"Ah." Fergal massaged his chin. "So you took the wrong path and Connaire knew you would, so he made his attack from hiding there."

Her eyes darted from side to side as if seeking an answer. "I . . . maybe--"

Fergal held up his hand to silence her. "Let us discuss the attack itself. You said that Bran never had a chance to draw his sword, that Connaire ruthlessly killed him and fled. Then why is Bran's scabbard empty? And I would wager there is a sword wound covered by a bandage on Connaire's arm. How did a sheathed sword do that?"

Deirdre looked confused. "Bran's sword must have fallen out of his scabbard when we brought him here. And . . . ah . . . ."

Fergal held up his hand again. "Let us talk of your three dead warriors. Archers, by the look of their fingers. The arrows that killed two of them came from below. Hard to explain, if you are riding a horse and the enemy is in a tree above, but easy if they were in the trees to ambush and shot from below." He paused, but Deirdre remained silent. "Perhaps the hound Cú Chulainn will tell us what happened. He would make far more sense than the fanciful tale you have just told us. Yours is a story, like the *Táin bó Cuailnge*, worthy of being told by a bard, except it is far less believable than the legend of the first Cú Chulainn."

Before Deirdre could respond, Gaeth stepped forward and

addressed the three warriors behind her. "You understand that to give false witness will incur a fine against you of the honor price of the person you defame, who in this case is a man of the rank of Aire forgaill. If you cannot pay the fine, you will be sold as slaves to pay it. Do you wish to change anything?"

They leaned together. They argued amongst themselves, keeping their voices low enough so that what they said could not be heard. Their disagreement became so intense that Connaire thought they would soon come to blows. Finally, they came to a consensus. One of them cleared his throat.

"I speak with the understanding that what we said previously will not be held against us, since it was under duress."

Gaeth studied the warrior. "Tell us your tale and I will decide."

The man hesitated before continuing. "We went with Bran to ambush Connaire. Rogan, Oran and Morc were to hide in the forest and shoot anyone with him. Then, if Bran were losing the fight with Connaire, they were to kill him too. That one," he pointed at Brid, "killed Rogan and Oran before they had a chance to let off an arrow. Then the hound killed Morc. We decided to leave."

Gaeth sadly shook his head. "And we have little doubt of what happened after that. Bran attacked Connaire and died in combat. There was no murder. But why did you agree with his sister's false account?"

The man glanced around nervously. "Deirdre told us that we would be exiled from the clann, become outside the law and killed without consequence, if we did not support her story."

Deirdre uttered a sharp cry and tried to push forward, but the guard was ready and held her back, roughly grabbing her arm. She spat out her words as she screamed at the three men. "You will pay for disloyalty." Then she glared at Connaire. "You will not walk away from this. You will pay, too."

Áedán banged his fist on the arm of his chair and abruptly rose, his forehead deeply furrowed and mouth tightly drawn. "You are the ones who will pay, both you and Ciarán. You owe honor price to both of those you falsely accused. Deirdre and Ciarán, you will both pay four handcounts of cattle to them." Then he cracked the start of a smile. "And a haunch of beef to the hound. My guards will take you to your settlement to collect your fine now."

Teasach moved from Connaire's side to Ciarán's, firmly grabbed his arm and marched him toward the door. Another guard followed with a struggling Deirdre in tow.

Many of the crowd gathered around Connaire and Brid to congratulate them, with Tian among the first. He seemed at a momentary loss for words, so Connaire spoke first.

"I am pleased you came to support us."

Tian grabbed Connaire's shoulders and gripped them tightly, staring into his eyes. "I was wrong about you. Will you forgive me?"

Connaire shook his head. "There is nothing to forgive. You did what you thought best for the clann."

Tian was about to say more when Áedán's guards pushed open a gap for the ri. Áedán smiled as he approached.

"I knew the accusations were false, but could do nothing. This was my first hearing and I had to take no side. But I hope you found the judgment fair."

Connaire returned the smile. "I did. I am not so sure about Deirdre and my brother."

Áedán wrapped his arm across the other man's shoulders. "That is their worry. Come, let us share some mead."

Chapter 76

The sun had started to sink below the trees by the time the clann mounted their horses and started their ride home. What had begun as a hearing of judgment had turned into a feast. Áedán had mead brought for everyone to drink their fill and had spitted a shank of beef over an open fire. Soon the air was filled with the fragrant smell of roasting meat and the sounds of laughter and singing.

Connaire had gone from being the accused to the hero of the day. Everyone wanted to hear the tale of how one warrior, his companion and a hound had soundly defeated the eight warriors who had ambushed them. At first, Connaire was loath to speak of it, feeling that he should not boast. But soon mead and camaraderie loosened his tongue.

"When I saw Bran with his sister and his warriors blocking our path, I knew there would be more of them." He glanced up at an attentive young woman who pressed her ample breasts against his arm as she stood behind him and smiled. "So I--"

Connaire jerked suddenly as something sharp jabbed his other side. He looked over to see Brid, who smiled up at him and wrapped her arm around his waist as she stood beside him.

He cleared his throat. "We . . . uh, Brid realized archers must be hiding in the trees. Before they could fire on us, she shot them both. There is no archer in Dál Riata that can match her."

He felt her hug of approval as one of the three warriors who had been a part of the ambush and then given false witness pushed his way close to Connaire. He had a sloshing half-full cup of mead in his hand, as he gestured to those gathered and spoke with an alcoholic slur.

"It is true. Bran promised us it would be easy. But he did

not tell us that we would be fighting such heroes as Fionn mac Cumhaill and Cú Chulainn." He glanced around. "After seeing what he did to Morc, I swear that his hound is Cú Chulainn returned."

Several in the crowd chuckled, which the drunken warrior took as a challenge to what he had said. He pushed Connaire's buxom admirer away, grabbed him by the arm and glared around. "I admit that I pissed my pants when I saw who we were fighting. I challenge anyone here to stand against any of the three, this warrior, the archer or the hound from the Otherworld. If you do, you will die."

Connaire looked uneasily around. He did not fear anyone there, but had no desire to ruin this celebration by killing some drunken, foolish warrior who took up the dare. With relief, he saw Áedán's guards pushing their way into the center of the crowd. The ri stepped forward and raised both arms. The din of conversations lessened enough for him to be heard.

"The haunch of beef is ready."

He momentarily glanced back at Connaire and Brid and smiled before he continued. "So who shall have the hero's portion, the swordsman, the archer or the hound?"

He cocked his head, as if listening to see who the most of them favored.

"Connaire!"

"The pixie!"

"The hound!"

Connaire had no idea who had the most or loudest yells of support, but Áedán smiled and nodded.

"The hero for this feast has been chosen. Summon Cú Chulainn."

Brid gave a short series of whistles. The hound wove his

way to them.   Áedán leaned over and rubbed him behind his ears.

"Cú Chulainn, Dál Riata has decided that you will receive the hero's portion for this feast.   Come with me."

Áedán followed his guards, with the hound and Brid at his side.   As Connaire started to follow, Bran's warrior pulled his arm.

"You must think me a coward, the way that I ran last night. I hated Bran for what he did and did not want to die for him.   I do not fear death, but did not want to die for a coward.   I ask you to let me come to your clann.   I would gladly die fighting alongside a man like you."

Connaire regarded him disdainfully.   "Die for a coward? Were you not a part of the cattle raid on our clann, the clann of my father Fergus?   Did you not kill the herders, mere boys?   Was that not the act of a coward?"

The man hung his head.   "I was a part of that raid.   There is no honor in it.   Nothing had been said of the killing of the boys before we went.   We thought it was a simple cattle raid.   Instead Bran and his friends killed them.   Rogan, Oran and Morc.   After that, our own clann turned against us and we had to flee."

Connaire stroked his beard.   "You would have me believe that you knew nothing of Bran's plans, that you had to follow him here because you were an outlaw to your clann.   Yet why did you not stand against Bran when you came here, remove him as taoiseach?"

For a few moments, the warrior was silent.   Then he sighed.   "I was a coward.   Any that stood against Bran died.   A few died fighting him, but more often it was by a dagger in the night.   We never knew who did it.   You never knew who you could trust.   Our clann here was a clann of fear.   You cannot understand what it is like to mistrust your own friends.   How it feels to be less than a slave. But once you have taken the path without honor, nothing matters."

Connaire remembered how he felt when he had left his brother when he thought he was dying. How it felt to abandon his vow to marry his brother's mate after he died. He angrily shook his head. He wanted to punish this man for acting much as he had himself a while back, for not following a course of honor and duty. But what right did he have to judge?

Connaire slowly exhaled, calming himself. "This is not the time or place for this. Come to our crannog tomorrow morning and you can speak with Cathal of this then. He is taoiseach."

The man nodded. He started to walk away, but stopped and turned. "There is something more you should know, whether you accept me or not. After we settled here, Bran bragged about your brother knowing of the attack before it happened. That he was going to use it for his advantage."

Stunned, Connaire had trouble finding words. "Cathal? Cathal knew of the raid?"

The warrior shook his head. "No, the other one. Ciarán. He was to kill Eoghan with an arrow so that Bran could become taoiseach. Then Bran would kill Fergus for Ciarán. And your other brother would be blamed."

Connaire shook his head. Not even Ciarán could be so base. "You lie."

"Did he have a bow when he rode against our clann? A bow, but no sword? Did he want you to have one as well so that he could claim you had killed Eoghan?"

Connaire said nothing, thinking back to when they rode against Eoghan. Ciarán, with a bow. Ciarán wanting him to carry a bow. It was no lie.

"Come in the morning. As I said, I am not taoiseach. It is my brother you will need to convince that you are worthy to be a warrior of our clann." Then he smiled. "My brother Cathal. Not Ciarán. But I give you no guarantee. So far, you have not shown yourself to be an honorable warrior."

The warrior shrugged. "I will be there. Where else do I have to go?"

That conversation was on Connaire's mind as he rode home with his clann. He had not yet spoken of it with Cathal, but knew he must. What else might their deceitful brother have in mind? He was obviously in league with Deirdre, whose ambitions knew no bounds. What a pair.

Some had overly enjoyed the festivities. Tian was singing some bawdy songs about women who willingly opened their legs for him. He sang of many women, Dubhain, Finola, Keira and more. Some men drunkenly joined him for a few words, perhaps remembering their own experiences. When he sang of Maille, no man joined him.

The thighs I most love to spread,
With a thatch of curly red,
Belong to the lovely Maille,
Who--

His song ended with a sudden yelp.

Connaire glanced back to see Tian leaning over his horse, clutching his stomach and gasping, while Maille rode close beside him. Very close, and with her bow clutched tightly in her fist. She gave Connaire a half shrug as if to say, "What else was I to do to silence him?"

Connaire chuckled.

As they neared their crannog, Connaire saw a long line of mounted men in front of them. Spears glinted in the last flicker of light as the sun dropped behind the far mountains.

The hound beside Connaire uttered a low, menacing growl. Connaire quickly slid from his horse, drawing his sword. Glancing back, he saw that his companions were also readying themselves for battle.

A warrior in front of him rode closer. It was one of Bran's men, the one who had been so friendly earlier. But this time he held a spear.

Chapter 77

The mounted warrior brandished his spear high, then cast it into the earth with so much force that the entire head was buried and the shaft quivered. He slipped from his horse and walked to Connaire.

"When I spoke to you earlier, you said to come here in the morning. But Bran's sister has made that impossible. When Deirdre returned to our settlement, she told us that we would ride against your clann before dawn. Our goal was to kill you and your brother, Cathal, so that Ciarán would become taoiseach." The warrior shook his head. "She has taken leave of her senses. She is not our taoiseach, but acts as though she were. And yet there are many who follow her."

"She is like a kelpie, a breathtaking mare who will take any who mount her to destruction." Connaire sighed. "I am amazed that any will follow her after what happened in the judgment of the ri."

The warrior gave a short, humorless laugh. "You are right to compare her to the water horse. She has taken the form of a woman, but only to devour any who fall prey to her wiles. There are those still who follow her. Like your brother."

Connaire shook his head. "So Ciarán stays by her side. That is no surprise. They are much the same, even if he is not as appealing to the eye." A quick smile flickered across his lips. "But there are others who will fight for her?"

The warrior shrugged. "Bran had collected quite a number of outlaw warriors before . . . before you defeated him. They have nothing but Deirdre. They will fight for her because they have no honor, so they have nothing else left to them."

Connaire eyed him suspiciously. "And you? Why did

you not stay to fight for her?   You were willing to give false statements to the ri for her."

The warrior stepped back.   For a moment Connaire thought he would reach for his sword, but he just stood silently for a moment.   Then he rubbed his forehead before he spoke.

"You are right to attack my honor.   I admit that I have shown little enough of late.   But I am trying to repair that now. We have come to warn you and to stand with you.   After this, you can either accept us as part of your clann or tell us to go.   We will accept your decision.   At least this time we can feel we acted with honor."

Connaire glanced over at Cathal, who had come close enough to hear all that was said.   "What is the will of the taoiseach?"

Cathal chuckled.   "The taoiseach wants his brother to handle this matter as he thinks best for the clann."   He paused. "But the council will decide if these men and women are worthy to be part of our clann."

Connaire nodded.   Cathal had given him the power of chief in this, but in a way not to irritate the clann.   "Then let them remain with us until this threat has passed."

Tian pushed his way in front of Cathal.   "Do you think this is wise, letting those who are our enemies stay with us?   They might well stab us in the night while we sleep."

Cathal glanced over at Connaire.   "I think I am wise in letting my brother decide."   His voice turned hard as stone.   "And anyone who disputes his decision will have both of us to contend with."

For a moment Connaire thought Tian might do just that, but then he stepped back and shrugged.   "As long as I can sleep with my sword at my side."   He looked back at Maille and grinned.

"And, of course, a warrior who is more fearsome than any of Deirdre's."

Connaire felt a great sense of relief. He had no desire to fight his own clannsmen. "Then let any that have room take one or two of our new allies into their homes. We will take a handcount of them to the crannog. And we will mount a watch for the attack we expect."

With some murmuring, the clann broke into small groups. They went to the new arrivals to offer housing. Hospitality was a sacrosanct tenet of society and no one in the clann would break it. As he watched, the crowd disbursed. The warrior still stood in front of him with a few men and women at his side.

Connaire smiled. "Although we have spoken much, I do not know your name."

"Faolan, son of Luigsech."

Connaire extended his arm and the men grasped each other's forearms in peace. "Well, Faolan, son of Luigsech, you have the name of my uncle, a valiant warrior. I will tell you of him sometime, but it is late. We all need some rest."

Connaire awoke with a start the next morning. A storm was raging outside. He had slept fitfully, waking with every creak or groan of the crannog. Since the wind had arisen not long after he had gone to bed, that had been often. But the rain must have started in the short time since he had last fallen asleep.

Groggily, he shook his head and brushed back his hair with his hand. Brid had already risen. He yawned, rolled out of bed and quickly dressed. Although he could hear a fire crackling in the hearth, it was cold in the outer areas of the crannog. Yawning again, he pulled back the curtain from his sleeping area and slowly walked into the main room.

Brid, Aislinn, Cathal and several members of the clann

were huddled around the fire. Faolan and a couple of handcounts of the warriors from Bran's clann were standing in a group to one side, talking softly among themselves.

Cathal turned and smiled as Connaire entered. Then he took a bowl and ladled porridge into it from a cauldron by the fire.

"Did you sleep well, Brother? You look as though the hound has dragged you through the storm."

Connaire shook his head as he took the bowl and he ate a bite of porridge. "I dozed a few times, but kept expecting the attack. I must have finally gone to sleep before everyone else arose. How long have the others been here?"

"Not long. The porridge has just finished cooking. Probably the sound of the storm hid their arrival."

Connaire sighed. "No attack. I am not sure whether I am relieved or disappointed."

"I know. It will make it difficult when the Cuirmtig meet this morning to convince them that these actually fled Deirdre and are not here to lull us into a false security until an attack comes."

"If it comes."

Cathal grasped his brother by his shoulder and looked directly into his eyes. "We both know it will come. Meanwhile, we need to make sure the clann stays alert."

Connaire shook his head. "I doubt that they will believe that there is a threat since nothing happened last night. Faolan seemed so sure that Deirdre's men planned to attack us. Why did they not do so?"

"Do you think that she is that stupid? A woman who plots and plans every move? She knew we had been warned. She probably figured that we would doubt these men because their warning did not come true."

Connaire laughed bitterly. "And now I look the fool."

490

"Perhaps. Or you might look like the canny leader. It is up to you how you will appear. Most of the Cuirmtig are here now. It is time for you to speak to them."

Connaire stared at his brother in surprise. Why was it up to him to convince the clann that he had not acted foolishly, that he had not been taken in by lies and deception? Cathal was the chief. But he saw the answer in his brother's eyes. Cathal had hinted, even mentioned, that he wanted him to become chief. This was a test to see if he was capable of being a leader. The clann had to be willing to make him chief or it would never happen, whether Cathal wanted it or not.

Connaire handed the bowl back to Cathal. He had only taken a couple of bites, but he was no longer hungry. He was ready for battle, whether it be with words or weapons. They walked into the center of the circle of clannsmen and stood in front of the hearth.

Tian, looking haggard from lack of sleep, stepped towards them. "Our enemy seems to be he who deprives us of our night's rest. Connaire, not Bran."

Connaire met his eye. Tian had made a mistake. "Between the two, you are right. Bran is dead, remember. I killed him."

"I, uh . . . ." The bard angrily shook his head. "You know what I meant. Lack of sleep has made me thick headed."

"Yes, I know what you meant. You would prefer to die in your bed, your throat slit, than watch for the attack we both know will come. At least then you would have your precious sleep. It is much more comfortable."

"Are you calling me lazy?" Tian's eyes narrowed to hard slits.

Connaire shrugged. "If the sword is comfortable in your

hand, perhaps you should hold it." Then he flashed a quick, friendly smile. "But, no, Tian, only a fool would think that. I know you too well. You are tired and weary of waiting for an attack that has not yet come. But if there is anyone I would want beside me when it comes, it would be you." He paused, seeing Brid looking at him with a raised eyebrow with Cú Chulainn at her side. "Well, except for my beloved Brid . . . or the hound, of course."

"So I come after a woman and a dog?"

"I, ah . . . ." But when he saw a smile flicker across Tian's lips, he realized the umbrage was feigned. "I am sure that I would come after Maille for you."

Tian chuckled. "As surely as the sun rises in the day." He quickly grew serious. "There is still the question of Bran's . . . Deirdre's warriors. Do they stay?"

Connaire glanced around the gathered clannsmen. The crowd had grown while he had been talking to Tian. The Cuirmtig was there. It was time.

"They have come to us abandoning their clann. That is not easy. I know." He waited to let any who might accuse him speak. None did. "I left because I was foolish and guilty for causing harm to my brother. These men and women came to us because they could not abide a leader who ignored two of the three legs of the cauldron of society, truth and honor."

Connaire walked around the circle of clannsmen surrounding the hearth, hands clasped behind his back. "Deirdre has proved she has no truth or honor. If there is only duty, the cauldron will fall. You can choose to turn them away, make them outlaws and hated by all clanns. Before you decide, think what you would do. How hard would it be to turn your back on your clann because you could not abide what your clann had become."

492

He paused, looking into the eyes of as many as he could see. "But then you already did that when you came here, did you not?"

The room was silent.

Cathal stepped next to his brother. "Do we remember what we ourselves have done and welcome these wanderers as clannsmen?"

For a moment, no one spoke. Then Tian pushed in front of them. "I was against allowing them to stay. I have changed my mind. We cannot do to them anything we would not want done to us. I say let them stay."

A few voices rose in agreement. Then a few more. Finally the clann's roar of approval filled the room. The door was flung open and the newcomers were invited in, soon mixing with all the others. The din of conversations rose as bowls of porridge were passed around.

Connaire breathed a slow sigh of relief. He wrapped his arm across his brother's shoulders. "I need a little cold air to clear my head."

Cathal smiled. "I do too."

As they walked around in the rain and wind, Connaire could hardly suppress his elation. "I cannot believe that I bested Tian in a battle of words."

Cathal laughed. "Do not be too proud. Defeating a man who is not fighting is no feat."

Connaire stopped. "Then . . . Tian let me win?"

Cathal stopped and turned to his brother, rain dripping from his hair and beard. "I spoke with him this morning. He has come to admire you. But he was like a dog who is not willing to release a stick he does not want. Stubborn. To his credit, Tian saw it. That is why he started as though he disagreed and then made foolish arguments, even bringing your defeat of Bran to the clann's mind."

"So he agreed with me all along?"

"No, not completely. But he respects you enough to trust your judgment. He will support me when I ask for you to be made taoiseach in my stead."

Connaire wiped the rain from his face. "I feel a fool to have thought Tian would so easily concede defeat. Do you have any other wise words for me?"

"Yes. It is cold and wet out here. Let us go back to the fire." He pulled his bratt close around himself and hurried to the door of the crannog.

Connaire quickly followed.

Chapter 78

Just before the night darkened the cloudy skies, Connaire was standing on the wood planking outside the house. The rain had recently stopped, but the air had become chillier. The day had passed with finding housing for the new members of the clann until they could build their own. While not physical labor, it had been taxing and he was tired. Faolin and a couple of his companions had gone hunting and returned with a large stag. It was now roasting on spits over a couple of hearth fires. That had helped gain favor with those who might still resent the newcomers. He sighed. The worst problems seemed to be over.

In the distance, Connaire saw someone approaching, threading his way through the trees. Although he was too far away to discern the man's features, Connaire was sure who he was. Ciarán.

With a feeling of foreboding, Connaire stepped inside and went to Cathal. He was seated by the hearth, cup of mead in hand, and was laughing with Tian, Gruagach and some of the other warriors. He glanced up as Connaire came near and smiled.

"So, brother, why so grim? Have you eaten something that does not agree with you? Or did you catch a chill standing out in the cold?" He patted the bench he sat on. "The fire is warm and we are all friends here. Come. Sit and drink with us."

"I caught a chill, but it was not from the cold." He took the cup from Cathal's hand and set it on the floor. "We have a visitor."

Cathal picked up his cup and drank deeply.

"And who is our visitor that causes you such concern?" He glanced around at his companions, grinning. "Has Bran returned from the dead?"

"About as bad.   It is Ciarán."

The laughter quickly died as all eyes turned to Connaire.

Cathal sighed, eyes closed.   Then he rose, set down his cup, and wrapped his arm across Connaire's shoulders.   "Then let us greet our brother and find what brings him to our settlement."

They stood together outside the house, watching as Ciarán came to the causeway to the crannog.   The guard looked to Cathal, who nodded, then let Ciarán cross the drawbridge.

He was alone, on foot and carried a satchel.   His bow was slung across his back.   His sodden appearance, his wet, black hair plastered to his skull, reminded Connaire of a rat swimming across a pond.

When he got close to them, Ciarán suddenly dropped his satchel and embraced Cathal.   "Brother, it is so good to be with you again."

Cathal did not respond.   Then Ciarán dropped his arms and stepped back, turning to Connaire.   But the young warrior held an arm stiffly between them.

"The last time I saw you, you were standing with the man who tried to kill me."

Ciarán bowed his head.   "It is true.   I was enchanted by Deirdre.   She convinced me that she loved me, that you and Cathal were my enemies."   He glanced up to Connaire with a slight, momentary smirk.   "But then you are familiar with how alluring she can be, how she can convince you to betray your own brother. Now I am returning to my family.   If they will have me."

Connaire felt his anger rise.   He was about to grab Ciarán and toss him into the lake when Cathal rested his hand on Connaire's shoulder.   Connaire glanced back and received an admonishing look.   Cathal must have sensed what he was thinking.

Cathal studied Ciarán. "Why are you here?"

Ciarán shrugged. "I will not lie. I had nowhere else to go. After Bran's death and many of the warriors and their families deserted to you, there were few of us left. Then Deirdre found a new lover and rode off with him and most of the others. The rest of us just wandered away. I came here."

Cathal eyed him suspiciously. "Why not return to our father?"

Ciarán gave a short laugh and shook his head. "I was too good at convincing Father that he loved Aislinn. After you fled, he told me to find her and bring her back or never return. I knew that would not be possible. That is why I went to Bran." He sighed. "Then I met Deirdre and was lost."

Stepping so close to Ciarán that he was forced to step back, Connaire glared at his oldest brother. "What of your plan to kill Eoghan while Bran killed Father?"

Ciarán looked confused. "Plan to kill Eoghan? I know nothing of this."

"Faolan told me after the hearing before Áedán. The one where you lied about what happened when you and Bran ambushed us."

Ciarán held up his hands in front of him. "I have freely admitted that I was taken with Deirdre and would do whatever she asked. That is why I was there. But I know nothing of this other plan, the one to kill Eoghan." He paused, as if considering what Connaire had said. "But Faolan hates me and will say anything or do anything to harm me. I think he loved Deirdre himself and was jealous."

Connaire leaned toward his oldest brother, teeth gritted. "That is--"

Cathal cut the argument short with a wave of his hand.

"Enough. It has grown dark and is getting colder. We will discuss this inside with the evening meal."

Clouds hid the moon and stars. Connaire followed Ciarán and Cathal inside, where the hearth fire lit the room with a smoky glow. Everyone seemed to be watching them. No doubt most of their words had been heard as well. Connaire pushed Ciarán aside as he found a seat by the fire.

Cathal took a piece of firewood and pounded on the floor to quiet everyone.

"Ciarán has come to seek shelter with us. He will sleep here tonight." Hearing the rumble of unhappy murmurs, Cathal pounded for silence again. "The clann will decide whether to accept him after that." He gave a hard look at Connaire. "But for tonight, he has hospitality." Then he smiled. "So let us eat."

Connaire heard some unhappy muttering, but people began to get their bowls. A large slab of roasted beef was on the table and the aroma of a leek soup wafted from a cauldron near the fire. Food soon took priority. But Connaire stayed on his bench, studying the fire.

Tian sat beside him, holding a bowl with a chunk of beef and soup in one hand and a cup covered by oat bread in the other. He set the cup down, crumbled the coarse oat bred into the soup and began to scoop out the thick, oaty soup and beef. Between bites, he spoke.

"Ciarán will be gone in the morning, you know. No one wants him with us. Cathal is only trying to be honorable before Ciarán is turned away."

Connaire shook his head. "I do not trust him. There is no truth, honor or duty in him. He must know that he cannot stay. So why come?"

Tian paused in his eating. "True. I will have Gruagach

watch him tonight." He nudged Connaire. "Now go and get some food before it is all gone."

When he went to bed with Brid, Connaire lay awake for a long time, thinking, wondering. He reached down, touched Cú Chulainn's fur and felt a sense of security in the hound's presence.

Finally, sleep overtook him.

Chapter 79

Connaire fought for his life against a large man in a dark room. They flailed at each other on the wooden floor, each struggling to gain the advantage. The man wrapped his thick hands around Connaire's neck. He grunted each time Connaire drove his fist into his stomach, but would not release his grip. Suddenly Connaire could plainly see his foe. It was Bran.

With a start, Connaire awoke, sweaty and breathing heavily. It was a still night, with no light from the banked hearth fire. But why did he still hear the grunts of battle?

Someone yelped in pain, a woman's voice, and something hit the floor with a clatter. Connaire realized Brid was not next to him and that the sounds were close to the bed where he lay. He rolled out of the bed, groping in the darkness.

"Get a torch, someone! Quickly!"

As he swung his arms back and forth in front of him, Connaire hit something. He grabbed what felt like an arm, Brid's he thought. She was kneeling on the floor, pushing down. As he followed her arm, he came to a woman's wet, soft breast. He could hear her gasping. Brid was choking her.

"Stop. Hold her down and we will see who she is when we get some light."

People scurried about, stirring the fire to life and igniting tallow-soaked torches. Their brightness pierced the veil of darkness and he could see who was under Brid. It was Deirdre.

"What . . . How did you get in here?" The drawbridge to shore was pulled up every night, mainly to keep out predators like wolves. But it should have kept away a she-wolf like Deirdre as well.

Tian ran to them with a torch and the others in the

household rushed to see what had caused the ruckus. Brid lifted Deirdre by the front of her léine from the floor and flung her against the wall, where she collapsed. The diminutive warrior woman stood, fist clinched, glaring at her larger foe who lay in front of her.

Deirdre wore a short léine and trews. Her léine had been torn from one side of her body in the scuffle, exposing a heavy breast and a stomach that had grown flabby since Connaire had last touched her. She was soaking wet, with her long hair dripping on the floor. There she lay, breathing heavily, and eyeing Brid warily.

Connaire knew how she got across the water to the crannog. She swam.

Oswald pushed his way to the fore, opening a way for Cathal and Aislinn. Cathal turned to Connaire, looking confused.

"What is she doing here?"

Connaire looked at Deirdre and shook his head. "I, uh . . . I have no idea."

Brid grabbed Connaire's arm and made a cutting motion across his neck with her hand. Then she pointed to the floor, where a long dagger glinted in the torchlight.

Connaire stared at Deirdre, filled with disgust at himself that he had ever been attracted to her. "She came to kill me."

Oswald stooped and retrieved the dagger, studying it. "Are you injured?"

Connaire shook his head.

"And your woman? Is she injured?"

Brid shook her head.

The Angle held the blade to the light. "Then whose blood is this?"

It hit Connaire like the flat of a sword.

"Where is Cú Chulainn? He should have been here."

Tian touched his arm. "And where is Gruagach?"

They both looked at Deirdre. She smiled smugly and said nothing.

Connaire headed for the door. He stopped and turned to look at Deirdre.

"Bring her."

Then he rushed out into the night.

Connaire could see by the moonlight that the drawbridge was down. Ready for Deirdre's escape? A dark form lay near the bridge, not moving. He ran to it.

It was Cú Chulainn. As Connaire rested his hand on the dog's chest he thought he felt a shudder. As those with the torches came closer, Connaire could see that there was a pool of blood around his head. His faithful companion was dead.

The hound's neck had been sliced. His eyes stared sightlessly ahead, but they seemed to have a look of bewilderment, of betrayal. Connaire threw back his head and roared in anguish, striking his forehead with his clenched fists. Brid fell to her knees beside him, uttering strangled, guttural moans. She buried her face in Cú Chulainn's side.

As he started to go to her, Connaire felt a hand on his shoulder and turned to see Cathal. A tear glistened on his brother's face. "I am sorry."

Oswald had brought Deirdre to them, dragging her roughly by one arm. In his other hand he held the dagger that she had used to kill the hound.

She sneered at Connaire. "You were always weak. It was only a stupid dog."

With a low, feral cry, Brid turned and sprang at Deirdre, grabbing the dagger from Oswald's hand as she did. She plunged the knife into Deirdre's stomach, jerking it upwards several times.

Deridre's screams pierced the night. She pulled her arm from Oswald's grasp and clasped the dagger. As she sunk to her knees, her blood flowed onto the wooden deck.

Brid dropped her hands and stood a moment, staring at Deirdre. Then she turned and knelt beside the hound again. Connaire knelt with her, one arm across her shoulders and his other hand resting in the hound's side.

Cathal came into the light of the torches. He looked at Deirdre, the hound, Brid and Connaire. He shook his head.

"Connaire, run for the healer."

His younger brother slowly rose to his feet. He glanced down at Deirdre before looking Cathal directly in the eye.

"She will die no matter what the healer does. If she did not, I would kill her." He paused, regaining his composure. "Cú Chulainn was raised by women. The only enemies he knew were men. He trusted her, probably came to her with his tail wagging. Then she slit his throat."

Brid had risen, holding the hound in her arms as if her were a puppy as his long legs draped across her arms. She had her cheek pressed against the dog's jowl, her eyes closed, tears flowing from them. Connaire rose with her, facing away from the light. His shoulders shook.

Suddenly Tian called from the drawbridge. "I need help! Gruagach is in the lake."

Tian was struggling to pull a dark form from the water and several others quickly went to help him. Connaire and Brid walked over to them, she carrying the hound and his arm across her shoulders, holding her tightly to him.

It was Gruagach, dead eyes staring, an arrow sticking thorough his neck, the arrowhead under his chin. Tian held his friend to his chest, face contorted in agony. With a wail like a banshee, his mate Niassa ran to him, dropped to her knees and buried her face in his side.

Tian looked around. "Ciarán. He did this. Where is he?"

Cathal looked around. "Has anyone seen Ciarán?"

Connaire sighed, his voice toneless, without emotion. "He is gone. He would never stay to fight. I am sure we are missing a horse as well. We will have to track him."

Cathal shook his head. "I have made many mistakes tonight, but not this one. We will track him in the morning. Even if we happened to find his trail, he would ambush us and escape in the darkness. If we are to die, Ciarán must too. We will wait until daybreak."

He walked over to Oswald, who stood looking down at Deirdre. She was still clutching the knife in her belly, uttering sharp, pained moans. Blood stained her léine, dripping to the ground.

"There is no reason for a healer? Will she die soon?"

The Angle shrugged. "Perhaps. Belly wounds can take time. But she will surely die."

Cathal stared at him. "Do you feel no pity for her?"

Oswald glared at her coldly. "No. She is without honor. She is nothing more than dung."

Cathal shook his head. "That is true, but I cannot let this go on. Kill her quickly."

Deirdre look up at him, fear in her eyes.

Cathal sighed. "Do it as painlessly as possible."

The Angle pulled the dagger from her stomach. She screamed as he did. He grabbed her hair, pulled it back and, with one smooth motion, slit her throat. Then he dropped her lifeless body into a pool of her own blood and threw the dagger into the water. It landed with a soft splash.

Cathal slowly rubbed his brow, eyes closed. "That is the last order I will ever give as taoiseach of this clann. Ciarán must have planned this with Deirdre before he ever came here. Gruagach heard Deirdre getting out of the water after she swam here and Ciarán shot him from behind. Then she killed the hound. I should have known that Ciarán would do something like this. I have failed to keep my people safe. It is Connaire's time now. May the gods . . . may God give him more wisdom than I have had."

He turned and slowly walked over to where his friend lay, slain by his own brother. Tears ran down his face. He did not wipe them away.

Chapter 80

Early the next morning, Connaire and several warriors rode out to track Ciarán, but found nothing. He had not taken a horse, so he had been able to leave no trace as he went through the forest. Cú Chulainn would have followed his scent, but the clan had no other hound so able. It started to rain, washing away any chance of picking up Ciarán's trail. Angrily, Connaire had finally called off the search and returned to the crannog.

After the midday meal, Tian, Maille, Cathal and Oswald carried Gruagach's body, tightly wrapped in his woolen bratt, to be buried. Niassa walked behind them, supported by Aislinn. Following them, Connaire carried the hound, covered with his own bratt. Then came the royal contingent.

One of Áedán's warriors had stopped for hospitality early that morning, in the aftermath of death. When he had heard what had happened, he took a hasty meal of some cold meat with him as he rode to Dun Ad. The ri's fondness for the hound who had helped save his life was well known.

Áedán had arrived just before the clannsmen had begun their sad procession. Along with him came a handcount of warriors and Brother Padraig. When they reached the burial site, two graves had been dug. Gruagach's bearers slowly lowered him into the larger one, followed by Connaire gently laying Cú Chulainn into the other.

Brother Padraig knelt by Gruagach's grave. He made the sign of the cross of the Christus and spoke softly in the language of Rome.

"Christus inquit, 'Ego sum resurrectio et vita.'" He paused. "'In domo Patris mei mansiones multae sunt si quo minus dixissem vobis quia vado parare vobis locum.'"

Then he sprinkled some water from a small flask on the body and made the sign of the cross again.

Cathal glanced at Connaire with a look of incomprehension. Connaire quietly muttered a translation. "They are the words of our Lord. 'I am the resurrection and the life. In my Father's house there are many dwellings. If it were not so, I would not have told you. I go to prepare a place for you.'"

Padraig rose from his knees and turned to go, but Áedán grabbed his arm.

"Cú Chulainn." The ri's voice was choked. "Bless him."

Padraig looked uncertain. "The dog? You want last blessing on the dog?"

"He deserves it as much as any warrior I have ever known."

For a moment, Padraig said nothing, looking at the ri askance. Then he sighed and nodded. "He was God's creature. One with a brave and loyal heart. That is more than I can say for many men I have blessed."

After the Brother had finished the blessing, they all went back to the crannog. A feast had been prepared in honor of the fallen. First Brother Padraig celebrated the Eucharist, then everyone filled their cups and began to eat.

On the table sat platters with haunches of venison and slabs of beef, slathered with honey. A thick beef stew simmered in a cauldron, giving an aroma of garlic, rosemary and thyme to the air. Bowls of boiled duck eggs, clams and mussels were scattered about on the table. Loaves of dark bread were piled high. For drink, there was an oaken barrel of ale and one of mead. The ri had even brought Gaulish wine in earthen jugs to be shared.

Áedán pounded on the table with his fist for silence, but the crowd finally quieted only after his guards had joined his efforts with the butts of their spears. He raised his cup of wine high.

"I raise my cup in honor of two heroes of this clann. I did not know Gruagach well, but I did know Cú Chulainn. Valiant warriors, both. We drink to them."

With a roar of approval, all there joined him in drinking to the two of the clann who had died.

Then Tian stood by the hearth and banged on the cauldron of stew with a piece of firewood, silencing the crowd. He spoke loudly, but slowly and carefully. Connaire could tell that the filidh of the clann had indulged too much in the solace of drink.

"My kinsmen, I have heard my closest friend honored equally with a hound."

As he paused and drank from his cup, Connaire glanced worriedly at Brid, who stood by his side. Her eyes narrowed, holding Tian tightly in her gaze. Connaire put his arm across her shoulders, pulling her close. If Tian insulted Cú Chulainn, he only hoped he could keep her from attacking the bard.

Tian set his cup carefully on a table and spread his arms wide. "If Cú Chulainn were just another hound, I would object. But Cú Chulainn was a warrior as brave as my friend. So instead, I will give you this eulogy in honor of both of them." He picked up his cup and took another drink before he began.

Treachery stalks the shadows and circles round the moon
You can hear it rush past your ear and fade into the gloom
The protected become hunters as protectors meet their
doom.

Gruagach, trusted friend, fierce of look and arm of might
His tousled mane and cold disdain of all danger in his sight
But he could not fight what he did not see, felled by arrow's
flight.

Cu Chulainn, Brid's friend, will be missing our next strife
The gallant hound of much renown has given up his life
For his noble trust of womankind was repaid with a knife.

So the protected become the hunters to mete out righteous
doom
And the traitor seeks the shadows and hides behind the
moon.

When he finished, tears formed at the corners of his eyes and trickled down his cheeks. Many others were moved to weep as well. Brid turned and buried her head in Connaire's chest. Tian walked over to them.

Connaire rested his hand on the filidh's shoulder. "I am glad that your eulogy was for both of them. For a moment I feared that you would say the hound should not be honored in the same manner."

Tian glanced down at Brid, then gave Connaire a wry smile. "I may be a little drunk, but I have not lost my sanity. Besides, that hound would have returned from the dead and run me to the ground if I had insulted him." He choked back a sob. "And, with God as my witness, I loved that mangy cur almost as much as you did."

With tears still flowing, he walked unsteadily over to Maille, who grabbed him and pulled him close to her breast.

Áedán worked his way through the crowd to Connaire. He surveyed everyone there before turning to Connaire.

"And what of this woman, Deirdre, who caused all this? I understand she . . . perished."

Connaire silently nodded.

"Well deserved, from what I have heard. And what did you do with her body?"

"Last I saw of it, it was being dragged behind a horse. Brid seems to have lost hers."

The ri lifted one eyebrow. "Behind a horse? Ah .... So what do you think happened to her body?"

Connaire shrugged. "Probably left as food for the wolves."

Áedán slowly shook his head. "I hope she does not sicken them."

They stared solemnly at each other for a moment. Then they both began to softly laugh. It was a sad laugh, without humor, only to break to the tension of the moment.

VI. THE BATTLE OF DEGSASTAN

Chapter 81

Slowly, Connaire rolled out of his bed. He rubbed the back of his aching neck. The smell of the fire and the aroma of porridge coaxed him to the hearth, where he settled into his chair with a groan.

Cathal was sitting beside him and smiled.

"Have over five handcounts of Samhains as being taoiseach taken their toll or are you just feeling the pains of age?"

Connaire sighed. "Perhaps both. Too many cold, wet nights raiding the Fortriu. But then, we are both getting older. I see more gray in my hair than brown and you have little but gray." He chuckled. "But at least we have hair. Not like Tian."

"Maybe that is because Maille stroked it too often when he sang to her."

They both laughed, but quickly stopped as Tian approached. He looked from brother to brother curiously.

"What was so humorous?"

Cathal shrugged. "We were just discussing how, ah . . . how cold it has turned in the few days since Samhain."

Tian absently rubbed his balding pate. "I noticed that, too. My bratt no longer seems to keep me as warm as it once did. I wonder why."

The brothers looked at each other and again broke into laughter.

Tian stared at them for a moment with a puzzled expression, but turned to the doorway as a short, pudgy man with graying hair cut in the St. John's tonsure hurried in. "I wonder what brings Brother Padraig to us in such a rush?"

Connaire's laughter died in his throat. "I fear that Áedán's summons has come, the one he spoke of in the last meeting of the Dal. We are to ride to Bernicia to stop Æthelfrith's Angles."

The brother stumbled to them, dropping to a chair, panting. Connaire placed a hand on Padraig's knee.

"So is it to be? Are we to gather our warriors and ride to Bernicia?"

Padraig nodded, gasping as he spoke. "Áedán calls to the Cenéls to meet at Dun Ad on the morrow. He wants to ride before the time of the snows. Many men have sailed from Eireann and have just arrived. Hering, the true Ri of Bernicia, will be with us with his Angle guard. He says that many of Æthelfrith's men will change to his side when we fight."

Connaire leaned back in his chair. "Then why have they not done so already? This fills my heart with dread."

Cathal cocked his head as he studied his brother. "Æthelfrith strikes down any who try to stop him. He will soon be at our hearths. We must protect our lands. Is that not what we do as warriors? Find glory in battle when we protect our clanns? I never saw fear in your eyes before, but do I see it now? Are you afraid to die?"

Connaire sadly shook his head. "No, I do not fear battle, nor do I fear death. But we will ride far from our homes, to meet our foes in a distant land. Let Æthelfrith bring his Angles to us. We will be rested, on familiar territory, and destroy him."

"So you want us to ignore the ri's summons?"

Connaire bowed his head. "No, we must heed the call of the ri. Truth, honor and duty. The three legs of the cauldron of our society. And this is our duty." He slowly rose from his chair, feeling very weary. "Send for our warriors."

The warriors, young and old, male and female, were crowded in the crannog. Connaire had opened several barrels of ale and their cups were kept full. Padraig stood next to him, sipping from his cup. Connaire pounded the flat of his sword against the table in front of him until the din of the crowd slowly ceased. Looking around the torch-lit room, he realized how many of those who had come with Cathal and him from Eireann those many Samhains ago had died, how many of their children now stood in their stead.

"My clann, Brother Padraig has brought a summons from Áedán, our ri. In the morning we must ride to Dun Ad and join him in the attack on Æthelfrith of Bernicia."

A cheer arose, filling the hall. Connaire held up his arms and waited until the noise had subsided.

"If there are two warriors in the household, only one will go. If it is a father and son, the father will go. If it is a man and a woman, they will decide which one will ride with us, unless there are young children in the household. Then the man will ride."

This time a roar of objection rose. Again Connaire raised his arms and waited for the crowd to quiet.

"I have been taoiseach since before many of you were born. I have always put the clann first in everything I have done. When we came here from Eireann, we were few. Over time, we have grown stronger. What I have said is to keep us strong, no matter what happens when we go to Bernicia. If you no longer trust my wisdom to lead the clann, then remove me as your taoiseach and do what you will."

For a moment there was silence. Those gathered looked from one to another in disbelief.

Then someone yelled.

"No!"

513

Then a few more.

Soon the hall was filled with the voices of the clann.

"No!"

"No!"

"No!"

"No!"

The shouts of support were deafening.

Connaire smiled. He was still their leader. What he had said they would follow. The clann would survive, even if he did not.

He walked out into the night and stood, gazing at the reflection of the moon on the loch. Brother Padraig quietly followed and stood next to him in silence.

"It has been some time since we last spoke, Brother Padraig."

"Yes, two handcounts of Samhains have passed."

"How is your community on the isle?"

Padraig sighed. "We thrive. But some of our friends have gone to be with the Christus. Colm Cille, for one, and-"

"Colm Cille has died? I thought he would live forever."

"He will, but not in this place. In the better one."

"Ah." Connaire gave a dismissive wave of his hand. "The life beyond."

"Do you believe that it is so?"

Connaire considered the question. He had been baptized, but sometimes he called upon Lugh instead of the Christus. Too many years following the old ways, perhaps. Did he believe? He touched his chest where the cross given to him by Brother Diarmuid still rested.

"Yes. Yes, Brother Padraig, I do. I believe, but I often do not understand Him." He pressed the cross, feeling the metal against his skin, remembering how it had saved his life with the Fortriu. "How is Brother Diarmuid?"

"He went to be with the Christus not long ago."

"He is . . . . I am sorry that I did not visit him after I left the isle. I should have. He was a good friend."

"You had your duties as taoiseach of your clann."

"I have been on hunts and raiding expeditions. I could have made the trip to Ioua."

Padraig rested his hand on Connaire's shoulder. "You sound like a man who is dying, regretting things he did and did not do in life."

"Perhaps I am."

The stout, little man rested his hand on Connaire's shoulder. "Perhaps you are not. Let God decide your fate. Trust Him."

Connaire shook off the hand. "So God is sending us to this battle?"

"No, Áedán is. But God can be with you."

Connaire gave a short, humorless laugh. "He is welcome to ride along." He paused. "I need to ready my people for war, not talk of God. So pray for us, Brother, for I fear that is the only hope we have."

Connaire turned and went back into the hall. Padraig stayed and prayed.

Chapter 82

The next morning, after their meal, the clann's warriors who were to join Áedán's army assembled by the loch. Connaire looked anxiously for Brid. She had gone to bed before him. He was sure that she had feigned sleep when he retired, angry that she would not be going with the other warriors. When he rose in the morning, she was gone and he had not seen her since.

As he wandered through those gathered, both warriors who would be fighting and those bidding them farewell, Connaire saw Cathal with Oswald. Oswald had grown heavier over time, but was a big man who could carry the extra weight. The Angle had a large, round shield covered with leather and a sword that was longer and heavier than anyone else's.

Connaire drew his brother aside. "The two of you should stay here."

Cathal smiled. "And why is that? So that you can claim the hero's portion at our feasts when we have won?"

"Brother, your sword arm is . . . almost useless. And Oswald is not only lame, but is an Angle. I cannot trust him to fight his own people."

Coldly, Cathal studied him. "Oswald is *our* people. He is a member of our clann. I would trust him with my life. I will be trusting him with my life. And we will fight as one warrior, so that our lamed limbs will not matter."

Connaire cocked his head. "Fight as one warrior? How?"

"I will fight with my good arm on one side of his shield, while his arm will defend the other." Cathal gave a short laugh. "We might move slowly, but we will be formidable."

"But think of--"

Suddenly Connaire felt a forceful tug on his arm. It was Aislinn.

She pulled him away, fire in her eyes. "What are you doing? Trying to destroy him?"

Connaire shook his head, confused. "Destroy? I am trying to save his life. This attack is unwise. Worse, foolhardy."

"It does not matter." Her eyes flashed with anger. "Cathal has stood by you whenever you needed it, even stepped down as chief and made sure you became chief in his stead. He would gladly die for you. Honor him as a warrior. Honor him as a man. Honor him as your brother." Tears welled in her eyes. "I wanted to go, but he said that he must do it. If he is to die, so be it. No one will mourn him as much as I. But, if you love him, do not take away his honor."

Connaire could find no worthy argument. He mutely nodded, turned and went back to Cathal.

"Mount up, Brother. We need to leave."

"And Oswald?"

Connaire shrugged. "If you want him to ride with you, as one warrior, that is your choice. But I think he should take his own horse."

His brother raised an eyebrow. "So, what did my gentle mate say to persuade you to let me ride with you?"

Connaire smiled. "That she would geld me and feed my bollocks to the pigs if I did not."

After a moment, they both started to chuckle, then to laugh. They walked to their horses, arms across each other's shoulders.

When Connaire's clann arrived at Dun Ad, they found a sea of people: warriors and merchants, men, women and children. It was like a giant fair, with everyone laughing, drinking and slapping each other on the back.   Tents surrounded the hill below the fort, with several large corrals spotted on the outskirts.

Connaire stopped, awestruck.   He had never seen so many people, so many horses.   He dismounted and stood silently.   For a moment he wondered he had been wrong, if this host of warriors might well win any battle.

He felt a heavy hand on his shoulder.   It was Oswald.

"You are right to worry.   They are many, but they do not understand what is to come.   They are heroes, each one of them.   They shout their name as they challenge their opponent to combat.   But they will face an army that does not care who they are.   And they will die."

Connaire turned to him, upset to hear what had been in his own mind.   "You think our Angle foes are better than these?   That we are weak?"

Oswald shook his head and sighed.   "No, you are not weak."

At first, Connaire was angry, but he saw sadness in the Angle's eyes.   Not arrogance.   He waited.

"You fight valiantly, but you do not fight to win.   You fight for glory.   For honor.   To be remembered as brave warriors in the songs of your bards."   His blue eyes bore into Connaire's.   "Angles fight with honor, but it is not the same as yours.   Your swords are short and your shields are small.   The worst is that you think your foes will fight as you do, one man against another.   Angles fight as an army, together.   And that is why the ravens will feast on our dead eyes on the morrow."

Our dead eyes.   Connaire heard those words.   Oswald was a part of the clann.   But that did not change what he had said.   The voice of doom.

For a three handcount and two days, they trekked toward

their Angle foes.   At first, their pace was slowed by carts hauling supplies over a difficult terrain and by those on foot.   Often riders would have to dismount to help the carts get through a muddy area. It was slow, tedious travel. Then the carts were abandoned and as much of the supplies loaded on horses as they could manage.   The pack horses were loaded with salted beef and fish, cheese, oats and hides of ale.

Soon some of the warriors began to grumble, wondering why they were venturing so far from their homes.   It was an unfamiliar land to them, more grassy hills than rugged mountains, with more farms and wooded regions than Dál Riata.   The Angles had fled their farms, taking all of their animals and goods that they could manage, leaving their homes deserted in fear of the advancing Dál Riatan throng.

Then, finally, Áedán called the chiefs together to tell them that a scouting party had seen the Angle army nearby.

He smiled.   "We will attack in the morning.   Æthelfrith has far fewer warriors than we and they will fall as grain before the scythe.   Tonight, we will open the hides of ale and celebrate tomorrow's victory."

Connaire shifted uneasily on his feet.   "Should we not wait until we have victory to celebrate it?   Is there not a saying that the boar gores the arrogant hunter?"

Áedán gave Connaire a hard stare.   "There is also a saying, 'The boldest warrior wins the battle.'   A little ale will make us even bolder, more fearless than we already are."

The younger chiefs shouted their agreement.

Connaire shook his head and muttered, "And the fool gathers his winnings before the die is cast."

But no one listened.

That night, the clann camped on a wooded hill, overlooking the rest of Áedán's host. It was a chilly night, not long before Samhain. The lights of their army's campfires filled the night as far as Connaire could see. They pitched their hide shelters and prepared for the night, everyone excited in anticipation of the coming battle. A woman, with the build of a warrior and not quite young enough to be his daughter, came up to him.

"Are you ready for our victory tomorrow, Taoiseach"

He smiled sadly in return. "I am as ready as I can be." Then he recognized her. "Are you not Eavan, the lass who had come across the sea in Cathal's currach? Why did your mate, Gair, not come in your stead?"

"I was with Cathal then and wanted to be fighting beside now. Besides, Gair is no warrior and would just get himself killed." She looked down. "Since I have proven not able to conceive, there was no reason for me not to die."

To Connaire, she was still the brave lass from so long ago and that made him angry. "Perhaps the fault is his. You are still young enough to bear, but you will never know."

She shrugged. "If I die in this battle and he takes another mate, Gair will."

Cathal patted her shoulder, unable to think of a reply.

After their evening meal, Tian sang the songs of their clann. He sang of Gruagach, of the hound Cú Chulainn, of their journey across the sea to their new homeland and the legends of their ancestors. These were familiar, heroic songs for the clann and heightened their fighting lust.

The warriors sharpened their swords with their honing stones, laughing and joking, boasting of the Angles that would fall beneath their blades. Connaire walked among them, encouraging them to make sure that their weapons were prepared. He tried to keep their ale-drinking under control, but some of the younger warriors made it a game to sneak away and see how much they could consume.

Suddenly he stopped, startled by a warrior crouched by the fire, sharpening iron arrow points.

It was Brid.

"What . . . . How did you get here?"

She turned to him and smiled, then spoke with the language of the hands.

I followed you. Since we fight tomorrow, I joined you.

"But you were to stay home." Connaire fought to contain his anger. "I said that only one warrior from each hearth could come."

I never agreed. Why should you go and not I?

"Because I am taoiseach. I had to go. And you were to stay."

I am your mate. I go where you go. We have no children. If you die, I will too. If not with you here, I would die if you did not return.

"But--"

She placed a finger on his lips and slowly shook her head. Then she grabbed the front of his léine and pulled him into the dark woods. She slipped out of her woolen trews and pulled Connaire's down to his ankles. He lifted her as she wrapped her legs around him. She was wet with desire as he entered her and they mated with feral intensity, saying nothing and panting heavily. His release was so intense that he would have fallen to the ground if there had not been a tree close enough to lean against. Brid buried her head on Connaire's shoulder, moaning softly.

They stayed, coupled together for a time. Finally, Brid

kissed him ardently and slipped down to her feet. They dressed and slowly walked back to the others.

Connaire felt such a closeness to her that he almost wept. While they might die on the morrow, at least they had that night.

Chapter 83

As the sun slowly rose above the ground fog that lay low along the horizon, Connaire stood with his warriors on a grassy ridge overlooking a shallow valley with a small stream flowing through it. The slope down was bare of trees and brush, with only a very few clumps of oaks along the stream. The damp, morning chill permeated his clothing and he wrapped his bratt tightly around him. Áedán's army stretched along the ridge as far as he could see. Below, across the stream, were the Angles. While not as many as the Dál Riatans, they were still a formidable force. An occasional glint of sunlight flashed off an Angle sword, spearhead or iron helm as they waved their weapons in the air and yelled taunts in their unintelligible tongue.

Although it was hard to hear anything above the answering insults from the Dál Riatans, Connaire managed to gather his clann's fighters together. He eyed each one, assessing. Some had obviously indulged too much in the free-flowing ale and now suffered the effects. Because of how Connaire had chosen his warriors, many were older. Good. They would be more wary, knowing better what to expect in a battle. Still, he gave them instructions.

"When the signal is given to attack, we move together. No one will run ahead. When we reach the Angles, we will attack as one."

Lunn, Gruagach's son, spat on the ground. He was young, tall and broad-shouldered as his father had been, but had the rashness of one who has never seen a true battle. "You want me to go as slow as old men and cripples? I can walk faster. I could challenge and beat a dozen Angle warriors in the time it will take all of us to cross the stream together."

Connaire shook his head. "Or you could be dead. We came here to stop Æthelfrith, not to die."

Lunn laughed. "You think I cannot take an Angle?" He gestured at Oswald. "Are you afraid of this old cripple?"

Connaire wanted to cuff the insolent youth, but refrained. "No, but I respect him, both as a member of this clann and as a warrior. You would be wise to do the same. His leg does not hamper his skill with a sword."

Lunn spat again and, with the other young warriors, turned and stalked away, grumbling loudly.

Connaire turned to Oswald and Cathal. "I apologize for Lunn. He already has the frenzy of battle in his mind and gives no thought to what he says."

Oswald shrugged. "We were all foolish when we were young. I hope he lives long enough to grow wise." He gazed along the ridge. "I see Hering with but a handful of his followers. Did he not claim most of the Bernicians would abandon Æthelfrith for him? He appears to have overestimated his popularity."

Cathal nodded. "Yes, and why are we attacking from here? It is a long way to the Angles. Would it not be better to let them come up the hill to us? Then they would be tired, not us. By the time we reach them, we will be scattered and exhausted."

Rubbing the bridge of his nose with his thumb and forefinger, Connaire sighed. "I told the ri the same. But he insists that the force of our attack as we run at the Angles will overwhelm them. Nothing I said could dissuade him."

Cathal shook his head. "Then, as Oswald has said, we are doomed."

A short, plump brother with only a fringe of gray hair skirting his head approached with a broad smile. It was Brother Padraig.

"I have come to celebrate the Eucharist with you and your clann."

Connaire embraced Padraig. "You are welcome, Brother. And will the Eucharist protect us in battle against these pagan Angles?"

The brother stepped back and shook his head. "Sadly, no. Our sainted Colm Cille realized that no battle is truly blessed when he saw the followers of the Christus slay each other. It is only that you may be close to God in case . . . ."

Padraig turned his face, unable to finish. He took a deep breath. "I will rescue the wounded and anoint the dying. It is all I can do."

Connaire rested his hand on the little man's shoulder. "Let me summon the others."

They stood ready, awaiting the signal to attack. Then it came. First one war horn made from the horn of a bull sounded, soon joined by the droning of more and more horns. They rose in in deafening crescendo that filled the air. Then, with fierce cries the warriors charged down the slope in ragged lines towards the enemy.

Connaire's clann trotted slowly toward the Angles, keeping together. If one of the younger men started to run ahead, Tian, Connaire or one of the other older warriors would slap him with the flat of the sword. By the time they reached the valley, Áedán's host was scattered. The fleeter warriors were far ahead of the slowest.

Periodically, Brid would stop and loose an arrow. An Angle would fall. The clann's pace was slowed by Oswald, but Connaire forced them all to match his awkward trot. By the time they reached the stream's muddy bank, most of Áedán's army was already across, breathing hard and tired.

The Angles were rested and ready.

No Angle came out to do individual battle with a Dál Riatan hero, so Áedán's men attacked one at a time or in small groups. Some cast aside their shields and tried to clamber over a veritable wall of shields, only to fall to spears of their enemy. Some stood and beat against the Angles' shields, only to be slain by the enemy's longer swords. By sheer bravery and strength of will, pockets of warriors would force their way through the Angle shields and slash those holding them. But the Angles would quickly close the gap and annihilate those Dál Riatans. Their war cries turned to cries of pain. As they lay, bleeding and dying, some raised an arm as if to plead with their comrades to save them. But there was no salvation.

As he slogged through the clinging mud of the stream bed, Connaire saw it all. He called to the clann to stay together, but the droning of a dwindling number of war horns, the din of iron swords clanging, men yelling in anger and screaming in agony drowned him out. Bodies of those dead and dying with their pooling blood made footing treacherous. There was no time to help the wounded. Only after a victory was there time to see to the wounds of fallen comrades.

The Angles had stepped back to gain better ground, with the perilous, bloody muck in front of them left to their attackers. Oswald slipped and fell to one knee. Cathal pulled him to his feet and they pressed on. A few of the clann's young warriors ran ahead at the Angles and were cut down, adding their bodies to the bloody mass in front of the Angle line.

Then the clann hit the Angle shields and Connaire had to concentrate on keeping alive.

As he struck an Angle's shield with his sword, Brid bent

low and jabbed under the shield with hers.   His foe dropped his
shield to protect his legs and Connaire slashed.   As his sword sunk
into the Angle's neck, blood spurted in a thick stream.   For a
moment, Connaire saw surprise in the blond, young man's blue
eyes, then life left them and he slumped to the ground.

After the Angle fell, he and Brid attacked the men to each
side through the gap made when the young Angle fell, taking them
before they could react.   Connaire swung his sword low, sinking
his blade into his foe's back.   The man collapsed, his legs no
longer supporting him.   He looked as old as Connaire, with
grey-streaked hair and a thick mustache.   In his eyes Connaire saw
death as he brought his blade down on the man's head, cleaving his
skull.   As he pulled his sword back, he turned to see Brid fell
another Angle.

They had opened a hole in the Angle line and his clann
followed them through it.

Connaire felt a rush of power as he swung his sword.
Caught in the blood-lust of battle, he yelled at the top of his lungs
as he struck the neck of another Angle who was trying to bring his
shield around.   Then he blocked an enemy's sword with his round
shield and stabbed the warrior through the ribs, blood spurting
from the wound and running down Connaire's arm.   As Connaire
pulled this blade from the Angle's fallen body, for a moment no
other Angle attacked him.   Although he could not keep track of all
of his warriors, he saw more Angles fall by their swords and spears,
widening the gap.   They had a chance to turn this battle.   The
other Dál Riatans must see the gap and would follow, turning the
line of the Angles and driving them from the field like a herd of
cattle.

But no Dál Riatans followed and soon more Angles joined
the fray in front of them, pressing them back.   With their huge

shields and heavy swords, the Angles forced the clann to retreat, step by step.   Connaire saw warrior after warrior of the clann fall. No other Dál Riatan warriors came to help them, to shore up their line.   The Angles were attacking from three sides, leaving them no way to protect themselves with their smaller shields.   Their only hope was to reach the hill above the valley and there make a stand.

"Back!   Back to the hill!"

Did anyone hear him above the noise of battle?   He was not sure, but most did follow Brid and him as they backed towards the stream.   Suddenly, a small group of Áedán's bravest warriors ran past them to attack the Angles, yelling and wildly swinging their swords.   While it was a hopeless, desperate charge and they were slaughtered, it did slow the Angles.

Connaire and the remnants of his clann pushed through the clinging mud of the stream, reaching the other side before the Angles did.   Brid unerringly sent her arrows into their vanguard, killing the leading warriors, and the rest slowed as they raised their shields.   The clann continued their retreat, but held together, protecting each other as best they could.   Then the Angles turned to pursuing Dál Riatans who had dropped their weapons, making them easier prey when they had turned to flee in the muddy stream. They were cut down like ripe grain before the scythe, but their deaths gave the clann time to escape.

By the time the clann reached the top of the ridge, they all collapsed on the ground.   Gasping for air, Connaire took a quick assessment.   His heart sank.   It was a disaster.   Tian and Brid were there, as well as less than a handcount of the clann's warriors. Then he realized that Cathal was not there.   Connaire stood and peered into the milling mass of warriors at the base of the hill.

He saw Cathal.

Along the stream at the bottom of the hill was a copse of

oaks. Cathal and Oswald were there, as yet unseen by the Angles.

Connaire turned to what was left of the clann.

"Quick. Grab your swords. We must save Cathal and Oswald."

One of the men, a young warrior lying on the ground, turned to him. "Why? We are outnumbered now. We will only die. Let us flee to our homeland."

Connaire grabbed him by the front of his léine, quivering with rage. "You are one of the ones that scoffed when I said we should stay together as a clann in the attack. Now you scoff when I say we should stay together as a clann when we retreat. Learn this, boy, I am still taoiseach and you will follow me or I will break your sniveling neck."

Brid laid her hand on his arm. She looked in his eyes and shook her head. This young man was not the enemy. Connaire released his grip, letting the warrior drop to the ground, and turned to the others.

"I go to save our clannsmen. Come if you want. Flee if you want."

Eavan stepped next to him, bloody sword in hand. Connaire looked down at her. Her léine and face were covered with mud and blood, how much was hers, Connaire did not know. She looked him in the eye. "I will follow my Taoiseach. We need to save Cathal."

Taking up his sword, he walked to the edge of the ridge and looked down.

Cathal stood with his back to a small oak and peered around. The Angles were moving across the valley, pursuing the fleeing Dál Riatans. Like a pack of wolves, they cut down the slower of their prey. Oswald was leaning against a tree close to him, also watching. Temporarily, they had not been spotted by the Angles.

Cathal wiped some blood from his face with the back of his forearm. He was not sure if it was his own or a fallen foe's. "Oswald, I see little hope of our escape."

Oswald shrugged, but said nothing as he kept his eye on the enemy warriors.

Cathal laid his hand on his companion's shoulder. "But you can."

The Angle turned to him. "No, I cannot."

"You are an Angle. Surely you could pretend that you had fought with them instead of us."

The Angle swung his sword, slicing through a sapling. "Do you think I could do that? Do you think I have so little honor?"

"No, but I had to offer. My dear friend, I had to offer."

Oswald smiled grimly. "Offer refused. We will die together. As brother warriors."

The Angles had reached their copse and warily entered.

Oswald gave a nod and Cathal joined him behind his large shield. With a yell, they went at their foes.

"Wōden!"

"Christus!"

Cathal felled two Angles, attacking from the side of the shield they did not expect. Then Oswald fell to the ground with a spear through his neck, eyes sightlessly looking skyward, taking his shield to the ground with him. As Cathal swung his sword, yelling in rage, a searing pain shot through his side.

Tian came up and grasped Connaire's arm.

"It is over. If you throw away the lives of those of us who are left when Cathal is already dead, it may mean the end of our clann."

"No!" Eavan cried. "We cannot leave him."

Connaire watched as the Angles swarmed around Cathal's body. Tears filled his eyes. He never had been able to save his brother.

"It is over." Connaire numbly said. "There is nothing we can do."

Eavan dropped to her knees, wailing and weeping. Connaire rested a hand on her battle-matted hair, unable to speak.

"Hallo!"

Connaire looked down the hill to where the greeting came.

Brother Padraig was struggling up with Lunn across his shoulders. He stopped and bent over, hands on his knees, to regain his breath before he spoke.

"He is still alive. This lad is still alive."

The battle was lost. Now Connaire had to save the few surviving warriors of his clann. He and Brid rushed to help Padraig with Lunn. When they reached the top of the ridge, Connaire paused to speak.

"Let us go to our horses. There will be more horses than we need with so many dead, but take all of ours. Our clann will need them when the Angles attack."

When they reached where their horses were corralled, Connaire realized how many of Áedán's vast army had fallen, a multitude of their mounts waiting for riders who would never return. He saw Áedán and his guard riding away and knew it was time for them to flee as well.

VII. AFTERMATH

Chapter 84

Connaire stretched his legs and sighed as he relaxed in his chair before the hearth fire. Outside, an angry storm lashed at the house with sheets of rain, but inside it was warm and comfortable.

Many Samhains had passed since their disastrous defeat by Æthelfrith's Angles, but the expected invasion had not happened. Why, he had no idea. When he and the few survivors had stumbled back from Degsastan, Connaire had posted a constant guard. After such a victory, surely Æthelfrith would attack. It had not happened and Connaire had slowly relaxed. The battle had become but a memory, one that would haunt him as long as he lived.

He was drowsing, comfortable after his evening meal, when Lunn came to him, standing with spear in hand.

"Your brother is at the door and asks to enter."

Connaire was stunned. Cathal was still alive? He had been sure that his brother had fallen to Angle swords. How had he escaped? He sprang to his feet and ran to the door.

Then it hit him. He had not fought his way down to be sure that Cathal had died. He had left his brother lying on the battlefield, left him to die. And yet he had survived. Again.

Connaire shoved the guard away from the door. In the dim light glowing from the hearth fire behind him, he could see a man. Bent over in a spasm of coughing, his long, scraggly grey hair almost covered his face. His clothes were rain-drenched, tattered rags. He wobbled on a makeshift crutch.

When his coughing stopped, he straightened enough to look up at Connaire and smiled crookedly. Water dripped from his long, matted hair.

"Hello, Brother."

It was Ciarán.

Shock, then anger and finally disgust flashed through Connaire. He felt like gripping Ciarán's neck and squeezing the life out of him. This was the man who had betrayed Cathal's hospitality and murdered Gruagach.

Ciarán bent over and went into another coughing spasm, almost falling over. When he finally stopped, he slowly raised his head. Blood was dripping from the side of his mouth and he shakily wiped it away with the back of his hand.

This pathetic creature at the door was not worth the effort of killing. Connaire started to shut the door, but Ciarán stopped him by leaning against it.

"Wait! I claim hospitality."

Connaire gave a short, humorless laugh. "And the last time you did, you killed one of the clann, a good friend. Shot him in the back. Where is your bow now?"

"I have no bow, no sword. Only my dagger and I will gladly give it to you. You can keep it. Just let me inside where it is warm." He paused. His voice was hoarse and weak. "I am dying, brother. Let me die where I am not cold, wet and alone. I beg of you, in the name of our father."

Connaire stopped. Our father. Our Father. The holiest prayer, the one from the mouth of the Christus himself. Forgive us as we forgive others.

He glared at Ciarán. "Wait here."

"Can I at least come in from this horrid rain?"

"Wait here. Or leave. Pray, do the latter."

Connaire turned to the guard. "Get some firewood. Take it to Barthionn's hut. Make it ready for . . . for this man. The house has been empty since Barthionn died, so you will need to see if the bed is usable. Then return here."

When he had finished his orders to the guard, Connaire turned to see Tian and Brid behind him.

"Who is outside, Connaire?" Tian looked puzzled. "Why do you not invite the traveler in from the storm?"

"It is Ciarán."

Tian's mouth gaped. "Ciarán? Alive? Here?" Then his jaw set. "Why did you not kill him?" He tried to push past Connaire. "I will do it with my bare hands."

Connaire gripped his shoulders, holding the smaller man tightly. "No. He is almost dead. We will give him a place to die that is warm and dry. In the name of the Christus."

"In the name of the Christus?" Tian's voice shook with rage. "Have you somehow forgotten he killed my best friend, shot him in the back? You are going to bring him into our home that he can kill another of us while we ply him with food and drink? Do you want me to sing a song of his praises as well?"

Connaire sighed, releasing Tian and rubbing his forehead. "I do not like this any more than you. But it must be. He will be in Bathionn's hut until he dies. He will be fed and given water. Nothing more."

As soon as Connaire had said that, he turned and strode over to the fire, standing with his hands clasped behind his back. Tian started to follow, but Brid grabbed his arm and spun him around. She had lost a beloved friend that awful night as well and found it as difficult as he to accept Connaire's decision. Her glare told him that he must say no more. Then she went to Connaire, wrapping her arm around his waist and leaning her head against him.

When the guard came to him and told him that all he had

ordered had been done, Connaire went with Brid to the hut where Ciarán had been lodged. Everything was covered in dust, but a welcoming fire roared on the hearth. Ciarán was lying on the bed with a woolen blanket over him. He recovered from yet another bloody coughing fit while Connaire and Brid stood by his bed.

"Brother, you have made me comfortable. More than I have been for some time. Sit and I will tell you my sad tale."

Brid plopped down on the side of Ciarán's bed. He recoiled, but she roughly pulled him back. She motioned for Connaire to hold his torch closer and he did. She felt Ciarán's forehead, then pulled up his eyelids and looked in his eyes. Finally she jerked down his chin and peered in his mouth. As he again broke into coughing, she released his chin and stood. She spoke in the language of the hands to Connaire.

Ciarán raised up on one elbow. "What was that? Is she signaling you about something?"

"She said you will not be alive in the morning."

Eyes wide with fear, Ciarán grasped Brid's hand. "No. Not so soon. I . . . I am not ready."

Brid twisted back Ciarán's thumb on the hand that held her and he released her with a yelp. She spat in his face and stomped out of the house.

Ciarán massaged his hand. "She is a mean one, that woman of yours. Now pull up a chair and I will tell you stories to add to the lore of our clann before I die. I will live on in the tales of our people. And we will be together to the end. Well, my end." He gave a sad half-smile and glanced around. "Do you have any mead?"

Connaire stood with fists clenched. "I have given you far more than you deserve, but I did it only because of the Christus. You are not of this clann. You are outside the law of any clann.

You do not know what truth, honor and duty are. All memory of you will be like a doused campfire, soon dead and forgotten. You have a jug of water and a cup. There is a bowl of cold beef. Now die and leave us in peace. For once in your life, do no more harm."

With that, he turned and strode out of the house. As he closed the door, he heard Ciarán calling to him. "Connaire, do not let me die alone. I beg you, do not make me die alone and forgotten."

Connaire turned to the guard. "No one is to enter. In the morning, when he is dead, bury him somewhere far away from the graves of our clann. Do not tell me where."

As the night grew later, Connaire sat in his chair with a cup of mead, staring at the dying fire. Brid came to him and curled in his lap like a contented cat, her head resting on his chest. He looked down at her. Her hair was still black, while his had turned gray. Her face had changed little since when they had first met. Pehaps she was part pixie.

He sighed. "I left him alone to die. He feared that most of all. But I could not stay. I am not the Christus. I could not forgive all his sins. I could barely keep from killing him myself."

She smiled up at him and gently caressed his cheek. He reached up and grasped her hand tightly, fighting back tears. She pulled his hand to her and kissed it. He relaxed, closing his eyes.

Connaire remembered that night long ago, when Cathal and he had sailed across a stormy sea with but a few followers. Of the adults in that original band, only Tian and he still lived, and Tian had grown much weaker of late. He walked with a stoop. Although still a proud man, the younger warriors did not challenge him out of respect rather than fear. Connaire knew that he himself must step down as taoiseach, chief of the clann, soon.   Cathal and Aislinn's son, Fergus, would make a fine replacement, having a handcount of his own children.   The clann had grown strong, filled with the young and healthy.   His turn of the wheel was almost over.   He was ready to go to the better world, the one promised by the Christus.

Tian sang softly from his chair across the fire, his tenor voice softer and breathier than when he was young, but still rich and beautiful.   It seemed to Connaire that since Maille had passed to the next world last Beltane that all of Tian's songs were sad. This one was no exception.   But in it there was still courage and hope.   It was the tale of Cathal and Oswald.

> *Oswald pagan Angle born*
> *Sided by the Angle-bane,*
> *Mighty Cathal by him stood*
> *One armed and fierce of mien.*
> *Made as one by battle's turn*
> *Standing in the arbor lane*
> *Awaiting fate's last laugh*
> *As the wheel turns again.*
>
> *Oswald calls on Wōden dire*
> *And the gods that follow him.*
> *They march across the rainbow bridge*
> *Toward Ragnarok's bloody end.*
> *Cathal wears a cross of wood,*
> *"Christus, killed for me and raised."*
> *For men's salvation, hope eternal.*
> *He knows what comes with mankind's end.*

Sleep now both until the trumpet,
Oswald will think it Wōden's horn,
Cathal will know the angel's summons
When all men will see Christ our Lord.

GLOSSARY

Terms

Aire- Nobility and freemen

Aire Désa- The lowest level of nobility.

Aire forgaill- The highest level of nobility, just below royalty.

Anruth- Second highest level of a Brehon, normally the final judge of a dispute.

Banrion- Queen.

Bean sídhe- Also known as banshee, a female spirit whose wail was the harbinger of death.

Beltane- May 1st, the third of the Gaelic fire festivals that are spaced equally through the year (the others being Samhain, Imbolc and Lughnasadh) when bonfires would be lit for a celebration at night. These celebrations were primarily based on events in the herding society. This was the time when the livestock would be put out to pasture.

Bratt- A blanket-like cloak of wool that was fastened around the neck or across the shoulder with a brooch. It could be a single color, speckled or checked. Also spelled brat.

Brehon- Law-interpreters of Ireland who, depending upon the circumstances, acted as both lawyers and judges.

Briughu- A wealthy man who was a "hosteller." He had considerable standing in society because of providing hospitality in housing, food and drink at his own expense.

Broch- Round dry-stone towers that were up to 60 ft. inside diameter and 40 ft. high that were built in Northern and Western Scotland in the 1st to 3rd c. A.D. They had outer walls and inner walls with a staircase between them. Livestock would be kept on the bottom level. Although no written record exists of why they were built, their defensive nature speaks for itself.

Cairn- A burial mound of stone, sometimes hollow.

Cenél- Many fines together, normally with a claimed common ancestor. Similar to the later form of Highland Scottish clan.

Clann- A smaller group with a claimed kinship within a fine. Not to be confused with the larger Scottish Highland clan.

Crannog- Dwelling built on an artificial island on a lake or river, normally with a wood-plank floor. Often it would be surrounded by a palisade and have a causeway, with or without a drawbridge, leading to shore.

Crossans- Traveling bands of entertainers, including jugglers, known for their impudence.

Cuirmtig- An assembly of all the aire, freemen and nobles.

Currach- A wicker-frame boat covered with greased hides that accommodated two to twenty people and powered by oars and/or a square sail.

Dal (Dáil in modern Irish)- A meeting of the nobles for a specific purpose.

Dalaigh- Entry level as a brehon.

Derbfhine- Those related, up to second cousins, on the male line.

Druid- Pagan religious leaders who were known for prophesying. Although the exact form of their worship is unknown, they held oak groves as sacred and worship was likely done there.

Filidh- A poet, but of the highest standing. He would be honored and feted by kings. If he satirized a king, it would shame that king.

Fine- Large circles of relatives with a claimed common patrilineal descent.

Glasaigne- A Brehon who has just finished his first course of studies of the law.

Handcount- Five.

Honor price- A payment system for offenses, civil or criminal, based upon damage done and the injured person's standing in society.

Imbolc- February 1ˢᵗ, the second of the Gaelic fire festivals. The onset of the lambing season.

Léine- Gaelic for "shirt" or "tunic" and worn by men and women as an outer garment, the léine varied in length from the lower calf to the upper thigh. Léine's were worn pleated with a belt at the waist and had bagged sleeves.

Lughnasadh- August 1ˢᵗ, the fourth of the Gaelic fire festivals. Literally, "the assembly for Lugh," it marked the beginning of the harvest.

Oenach- A seasonal gathering that had aspects of a fair, but could have a legal and jural aspect.

Psalter- The book of Psalms in the Old Testament of the Bible.

Ri- King. There were four types of kings: king of the tuath; the king of the mór-tuath (large tuath); the king of one of the five regions; and the king of all Ireland, known as the aird ri (high king).

Samhain- November 1ˢᵗ, the first of the Gaelic fire festivals and the Celtic New Year. Since the day began at sunset, it was also the origin of Halloween when the portals between the world of men and the sidhes opened, allowing the fairies and the dead to walk the earth. It was when the livestock were brought in from summer pasture.

Senchus Mór and the Book of Acaill- The written, compiled

Brehon Laws regarding civil and criminal law.

Sídhe- Also known as a fairy mound, a hillock or knoll that is a mythical entrance to the realm of the Other World of the Tuatha dé Danann, pixies, fairies and other supernatural beings.

Saint John's tonsure- the tonsure of the monks in early Ireland and Scotland that is derived from that of the druids. The front of the head is shaved going across the top of the skull from ear to ear and forward, while the hair behind it is left long. The Roman church replaced it with St. Peter's tonsure, which had the top of the head shaved to leave a ring of hair reminiscent of Christ's Crown of Thorns.

Standing stones- Neolithic-era stones set upright, either in a pattern or individually, probably for religious or monumental reasons. In Scotland, there are many sites with such stones arranged in a circle pattern.

Táin bó Cuailnge- The epic tale of the Cattle Raid of Cooley, when Queen Medb and the warriors of Connacht attempted to seize a prize bull in Ulster, opposed only by the young warrior Cú Chulainn who soundly defeated them.

Taoiseach- Chief.

Trews- Woolen trousers that fit tight to the leg.

Tuath- A petty (small) kingdom.

Historic and Mythical People and Places

Áedán (mac Gabráin) - King of Dál Riata from circa 574 A.D. to circa 606 A.D. and the nephew of Conall mac Comgail. He was the first king annointed (by St. Columba, who at first had reservations about him) on the British Isles. His disastrous battle at Degsastan was the last foray against the Anglo-Saxons by Dál Riata.

Æthelfrith- King of Bernicia. Considered the founder of the kingdom of Northumbria, a major power in England, after uniting Bernicia with another northern English kingdom, Deira.

Angles- Germanic people from Angeln, also known as Anglia, near Denmark. Along with Germanic Saxons and Jutes, they came to Britain as raiders, as settlers and as conquerers after the Roman troops left the island in the late 5th c.

Bernicia- An Anglian kingdom of Northern England.

Brude- Also known as Bridei, the king of the Fortriu, a people often termed Pictish. They often raided and battled the Dál Riatans. Some historians think he was converted to Christianity by St. Columba.

Colm Cille- Gaelic name of St. Columba, who founded the monastic house on Iona and is credited with bringing Chrisitanity to Western Scotland in the 6th century.

Cú Chulainn- Legendary hero of Ulster in the *Cattle Raid of Cooley* who single-handedly fought off the vast army of Connacht. So named after he killed the watchdog of the blacksmith Culann and took up the hound's role, becoming the hound of Culann, or Cú Chulainn.

Da Derga's Hostel- A vast, multi-roomed legendary hostel where Aird Ri Conaire Mór was killed while feasting during Samhain.

Degsastan- A major battle between Dál Riata and Bernicia in which the much larger forces of Dál Riata suffered a crippling defeat. The exact location is unknown, but was probably in the Liddesdale region of Southeastern Scotland.

Danu- Mother goddess of the Tuatha dé Danann.

Dian Cécht- God of healing of the Tuatha dé Danann.

Donn's house- In pagan Irish legend, an island to the West where the dead went before rebirth. Also known as the Land of the Dead.

Dun Ad- Hilltop fortress that was the stronghold of the kings of Dál Riata

Eilean nam Ban- A very small island, just off the coast of Mull, much smaller than Iona, that housed all females in St. Columba's community.

Eireann- Present day Ireland.

Eireannach Sea- Present day Irish Sea.

Fian(na)- Independent bands of warriors, often acting as paramilitary keepers of the peace.   The most famous, legendary one was last led by Fionn mac Cumhail.

Fionn mac Cumhail- Legendary leader of the Fianna.   He gained wisdom by being the first to taste the Salmon of Knowledge that ate hazelnuts from a holy tree.   He had burned his thumb by touching the salmon when cooking it and had put his thumb in his mouth. From then on, he gained wisdom by putting his thumb in his mouth.

Fortriu- A powerful kingdom of the people often known as the Picts.

Hering- Failed claimant for the Bernician kingship, backed by Áedán at the battle of Degsastan.

Ioua- Present day Isle of Iona.

Kelpie- A mythical water spirit that would often take the form of a mare.   Anyone who mounted her would be stuck to her back and she would descend under water, drowning her rider as her next meal.

Lugh- Also known as Lugh Lumhfada, god of the Tuatha dé Danann that is the jack-of-all-trades, able to do anything the other gods can do.

Manannán mac Lir- Sea god of the Tuatha dé Danann.

(the) Morrigan- Goddess of war of the Tuatha dé Danann, who encourages strife. She is three-in-one, but it is unclear what parts make up the three and they vary from myth to myth.

Mumhan- Roughly present day Munster.

Muile- Present day Isle of Mull.

Niall of the Nine Hostages- The Uí Néill king, possibly 4th c., who is credited with the onset of Uí Néill family power. Hostages were often given by client kings to guarantee their loyalty and Niall had one from each of five kingdoms of Ireland and four others, possibly from Scotland, making nine.

(Saint) Padraig- Also known as Saint Patrick, the former slave from Britain, who is considered to have brought Christianity to Ireland in the 5th century.

Rheged- A Brittonic kingdom whose language was very similar to Welsh. It was taken over by Northumbria in the late 7th c.

Scáthach- The legendary woman who trained warriors at her home in Western Scotland, possibly the Isle of Skye. Cú Chulainn was her most famous student.

Seagais well- Mythical well where hazelnuts fell from a holy tree and were eaten by the Salmon of Knowledge.

Tuatha dé Danann- The "tribe of the goddess Danu," they were the gods that inhabited Ireland before the Mileseans (Gaels) invaded. The land was divided and they were tricked into taking the underground portion of the kingdom.

Uí Néill- A powerful family that came to dominate Ulster politics.

Ulaidh- Ancient Irish kingdom that is roughly present-day Ulster.

Wōden- Chief god in the Germanic pantheon.

SUGGESTED READINGS

Alcock, Leslie. *Kings & Warriors, Craftsmen & Priests*. Edinburgh: Society of Antiquaries of Scotland, 2003.

Armit, Ian. *Celtic Scotland*. London: B. T. Batsford Ltd, 1997.

Bannerman, John. *Studies in the History of Dalriada*. Edinburgh: Scottish Academic Press, 1974.

Crone, Anne and Ewan Campbell. *A Crannog of the First Millenium AD*. Edinburgh: Society of Antiquaries of Scotland, 2005.

Cross, Tom Peete and Slover, Clark Harris, ed. *Ancient Irish Tales*. New York: Barnes and Noble, 1996.

Fraser, James E. *From Caledonia to Pictland Scotland to 795*. Edinburg: University of Edinburg Press, 2010.

Joyce, P. W. *A Social History of Ancient Ireland*. 2 vols. Dublin: M. H. Gill & Son, Ltd, 1920.

Kinsella, Thomas, trans. *The Tain*. Oxford: Oxford University Press, 1970.

Laing, Lloyd and Judy Laing. *The Picts and the Scots*. Phoenix Mill: Sutton Publishing, 1996.

Newton, Michael. *A Handbook of the Scottish Gaelic World*. Dublin: Four Courts Press Ltd, 2000.

Patterson, Nerys. *Cattle Lords & Clansmen.* Notre Dame: Univeristy of Notre Dame Press, Ltd, 1994.

Riotchie, J. N. G. *Brochs of Scotland.* Oxford: Shire Archaeology, 1998.

Young, Simon. *A.D. 500.* London: Phoenix, 2006.

ABOUT THE AUTHOR

I live in the Gold Country, the Sierra Nevada foothills in California, with my life-long love, my wife. If you come here in January, you can find me at the local Robert Burns Dinner, dressed in my kilt and Montrose, perhaps giving a toast or an Immortal Memory. Although, like most Americans, I am a mutt, I do have Celtic blood in my veins. My ancestry includes Scottish, Irish and a wee bit of Welsh. I have long been involved with the worldwide Scottish-American community and with a local Celtic cultural society. I also have long had a great love of history.

While living on the Isle of Man for five years with wife Kelly, daughter Noelle and our sheltie, Fionna, I finished my Master's degree in history from Cal State Dominguez Hills. My thesis was on 17th century Manx history, which was part of Dál Riata for a time, and a copy resides in the Centre for Manx Studies there. During my sojourn on the Isle of Man, I made several trips to Scotland, some that included the region of Dál Riata. In fact, I have been to every location named in the book. I also hiked the mountains described in it.

In this book I have combined my love of history and my love of my Celtic heritage with my love of writing fiction. Since I often find factual errors in other works of historical fiction that I read, I have long been loath to write one myself. Better to write mysteries and throw in a few historical facts than to expose myself to such possible criticism. Yet, I felt compelled to write this Celtic saga. Cathal, Aislinn, Connaire and Brid made me do it. Cú Chulainn also had his part. That's the way it is with characters when you write. They tell you how their story must be written and you merely follow their commands. We all hope you enjoyed their tale. If you find any errors, pray be kind in your corrections, if for no other reason than self preservation. Brid has a short temper, does not take criticism well and is inclined to be rather protective of those in her clann. I, on the other hand, do want to know if I have made any historical *faux pas.*

For more about me and my writing, go to www.rlcherry.com. You can contact me there and let me if you enjoyed this Celtic journey.

Made in the USA
San Bernardino, CA
26 March 2016